I0564547

PRAISE FOR

Every Inch a Saint

"An immersive journey into the tumultuous times and faith-filled culture that calls forth a miracle—a severely disabled woman whose entire life is devoted to the healing of her community. Meeting the extraordinary Eileen O'Connor in this rich and compelling novel is an unforgettable experience—and I am sure many readers, like myself, will find themselves devoted to her by the final pages."—**PERDITA FINN, author of** *The Way of the Rose* **and** *Take Back the Magic*

"I was enthralled by this gorgeously written novel about Australia's next potential saint, Eileen O'Connor. The plot leaps and circles, propelled deftly across two timelines: that of Eileen in the early 1900s; and a modern-day family suffering their own crises of trauma and faith. The privations of life in Australia before and during World War I, as well as Eileen's specific and devastating health challenges, are incredibly well drawn, in rich and unflinching detail. But this is no bleak read—as one character notes, 'This is an unconventional love story. On many levels.' The elegant balance of the contemporary family's story against that of Eileen and her circle not only emphasizes the reality of generational trauma, but also the very real possibility of generational healing, and hope." —**KRISTEN HOLT-BROWNING, author of** *Ordinary Devotion*

"Inspiring and engrossing time travel story of one tiny woman's giant achievements. Amazing! Let Eileen's incredible life inspire you to just—get on with your own!" —**MARY LEA CARROLL, author of** *Saint Everywhere* **and** *Across the Street Around the Corner*

"Kate Clinch has written an engaging portrait of Eileen O'Connor, Australia's saint in waiting. Full of firsthand recollections and skillful reenactments, Eileen's short but remarkably well-lived life is brought vividly to life with wonderful care. A fascinating read." —**TRICIA STRINGER, author of many books including** *The Road Trip* **and** *Queen of the Road*, **winner of the Romance Writers of Australia's Romantic Book of the Year award**

"Kate Clinch has created such a vivid story of young Eileen O'Connor. She has brought to life Eileen's unstinting energy and commitment for those who were left on the fringes of society. This novel shines a light on the remarkable strength of a young woman who, despite the extraordinary physical pain she endured, refused to compromise on the call she felt from her God, inspiring others in the journey and leaving a legacy that shines on even today." —JANE WOOLFORD, CEO, Mary MacKillop Today

EVERY INCH *a* SAINT

A Novel about Eileen O'Connor,
Australia's Second Saint-in-Waiting

KATE CLINCH

MONKFISH
BOOK PUBLISHING COMPANY
RHINEBECK, NEW YORK

Every Inch a Saint: A Novel about Eileen O'Connor, Australia's Second Saint-in-Waiting © Copyright 2026 by Kate Clinch

All rights reserved. No part of this book may be used or reproduced in any manner without the consent of the publisher, except in critical articles or reviews. Contact the publisher for information.

Paperback ISBN 9781966608417
eBook ISBN 9781966608424

Library of Congress Cataloging-in-Publication Data Pending

Illustration of Eileen O'Connor and photograph on front cover by Kate Clinch
Book and cover design by Colin Rolfe

Monkfish Book Publishing Company
22 East Market Street, Suite 304
Rhinebeck, New York 12572
(845) 876-4861
monkfishpublishing.com

To everyone who, like Eileen and her Sisters,
has ever let kindness, compassion and love lead the way.

If you are reading this, that probably means you.

To Sister Greta Gabb and the late Sister Margaret Mary Birgan
whose prayerful, loving kindness infuses the pages of this book.
You are written in my heart forever.

For Eileen.

ACKNOWLEDGEMENTS

This book resulted from the teamwork of many people. My heartfelt thanks go to all of them, and particularly:

To my special writer-friends, made at Fiona McIntosh's 2018 Masterclass, who have companioned me through beta-reading, blood, sweat, and tears ever since. To Carolyn McCarthy and Kerrie Thomson: I can't imagine living life without your endless, loving support, let alone writing books. To Donna English, who came up with the original working title. To Amanda Dale and Eleni Konstantine, who were part of the first aid team on hand when I collected my first rejections.

To my dear friend in prayer, Perdita Finn, whose long career as a writer and brilliant intuition nudged her to generously offer to read my manuscript. Having fallen in love with Eileen, Perdita took a chance on me, for which I will forever be grateful, and brought it to her friend, who is now my publisher.

To my publisher, Paul Cohen, thank you from the bottom of my heart for believing in Eileen enough to add this book to your incredibly impressive stable. I am deeply humbled.

To my editor, Jon M. Sweeney, a talented and exacting author, scholar and editor, and an experienced guide who has patiently helped me navigate the pathway to publication. It isn't chance that the man deciding whether Eileen's story was worth publishing had himself written a book about someone under investigation for sainthood.

Thank you to Colin Rolfe for designing the beautiful, unique cover.

To Steve Evans and Sandy Vaile, thank you for your editorial input to earlier versions of the manuscript, which encouraged me to keep believing in my ability to tell this story, and make it better.

To my wonderful children, Amy and Lance, who have been my reason for getting up in the morning for a quarter of a century. I am a better human being because you came into my life. Thanks for everything.

To Jessie Merle. Decades ago, you told me the story of your husband who came home from World War I with osteomyelitis in his leg, and how you could never forget the look on his face whenever the dressing was changed, and he saw it wasn't getting better. I never forgot and I couldn't have written George without you. We will remember them.

Thank you to Chantal Celjan, former archivist for Our Lady's Nurses for the Poor for her help and for access to the Archives.

As befits a book about a saint, my humble gratitude to all those who have prayed Eileen's novel will be published. Prayer works.

Special mention goes to two of Eileen's Sisters, Greta Gabb, and Margaret Mary Birgan, who, in addition to providing information and feedback on the manuscript, prayed for this for years. It was a joy to finally phone Sr. Greta and tell her I had a book contract.

My deep gratitude for your prayers, Greg Casale. Thankfully the contract came through before you could action your promise to sacrifice a pig in Central Park. I believe the pig is thankful too.

CONTENTS

I remember the first time I saw her. Well, I didn't really see Eileen O'Connor then. But I saw her arrive. It was 1903.

I was Kathleen O'Brien, an ordinary twelve-year-old girl living in the treeless, dusty streets of Redfern, Sydney. There was no reason to guess I'd have a story to tell. Not until Eileen arrived on a stretcher in the back of a horse-drawn ambulance. That was the moment our story began. The hairs on the back of my neck stood up, and they're standing up now. Maybe that's how saints announce their presence?

Arriving on a stretcher seems like an unlikely start, but you can't judge a gift by its wrapping. Eileen O'Connor blessed the lives of everyone she met. No matter how sick she was, no matter what she was suffering, her kindness and compassion transformed people.

I once thought life begins when we are born and ends when we die. But I know differently now. I saw Eileen's story outlive her frail young body.

Fifty years after she died, I tried to tell her story. Not just hers, mine too, and Georgie's. That's how stories are: they weave together like a tapestry. If you leave one thread out, the whole picture unravels. Poor George. I did try to tell our daughter, Evie, what happened to her father, but there was never a good time. Some stories are too hard to tell.

I thought the tapes were my last chance, and Evie would listen to them after I had gone. But things didn't go to plan. Despite the effort I put in, lying in my hospital bed, making tape recordings almost with my dying breath. Going through my memory box and making sure my mementos were arranged in the right order, so they'd fit with the story. I thought I'd made it clear to Evie that she should go through the boxes, and she understood there was something important there. But maybe my brain was a bit addled at the end, with all those painkillers. Or maybe she was too upset when I died. The fruits of my efforts got pushed into a space in the cupboard under the stairs, and stayed there, though I tried to whisper in Evie's dreams to remind her. I even tried to push the boxes off the shelves a couple of times, so she'd find them on the floor, but that's harder than you'd think, more's the pity.

Fifty more years have passed, and I've been given another chance. The boxes have been found at last. Caitlin isn't the sort to let sleeping dogs lie; she'll be busting to find out what I was doing with a tape recorder all those years ago. It's high time we laid the old family skeleton to rest, but the most important thing is that Alex and Caitlin hear Eileen's story: it's their turn to get caught in the thread. My precious great-great-grandchildren need help and I'm praying Eileen still has the power to transform people's lives, just like she used to. Maybe that was the plan all along, and I just didn't know it until now?

SEPTEMBER 2, 2019–ADELAIDE

Alex didn't like distractions. Noise-cancelling headphones crowned his tousled, dark hair, cutting out the ambient sounds: a lawn-mower next door, hidden by his drawn blinds, and his mother's Sixties playlist, abandoned in the kitchen. Blue reflections flickered across blue blocking glasses as numbers scrolled across the dual computer screens in front of him. He was lounging back in his body-hugging chair, but the muscles in his cheeks were taut as he unconsciously ground his teeth.

His breath caught as his phone buzzed. He pressed speakerphone on the first ring.

Silence on the line. He thought it was a bad connection. Before he could hang up, he heard a muffled sob.

"Mum? What's happened?"

A loud sniff. "She's gone."

"Nan's gone?" A vision of his grandmother, with her mischievous smile and wispy white hair, flashed through his mind. "But she was so well on Sunday …" He shook his head. "Where are you?"

"At the nursing home." His mother switched into business mode. "Your Uncle Tim wants to see her. And Caitlin. I told them you'd pick them up on your way here."

He swung out of his chair, his phone in one hand, reaching for his keys with the other. He kept his voice level. "Okay, Mum, I'm on my way." He paused, wondering what he could do to comfort her. "Do you want me to stay on the line while I drive?"

The soft gasp was barely audible over the phone, but it reminded him how she responded when he showed her he loved her. It stabbed his heart. Poor Mum. He should show that more often, so it didn't surprise her.

"No, thank you, sweetheart. I'll be okay. I'll see you when you get here."

Alex gritted his teeth as he buckled his seatbelt, steeling himself. The engine came to life at the turn of the car key. He shivered despite the warm sunshine flooding through the windscreen.

Familiar unease grew in the pit of his stomach. He deliberately turned his thoughts to his grandmother, who had only moved to Adelaide to be near them six months ago, after it was clear she couldn't manage in her own home any longer. How she had loved that house. It was only an ordinary little terrace, but it had meant the world to her. Maybe that's what happens when you've lived in the same house all your life. And not just his Nan: Nan's mother and grandmother had lived there before her. He remembered her saying with pride her family had lived in that house for over a hundred years. But when she had her second stroke, Nan agreed to come from Sydney to Adelaide to live. Alex's mother managed to pull strings and get her into a nursing home after flying to Sydney and helping her pack up the old house.

And now she was gone. She was a wonderful old lady, and Alex knew he was very fond of her, but he wasn't sure how he felt about her death. It was just one more thing to deal with. He grunted. He already had enough on his plate.

He pulled into the empty driveway at Uncle Tim's. Scowling slightly, his eyes roamed over the uncut grass, the couple of half-dead rose bushes with escaped kikuyu grass climbing up their trunks, the shabby paint work. Before he could knock, the front door opened. The odor of stale beer and cheap aftershave engulfed him as he stood awkwardly on the step.

His cousin Caitlin's shy smile was damp with tears. She wheeled toward him, blocking the dark entry. "Thanks for coming to get us." She called over her shoulder. "Alex is here, Dad, are you ready?"

Rhythmic thuds echoed in the hallway and Uncle Tim appeared on his crutches, one leg of his faded blue jeans pinned up. Gray stubble covered his cheeks, and despite the nostril-filling aftershave, Alex smelled the sharp stench of sweat.

After Alex got everyone into the car, and loaded the wheelchair and crutches, he cast a long sideways glance at Caitlin, settled in the front passenger seat, her braced leg held stiffly in front of her.

"Have you got enough leg room, cuz? I put your seat back as far as I could."

"Yes, thanks." Her voice was raw with bottled grief.

"You right back there, Uncle Tim?"

Tim nodded. For a moment, his eyes almost met Alex's in the rear vision mirror, but Alex moved his head. Not meeting people's eyes had become second nature to him now. He knew the scars around his eye had faded, but he couldn't meet the pity or horror they still conjured on the faces of people who saw them.

Locked inside their own thoughts, they made the trip in silence.

* * *

As soon as she was in her wheelchair, Caitlin propelled herself towards the entry of the nursing home, leaving Alex to close the car door. She felt his gaze like a weight on her back, but she needed a moment to collect herself. Thank God, Alex was still handsome, even with his scars, but she could hardly bear looking at his face, marred as it was, because of her. Her cheeks flushed with exertion and a deadly cold rage as the glass door slid open in front of her. Down that passage, her Auntie Cara was waiting for them. Cara's face was habitually pinched with worry in a way that almost broke Caitlin's heart, because Caitlin knew she was the root cause of it. But now, the body of her dead grandmother was lying in the neat-as-a-pin bedsit, alongside her aunt's motherly concern. The last time she saw a dead body ... memories of her mother, ash-gray in a hospital bed, threatened her self-composure and she pushed them away. Too much to bear. Breathing slowly to calm herself, she waited for the steady rhythm of the crutches to stop behind her.

Her father cleared his throat, but his voice was raspy as he asked, "You alright, love?"

She didn't turn to meet him, just nodded, squirming under his attempt at paternal care. They both knew he had nothing to give.

Alex laid a proprietary hand on the handle of her wheelchair. "Let's go then," he said. They followed the linoleum-lined corridor to their Nan's door. The room was unoccupied, except for the bed, where a shock of white hair stuck out above a crisply folded, turquoise bed sheet. Her face was peaceful, almost smiling, but still and empty, like a deserted tomb.

Caitlin's wheelchair filled the doorway, and she reached the bedside first, resting her hand lightly over the cold wrinkled hands folded on her grandmother's breast. She was silent for a few moments, before a strangled sob escaped the confines of her throat.

Later, when their first, shocked grief had ebbed, they sat around the bed. No one spoke. The silence was jarring. Caitlin stared openly at Cara, who had returned after attending to paperwork, wishing she would take the lead and say something, anything. But Cara was clearly lost in thought. Alex had never been one for idle chatter, and her father was staring morosely at the floor.

Caitlin's eyes hunted around the room, settling on the Overway table that was usually near Nan's bed, but had been pushed out of the way against the dusky pink painted wall. "Has anyone seen this before?" she asked.

Three heads startled and turned to follow the direction she indicated. Alex took a few steps to investigate. "It's a tape deck. Ancient. From the Seventies, maybe. It looks like she was listening to an old tape."

Tim shuffled in his plastic chair. "I haven't seen a tape reel like that in years." Something stirred in his memory. The smell of disinfectant, the sight of a tape recorder on an Overway table long ago. He shut his bloodshot eyes for a moment and rubbed his furrowed brow as if trying to clear his head. "Well, that's weird. I reckon the last time I saw an old tape reel like that, was in a tape recorder on the table at my great grandmother's bed, not long before she died."

"Granny Kathleen?" Cara's voice was warm with remembered love for their great grandmother.

"Yes. Do you remember it?"

Cara shook her head. "I was too young, Tim. It was 1974 when she died. They didn't let children visit in those days." Her gaze wandered back to her mother's still form on the bed.

Tim squirmed in his seat again, and Caitlin was sure his stump was hurting from the pressure of the hard seat. She tried to force the conversation. "Did you know Nan had the tape player, Auntie Cara? Do you know what's on the tapes?"

Cara shook herself as if she was wearing a mantle of weariness that was so heavy she couldn't think. "I don't know what's on them, no. But when I was clearing out her house, I found the tape player and some old tapes tucked into the back of the cupboard under the stairs with some other stuff. Mum didn't know they were there. She said she thought they must be Kathleen's. I forgot about them, but once she was settled in here, and was feeling better after the last stroke, she asked me to bring them in for her. She was curious to find out what was on them." Cara gave a short half-laugh, warming to reminisce about her mother. "You know what she was like, always curious about everything. She was busting to find out what was on those tapes. She said she'd love to hear her Granny Kathleen's voice again." Cara's lips trembled and tears spilled over her eyelashes. "I feel so bad, now. I'd been meaning to ask her if we could listen together, but I didn't get around to it. The nurse said she had been listening to the tapes, in fact, she had asked the nurse to plug the machine in for her, not long before … She was listening to it at the end." She sobbed again.

Caitlin wheeled closer and took her hand, then turned to her cousin. "Alex, do you think you can rewind the tape, and play it for us?"

He frowned, squinting at the magnetic tape on its three-and-a-quarter inch reel. "It's really old tape. She's lucky it didn't break. Honestly, I'd be scared to damage it."

Disappointment settled in Caitlin's chest. "Oh dear."

He managed a smile. "It's okay, cuz. I know a bloke who knows a bloke."

"What?"

"A bloke who can take these old tapes and copy them onto CDs for you, if you'd like?"

"I'd like to know what Nan was listening to in her last hours. And your mum would too."

Cara nodded and blew her nose. Tim cleared his throat. "If they're Granny Kathleen's, I might like to hear them too," he said softly, studying his shoe.

"Right," Cara said. "I'll drop them off. Bradley should have them done within the week, I reckon. Where are the rest of the tapes?" She retrieved a box of tapes from the wardrobe and put them next to the tape recorder. "That's funny." She looked again in the wardrobe. "There was an old toffee tin as well, I can't find it."

Caitlin spotted the top drawer of the bedside cupboard was ajar. She opened it, and with a brave grin said, "Is this what you're looking for?"

"Oh yes, that's it. She must have been looking through it, I guess. It was packed up with the tapes when I found them."

"What's in the box, Mum?"

"I didn't have a proper look. Old papers and letters and stuff, I think."

Alex turned to Cait. "Well, finders keepers. You're the history buff in the family. You can work out what's in there. I'll get the tapes to my mate tomorrow. You'll be listening to them before you know it."

I remember the first time I saw her. Well, I didn't really *see* her then. But I saw her arrive. Horse drawn ambulances didn't come down Baptist Street.

Patrick whooped and brandished the broken fence paling in triumph. "Six! Did you see that, Kathleen?" he called, flushed with pride and exertion, as several barefooted children scampered to retrieve the ball. I looked up from the doorstep where I was sitting, gossiping to Becky from a few doors down, and peeling potatoes for dinner which was my first after-school chore. The kids fell back, suddenly quiet, as the ambulance made its ponderous journey to Number one-hundred-and-forty-four. My gaze was rivetted to it and the potato I was peeling dropped back into the bowl.

Beside the driver sat Mary O'Connor, her face pinched with worry, one arm securely around her younger brother, Frank, who was about five years old, squirming on the bench to study the silent honor guard of children flanking the road. Mr. O'Connor walked alongside the wagon, with his other son, Charlie. He smiled at me, but the smile didn't reach his eyes.

"He must be tired after moving their furniture this morning," I suggested to Becky.

She replied with the question I hadn't been able to ask. "Who's in the ambulance?"

"I don't know."

The wagon stopped. Mr. O'Connor swung Frank to the ground, then Mary. The driver jumped down and walked around the wagon, its lower half a dirt-spattered grayish blue, its top white, emblazoned

Civil Ambulance with a red Maltese cross on the sides. He opened the doors at the back and peered in as Mary ushered the boys into the single-fronted terrace house, propping the door open behind her.

Mr. O'Connor hovered at the back of the wagon, his body taut, rocking on his heels. His wife stepped out and stretched her back wearily, before meeting his eyes. Her mouth twisted into a tight smile then she shook her head. Her lips moved, but I couldn't hear what she said.

The two men climbed into the back of the ambulance, then the driver backed out holding the foot end of a stretcher. "It must be one of the grandparents, frail and old, needing to be cared for," said Becky, as the driver inched backwards, minimizing the jerking of the stretcher.

Horror twisted in my stomach: the blanket at the end of the stretcher was flat. As more of the stretcher crept into view, my paralyzed gaze waited, until there was a slight rise in the covering, indicating where the patient's legs began. Nausea rose. The patient was too short to be a grandparent. It was only a child. I snapped my eyes away and, snatching up the potatoes, bolted into the house before I could see the child's face.

Mum didn't look up from the stock pot she was tending on the stove. "I wondered where you'd got to with them spuds."

"I'll just finish peeling them in here." I put the bowl on the scrubbed timber table.

Mum blinked at me, but my eyes were adjusting to the darkness after being outside in the sunshine, and I couldn't read her expression. "Did something happen out there?" She dropped the spoon into the pot, and wiped her hands, moist from steam, or sweat, on her apron.

"They're moving into Number a-hundred-and-forty-four. One of them is a patient in an ambulance," I answered, so she would know nothing had frightened me, and I hadn't left the kids out playing in the presence of a drunk or other undesirable.

"Goodness, whatever next?"

Becky trailed in after me, bringing the tin pail for the peelings. "It's a little girl, she doesn't look very well at all, poor thing."

"Oh, dear. They won't have time to get a decent supper if they are settling an invalid. Scrub a few more potatoes, will you, pet?"

And so it was that the mutton stew was stretched with more water and potatoes and a handful of barley from the cupboard, and Mum sent me carrying a pot over to the O'Connor's house. Mr. O'Connor answered the door, uncertainty in his eyes.

"Hello. I'm Kathleen O'Brien from over the road." I thrust the pot towards him. "Mum thought your wife would be too busy to cook tonight."

He took a step backwards, then recovered from his surprise and light shone from his smile. "She'd be right about that. She's not made you all go hungry?"

I hurried to put his mind at ease. "No, we put in some extra potatoes and barley."

"You be sure and thank your Mum for me." He picked up a cloth to take the pan from me. "You're just opposite, aren't you?"

"Two doors down on the left." I nodded.

"I'll get Mary to run your pan back later."

I hovered, standing on one foot, the toe of the other foot stretching out through the hole in the end of my boot, scratching a scab on the back of my leg. Curiosity about the new family, and especially the sick child, quelled my desire to run away, to not see suffering that might remind me …

A slight crease formed at the corners of Mr. O'Connor's eyes. "How about you come in? I'll introduce you to Mary, so you'll know her when she comes with the pan."

I drew myself up to full height—all of four foot ten but I was hoping I'd grow another couple of inches yet—and made my voice sound polite and reserved. "I don't want to be any trouble, Mr. O'Connor. You're busy moving in, and Mum's got our supper ready."

"It'll only take a minute to be properly introduced." He was grinning now, though he looked worn out. He balanced the pot on a narrow table against the wall of the hall, then held the door open and stuck out his hand. A clean, white hand, an office worker's hand, with neat fingernails. "Charles O'Connor, at your service, Miss O'Brien."

I giggled and shook his hand.

"Come in, Miss O'Brien." He retrieved the stew and led the few paces down the hall to the back room. "We've got company, Annie." His Irish accent seemed even stronger as he spoke soothingly to his wife. "Kathleen O'Brien from over the road. Her mother has kindly sent us a gift of some supper."

Mrs. O'Connor looked up from the loaf of bread she was slicing. A delighted smile chased a darker expression from her face before I could work out what it was.

"You tell Mrs. O'Brien thank you." She waved her hand over the scrubbed wood tabletop. "Bread and dripping was all I had time to make for my family tonight, and it doesn't go far with growing boys and our Eileen not well."

I'll never forget how her eyes lit up as she told me her daughter's name, though they almost instantly shuttered as if she had said too much.

"I'll tell Mum you're grateful," I assured her. "I saw the ambulance when you moved in. Mum thought you'd not have enough time to make supper if you were settling an inv— a sick child into a new house."

"That's very thoughtful of her."

I shook my head. "Mum had a sick child to look after too, once. She understands." A wild panic flashed in her eyes.

I squeezed a few words through the choking constriction in my throat. "Is Eileen very sick, Mrs. O'Connor?"

She turned away and made a show of spreading dripping on bread. Mr. O'Connor put the stew on the table. "Eileen fell out of her pram when she was three. She broke her back. She's had to have several operations on it, but it still isn't right."

"She'll be having another operation as soon as she's well enough," said Frank peering around his mother's skirt, a piece of crust halfway to his mouth. "That'll make her better, won't it, Ma?"

"Yes, Frank, that'll make her better," agreed Mrs. O'Connor, but her heart wasn't in it. She lifted the lid of the stew pot and sighed softly as she inhaled the steam. "Oh, this is perfect. Thank you." She put a piece of soft bread from the middle of the loaf into a china bowl, then spooned some of the broth from the top of the stew over it, hiding part of the blue willow pattern. She fished for a few potato pieces and crushed them into the bowl with the back of the spoon. "Would you like to come and meet her? She's in the front room with Mary."

I hesitated for a moment before nodding my assent. Meeting a girl with a broken back couldn't be as daunting as watching my little sister Cara wasting away in front of us, coughing blood into her small hands, her wide eyes staring out from deep hollows under dark brows.

Two heads turned towards the door as Mrs. O'Connor opened it. "Girls, I'll just introduce a neighbor to you. She can't stay as her mother is wanting her home for supper. This is Kathleen O'Brien. Kathleen, these are my daughters."

"Hello, Kathleen, I'm Mary." Her hair was plaited into two dark brown braids which bobbed on her white pinafore as she nodded to her sister, whose untamed locks were spilling over her shoulders. "And this is Eileen." The pride in her voice surprised me. What could make a big sister so proud?

Mary's arm was draped around Eileen's shoulders, protective and affectionate, as they sat propped against pillows on the bed. Her free hand held a scrapbook, and Eileen's arm was frozen in mid-air as if she had been about to turn the page.

Eileen was much smaller than Mary, the size of a five-year-old child, but her seriousness and manner made her look older. Eileen fixed me with her gaze and everyone else in the room disappeared as if just the two of us were floating in an iridescent soap bubble, and the rest of the world had stopped. The hair on the back of my neck stood up. This must be what people felt when they said someone had just walked on their grave. My mouth gaped open, and I ran my tongue over my drying lips. Eileen's eyes seemed to see right inside of me, as my heart seemed to hang in space for seconds, waiting to beat. And then it was over. She extended her soft, little hand, peeping out from under the cuffed sleeve of a white, cotton nightdress too big for her, to shake mine.

"I'm pleased to meet you," she said, seriously. "Why don't you ask your mother if you can come back after supper, and we'll show you my scrapbook?"

I looked to Mary, as the older sister, for confirmation. Mr. O'Connor answered for her. "What a good idea; you can pick up the saucepan at the same time."

"Thank you. I will come back after I do the washing up. I'd best be going now." I turned and fled those piercing eyes. Our house was silent as I hurried in, slamming the door and leaning my back against it for a moment. Images and questions whirled in my mind so fast that they made time run slow, and I needed to settle them before I faced my family in the kitchen.

Chair legs screeched across the bare slate floor, and Mum's lean frame filled the doorway. "You all right, love?" It was too dark inside to see the concern in her eyes, but I heard it in her voice.

I nodded. "Mrs. O'Connor was very grateful," I managed to say.

Mum was staring at me now. "You alright? You look like you've seen a ghost."

"No. Not a ghost, Mum." My head shook from side to side. "She's not a ghost."

"What exactly did you see, then?"

"Eileen. I saw Eileen."

Mum turned her head and called over her shoulder, "Please start eating. We'll be there in a minute." She took my elbow, her hand warm through the blue-sprigged calico of my sleeve. Squeezing my arm to reassure me, she led me into the tiny parlor, even though it wasn't Sunday, and sat me down on an aging armchair, the worst of its shabbiness hidden under an embroidered antimacassar. She sat opposite me.

"What happened?"

"Eileen fell out of her pram when she was only three. She broke her back. She's had lots of operations, and needs another one, but she's not strong enough yet."

"Poor little pet." Mum tutted her disapproval of the ways of the world.

"Why does God let the little children suffer?" My question tumbled out, even though I knew it was best unspoken.

Mum's eyes pricked with tears. They always did when she thought of Cara. "God's ways are beyond our understanding, love."

SATURDAY, SEPTEMBER 14, 2019 – ADELAIDE

Silence draped the somber, gothic interior of Adelaide's State Library's Mortlock Wing after Kathleen's voice faded away. A click indicated the tape recorder had been turned off.

Alex stroked the stubble on his chin for a moment, then removed his earplugs and set them deliberately on the table before meeting his cousin's eye. "So, what do you think, Cait?" He glanced around at the disapproving stare of a woman studying a display of antique toys in a nearby cabinet, and lowered his voice. "You've been listening to our great-great-grandmother."

Caitlin shifted restlessly in her wheelchair. "We know somehow the tapes were lost in the back of a cupboard for decades. But what do we know about Kathleen?"

"She was Nan's granny," Alex began.

"I know who she was. What I want to know is why did she make the tapes?"

He sat taller in his chair. "Ah, I can help you there. I did a little bit of editing. Just to skip the boring bits." He kept talking, cutting off Caitlin's attempt to interrupt. He didn't want to admit she was right, and he saw now his pursuit of efficiency had kept her in the dark. "I don't know exactly why Kathleen was telling a story about some kid she met way back when, but I do know why she had a tape recorder. It was an oral history project. Kathleen knew the history of the Rachel Forster Hospital in Sydney. One of the nurses arranged for her to record it." Light danced in his eyes as he fixed them on her. "Now I think of it, I reckon Kathleen was a lot like you: a history nerd, and a bit OCD." He ducked away from Caitlin's playful swipe. "She wrote notes, that she put with the tapes. To say why she made them." He pulled a dog-eared exercise book out of his backpack and pushed it across the table to her. "I found this at the bottom of the box."

"Why didn't you tell me before?"

He shrugged. "I just skimmed the notes. I didn't read them properly. I figured I could leave the paperwork to you."

She pursed her lips at his sheepish grin and opened the book.

Well, here I am, eighty-two years old. I must be made of tough stuff, apparently. But I don't feel tough now.

Everyone's pretending I'll be alright, and I'll recover from this surgery. That it was just a simple bowel obstruction. I guess they're trying to give me hope. Spare my feelings. But I know I'm dying. I know it's cancer. I see them talking in hushed voices at the nurse's station, glancing at me under their painted eyelashes, as if I am not only old; as if I am also deaf and stupid. Sometimes, heat surges up in my chest when I'm watching them, before fading away, like everything else about me, too weak to hold itself for long.

I'll play along with their game because it's easier for poor Evie. She's upset, of course, but as long as we pretend, we don't have to talk about any of the hard things. Maybe it's all for the best? Except for the promise I made, that's the sticking point. Over fifty years ago ... Do promises expire if you leave them unfulfilled long enough?

I promised Eileen I would tell Evie what happened to her father. When she was old enough. She's pushing sixty now, and I've never found the right time. But I did my best for her, all those years. We had a good life.

Maybe I can just tell the story on the tape recordings? Evie can listen to them after I'm gone.

It's funny. There I was complaining they treat me like I am stupid because I am old, and yet, being old has given me this opportunity. All because I was telling Sister Murphy some stories about the history of this hospital.

Suddenly I am an expert, and they want to record what I know. Before it's too late.

Sister Murphy came to see me between her rounds, looking like the cat that got the cream. She brought a young man with her, who was training as the hospital's fourth male nurses' aide. His freckled face blushed pink and he looked so bashful, I longed to offer some encouragement. "Seeing how much heavy lifting these nurses do, I can imagine a few nice strong men like you would be a godsend to them," I said.

He rewarded me with a shy smile. "I'd like to train as a nurse, maybe, later."

The women in the next beds were staring at us, scandalized, the bedsheets pulled up to their chins. Silly old biddies. I offered him my arm, showing I didn't mind a male nurse's aide helping me get comfortable. But he wasn't here to nurse me; he was on his dinner break. Sister Murphy had arranged for him to lend me a tape recorder to tell stories about the old hospital.

He moved aside the women's magazine on the Overway table across my knees. I'd been pretending to read it, but honestly, I'm not interested in its reports of what people are doing in 1974, or recipes I will never have time to try. I prefer my memories now, but I watched him with a mixture of curiosity and distrust as he slid an ivory-colored plastic contraption out of his satchel and put it in front of me.

I squinted at it. I'd never seen one before; I have never trusted new-fangled gadgets. "I don't know how to use your fancy machine," I said. My arms were folded defensively across my chest, but I made sure my voice was kind.

He swelled with pride in front of my eyes. "It's the latest thing. I bought it for my Mam. Her folks are all in Scotland, and her parents are getting old. Once a month she records a message on tape to send to them. One of her nephews has a recorder and plays the messages, and then her family records a tape to send back. Much more modern than letters, and you should have seen Mam's face the first time she heard her mother's voice."

It's a long time since I heard my mother's voice. Maybe Evie and my grandchildren would like to hear mine one day, after I've gone. My great-grandchildren, even. Most of them will be too young to remember me, but Timothy. Jesus, Mary, and Joseph, what will happen to Timothy? I can't afford that line of thought. There's comfort in the past; no need to worry about how things end up in the past, because we already know.

You don't need faith to face your past, not like you do to face the future.

I turned back to the earnest young man. "Are you sure I won't break it?"

"Of course, I'm sure."

"I wouldn't know what to say." The words tumbled out in an embarrassed rush, although perhaps I do have a story to tell.

"We thought of that. Sister Murphy will get you started."

"You want me to start now?" Panic rose as I watched him plug a black wire into the box and point a small black rectangle towards me.

"Why not? This is the microphone, and it's also the remote control. See this little switch on the side of it? Slide it up when you want to start recording, and down when you want to stop." He winked like a stage actor. "You don't have to touch the machine itself, see. It's completely fool-proof. You can't break it."

"That's good."

He laughed and told me all I needed to do was keep the microphone near my face, so it could pick up my voice.

Possibilities were firming in my mind, and I started to smile.

Saying thank you seemed too trivial in the face of being trusted with such a special machine, by a young man who didn't know me from a bar of soap. I locked my eyes on his, determined he pay attention to what I was about to say. "Here you are, setting me up to record past history, when you yourself are making history as we speak." Confusion registered in his eyes. "The fourth male nurse's aide to train at the Rachel Forster Hospital. Young man, you are clearly following your dreams into uncharted waters, stepping into territory that was once exclusively women's work. It's easier to record history than to make it, isn't it? Your Mam should be very proud of you."

For a moment, tears glinted in his eyes, or perhaps it was a trick of the light. "Thank you, Mrs. O'Grady. I'll call back in a couple of days and see how you're getting on."

Sister Murphy watched him walk out through the ward, then bent towards me. "Ready to try? I'll ask you a question, to get you talking, then you can talk about whatever you want as you go along. Any memories you think will interest people when this old place is gone."

She shivered and I caught it, a deep shudder that reminded me time never stands still.

I nodded. I've got interesting memories, all right. Eileen's story is a story worth telling. I can't do that without telling my own. And Georgie's. But at this point in my life, what've I got to lose?

STATE LIBRARY, ADELAIDE

Caitlin shifted in her wheelchair, trying to get comfortable. "Okay, so Kathleen was asked to record local history, but she took the opportunity to record Eileen's story. What did she say? She couldn't tell Eileen's story without telling her own."

"Yeah."

"I wonder what happened to the tape with the hospital's history on it?"

Alex shuffled his feet under the table. He'd been in trouble with Caitlin so many times when they were children, he knew he couldn't win. But that didn't mean he would concede she was right straight away. He glanced at her sideways and couldn't help smiling. It was a long time since he'd seen Caitlin looking animated. "Well, I thought I'd save time. There was a tape labelled History of the Rachel Forster Hospital. It sounded boring so I kept it separate."

"Did you listen to it?"

"No, the title was bad enough."

"You're incorrigible. I suppose it was labeled Tape One?" She sighed and put on her serious face. "All history buffs know history starts at the beginning. Play the first tape. We might have missed something."

Alex shrugged. "One way to find out." He gestured to his phone, waiting on the table, and Caitlin pushed her earbuds into place. "Ready?"

She nodded and he pressed the play button. There was a click then a woman's voice, loud and carefully enunciated. "Testing, testing."

"That can't be Kathleen, she sounds wrong. As if she's talking to someone deaf, and that accent! She sounds like she's from a rerun of Paul Hogan." Caitlin stopped talking after the voice counted to three.

"Mrs. Kathleen O'Grady, thank you for agreeing to record what you know about the hospital's history for us. You've lived in Redfern all your life. You're here in the Rachel Forster Hospital in July 1974. But you've been in this hospital before. Pretend you can travel back in time and tell me all about it."

There was a long pause followed by a deep, sighing breath. Then a soft, hesitant voice. "You're sure I won't break that nice young man's new-fangled machine, Sister?"

"She'll be right, Mrs. O'Grady. Blind Freddy could work it. You remember how to turn the tape off?"

"Yes, Sister." Another deep breath, then Kathleen's voice began again, quavering with age, hesitant at first, and then gradually gaining confidence as she warmed to the task.

"It's hard to imagine there was a time when people couldn't get hospital care. When there weren't hospitals to go to, or when poor people couldn't afford to go. We're lucky now, having this lovely big hospital with its paid nurses and all the modern equipment, and anesthetics, and medicines. The Rachel moved to Pitt Street during the Second World War. There's an air raid shelter in the basement, did you know that? No, why would you? It's probably used for storage now. After the war, the second one, the hospital was given an old ambulance, from the Emergency Services. Oh, my, the uses that ambulance was put to. It used to get driven all around the district to help with fundraising. The whole community chipped in, collecting bottles, and donating eggs, all for the cause. We gave eggs when we could. We had hens. And a lemon tree. My mum planted a Granny Smith apple tree. In the Depression, we grew cabbages and potatoes, anything we could cram into the narrow terrace garden. Sometimes Evie and her friends would slip down to Centennial Park and bring back whatever weeds they could find, to feed the chickens. Sometimes I'd put some of the weeds in the soup pot: dandelion greens or dock.

"But I'm rambling, that was long before this hospital was here, of course. Eggs, we used to donate eggs for the egg drives. And I used to sew baby clothes for the hospital too. One night a week we'd have a sewing bee. We helped raise the money to buy the land here and build the buildings. Had a tearoom at the Easter Show, too. There's an old stone well in the basement, that was built by convicts. From way back, when this was farmland. Would have come in handy, maybe, if the air raid shelter had ever needed to be used.

"Back before the Second World War, the hospital had moved into a nice, big house in George Street, just around the corner. It was opened in 1925 by the Governor-General's wife, Lady Rachel Forster. It was named after her, you see. So smart she looked in her nice fur coat and patent leather shoes. We all lined the streets to see her. It wasn't every day a baroness came to Redfern. But even though they added a few wings, the building in George Street soon got too small. Back in the twenties and thirties, this whole area was teeming with people, factory workers, migrants, the unemployed. No one could afford a private doctor or to call a nurse to their house. That's why the lady doctors chose Redfern in the first place.

"But the very first hospital those lady doctors set up was in Surry Hills, less than a mile from here, back in 1922. The hospital had a different name then: The New Hospital for Women and Children. Well, it was a new hospital alright, but it was in an old building. A tiny terrace house. Two stories. The funny thing was, it was a very run-down house. The floor upstairs was alarmingly rickety, so they didn't take any heavy furniture up there. They couldn't even treat weighty patients up there, in case the floor gave way.

"That house has gone now. I think it fell down of its own accord before the slums were cleared.

"There wasn't a hospital here at all during the First World War. So, it couldn't have helped my husband, Georgie, in any case. When he was wounded, Eileen's Brown Nurses came to help us. Which brings me to Eileen …

"Oh, Eileen. I'm sure the nice young man won't mind if I use his machine to record your story.

"Evie's upset, Eileen. Did you see her yesterday, in visiting hour? She was sitting taut beside my bed, with her knees pressed together and her hands folded over the strap of the black, leather handbag balanced on her lap. Poor Evie. I reached out and patted the yellow-and-white crimplene of her sleeve. She was blinking away tears. I pretended I couldn't see them through her cat's-eye glasses. I thought it was best.

"I never did tell her, you know, even though I promised you I would. It's too late now, isn't it? Unless I tell the story on these tapes.

Your story, and my story, and she can listen to them afterwards? What do you think? —"

Another voice cut across the whirring of the tape, sharp with worry. "Are you alright, Mum? You were mumbling to yourself. I couldn't work out what you were saying."

"I wasn't mumbling, Evie. I was talking to Eileen."

"Eileen? There's no one else here, Mum. Just the other patients and their visitors."

"She was here as clear as day. You just didn't see her."

"Oh, Mum." A shuddering half-sob. "She's seeing things, Sister."

The nurse's voice again. "Things?"

"A woman. She was talking to her. Someone called Eileen."

"It's alright, Evie, Eileen's gone now. But she'll come back. She always came back when I needed her."

Footsteps and the sounds of movement, Evie's voice saying, "I'll see you later, then, Mum."

Calm returns. A breezy sigh. Then Kathleen, content and dreamy, speaks again. "Ah, where was I? Eileen O'Connor … I remember the first time I saw her. Well, I didn't really *see* her, then. But I saw her arrive. We were just children.

"I'm tired, Little Mother. I don't know if I can go on. Your face is as serene as ever, Eileen. Though somehow, it's changed … Ah, I see what it is now. The little pucker lines between your eyebrows are gone, smoothed away."

"You still understand my thoughts, because you answer me, 'There's no pain here, Kathleen. You'll have no pain when you get here.'

"Do my eyes look as round as they feel, Eileen? No pain?"

"None at all." Your smile is soft as moonlight and, as you nod encouragement, your hair spills over your shoulders like a curly waterfall and brushes against my cheek …

* * *

A click on the recording marked the moment the microphone was turned off. Alex pressed pause while Caitlin popped her earbuds. She laid them on the polished timber tabletop, making sure the snaking wires didn't tangle with his.

"Trust a geek to have a jack that lets us plug two sets of earplugs into the same phone." She spoke in a hushed, library whisper. "Are you expecting a message from someone?"

He shook his head in eager denial, ashamed she had noticed him checking messages, and deflected her question. The deflection seemed effortless in the same way a prize fighter evading an opponent's blow can look effortless.

"So that's how come the tapes got made," he said with feigned nonchalance. He had set this weekend aside for Caitlin. He put down his phone and pushed it just out of reach. Okay, so he wasn't interested in poor Nan's tapes made by a batty old lady on her deathbed, but this weekend was about Caitlin, and he just had to keep focused on her. He dredged up a childhood memory and a smile played around the corners of his mouth.

"What are you thinking about?" asked Caitlin.

"Remember when I was four and went paddling in the creek? You dobbed me in for ruining my new sandals *and* going in the creek without an adult."

She flushed. "I was eight years old. Our parents were terrified one of us would drown and had drummed the rules into us."

"You always were a goody-two-shoes." Alex grinned, his head on an angle so his fringe flopped across one eye.

"Well, you didn't drown, did you?"

"Hmm. Apparently, you saved me. Though the water *was* only ten centimeters deep."

Her smile faded. "We did have fun, when we were kids, didn't we?"

He nodded, then shrugged, baffled by the sadness etched into her face. "Yeah. Then we grew up, I guess, went off in our own directions, and lost touch a bit."

"But not completely, Alex." Tears welled up in her eyes. "You came when I needed you."

"You would have done the same for me, cuz."

He was certain of it, but she hesitated. Her tears hovered, threatening to break over the barrier of her lower lids. He kept talking, bringing her back to the present, wanting to make sure the dam didn't burst. "Maybe I owed you, from you not letting me drown when we were kids, Cait. What about the tapes? What do you think of the tapes?"

She took a deep, steadying breath. "They're awesome. We're listening to our great-great-grandmother's voice. Hearing what she sounded like."

His tone bright, urging her to stay cheerful, Alex focused on the task at hand. "I reckon Kathleen was as nervous learning to use the tape recorder as Nan was when we taught her how to Skype."

"Yes, the generation gap strikes again." A knot untied in Alex's stomach as he savored the fleeting twinkle of humor in her expression. "I love Kathleen's accent, that hint of an Irish lilt in her voice. She must have inherited it from her parents seeing as they emigrated only a few years before she was born. I'm so glad Nan got to hear it before she died." Caitlin's voice was even, but Alex saw the tension in her neck muscles that kept it that way.

The hospital history hadn't caught his interest, and he shivered at the thought of spending more time hearing about a poor, sick little girl, but he sighed and chose surrender. This project was bringing Caitlin out of her shell already. After everything she'd been through because of him, he was determined not to let her slip back.

"So, I know who Kathleen is," Alex said with mock pride as if he had deciphered some complicated mathematics equation. "But who's Evie again?"

Caitlin shook her head. "Come on, Einstein. Evie's our great-grand-mother, Nan's mother."

"Who else did she mention? Timothy? She was worried about Timothy."

"That's not surprising, in 1974."

He appraised her with interest, and his features relaxed into a grin. "I don't get it," he claimed, teasing. "Who was Timothy?"

Caitlin clapped a hand to her forehead, playing along. "Kathleen's grandson. My father. Your Uncle Tim."

He rolled his eyes theatrically. "Silly me." Growing serious now, his eyebrows drew together. "So, we know who Evie and Tim are. And she talks about the nurse and the guy with the recorder, but what was going on with Eileen? No one else could see her when Kathleen talked about her on the tape. Was she hallucinating?"

Caitlin chewed her lip. "We don't know for sure it's the same Eileen, do we? Maybe it was another Eileen she knew, come to visit her?"

"Then why couldn't anyone else see her?"

"I don't know."

He studied her with a sideways gaze, treasuring the genuine interest in her eyes. "You're enjoying this, aren't you?"

She looked surprised as she answered without hesitation. "Yes, yes, I am. And meeting here at the State Library was a great idea. I love the architecture, but, honestly, being anywhere that's not a hospital or the four walls at home makes a nice change."

He struggled to find an answer to that. Guilt chewed at his insides. It was his fault she'd been hurt. His gaze turned to the imposing interior of the building for a moment, but, from his seat in their alcove, even craning his neck he couldn't see up to the windows of the mansard roof above the second gallery with its wrought iron balustrades. French Renaissance, why would mid-nineteenth century gentlemen in the then colony of South Australia have chosen something so un-English?

Alex snapped his mind back and chose the first safe topic that popped into his head. "Is it time to take the first thing out of the tin? You said everything seemed to be in order. Maybe they fit the tracks on the recording?"

"Well, you've already got us out of order, haven't you?"

He groaned, but his eyes were smiling. "You mean you want to listen to the first track again?"

"The one where Kathleen meets Eileen. We don't want to miss anything."

A thought that was bouncing around in the furthest recesses of Alex's mind took shape. "Back up a bit. If Kathleen wasn't hallucinating …"

"Hmm?"

"How could it be the same Eileen? She was so sick when she was a child, I can't imagine she could have lived to be in her eighties too. What was going on when Kathleen was on her deathbed?"

Alex relaxed again as a smile twitched on Caitlin's lips before she swallowed it, putting on the serious look she used to wear when they were children, when she would play up the fact she was four years older than him. She pushed the tin away and picked up her earbuds with a flourish. "There's only one way to find out."

He reached for the play button. "Listen to more of the recording?"

"In the proper order from now on," Caitlin reminded him, waggling her finger playfully.

Kathleen's voice, steeped in awe, again crossed the decades, and flowed through their earbuds. The hairs on the backs of their necks stood up.

I remember the first time I saw her …

* * *

"How awful that Eileen broke her back." Caitlin's face was wreathed in sympathy. "And had lots of operations. They barely had anesthetics in 1900. I can't imagine what that would have been like for a child." The sleeve of her blue denim shirt slid up as she took out her earbuds.

Alex shook his head, tearing his eyes away from the small puncture scar on the side of her wrist, where a drip had been. "I can't imagine either. And how did she break her back falling out of a pram? Kids must fall out of prams all the time."

"I don't know, Alex. Maybe her back was weak to start with?"

"Maybe we'll find out more on the next track. It wasn't a good time to be sick or injured, back then. And Kathleen's sister Cara, my Mum was named after her. What did she die of, do you think?"

"Coughing up blood? Tuberculosis, probably. It was common back then. They built isolation hospitals for sufferers. Could even order people to live in them, until they got better, or …" She shuddered as if a cold breeze had swept through the stillness of the library.

"Or what?"

"Died."

"No shit." Alex's eyes widened with horror.

"But Cara sounds like she died at home. Maybe that's why Kathleen wanted to record there weren't any hospitals back then?"

"Or maybe the family couldn't afford a doctor." His voice was harsh. "That's awful to think, isn't it?"

"Yes. Let's change the subject." Caitlin shuddered again, as if she was shaking off thoughts of death and hospital wards.

Of course, Alex thought, she'd had enough of hospital wards to last her a lifetime. He spoke quickly. "This place reminds me of Harry Potter. Watch out for Professor McGonagle. She'd give you demerit points for laughing in the library."

Caitlin shook her head. "Madam Pince. Madam Pince was the librarian at Hogwarts."

"Whatever." He pushed the box over to her. "Let's see what's in this."

Her eyes lit up as she inserted her nails under the flower-speckled lid of the toffee tin and prized it open. "Should I be wearing gloves to handle these?" she breathed.

"Nah, I looked it up. Some experts are saying gloves don't actually do anything to protect papers. Just hold everything from the edges as best you can."

With cautious reverence, she lifted a sepia photo off the top of the pile of papers. A young woman with sunken eyes and a big, joy-filled smile gazed out of the image. Her curly hair blowing free in a light breeze. Dressed in white and sitting in a cane wheelchair.

"Who's this?"

"I don't know." He shrugged. "Read the back."

"Not yet." Caitlin studied the image, then pushed it in front of Alex. "What a beautiful smile she has. But something's wrong. Look at how dark the shadows are around her eyes."

Alex squinted. "Yeah, maybe. Unless it's the lighting; she's out in a garden."

"In a wheelchair, Alex. She looks like she's in pain to me. And her foot's in a funny position. As if she is paralyzed." Her breath caught and she turned eyes full of appeal on her cousin. "What if it's Eileen?"

Alex took the picture, careful to only hold its edges, and turned it over. "For my dear Kathleen. 1918. That's not much to go on."

Caitlin stared at the back of the photo. "It doesn't have any photographer's details on it. Maybe someone was an amateur photographer and developed the photo themselves?"

Alex put the photo down beside the tin. He didn't want to look at Caitlin with her leg stiff in its brace and confined to the cheap, hired wheelchair. He couldn't meet her gaze. He was afraid he'd see the ghost of pain in her eyes too. Pain he'd caused.

Caitlin's excitement was palpable, but Alex's mind was too full of the echoes of screeching tires and scrunching metal to notice. He jumped when she spoke.

"That smile would light up a room. And her hair is long and curly, like a waterfall. I think it's her ... *Eileen!*"

REDFERN–1903

I was reluctant to open the door, in case she was sleeping, despite Mrs. O'Connor's smiling invitation. Eileen looked up at me, and a contagious smile formed on her joyful face.

"Oh, Kathleen, I am glad your mother allowed you to come back," Eileen said.

"So am I." And I was, even though I didn't understand why, not then.

"Come on in," invited Mary, who was perched on the end of the bed.

"Won't you come here and brush my hair?" Eileen wriggled herself up from her lacy pillow into a sitting position and waved her frail hand over the silver hairbrush lying partially obscured in a fold in the quilt. I wondered if she was too weak to lift it. A question which distracted me from feeling awkward at the intimacy of the act she asked of me, a complete stranger.

"If that's what you want?"

"She loves having her hair brushed," Mary confided. "But tonight, I'm sticking some pictures in her scrapbook, so my hands are busy." She held up a picture, a bulldog, cut from a newspaper. "Just be careful not to bump her back."

My breathing quickened as I scooped up her hair and draped it over my left forearm, hoping I could brush it without touching her spine. As I did so, I noticed a lump on her back, running from shoulder to shoulder. My eyes fixed on it, below the curtain of reddish-brown hair. Part of me didn't want to look, but another part stared at that lump, and thought it was shaped like a little wing. Eileen let her head sway, keeping time as the brush swished rhythmically through her hair.

A hundred strokes later, she held up a fresh, blue ribbon for me. I remembered how she had it before supper, looped under her hair and tied in a big bow at the top of her head.

She smiled. "I enjoyed my delicious supper. Your mother is very kind."

"She always says people should stick together and help each other when they can."

"I think I will like your mother very much. But right now, I'd like us to get to know each other. Where were you born?"

"Right here in Baptist Street. A few doors up from where we live now."

"We moved to Sydney last year. See the photograph on the mantelpiece? Could you get it for me? This was taken five years ago, at our old house in Richmond, Melbourne." A hint of mischief shone in her eyes. "Can you work out which one I am?"

I studied the photograph. Mr. and Mrs. O'Connor were seated in front of a timber trellis, with four children. Something didn't make sense. There were two older girls in the picture. Mary was the only older girl now. Had this family lost a daughter too? "Five years ago? Frank must be the baby," I guessed. "And this one looks like Mary, but I don't see you. Are you sure you were in the photo?"

Eileen laughed, her pale face shining with the pleasure of having a secret joke. For a split second, my body stiffened, but the instant I realized she wasn't laughing at me, I couldn't help myself and started to laugh too.

Mary rolled her eyes. "Don't mind her. She likes to tease."

My eyes met Eileen's like magnets snapping together, savoring our mutual mirth, but not just that, something much deeper for which I have no words.

"Don't mind her. She has too much starch in her ..." Eileen paused dramatically. "Petticoat."

Skating so close to being risqué was too much even for Mary's attempted dignity, and we exploded into laughter, Mary and I flopping back onto the bed, but despite our merriment we were still mindful not to bump Eileen.

"Oh, look, I like this. I'm taller than both of you now," Eileen giggled.

I rolled over to look at her, mock triumph in her pale little face, and dried my tears that, suddenly, weren't just from laughter. She broke the tension, beckoning me to hold the photo closer to her. "That's me." She pointed to a serious-faced girl, sitting stiff and awkward on her father's lap. "About four years after I broke my back."

I ran sums through my head. "You broke your back when you were three, and this picture was taken in 1898." She was only about as tall as Cara was, and Cara was six when she died.

"It's hard to fathom, isn't it?"

"I don't understand."

"I was born in 1892, so I'm eleven years old now."

My tongue tied itself into knots.

"Breaking my back stopped it from growing properly, and all the operations I've had, haven't fixed it."

"Does it hurt very much?"

Her brows drew closer, and she turned to the lithograph of Jesus of the Sacred Heart, in a dark, wooden frame hanging on the wall beside her bed. Her voice was low, reverential, almost as if she was whispering in church. "Oh, yes. But I welcome it, because it reminds me of Him. He suffered so much more for *me*."

Her gaze returned to me, and I swallowed the lump in my throat. She held out her hand and I took the thin, bony fingers in my own. "Oh, Eileen."

"Don't worry," she nodded with grave sympathy in her eyes, as if it was I who was suffering. "Kathleen, we will always be friends."

Although I had met her less than two hours before, I sat straight on the bed. "Promise?"

Eileen's response was a serene smile, but Mary spoke. "She doesn't have to promise. Sometimes, she just knows things."

"Like what?"

"Oh, just things." Mary's attention was back on the scrapbook.

An idea occurred to me. "Do you think you'll be going to the same school as me?"

"Which school do you go to?"

"Sisters of Mercy." My breath caught, waiting for Mary's reply.

"At Mount Carmel, Waterloo?"

"Yes."

We smiled like conspirators plotting world domination.

* * *

It took months for Eileen to recover from her operation and be ready for school. I hadn't seen her legs before, but her skirt slipped up towards her knees as she slid off the edge of her bed to stand on the scrubbed, timber floor in her well-polished, brown boots. Thin. Too thin. Like two little sticks. "You'll like school, Eily," Frank reassured her. "There's nothing to worry about."

"I'm not worried," Eileen said, but her jaw was clenched enough to make her lips blanch. With painful, shuffling steps she made her way to the narrow entrance hall.

"Everyone's been hoping you would be well enough to come today." Mary was ready, holding their shared lunch pail and little bundle of books and a slate strapped together with an old, brown belt.

Mrs. O'Connor appeared in the kitchen doorway, drying her hands on her apron. She bent over to kiss Eileen's forehead, and whispered, "Your first day at your new school, Eileen. Be brave and strong."

"I will."

"Mind your sister."

"We will," chorused her two brothers and Mary.

Charlie stood soldier-straight, assuming whatever authority he could at nine years old. "Father's the man of the house, but when it comes to Eileen's education, I'm the man of the school."

His mother held him close, a swift, fierce movement, as she turned away, not wanting anyone to see her face. "Off you go now; you can't be late on Eileen's first day at school." She kept her face averted till we had gone out into the street, but I felt her anxious eyes on my back as we began the walk to school.

Mrs. O'Connor was worried how Eileen would manage. But perhaps she was relieved too, to not be nursing her. She had two boarders to cook, and wash, and clean for, as well as her own family.

Normally we would walk faster, keeping up with Frank and my brothers Patrick and Jo as they scurried about in front. But now the younger boys were walking arm in arm chatting, and my sister, Betty, and some of the smaller girls were playing free-form hopscotch, stooping to pick up little stones to toss on the road and jump over. Everyone tethered themselves to Eileen's pace, the careful, little steps she took as she tried not to jar her poor back.

I watched her out of the corner of my eye, as she leaned on Mary's arm. Her skin grew paler despite the flush of exertion on her cheeks, and perspiration beaded on her face. Not for the first time, nor the last, I wondered if the doctors knew what they were doing, because she didn't seem to be getting any better to me.

"Halfway there, Eily," Frank called as we turned left into Elizabeth Street, passing a strip of shop fronts and terrace houses as Eileen's pace slowed again.

Charlie came closer to his sister and murmured, "I can carry you, if you like?" But she shook her head resolutely and kept taking her little steps. The excitement that had been in her eyes at the beginning of the trip was gone now, replaced by grim determination, but as the road rose to the hill of Mount Carmel, she stopped, gray and panting, beaten. Handing her books and pail to me, Mary cradled her sister in her arms, and carried her up the hill to the school, past the curious stares of other children.

"You made it," Mary said with forced cheerfulness, setting her down near the schoolroom step. "Your first day at school."

Eileen grew a little stronger after that, and eventually, determined as ever, she struggled her way up the unrelenting hill and its steps, to either school or Church. She'd refuse any offers of assistance, but her slow progress and painful dignity was so obvious that passers-by and churchgoers alike would stand aside and watch her, sometimes whispering to their companions. Sometimes keeping silent watch like a guard of honor, heads bowed and dabbing at their eyes.

But by the end of the day, she was exhausted, and her brothers would have to carry her home. And then she fell ill again.

STATE LIBRARY, ADELAIDE

Alex studied Caitlin's face from under his downturned eyelashes, quiet anxiety twisting in his gut. The shadows under her eyes had deepened, and her shoulders hunched forward as if the effort of sitting upright was tiring. Self-recrimination filled his brain: was this all too much for her? Maybe he should have listened to the tapes first? His Mum was right, though, after all she'd been through with the car accident, she needed something to get her involved in life again.

Although Alex had no trouble getting digital copies of the tapes, he didn't have the patience or the interest to sort out the historical context on his own. He sighed, just as the track ended and Caitlin turned towards him.

"She was one tough young lady." Alex grinned, but he felt weighed down with sadness and worry.

"Yes. She didn't give up, did she?"

"Doesn't look like it."

Caitlin fell silent and Alex reached across the timber table to take her hand. His eyes found their way to the small puncture scar on her wrist.

"What would it have felt like, to have to be carried in to school in front of all the other kids?" Caitlin asked, squeezing his fingers before gently pulling her hand away.

He drew a deep breath, his eyes rivetted to her face, watching her brief struggle with emotion before she closed down again. He towed the line, taking the opportunity to show he empathized, without risking her self-control by overwhelming her with sympathy. "It would have sucked. Her exhaustion was obvious, she didn't look well, and although she was eleven, maybe twelve by now, her growth was so stunted that she looked like she was six, and her younger sister could carry her. I would have felt humiliated."

"Yeah. And kids can say such unkind things. I wonder if she was bullied?"

"I hope not. She had enough on her plate." Alex felt the heat rush to his cheeks. "No one should be bullied just because of who they are." He watched, half-relieved, as Caitlin missed his reaction and continued to focus on Eileen's story.

"She must have been absolutely determined to go to school. I wonder if she was behind, because of all the time she missed?" she asked, frowning.

"I guess her parents might have taught her at home."

They lapsed into silence. Alex worried about the effect Eileen's story was having on Caitlin, but he was afraid to ask. It was safer to keep talking.

"Cait, what do you think happened to Eileen? She clearly had a huge impact on Kathleen, because she's all she talks about, more than her own family. Even in that first part of the tape, where she was recording the history of the hospital, because the nurses wanted it, it was like Eileen was still in the front of her mind."

"Well, one thing's certain. This photo must be Eileen. A girl with long hair in a wheelchair. But the date here is 1918. Fifteen years after Kathleen first met her. At least we know Eileen lived till then." She sighed her relief.

"What's next in the box?" Alex leaned over to look.

Caitlin lifted a much-folded, yellowed newspaper article from its protective, tissue-paper bed, and frowned in concentration as she opened it and spread it on the table. The two pages of small, dense print seemed uninviting, but they drew closer regardless, reading the headline from The Catholic Press, "August 19, 1909. The Golden Jubilee of the Church of Our Lady of Mount Carmel."

"1909. I bet Kathleen and Eileen were both there, with their families."

Alex picked up a corner of the top page and peeked underneath. "Oh, look. Kathleen has circled part of the article. That must be the bit she thought was important. Thank goodness we don't need to read about the sermons and stuff."

Caitlin's brow creased as goosebumps tingled over her skin. "Maybe Kathleen wanted to make it easy for you." She laughed abruptly, and pulled the paper closer to her, reading aloud before he could answer. "Viewing the Future. If Father Collins' wishes were fulfilled today, he would have this hill upon which his church stands disappear entirely, so that the good, old people of the district would not have to labor up its sides, and, when they reach its crest, have to ascend so many steps, like the ladder of Jacob. (Laughter.) I do not know whether another church could be built below, or whether this one could be put on rollers and transferred to a lower level. (Laughter.) I am told that Father Collins was thinking of getting a small railway to bring the people up, but as the efficiency of the aeroplane is developing so rapidly, who knows that he will not bring his people to this height in airships."

"Father Collins sounds like he knew how to play up to an audience. Maybe his sermons wouldn't have been as bad as you imagined," Caitlin teased.

"If Eileen's school was on the hill with that church, no wonder she struggled getting there," Alex said, serious now. "But I wonder if she would have wanted to take a plane ride?"

"In 1909, even a car ride was a novelty." Caitlin shuddered. "And they didn't have seatbelts."

REDFERN–1906

"Hello, Eileen. Are you awake?" I whispered through the open front window of her house, unable to see her through the fluttering lace curtain.

"Hello, Kathleen. I'm awake."

In the long weeks of Eileen's being bedbound after another surgical attempt to drain pus from her back, it had become my custom to say hello to her through her window on my way to and from school. The front parlor had been converted to her bedroom, so she could see people passing by in the street, and she often had a steady stream of visitors peeping in.

"How are you today?"

"I can see a little better."

"I'm glad." I poked my head in through the curtains.

Eileen laughed. "You look like a nun, all that white around your head."

"A nun? Not a bride with a veil?"

"Maybe. But I'll never get married."

"Why not?"

Eileen's gesture encompassed her distorted little body. "Not cut out for it, I don't think. Anyway, I want to be a nun."

"A nun?"

"I've always wanted to be a nun. That way I can do some good in the world."

"Do you want to come over later? The girls from school collected some magazine pictures for you. If you bring your scrapbook, we can stick them in."

"Yes, please."

"Dad will come and get you after supper."

While I finished washing the supper dishes, Dad carried Eileen across the road and tenderly settled her into the armchair that we now thought of as especially hers. Even though I had seen Dad play with my brothers and sisters when they were little, and remembered him helping nurse Cara years before, it still surprised me to see this coarse, muscular factory worker, with oil stains he could never scrub off his hands, and broken fingernails, cradling Eileen's broken body as if she were made of eggshells. With one hand, he supported her, while the other slid a soft pillow behind her back. She just had that effect on people. Brought out the best in us.

While Dad arranged Eileen's feet on a cushion laid on top of an old apple crate, I opened the envelope of pictures and put them on Mum's tin tray. Eileen's legs were so thin, we always laid yet another cushion on her knees before putting the tray in her lap. During her latest bout of illness, I had made two more cushions out of an old frock too worn to be cut down again, because we'd never had enough to keep her comfortable before.

Her long, thin fingers separated the images and sorted them on the tray. Her eyes lit up. "Three bulldogs."

"Your favorite."

"Yes. I don't know why. It's something about their funny little faces. And how they don't look at all like bulls."

"And they're all wobbly when they are puppies."

"Oh, yes, maybe that's why. They're all wobbly like me."

I handed her the scrapbook and watched her curly-haired head bent closely over it. She squinted to see the pictures better, as she arranged them into designs that pleased her. A page of dogs. A page of plump children from advertisements, wearing bright clothes, many of them eating.

"Why do you like pictures of fat children eating so much?" I asked, conscious of her thinness and her delicate appetite.

"Because, when I am able, I will work to make sure children are healthy and have enough to eat."

"What will you do?" I couldn't imagine Eileen ever being strong enough to work.

"I told you. I will be a nun. I will be in an Order that looks after poor people, especially women and children. In their own homes."

"Are there any nuns who do that?"

"I don't know. If there are, I will find them. Or I will join the Sisters of Mercy." Her face was lit by ideals.

"What if they don't take you?" I clapped my hand over my mouth, horrified such a callous question could have slipped so easily from my tongue.

Eileen's eyebrows drew together for a moment, then the familiar determination lifted her chin. "If I have a vocation to be a nun, nothing will stop me. Even if I have to found my own order."

Still embarrassed, I laughed. "What a rebel you are, Eileen. You won't let anything get in your way, will you?"

"No, of course not. If the Blessed Virgin could be the mother of Baby Jesus, then I can find a way to serve God. Even if it seems impossible."

Dad hovered in the doorway to offer Eileen some bread and milk. "Heaven help the pope, if the Church gets in the way of Eileen's vocation," he muttered, shaking his head, his eyes shining with amusement.

"The Church." Eileen caught some of his words. "It's been so long since I was well enough to go to church. I do miss it, even though Father Collander brings me Holy Communion at home. I miss going to school, too." Never one for self-pity, she shook her head gently and summoned a smile. "I am grateful Mum and Daddy can continue my education at home, though. And it was lovely of the girls to send these pictures. I'll write a thank you note; will you take it to school for me, Kathleen?"

"Of course."

Eileen's face became serious, and dread seeped through my belly. "Kathleen, I need to tell you something. We'll be moving house soon."

"No," I protested. I couldn't imagine life without Eileen's constant presence. "Where to?"

"You won't need to miss me. Just around the corner. Telopea Street. The rent is good, and the house is bigger, so Mum can take in more boarders. It's my fault. The medical bills …"

"It's not your fault you fell out of a pram when you were little, Eileen. That was an accident, or maybe the carelessness of the maid. But definitely not your fault."

She frowned. "Well, fault or no, my family are caught up in my suffering." Our gazes connected. "As are my friends. My journey through suffering is like Jesus' journey to Calvary. I've been praying my suffering redeems you all, as His redeemed me."

My mind raged against her words. I was a Catholic, brought up on the suffering of Christ since infancy. But I didn't want *her* suffering for me. I didn't want her suffering at all. It didn't seem right that God should allow it. And yet, looking at the expression of peaceful, almost blissful, surrender on her face, I couldn't say any of that.

I took her hand in mine, averted my gaze to study its pale boniness, and whispered, "Thank you for your prayers, Eileen. I hope I am worthy of them."

"Of course you are. Just be good, and love me, and love Them." She tilted her head to the lithograph of Mary and Jesus with their Sacred Hearts exposed, that we, like every Catholic family of the time, had on our wall.

"We won't be able to talk through your bedroom window anymore." My mouth turned down as the loss hit me hard.

"We will, just a different window. I'll make my room in a glassed-in balcony off my parents' room, facing onto the street. It will be further for your father to carry me here, but you can call by after school, can't you? If your mother can spare you."

"Of course, I can. I'll make sure of it."

Alex sighed as he pressed pause. His stomach rumbled and he rubbed his eyes and forehead vigorously.

"You're hungry?" Caitlin asked.

"Not exactly. I'm not sure I'm … comfortable with this idea of Eileen's about her suffering. I don't know." He glanced around the library looking for inspiration then spoke in a rush. "This is going to sound weird. Don't laugh. It's kind of hurting my brain to think of a kid like her, so terribly ill and not wanting to get better."

Caitlin had been about to drink, but put down her water bottle and gave him her full attention. "What do you mean?"

"Well, she was clearly bedbound then. And what was that about her eyesight being poor too? But she accepted being ill, deformed, in pain, having loads of operations—though I can't see they did any good, and that's pretty upsetting too—accepted suffering because Jesus was crucified, almost welcomed it. What did she say about praying her suffering should redeem others? She was just a teenager. It's enough to turn my stomach." He picked up the photo of Eileen, the older Eileen, taken when she was a young woman, not a girl, and looked into her haunting, shadowed eyes. "Look at her: she's a beautiful person, inside and out. It just isn't fair." He was shocked to find himself fighting back tears and turned away.

The student in the opposite niche scowled at them again.

A shadow crossed Caitlin's face as she looked at her cousin. "Come on, let's get some fresh air and then we'll find you some lunch."

Alex returned the treasured artefacts carefully into the box and nestled it into his bag, under Caitlin's watchful eye. He stood up. "Where would you like to go?"

She led the way, wheeling herself from the Gothic-style Mortlock Wing to the lift in the modern foyer, and out through the back door of the library. "Well, I've been cooped up indoors for months. Would you mind taking me to see the River Torrens?"

"Sure."

They made their way down a lane way, past the Migration Museum, and Caitlin stopped her wheelchair by its masonry wall topped with broken bottles.

"The problem is, we are thinking with our contemporary brains, about the attitude of a young woman a century ago, Alex. She came from a different world."

"Okay …"

"See this wall? It is from her era. What does it tell you?"

His eyes travelled to the top of the high stone wall, studded with broken glass. "I've always wondered about it. What's with the broken bottles?"

"Think home-made barbed wire."

"What?" The wall suddenly became an aggressor in their midst, and he scowled at it with distaste.

"This used to be the Destitute Asylum in the nineteenth century. No one wanted the inmates to be able to escape, so they built high walls and put broken glass at the top to stop people climbing over them."

"Who lived here?" Alex gaped, incredulous.

"The poor, the sick, unmarried mothers …"

Alex typed into his phone, then read from the screen, "They had to wear uniforms and do forced labor. Parents were allowed to see their children for *two hours* per week. And this newspaper article from 1872 said *seventy-five per cent will most likely never quit it except by death!* What the?"

"People thought differently then, remember. Being poor, sick, or an unwed mother marked people as mentally and morally inferior, because the idea of survival of the fittest had become pervasive in society."

"But that's bullshit."

"It was the culturally accepted bullshit of the time, Alex. Of the time and the culture that shaped Eileen's thinking."

He sighed. "Okay, I get it. You're saying to understand how someone thinks, you have to go beyond your own reactions to their cultural values and let yourself feel into what it was like to be them."

Caitlin grinned at him. "Sometimes, you're really smart."

Chuffed, he returned the grin. "Only sometimes?"

"Okay, Mr. Smarty-pants, what did Eileen have in common with the inmates of the Destitute Asylum, do you think?"

He counted off on his fingers. "Her mother took in boarders, so they must have been poor. She was crippled and ill. She didn't get much education because of her illness ..."

"Her surname was O'Connor. Her family might have been recent Irish immigrants."

"So, if things fell apart for her, she would have been one of the seventy-five per cent who didn't make it out alive." He punched his thigh, and Caitlin turned away with bleak eyes.

"Oh, Eileen. This is getting real now," she murmured, looking nervous as she wheeled herself down the sloping pavement towards the river.

"She gets under your skin, doesn't she?" Caitlin nodded her reply and Alex grumbled, "I still don't get this religious suffering thing, though. Come on, I'll steer you downhill." Alex took the handles of her wheelchair, and they fell into silence for a few minutes until they got to the bottom of the hill.

He took care to position the wheelchair where she could admire the tranquil vista over the river to the trees on the far bank and applied the brakes. Three airborne ducks slid into the breeze-rippled water, leaving V-trails behind them.

"Thinking about the religious thing," Caitlin resumed, enjoying the warmth of the sun on her skin, and the opportunity to talk, "Eileen was born in 1892. The Irish Potato Famine caused a million people to starve, and another million to emigrate. That was only forty years before she was born."

"So, you're saying the Irish were used to suffering, starving and being refugees, and that would have flavored how they interpreted their religion?"

"Of course, it would have. But there was more. Ireland was ruled by English overlords for centuries, who collected rents and made the rules. And even during the Potato Famine, when people were starving, huge amounts of food—meat and dairy and grain—were exported out of Ireland."

"But that's awful."

"Hmm …" A lone black swan sailed past them, through reflections of fluffy clouds and blue sky, and Caitlin took a photo. "It all depends on how you look at it," she said, her gaze still on the disturbed reflections in the river. A slight, thoughtful frown creased her brow.

"How?"

"Well, the Catholic religion focuses on how Jesus was humiliated, victimized, crucified, and died a horrible death. But something good came out of it; his suffering saved souls."

"I never quite got how that worked. Did you?" he asked.

"We don't have to. The Lord works in mysterious ways, remember? We just have to get into the mindset of the person we are trying to understand."

"So, an Irish Catholic of that time would believe Jesus—through no fault of his own—suffered to save her soul."

"Yes."

"And therefore, she could dedicate her own suffering to the salvation of others."

"Yes."

"Okay, I think I get it." He knit his brows again. "But we don't think like that now. Today, someone like Eileen might see suffering as an obstacle she has to overcome in order to fulfill her best potential."

Caitlin pursed her lips in thought, then nodded. "Yes, I suppose she might. Or she might get lost in the role of victim and give up."

"That wasn't Eileen's style." Alex surprised himself with his vehemence.

"I reckon you're right." She smiled up at him, her eyes wide. Something lurched in his chest, and he ruffled her hair with tender fingers.

"It isn't your style, either."

Her smile froze and shattered into a million pieces.

Alex clutched at the easiest topic of conversation. "Ready for lunch?"

Waiting until the road was clear of traffic, they faced the large, white building commanding a view over a bitumen parking lot.

"In World War I, soldiers used to muster for parade here, on the Torrens Parade Ground," Caitlin explained.

For a moment, their imaginations filled with images of lean, tanned diggers preparing to head off on their only chance of an overseas adventure.

"We'll have to see what we can find out about Nan's Grandpa George too, and what happened to him in the war."

"One thing at a time, Alex. We made a plan to go through the tapes in order, then see what's in the box. We want to get through as much as possible this weekend. We need to be systematic. We'll see what else we can find out this afternoon, and then we'll regroup."

"Okay, but let's go up ANZAC Walk, to the War Memorial, before lunch. We can pay our respects."

"That's a nice idea."

"Oh no! We can't get the wheelchair in here." Alex stopped at the base of the War Memorial, surveying the steps.

She smiled. "It's fine. I've been in there before. I like the outside," she reassured him. "I'll take some more photos. There was nothing to photograph stuck in hospital."

He hesitated at the narrow entrance, his cheeks flushed. "You could use me as crutches, Cait. It's not many steps. You'd manage."

"Then we'd have to leave the wheelchair out here. I'm fine. You go in and pay our respects." Caitlin winked encouragement at him before wheeling herself around to better see the large white angel hovering above statues of three startled civilians—a girl, a young man in scholar's robes and a farmer—as if he was ready to plunge his sword deep into the earth. *The Spirit of Duty.*

Circling around to the northern side, she looked up at a bare-breasted angel, ascending to heaven with a dead soldier hanging limp and naked, except for a laurel wreath, from one arm and a long sword in the other.

Emerging back into sunlight from the dark chamber, Alex circled the monument to find where Caitlin was waiting for him. "What are you looking at?" he asked.

"The *Spirit of Compassion.*"

"I can't see much compassion in that sculpture."

"No, I don't get it, to be honest. It gives me the creeps. How was the inside?"

"So many names, all engraved neatly in brass. George's name will be on a memorial somewhere. It should be easy enough to find him."

"Yes, there are lots of online records. But I'm starving, let's eat."

At the café, chewing on a sandwich, Alex couldn't find what he was searching for on his phone. He pushed it away in frustration.

"What've you found?" Caitlin asked.

"It's what I haven't found. There's no George O'Grady listed as killed in World War I."

"Maybe George was his middle name?" She took another bite from her salad wrap.

"I thought of that. But the only O'Grady listed is William James, from the Light Horse Brigade."

"Where did you look?"

"Commonwealth War Graves."

"Okay. Well, leave it for now. Didn't we agree we'd be working through the tapes in order? Kathleen's still a kid. The war's nearly ten years in the future. We'll get to George later. I want to know how Eileen's getting on. Let's finish eating and get back to the tapes."

Butterflies took flight in Alex's stomach. He pushed the remains of his sandwich around on his plate as a wave of goosebumps rippled down his spine. "Caitlin?"

"Hmmm."

"At the risk of being weird again."

That caught her attention, and she focused on him. "I've got the weirdest feeling someone's watching us."

Caitlin's eyes flicked around the café, where the patrons were all busy with their own lunches and paying no attention to them. Alex shook his head. "That's not what I meant. I've got the feeling that if Kathleen could, she'd be watching us, hoping we'd get hooked into the thread of her story, relieved someone's listening after all these years."

"Okay, that's a bit weird." She closed her eyes for a moment, as if she were thinking, and a dreamy smile dawned on her face. "But if she *was* watching, yes, sure, I think she'd know she's hooked us. We're both busting to find out what happens next."

Eileen's smile was warm, as usual, but today there was more excitement in it as I let myself in through her bedroom door. She fluttered her hand towards a blue-covered book on her coverlet.

"Oh, do look, Kathleen. I've been given such a nice present."

I picked it up: *52 Stories of Courage and Endeavor for Girls*. The front cover sported an illustration of a windswept girl silhouetted against a stormy sea, struggling at the helm of a boat.

"Something new to read." I smiled.

"It's too heavy for me to hold," she confessed. "And my vision isn't clear enough to read, in any case. Would you read some of it today?"

"Of course." I pretended not to see the grimace of pain on her face as she wriggled across on her bed, making room for me to sit. I adjusted the pillows behind her to make sure she was comfortable, before taking my place and opening the gilt-edged pages.

"Oh, look!" I held the frontispiece open for her and joined her giggles at the photograph of a young girl with a wistful expression and a crown of leaves and berries resting on her curly head. Her lacy décolletage was decorated with cabbage roses.

"She doesn't look very heroic in that garb," laughed Eileen, before her eyes became serious. "But sometimes, courage is found in the most unexpected places."

I surveyed my friend, pale and fragile as a porcelain doll. An image flashed into my mind: deep scars crisscrossing over her poor, hunched back, and I lowered my eyes to the book, so she wouldn't see them fill with tears. Eager for an escape, I turned to the preface, and, swallowing hard, began to read.

"There is no sphere of life in which Courage and Endeavor are not needed. It is a popular error, born of old tradition and masculine prejudice, to suppose the more robust qualities of character are limited to boys and men."

"I couldn't agree more." Eileen snuggled into her pillows, settling in for a story.

"Eileen." My voice was hesitant, and she turned to look at me, encouraging me to go on. "I think you're the bravest person I ever met."

"Me? No, you're wrong. I'm only brave because I have my family and friends to support me." Her hand patted her pocket, bulging with the rosary she constantly carried with her. "And I have *Them*. Of myself, I am nothing."

"Perhaps we all would be nothing, if we were alone."

"Oh, yes, but we are never alone. Jesus and Mary are always with us. That is where our strength and courage come from."

We shared a knowing smile, and then I continued to read.

* * *

My sister Betty, her pigtails swinging about her head as she skipped along Elizabeth Street, called, "Keep up, Kathleen." She was carrying a shopping basket with potatoes for the night's meal, while I carried Mrs. Plunkett's dirty laundry back home for Mum to wash and iron.

Burdened as I was, I struggled to catch up. Suddenly, an urchin grabbed at Betty's basket, causing her to stumble, and several potatoes tumbled onto the pavement. With the big, cane hamper limiting my view, I tripped on a potato and fell towards the street. Flailing, I saw the flash of sunlight off a motorcar windscreen. Brakes screeched.

Lightning fast, a firm hand grasped my elbow, and a blue-sleeved arm steadied my basket. I turned to see my savior, George, a nice young man I knew from when he was at school. George yelled, "Oi. You little mongrel!" after the retreating boy.

Once I had my balance, George darted onto the road and plucked up two spuds before they went under the wheels of a lumbering delivery wagon.

"You alright, ladies?" He placed the vegetables into Betty's basket and glared down the road, but the thief had disappeared.

"Thank you, George. I was startled, but I'm not hurt."

Betty smiled shyly at him.

"I'll walk you home." His crooked grin was disarming, and I found myself passing the washing basket into his outstretched hands.

My cheeks flushed hot as I watched him sideways, from under my eyelashes. How handsome he was, with his lean, tanned face and cornflower blue eyes. How his jutting Adam's apple bobbed up and down as he swallowed. And the shape of well-developed biceps bulging under his shirt sleeves. I'd admired him, when we were both in school, but now it was obvious he had become a man. My heart beat faster, and I couldn't think of a single thing to say.

"Did that mongrel take off with your tongues as well?" he asked.

"No," I laughed. "How've you been, George?"

"I'm keeping busy in my new position, Kathleen. Lots of deliveries, and when I finish them, I make myself useful in the shop. Reloading shelves, cleaning, odd jobs. But Mr. Jenkins is happy with me, and he even let me serve customers last week, when Billy was off with a cut hand."

I hesitated at the curb edge, remembering how smart he had been at school. He was bright enough to get a trade or be a bookkeeper, but he never got the chance. George had to leave school at twelve.

"Do you like it?"

"I'm grateful for steady work, and being able to help support Mum, and earn my keep. I wouldn't want to be stealing potatoes off girls in the street, like that urchin. And maybe something better will come up."

"Of course, it will. You're a good, honest worker and you can turn your hand to anything."

Surprised by my praise, George stared at me. Something warm came into his eyes, and, for a moment, he leaned towards me awkwardly, because of the hamper, as if he were going to kiss my cheek, and then he flushed and walked on, quicker than before.

"How are you finding working?" he asked, his voice husky.

"I have a position with Mrs. Murphy now. I do the heavy housework and prepare vegetables for their dinner and mind the little ones sometimes. It's just from nine to twelve every morning, except Sunday. So, I still get to live at home, which is what I wanted. I help Mum with the laundry and ironing she takes in, in the afternoons, and go to visit Eileen."

A note of quiet reverence slipped into his voice, as it did with many people who spoke of her. "How is Eileen?"

My lips drew thin, and I swallowed before I managed to answer. "She's recovering from her latest operation. She was encased in a plaster cast to straighten her spine, but her mother had to call the doctor again, because it was so tight, it was smothering her. She could hardly breathe. When the doctor cut the cast off, her whole back collapsed. It's bent worse than ever now, and I know it hurts her dreadfully." I shook my head. "But you know how she is, she never complains."

"Are you going to see her later?"

"Yes."

He swung the basket up onto the kitchen table, for we had made it back to my house by then. "Give her my best, won't you? And," he dug into his pocket and pulled out something wrapped in a handkerchief, unwrapping it and smiling in triumph as he held out an orange, "it got squashed in the wagon. See?" He showed me a split in the skin, leaking juice. "So, we couldn't sell it. Mr. Jenkins said I might bring it home. I was going to share it with Lizzie, but I think we'd both rather Eileen had it."

"Are you sure?" The thought of George's sister missing out on a treat slowed my hand on its journey across the space to the orange.

He grinned again. "Yes. Eileen's special. And a piece of fruit might do her good."

"Thank you. For everything."

"My pleasure. I'll see you later." And he winked at me. He whistled as he made his way home. Later that afternoon, Eileen's eyes lit up as she inhaled the aroma coming from the split orange skin. "That was kind of Georgie."

"Yes, it was. He thought it might do you some good."

"It will. Mary, would you get the boys?"

Mary put down the sock she was darning and went in search of her brothers.

"You divide it, Kathleen," Eileen pressed me, from her bed.

Mary had brought a plate, and I cut the orange into five pieces, with near surgical precision. We all took one and joyously sucked the sweet juice out before chewing the pulp off the skin. Mary sponged her sister's sticky fingers with water from the white, china basin and jug set on her nightstand.

"Thanks for sharing, Eily." Frank, now twelve, pecked her cheek before following Charlie to finish his homework.

I collected the pieces of orange peel under Eileen's watchful gaze. "I'll put them on the verandah to dry."

She liked fresh potpourri, a mixture of dried herbs and flower petals, to scent the air in her room. She was self-conscious about the scent of sickness that could linger, of bedpans and, sometimes, infected bed sores, though she never complained. And neither did we, or her other visitors.

When I returned from the verandah, she patted the bed beside her. "So how was Georgie?" She raised an eyebrow at me.

"He is well. He's glad to have the job and says Mr. Jenkins appreciates him."

"I'm sure he does."

"But when I think of how smart Georgie was at school … he could have been a bookkeeper like your father. Or a poet and had his work printed in the newspapers, like Henry Lawson. And now he's an errand boy."

"Perhaps he will get a chance to do something he's better suited to in the future, but at least he has work."

"Yes, these are hard times."

"And what else happened when you met him?"

"He was a knight in shining armor." I kept my voice calm, despite the sudden speeding of my heart.

"And you were the damsel in distress? How romantic."

I shrugged, and studied my fingernails so she couldn't see my face. "A young lad stole some potatoes out of Betty's basket, and she stumbled, so potatoes rolled onto the pavement, and I tripped with a basket of washing in my arms. George appeared just in time to stop me from falling and saved the washing."

"And what else happened?"

It had never been easy to pull the wool over Eileen's eyes and she was tenacious when she wanted information. "He paused at the side of the road before we crossed, and I thought …"

"You thought what?"

"Just for a moment, I thought he was going to kiss me."

She smiled knowingly. "He's always had his eye on you, you know."

Tempted as I was to act dumb, I couldn't lie to her. Not to Eileen. "I know."

"And you've always admired him."

"Yes, I have. He seems to me to be a very honorable young man."

"He is, and that's the most important consideration, although it doesn't hurt that he's handsome."

"We're too young; he's a year older than me, but I'm only sixteen."

"That will change, soon enough." She patted my hand and smiled demurely. "You'll never guess who came to visit me today."

"Who?" It was a relief to enter the safety of our regular game of Twenty Questions.

"Guess." Her eyes twinkled with mischief.

"Was it a woman?"

"Yes."

"Does she come regularly?"

"Yes."

"Does she come to sit quietly in your room with you?"

"No."

"Does she read to you?"

"No."

"Does she talk almost without stopping because she is lonely and no one else is kind enough to listen to her?"

Eileen nodded, but I could sense her reluctance to admit she was offering a kindness that no one else would.

"Do you feel she gives you an opportunity to be of service by listening?"

"Yes."

"If you try to say anything, does she listen or does she just interrupt and say, *I know*?"

Eileen laughed cautiously, as ever protecting her back from any sudden muscle movements.

"Was it Mrs. I Know?" I used the cheeky nickname Eileen's brothers bestowed on the lonely woman.

"Yes."

"I feel a bit sorry for her."

Eileen yawned and paled.

"You need to rest."

"I won't sleep. But perhaps I could lie here quietly, and you could read to me?"

I leaned over and kissed her clammy forehead before picking up the book on her bedside table. I read another tale of moral fortitude to a real flesh-and-blood girl who outshone the fictional heroines in every way possible. Eileen's eyelids drifted closed, and her breathing became shallow but, instead of leaving to attend to my chores, I sat, transfixed by the sheer delight of watching her dear face freed from pain, wondering if she would ever be well enough to leave her room again.

"So, is that *the* George, do you think?" Alex asked, stretching in the straight wooden chair at the back of the library. They were alone now, so he didn't need to whisper. "Our great-great-grandfather?"

"Maybe. He's the right age and Kathleen obviously likes him."

"But when's this set, 1908? He couldn't have been the only George in Redfern. Maybe when Kathleen got older, she married a different George."

"Perhaps." Caitlin searched her cousin's face. "But I don't think so."

"Why not?"

"Well, the way she described him, I thought you were a dead ringer for him."

"What do you mean?"

"Smart. Lean and handsome. Prominent Adam's apple. Cornflower blue eyes. Muscular. Sounds like you."

Alex choked back a snort of self-deprecating laughter. "I'm only muscular on my computer mouse arm from all the gaming, and I'm certainly not tanned."

"You could be, if you spent any time in the sun," she teased. "Oh, and humble, she made it very clear George was humble. I think he's our man."

"Why didn't I find his name on a war grave?"

"Maybe the records were incomplete. Maybe we'll find him listed somewhere else. Maybe, if we're patient, Kathleen will give us a clue."

"Don't jump ahead," Alex chastised, "just keep going step by step, hey?" He winked.

"Exactly. Follow the plan." She checked the time on her phone and reached into her bag, then swallowed two pills.

"You alright?"

"Yes, I'm fine. Just painkillers. Nothing too strong, so my head will stay clear."

"What's next in the box?" He pushed it across to her and waited for her to prize the lid off and take out a small manila envelope with brown spots of foxing attesting to its age.

Caitlin's eyes misted as she studied the postcard that slid out of the envelope. "Oh, look." She turned it for Alex to see.

A lean-faced young man stood with his arms spread wide, in an unbuttoned shirt, with the sleeves rolled up. His Akubra hat perched at a rakish angle, but despite the way he was hamming it up for the camera, there was tenderness in his face, which was reflected in the message scrawled on the back of the card.

> *To my darling Kathleen—*
> *Who'd have thought I'd ever see the pyramids? We climbed*
> *one yesterday. I could see for miles up there, how I wished*
> *I could have seen far enough to see you!*
> *Always in my heart, George*

"It's him," Caitlin murmured, turning the card over to study the picture again. "And the pyramids are in the background."

"What were troops doing in Egypt?"

"There were some battles in the Middle East. But mostly, I think the soldiers who were evacuated from Gallipoli got some R and R there, before they were sent to the Western Front."

"Oh. Shit. Poor bastard." Alex picked at his fingernails for a moment. "Am I allowed to look him up yet?"

"No. Good boy for asking." She treated him to a stage wink. "But we're only up to 1908 in the story. They've only just started courting. The plan, remember?"

"The problem with the bloody plan," Alex blustered to hide how deeply he was moved by George's love note, "is that I didn't know I'd get interested in any of this when I agreed to it."

Caitlin giggled. "You were just doing it to please your mum?"

"At first." She waited for him to continue. "And then, I thought it was a history project, so you might like it. And maybe it would be good for you." He flinched at her momentary look of consternation. "Was I being patronizing?"

She lowered her eyelids, and then smiled her reassurance. "No. It was really nice of you."

She reached over and, just for a second, rested her hand in his. Treasuring the warmth of her gesture, quick as thought, he squeezed her hand, before she shifted to reach for his phone. "Next track," she commanded. "Before we both get mushy."

Eileen sighed her delight. "Thank you for arranging this picnic, Kathleen. I sometimes think Centennial Park is my favorite place in the whole world." She surveyed the sweeping, open landscape from her cane wheelchair, squinting against the sun reflecting off the lake. Mary and I busied ourselves, arranging a picnic blanket and a nest of cushions, and Eileen took her beloved box camera from her bag, eager to find a good shot.

She tore a stale bread crust to pieces, before throwing it to the army of ducks marching towards her, who halted their advance accordingly.

"You look pretty enough to be photographed," I told her, taking in her powder-blue lacy gown, with matching blue slippers, and the big satin bow in her hair.

"Me?"

"Yes, you. Not an ordinary belle-of-the-ball kind of photo. There's something more ethereal about you, like you're a fairy who's just visiting from a better, lighter place."

Frank grinned. "You've described our Eily exactly, Kathleen. I couldn't have put it better myself."

Georgie laughed and snatched up Eileen's camera, pressing it into Frank's hands. "A picture's worth a thousand words. Take a photo, won't you?"

"Do I really look all right?"

Mary stepped forward and adjusted the ribbon. "Yes, really. Just like Mary Pickford, the movie star."

A light breeze arose and teased Eileen's long ringlets away from her shoulders as she smiled for the camera. "Now, one with you girls," she invited. "And Georgie and Charlie. We can look back on this picture in the future and remember being together in happy times."

We crowded, laughing and joking, onto the blanket, and Charlie gently lifted Eileen and settled her in the pillow mound where she nestled into Mary's supportive arm. I sat to Eileen's right; Georgie threw himself down at my knees and seized my left hand in his, stroking my ring finger and staring up at me earnestly with those disarming blue eyes of his. I was photographed in the act of snatching my hand away from him, the moment immortalized by the blurring of my hand and the shocked expression on my face.

Eileen laughed when she developed the photo in her improvised dark room.

I folded that photo into a piece of butcher's paper and slipped it into Georgie's kit bag, the night before he went to war. I liked to imagine him huddling in some foxhole somewhere, pulling the picture out of his breast pocket, and remembering this happy day, just as Eileen foresaw. I hope it brought him comfort.

Eileen developed a second copy for herself, because she needed a memento too.

That was the last time we all were together in Centennial Park, one of her favorite places. Disaster was soon to strike.

* * *

Caitlin ran her hands through her hair. "Oh, dear."

"You okay?" Alex asked.

She nodded. "Yes. That was just sad. We found George. And we are soon to lose him again."

"He's been dead all along, Cait. Since World War I."

"I know. But he doesn't feel dead, listening to the tapes, does he? It brings them all to life. There he is, handsome, and rugged, and cheeky. His whole life ahead of him. Falling in love and we know he'll get married." She sighed, a faraway look in her eyes. She hadn't seen her own disaster coming, either. "But we know it will all go horribly wrong, and he'll end up dead, buried in some forgotten cemetery on the other side of the world, after going through who knows what hell?"

Alex shivered. "That's the trouble with knowing the future. There are some things you just don't want to know in advance."

* * *

Eileen's father, Charles O'Connor worked as a bookkeeper in Anthony Hordern and Sons, which was once the largest department store in the world. Every day he caught the tram into Sydney, and gossips said it was an extravagance to spend money on the tram fare for a journey of little more than a mile.

He was always well-dressed in his suit and carefully pressed shirt, with a splendid moustache. But under that, I noticed him getting paler and leaner over time, and worried he was not well. And so it was, in 1911, he was diagnosed with liver cancer and sent to a sanitorium in Katoomba. He sent Eileen a lovely letter encouraging her to be brave, and saying he was feeling much better, but contracted pneumonia and died in April, only a month after he went to the infirmary.

Eileen's grip on life and health had always been tenuous, but the shock of losing her beloved daddy was a devastating blow to her frail body. She became bedbound, having lost the use of her legs and her right arm. In the depths of her illness, she sometimes was blind.

There was a steady stream of visitors, of course. Long-term friends bringing flowers or meals. And a devoted band of Eileen's admirers, hoping for news of an improvement in her condition. The landlord, however, offered no grace to Mrs. O'Connor, and demanded the family move out as they could no longer pay the rent.

Mrs. O'Connor entreated the Sacred Heart Fathers in Randwick to help them find an affordable new house to rent. Somewhere big, so she could take in enough boarders to make a living. Father Edward McGrath was assigned to the task, and they didn't know it then, but none of their lives would ever be the same again.

* * *

I visited Eileen whenever I could, always hoping for a sign she was getting better, and eager to help Mrs. O'Connor in any way I could.

One day, as I turned the corner into Eileen's street, I was confronted by a woman I recognized from chance meetings at Eileen's house. She was walking towards me briskly, her lips pursed in disgust.

I bade her good morning, and she paused long enough to mutter, "Scandalous! She's got," she lowered her voice to emphasize her gossip, "a man in her room. What sort of example is she setting? I don't know how her mother allows such goings on. You be careful, young lady, or you'll end up tarred with the same brush." Resettling her bag over her arm, she continued her march down Telopea Street, leaving me staring after her stiff shoulder blades.

Confused, I let myself in through the O'Connor's front gate. I was only nineteen then, and I confess that I peered in through the glassed-in balcony of Eileen's room. Eileen was lying in bed, as was now usual, and although I couldn't see her face, she looked like she might be asleep. Next to her, hands folded in prayer, knelt a tall man in a dark jacket.

Mrs. O'Connor greeted me at the door, her face more care-worn and creased than it had been mere weeks before.

"Father McGrath is praying with Eily just now. You can sit with her when he finishes."

"Any news on where you can live?"

Mrs. O'Connor shook her head. Words tumbled out as if a stopper had been pulled out of her bottle of woes. "Our landlord hasn't got a merciful bone in his body. We used all our savings while Charles was ill. And Mary's wage isn't enough to live on. I'm sure we'd be able to get friends to help us if he'd just give us time. But Father McGrath is working tirelessly on our behalf. He suggested Coogee. It's cheaper rent, because it's further out of town, and the streets are rough. But Father says there are some big houses there, where we'd be able to fit in more boarders. That's the only way I'm ever going to be able to pay rent and buy enough food to keep body and soul together, through running a proper boarding house. By the beach, so people would come for their holidays. Nice families, not just single working men."

"That sounds like a good idea." I nodded encouragement as she paused to catch her breath. What else could I do?

"And, Kathleen, love, I was thinking when Eily gets better, she'd like to go to the beach. The sea air might do her good. Maybe we can even find somewhere with a view of the water for when she's too ill to go outside."

"That would be lovely." I recalled the image of the windswept girl at the helm of a ship, from the cover of Eileen's book, *52 Stories of Courage and Endeavor for Girls.* "I think she'd like to be near the ocean."

"She's never been, you know."

Father McGrath came into the hall then. He was so tall that by the time my gaze crawled up from his lapels, to his dog collar, and finally reached his face, my neck was cricked backwards. He was over six feet tall, and handsome in a boyish way, even though he must have been thirty years old at the time.

Mrs. O'Connor introduced us. "Kathleen is one of Eily's oldest friends," she said, which made me glow with pride.

Father McGrath looked at me with his clear, earnest eyes, "Then you are very fortunate. She is an exceptionally saintly child of Jesus and Mary." He shook his head, as if he couldn't quite believe his experience. "I had never realized how much spiritual power could be locked in such a frail body, until I met her. Her spirit touches souls."

I nodded absently, but as his words sank in, I realized I had become so used to being in Eileen's company that I took it for granted. When she was desperately ill, the sense of fun, the singing and laughter, the keen interest in everything and everybody's welfare—which Father McGrath hadn't had the chance to see yet—fell away, leaving only the sense of beatific peace emanating from her, even when she was barely conscious. And the unfathomable courage and surrender with which she accepted her suffering, the paralysis, blindness and fevers, and the relentless pain of a collapsed spine whose vertebrae were being eaten away by infected abscesses which pressed on her nerves and spinal cord.

The familiar softening of my heart and body, that I experienced when I sat with her, washed through me, and I smiled. My voice sounded dreamy and far away when I slowly assembled my thoughts into words. "Oh, yes, I know exactly what you mean. She is saintly. She always wanted to be a nun."

Surprise widened the young priest's eyes for a moment before his face crumpled into sorrowing sympathy, as if he hadn't thought a young woman so close to death's gaping jaws would have aspirations for the future.

I spoke quickly, slapping away the ever-repressed fear of losing her. "She made enquiries, but she was refused, because she was too ill to be a nun," I said, with a measure of spite for the mother superior who couldn't see what an asset Eileen would be. Spite was easier to harbor than grief at the quashing of my friend's deepest desire. Even if the mother superior was clearly right. "But she is devoted to caring for the sick and the poor."

Father McGrath's face became more animated now. "She is certainly devoted to Our Lady," he said, lost in thought. "If Our Lady spares her, we will see if she is called."

"When," I insisted, clinging to the impossibility of life without Eileen.

He frowned at me, not following my train of thought. "*When* Our Lady spares her. Eileen can't die, Father. When Our Lady saves her, you will know she's been called."

Father McGrath folded his hands as if in prayer and closed his eyes. His lips moved soundlessly, but clearly enough for me to read their words in the sudden silence of the front hall. *Holy Mother, is it true? Have I found my helper?*

STATE LIBRARY, ADELAIDE

Caitlin arched her back, stretching in the silence after Alex paused the tape. "What's going on with Eileen? You don't get paralyzed and go blind, because someone in your family dies, no matter how much you love them."

Alex frowned. "No, you don't. I'm thinking she had a lot more than a broken back going on."

"Yeah. Unlike me, three-year-olds bounce. Something must have been wrong for a fall from the pram to break her back in the first place. If that's what really happened."

A fleeting revulsion darkened his face but he made sure it was gone before Cait lifted her eyes. Don't go there. He didn't want to think about how she didn't bounce.

He kept talking to cover his feelings. "What medical conditions make it easy for kids to break bones? And then get pus in them?" He typed into his phone, then read, "Fractures commonly occur after trauma, such as falls or motor vehicle accidents." Screeching tires and blackness replayed in his mind, and he shuddered as he blocked it out. So many things were too difficult to face. "But there are also pathological fractures, when bones fracture with minimal or no trauma, due to an underlying bone pathology, such as a tumor, Rickets, or other bone disease … blah blah … bony destruction can also occur in long-standing infection, such as Pott's Disease caused by tuberculosis."

"You're not sticking to the plan," Caitlin objected, but she sighed to indicate she'd go with the flow. "I think Rickets affected the legs, made kids bow-legged; I don't think she could have had that. And she's nineteen now, she couldn't have lived so long if she'd had cancer since the age of three." She sighed and chewed her lip, her head on one side, remembering. "That's right, tuberculosis can infect bones," she mused. "I remember now, Pott's Disease is an infection of the bones in the spine, causing deformity and compression of the spinal cord, and could cause paralysis."

Understanding dawned in Alex's eyes. "Cara died of tuberculosis, you thought, and we know it was endemic then. That would explain Eileen's health problems."

"Yes. But not the blindness episodes."

"Hmm. They seemed to come and go?"

"Yes. It sounds like it."

"Mum has a friend with multiple sclerosis," said Alex. "She gets optic neuritis that makes her blind, and then she takes medication, and it gets better."

"I don't know if they had MS back then."

He shrugged. "It's an inflammatory auto-immune thing. Maybe TB can cause inflammation of the nervous system too?" He started to type on his phone.

"Let's get back on track," she said.

"There's something here about transverse myelitis, an inflammation of the brain and spinal cord, from TB. Don't you want to hear it?"

Caitlin tutted, shushing him. "No, I don't. Not now." An uncertain smile stirred then spread across her face. "We're agreed, aren't we, Kathleen organized the tin, so its contents dovetailed with the tapes."

"Yeah." He was reluctant to admit it. "How she did that, when she recorded the tapes in hospital and died there before going home, doesn't make sense, though, does it?"

Caitlin shrugged. "I don't think they rushed patients out of hospital as fast in those days. Maybe Kathleen got someone to bring her memory box to the hospital for her to go through. Or maybe she had it in careful order all along. In any case, she went to a lot of trouble to lay everything out. It must be time to see what's next in the box."

Not waiting for his reply, with loving fingers, she lifted the next item out; a folded sheet of paper, yellowed with age, which she opened and laid on the table. Alex, watching her, began to laugh.

"What now?" Caitlin scowled at him.

"Kathleen, carefully folding papers, and filing them in sequence in a toffee tin, you unfolding them carefully, in the same precise order she intended, decades later. You take after her, Cait. She was a bit OCD too."

Caitlin pursed her lips into a tight grin. "I'm not OCD, really. I just like to do things properly."

"Yeah, yeah, sure," he teased, enjoying that she was able to banter. She stuck out her tongue and pushed the paper closer to him. It was a short letter, in an untidy scrawl. They bent their heads together to read it.

> *Dearest child,*
> *I am sorry I am not well enough to write a long letter.*
> *Think of me often, and love me.*
> *Give my best love to your family. Come soon to see me.*
> *Eily the Pest*

"Eily the Pest? Why would she say that?" asked Alex.

"Because she was paralyzed. Unable to move or do anything for herself. Stuck in bed for months. Needing people to do everything for her, even to bathe her and help her to the toilet!"

Caitlin spat the words, causing raised eyebrows from a woman inspecting the display of nineteenth-century children's toys. She gestured with her hand, taking in her body, her right leg, stiff in its brace, angry, red scars showing where pins had protruded through her skin, to hold the pieces of her shattered tibia and fibula in place, until she was stable enough to have them screwed together. Lowering her voice she said, "I know just how she felt."

Alex's grief and shame, never far below the surface of his mind, oozed up like pus from a boil as her words and the raw pain in her voice catapulted him right out of the library, back in time so he could see her lying in her high-dependency hospital bed, with tubes snaking into her. He couldn't bear it. He screwed his eyes up, trying to shut out the images, and jolted his chair away from the table, dropped to his knees beside her and clutched her hands in his. Tears trickled down his cheeks and he rasped, "Oh Cait, I am so, so sorry."

She slipped her hands out of his, and cradled his face, watching a tear follow one of the scars on his cheek, one that came perilously close to his eye.

"Don't say that, Alex. It wasn't your fault. None of it was your fault." With one finger she traced his scar, fading now, and gave thanks the plastic surgeon did such a neat job. "I'm very glad you're still hand-some," she said, trying to lighten his mood.

He looked straight into her eyes. "Thank God the operations you had will make you better, Cait. You'll be strong again and walking without assistance in a few months. Unlike poor Eileen."

COOGEE – MID-WINTER 1911

I sat on Eileen's bed, unable to stop tears from running down my cheeks. I held her left hand because her right arm and legs were still paralyzed, and she couldn't even roll herself over in bed. Surrounded by packing crates, her family and I held our strange vigil. I wondered silently if Eily had the strength to survive the five-mile journey to Coogee. I'm sure her family did too. But some superstition left our fears unspoken.

The cold, bleak sky mirrored my emotions as Eileen was loaded into the back of a horse-drawn ambulance for the trip to her new home. My life had changed the day an ambulance brought her into my life, and now it was changing again, because she was leaving.

Father McGrath's lean face was grim as he waited to climb into the ambulance beside her, determined to pray for her safe deliverance throughout the trip. He caught my eye, and I summoned a brave smile, encouraging him to do the same before he moved into Eileen's line of vision.

Thankfully, my employer had agreed I could start work early, so my three hours was up in time for me to be here, and join the small retinue walking beside the ambulance. Charlie would be following with the removal wagon, once the last few items had been packed, and Mrs. O'Connor would be riding on the wagon seat with the driver. Frank, Mary, and I would walk the whole way beside the ambulance. Neighbors fell in beside us for the start of the journey, chatting amongst themselves.

"Redfern won't be the same now our saint has gone," said the thin old man who had volunteered as her gardener at Telopea Street, and often brought Eileen flowers.

"Never a truer word was said," agreed another.

"May the saints in heaven ease the journey of our suffering saint on earth," whispered Mrs. Murphy, her baby sleeping in her arms under her shawl.

And so it was, the end of an era came, and Eileen O'Connor made her journey, every moment in excruciating pain, as the ambulance, slowly and carefully though it was driven, lurched on every uneven spot on the rough road, jarring that scarred, broken back, and jolting the deep bedsores Eileen had developed during her paralysis.

One by one, the well-wishers fell away, until it was just the three of us, trotting along in silence, lost in our own thoughts, the cold wind forcing its fingers through our clothes.

It took almost two hours to make our anxious way to Eileen's new home at Coogee. The gray-green sea was choppy and uninviting at the bottom of the steep street. The ambulance driver pulled the horse to a stop, and Frank hurried to put a brick under the front wheels, to act as brakes. We huddled around the back of the vehicle as the door was opened. Father McGrath stepped out, his face green. Afraid he would vomit, I took the liberty of seizing his elbow, and guided him to the side of the street, where a few shrubs could screen him from view.

He shrugged my hand away, and leaned over to whisper, "She's been unconscious nearly all the way."

Still comatose, Eileen was settled into a makeshift bedroom on the ground level, with a window overlooking the sea. The bedrooms were downstairs, but when the move was planned, everyone balked at the idea of carrying her down a narrow staircase. She looked smaller than ever, hunched beneath the white coverlet. Father prayed over her again, before reluctantly making his way back to his other duties, leaving Mary and I sitting in silence by the bedside, a place I returned to as often as possible over the three months she lived at St. Elmo's in Neptune Street.

It was a terrible time, during which Eileen had frequent bouts of unexplained unconsciousness. Mrs. O'Connor's face grew ever more haunted, as she hurried through her duties of caring for Eileen and keeping her boarders comfortable.

And then another blow hit the family. Their new landlord informed them he needed the house for his own use, and they were compelled to leave. Father McGrath was tireless in his search, and soon located another large house suited to their needs, not far away, and named, perhaps as an omen, *Restwell,* in Beach Street opposite a park.

"Maybe the removal will be easier for her this time," I ventured to Mary. "It's such a short distance."

"Surely you are right. I dread to think what will happen otherwise; she's barely recovered from the last move." Her eyes drifted to the door, and she lowered her voice. "The doctor's not happy about moving her. I heard him telling Ma so, but what are we to do? The landlord will turn us out onto the street. Ma's beside herself." She shook her head and tears welled in her eyes.

"Is there nothing the doctor can do?"

Mary swallowed tears. Her reply, when it came, was barely audible. "He said she's in the Lord's hands now."

Father McGrath, silently brooding over his tea until now, set his teacup down with care, his big hand looking almost ridiculous against Mrs. O'Connor's best porcelain. He cleared his throat. "The Lord's hands are good hands to be in. Her spirit is strong, though the pure body that harbors it is weak. I have never seen such suffering. And yet, when she is well enough, I have never known such radiant happiness or welcome expressed by anyone else. We will pray that Our Lady delivers her again."

There are times when prayers are cold comfort and are left unanswered. This was one of those times ... or so it appeared.

* * *

On the twenty-seventh of October, Father McGrath could not be with us for the O'Connor's next move, much to his regret. Hurrying to Restwell as soon as he had finished his parish duties, he was met at the door by an ashen-faced and silent Mrs. O'Connor, who shook her head and ushered him to Eileen's room, where I was standing quietly in a corner, trying to keep out of the way. My heart, lumpy like cold porridge congealed in a pan, thumped a new rhythm, it's familiar lub-dub replaced by a half-choked *Don't-be-dead, don't-be-dead.*

He paused in the doorway, arrested by the grief in Mary's expression, before willing himself to approach.

"She's not … dead?" he mumbled, leaning over the lifeless body.

He felt in his breast pocket, and, bringing out a small piece of mirror, wiped it on his handkerchief before holding it near Eileen's mouth and nose. Seconds crawled by. Her sister and mother crowded around him, and, shaking his head, he showed them the mirror, still clear. Not a hint of condensation from breath on it. Dropping to his knees like a marionette whose strings had been cut, the priest began to pray.

After long minutes, as if answering our prayers, Eileen writhed in agony for a fleeting second, before falling still again.

Mrs. O'Connor was through the door in an instant, calling Frank, who had been helping Charlie carry chairs into the dining room. "She's alive! Quick, go get a doctor."

Knowing Eileen was carefully watched over by Father and me, the frantic family filled the nervous wait till the doctor's arrival with the mindless activity of moving furniture and unpacking trunks.

The doctor's examination was brief. "There's nothing I can do," he said, shaking a tousled, gray head filled with professional regret. "But in the name of Mercy stop all this noise and bustle of settling in and let her die in peace."

That first night in Restwell was a night of silence and tears. Eileen's teeth were gritted together, and any attempt to prize them open was met with the vomiting of a tiny amount of green bile. Father McGrath kept vigil all night, on a straight-backed chair, pulled close to the bed so he would hear her if she stirred.

Early the next morning, he administered the Sacraments, and somehow, she accepted them. Then he prepared to leave, to fulfil his other duties, including seven o'clock Mass, promising to hurry back as soon as he could.

He cleaned the glass and packed it with the little silver-lidded wine bottle and silver wafer plate engraved IHS, into his compact, leather-covered, traveling communion box. Watching him under fluttering, translucent lids sunk deeply into blue-black shadowed sockets, Eileen moaned softly through cracked lips. In a moment of desperate clarity, she clutched feebly at his sleeve. "Father," she croaked, as he strained his ear towards her mouth. "Whenever you leave me, the evil one comes. And as soon as you come back, he leaves me."

"What a coward he is to come to you when you are sick and alone!" Father's eyes flashed with anger, and for a moment I saw such determined power in them, I could understand why the devil wouldn't dare to torment Eileen while her protector was there.

"He glares at me and tries to terrify me, but I pray and remind the Old Boy that as soon as you are here, I will be safe." The 'Old Boy,' that's what she called the devil then, using an old Irish term, I suppose to make him seem smaller, and lessen his capacity to terrify her.

For six days, Father McGrath's every spare moment was spent at Eileen's side, and he sat with her every night. Watching over her like the chivalrous champion of a vulnerable lady in lace.

During one of those dark days, I slipped into the room to take the young priest a plate of sandwiches. He turned red-rimmed eyes upon me. "There are those in these modern times who believe the Devil is merely a figure of legend," he said, "or even an imaginary embellishment in old stories of temptation."

I nodded, unsure of what to say, and worried by his exhaustion. "But mark my words, Kathleen. That the Devil would torment one of the Lord's greatest servants is surely proof that he is at work amongst lesser mortals."

As if she were giving a sign, Eileen stirred, and we both turned to her. "Father, when I die …" she rasped.

I heard no more. Abandoning the plate on the nearest table, I fled the room.

"This is when? 1911, did she say?" Alex's tone was urgent.

"Yes."

"When was that first photograph taken?" He rifled through the neat pile of papers stacked next to the tin. "1918." He sighed and his face relaxed into a sheepish grin. "She had me worried for a minute there."

Caitlin studied his face, noting the muscles in his cheeks were still tense, as if he was clenching his teeth. Sometimes, Alex really worried her; she knew there was something going on behind his cultivated attitude of nonchalance. She waited, wishing he would say what was really on his mind, but when he spoke, it was clear he wasn't going to open up.

"Cait, I need to get out of here. This is doing my head in."

"Let's call an access cab, then. Do you still want to come back to my place? We can order something for dinner."

"Yes. I'm not standing you up. I just need …" He shook his head as if there were cobwebs in it. "I need to think. Or something."

"Sure, let's go home, then." Caitlin hoped her home would be a good place for Alex to think, despite the familiar worry that she never really knew what the atmosphere would be like when she got there. It was only because he was a relative that she'd invited him. She hadn't let friends visit her since the accident, claiming she didn't feel up to it, but it was easier to just talk on the phone. She called a cab.

The odors of stale beer and perspiration met them as Caitlin opened her front door. The despondent form of her father, slumped in his armchair, glanced up as they reached the living room door, made a brief gesture with his beer can, and returned his blood-shot gaze to the sports channel.

"Hello, Dad." The brightness of Caitlin's voice fell flat, landing pointlessly on the grubby carpet. She didn't attempt to maneuver her wheelchair towards her father. She had told him she'd bring Alex to sleep over, so they didn't have to waste time traveling. Her father could have at least showered.

Alex's body was taut, and he reached to squeeze her shoulder. He took a deep breath before he spoke. "Hello, Uncle Tim. We've ordered Chinese for dinner."

Tim grunted something incoherent about football.

"We'll bring yours in when it arrives." Alex shrugged, defeated.

It was twilight when the takeaway arrived. The cousins ate at the ancient kitchen table, mindful not to make much noise in case they disturbed Tim. Alex chewed his last mouthful of special fried rice, studying a scratch in the table's fake veneer.

"Is he always like that?" Alex asked, his mouth close to her ear.

Caitlin breathed in a sudden gasp. For a moment, it seemed she'd do anything to avoid answering his question. But looking at his scarred, earnest face, she knew in her gut she couldn't lie to him.

"He's having a rough patch," she said, her eyes cautious. "He's never been this bad before, not that I can remember. My ... the accident seems to have made him worse. He can't even look at me." Her lower lip trembled.

"Oh, Cait. Why don't you come and stay with us for a while? Mum would love to have you."

"I can't." She wiped her eyes with the back of her hand. "I'd never manage the stairs at your place. And here domiciliary services have put rails and stuff in the bathroom." She lifted her gaze to meet his concerned one, preparing to tell the whole truth. "I couldn't leave Dad, Alex. I don't think he'd be," her voice quivered, "safe to leave alone. Not now."

"He's always been a selfish bastard!"

Caitlin jumped in the face of his raw fury. "Sorry." She made her voice low and patient as she prepared to defend her father. She was also defending herself. She'd felt responsible for him for years. "It's okay,

Alex. You just don't understand. Something in him has been broken. Since the war. I promised Mum I'd look after him. It's like the accident triggered him somehow."

Alex's jaw muscles bunched as he swallowed his rage at his uncle. He took some slow breaths, willing it away. This anger wasn't something he could lay on Caitlin; she only had one parent left.

Caitlin's expression was soft. "I know it's not — ideal, Alex," she admitted. "And I know you're only mad at him because you care about me. But I can manage him. I've learned how."

A sad smile cracked through Alex's stony expression. "I know, Cait. I know you can."

"Aw, cuz, you're the best." She looked at him sideways. "I don't know why you haven't been snapped up by some gorgeous girl yet."

He laughed. "What with you and Mum and dear, old Nan, I've been surrounded with women. I don't think I could handle another one."

There was something else he was hiding, Caitlin decided. But it was safer to leave some secrets alone.

COOGEE–NOVEMBER 1911

"Kathleen, she's back with us, Lord be praised," Mrs. O'Connor greeted me as I entered the house called Restwell.

I squeezed her hand, too relieved to speak, and at her nodded invitation, I headed into Eileen's room. Eileen's eyes were bright, like one with a fever, but, propped up on pillows, she smiled at me. Frank was sitting near the bed, a book on his lap. "Hello," he said. "You must be tired after working and then walking all the way here. Take a seat. Can I get you something to drink?"

I was barely listening as my gaze hungrily took in Eileen's gentle, welcoming smile. Her face was thinner than ever, and her eyes shadowed. But she was alive. My heart soared like a bird. Against all odds, Eileen was alive.

"Tea, Frank. Please," she murmured.

Frank leaped from his chair with a speed that showed he, too, was delighted Eileen was still with us. "I'll be back," he promised.

She fluttered her left arm in invitation, and I very gently lowered myself onto her bed. I imagined she was too weak to talk, and after a few moments, I voiced the thought that kept going around in my head. "I thought we had lost you."

She made a slight movement of her head, a little shake. "I came back." Her smile broadened until she was beaming. Her eyes weren't bright from fever: it was a different kind of light shining from them now. I'm sure Eileen's smile could have changed the world.

"I'm glad. Rest. Don't talk; I can read to you if you like."

"No. I'll tell you."

I leaned closer so she didn't have to make the effort to project her voice. "On the eve of All Saints Day, I was very sick. As sick as you can be, without dying." Her eyes widened in wonder, and she caught her breath, as if she were finding the right words to tell me the story which filled her heart. "Our Lady came. She said I could choose. I could stay in heaven with her. Or I could come back healed, and live an ordinary life; or I come back still sick to suffer for Her, and Her work."

"Which life did you choose?"

"To live and suffer for Our Lady, and Her work."

I rubbed my head, hoping it would clear and I would understand her. "What work?"

"Our Lady loves the poor and the children. I will work for them. I will offer my suffering, trusting that because of it, they may suffer less." Her voice dropped in volume, but its power was magnified with a humble splendor as she continued, "I am going to save souls."

My body stiffened. A voice in my head was screaming, Oh Eileen, what have you done? What bargain have you made? Haven't you suffered enough?

But when I looked into Eileen's steady eyes, there was no fear there, no hesitation. Serene acceptance and happiness radiated from her, and all doubt left me. She had been close to heaven, I was certain, because it seemed a heavenly light shone around her. By some miracle, she had returned to us.

I'd grown up beside this otherworldly girl, and watched her become more holy, more godly. I'd heard neighbors say she was a saint and made light of their opinions. But that day, I knew in my heart, beyond doubt or reason, we had a saint in our midst.

I noticed at last that she was watching me. Waiting for me to respond. "What form will the work take?"

"I don't know exactly. We will help the poor and the sick and the children, whom Our Lady loves so much. Our Lady promised to guide me. When I told Her my decision, I went to Jesus. As close to Him as is possible, without dying. Our Lord spoke to me. He promised to help me." She smiled again, and another layer of light shone in her eyes. "He will help me through Father McGrath. We will love the least of Our Lord's brethren together."

The image of the exhausted priest sitting at her bedside came back into my mind. It was obvious he was devoted to her. Loved her. The perfect, pure love of a vital, healthy, young priest for a fragile invalid, lying paralyzed in bed, hovering between heaven and earth. And she adored him, too.

I closed my eyes for a moment as a wave of emotion flooded through me. Head bent, recalling the feel of Georgie's strong arms around me, the taste of his kiss after we shared a slice of Mum's apple pie, warm from the sun in Centennial Park. An electric shock tingled along my spine and into the top of my head. True love comes in many guises.

Maybe Mum was right all along. The Lord works in mysterious ways.

Eileen gradually grew stronger. Stronger in spirit, more so than in body, perhaps, as she remained paralyzed and was often bed-bound. But her mind was clear, and she often bubbled with a contagious excitement because her vague ideas of caring for the poor and the sick had crystalized in her conversations with Father McGrath, and they were determined to found an order of nurses to care for the sick poor in their own homes. My breath caught in my throat as I arrived at Restwell and saw her propped in her wicker wheelchair in its small front garden, her hair dancing around her in the gentle breeze, as she watched the goings on in the street. An elderly neighbor was caught in the act of handing her a posy, which Eily took in her left hand and buried her nose into, closing her eyes and transporting herself to who knows what sacred place on the scent of lavender and cabbage roses. Her eyes fixed on Eileen's tranquil face, the old woman crossed herself, and as she turned to leave, I saw tears glittering on her lashes.

Eileen grinned a welcome as soon as she saw me. "Get Frank. We're going to the beach," she said, as if it were the most natural thing in the world. "We're celebrating."

Frank carried her, and I wheeled the empty chair on the unsealed road, grateful for the maneuverability its lightness gave it, and watching the little bag of sandwiches and sponge cake that Annie O'Connor had made us, to make sure it didn't bounce off the seat.

"What are we celebrating?" I asked, my cheeks already aching from smiling so much at seeing her this bright and mobile.

Eileen, cradled in her brother's tender arms as he walked cautiously beside me, giggled, a peal of childish laughter, before her eyes grew round with wonder. "We're celebrating *everything*." She took a slow, contented breath. "All the wonders that the Lord has made. But especially, we are celebrating the wonderful progress of the work we are doing. Did I tell you we decided its name?"

"No," I said quickly, feeling lucky to get a word in, given her exuberance.

"It's going to be called Our Lady's Nurses for the Poor. We're going to arrange nurses for the sick poor, to care for them in their own homes, for no charge. Father is already searching for a house for us to rent, so we can make a home for the nurses to live in. I'll live there with them and look after them and devote my life to praying to support the work they do."

She was starting to pant with the exertion of talking and her color was fading. I seamlessly filled her silence, so she could catch her breath, watching her sideways under discreet eyelashes, for any signs we should abort our holiday. "That's wonderful, Eileen. It's a very good name and I'm sure you'll find plenty of people who need your help. Especially as you won't be charging them any money. Just let me concentrate on wheeling your chair over this sandy bit, and explain how you will fund it when we have got you settled." Did Eileen understand I had orchestrated a chance for her to rest already, I wondered. Probably. She seemed to just see through you. But she didn't say anything, and I was relieved to see her breathing was returning to its normal, shallow pattern. By the time Frank and I had fussed her into a comfortable position in her chair, she had recovered.

"I didn't tell you the best part," she said, her eyes coy.

I merrily took the bait. "What's the best part?"

"The best part is that we will set it up so it can become a convent later on, when everything is properly established." I began to comment, but she shook her head slightly, enough to cut me off, without hurting her back. "The better-than-the-best part, is that we already have some young women who have promised to join."

"Oh, Eileen, how happy you must be. Your dream is coming true. You've always wanted to be a nun."

Her smile was serene, but I caught a momentary sadness in her eyes. "It will take years and years to become a convent, Kathleen. Maybe after my time, but my girls will become nuns."

I blinked back the sudden sting in my eyes and plunged the conversation forwards as the roiling green tide crashed against Coogee Rocks below us. "How will you fund a house full of nurses?"

"We have a lot of fundraising to do. But Father is wonderful at recruiting. He's been talking to his fellow fathers and sending them to talk to me. One of them has promised to pay our first month's rent. And I have met with Father Gell a few times. He and his sister, Frances, are very kind. They have a lovely motor car, and they take me for rides in it. Such fun. They have promised to help us. He has sent a few girls for interviews too. And then, when we secure a place, we will start fundraising proper, with garden fetes, and concerts, and things."

How on earth would this frail young woman manage all this? I kept my lips tightly closed, but she must have read the question in my face.

"Our Lady will help us. And God's Bank of Providence will be open to us." She became almost stern. I hadn't been quick enough to hide my doubts. "It's Our Lady's work. It will not fail." There was no hesitation in her voice. I marveled at her confidence, her absolute trust in divine providence, before they swept away my concerns and bore me along with her enthusiasm.

"Then it will come to pass," I said with reverence.

Frank, sprawling at her feet, said, "All this talk about work makes a man hungry."

Chuckling, I unwrapped the sandwiches. He grabbed one and took a ravening bite. "Fish paste." He swooned with melodramatic delight amid the grassy tussocks. "The Lord does indeed provide great bounty."

I cut the crusts off a quarter of a sandwich and offered it to Eileen, but she shook her head. "Won't you eat just a little?" I pleaded, cutting my offering in half.

I sometimes think Eileen ate out of pity for those of us who watched over her, more than for the physical needs of her body, but she slowly chewed the piece of sandwich, and swallowed with effort, as if it threatened to stick in her throat. How such morsels could sustain her, I will never know. But saints be praised, they did.

Over the following months, Eileen kept busy interviewing benefactors and potential nursing recruits. She happily reported the climbing number of girls until she reached twenty who had promised to come to the home of Our Lady's Nurses for the Poor, which would be set up in a large single-story bungalow overlooking the sea, at 35 Dudley Street, Coogee. Eileen beamed when she announced the house had been secured. She hadn't been well enough to inspect it, but Frances Gell had given her a rough pencil sketch showing its long, enclosed verandah.

"That's where the girls will sleep. It'll make a lovely dormitory for them, with its views of the ocean, and all those windows will let in the sea breezes at night. We'll do lots of fundraising, so we can have every comfort for twenty girls and everything they need to perform their nursing duties." She deftly turned the paper over with her one good hand and showed me the floor plan sketched on its reverse. "And see, there's the room that will be my bedroom. Nice and close to the girls' room, so they can visit me before and after their rounds and tell me all about their work. We'll make it the chapel, one day, when we become a convent." Sighing, she smiled more deeply and held the picture to her heart. Closing her eyes in awed reverence, she murmured, "Here begins the work of heaven."

CAITLIN'S HOUSE, ADELAIDE

Alex tossed their empty Chinese food containers into the recycling bin, then wiped the kitchen table, and dried it with a tea-towel. "What's next?" He dragged his chair close beside Caitlin's, bending over the box as she opened it.

She untied the faded blue ribbon around a folded piece of paper. The thought that no one else had untied this thin piece of fabric or seen what was on the paper hit Caitlin like a gust of air from a long-lost tomb. "Kathleen has been dead for nearly fifty years. I wonder how long it is since anyone saw what was written on this page?"

"The suspense is killing me," groaned Alex. "Just open the bloody thing."

"It's not just one page. There are three sheets here."

"Well, read the first one to me, then." He relaxed back into his chair.

"Time for a bedtime story?" She grinned, relaxing herself. Her dad had meekly accepted his beef in black bean sauce, and she could hear the water running in the bathroom. He was capable of making an effort, after all, and seeing that made her feel good. She read out loud.

> *There was a grand girl from Redfern.*
> *Whose virtues I watched unfurl,*
> *Till the love in my heart did burn.*
> *I got on my knees, and said won't you please*
> *Come and give marriage a whirl?*

Caitlin sighed wistfully. "Was that a marriage proposal?"
"Sounds like one. A bit unorthodox."

"Well, we knew George was cheeky."

"And a real Irish lad, by the sound of this. What's next?"

Caitlin smoothed the next page, then read:

> *I can't afford much of a ring, Kathleen,*
> *But I'll fund our board and our bed,*
> *Don't worry your head.*
> *We don't need much treasure to bring ourselves pleasure,*
> *And riches or no, you're my Queen.*

Alex watched, his eyes twinkling, as Caitlin reached up her sleeve for a tissue and blew her nose. "That's really cheesy, you know."

"Yeah, but it's so …" A look of tenderness softened her features.

"So what?"

"Kind of innocent. And very romantic."

"You're a big softy."

"Yeah. But you love me anyway, right?"

He grinned and winked at her. "Yup. I'm scared to ask what's next."

"It's a tiny painting," Caitlin exclaimed as she unwrapped the third item from its protective tissue.

The watercolors had faded over the years, but the miniature image was still clear: two lovers, standing hand in hand, facing a sun rising over the water. Under the picture, the words: *Yes, George, I'll take your hand and walk into the future with you. Kathleen.*

"You need a new box of tissues?" His smile was affectionate, despite his teasing.

She shook her head. "I wonder how long they were together, before he went to war?"

"We'd better listen to the next tape."

COOGEE-1912

I sat on the tram, savoring the novelty of riding instead of walking. I closed my eyes and replayed the scene of Georgie pressing the pennies for the fare into my hand. I had tried to argue, but he silenced me with a kiss.

"No arguments, Kathleen. You'll be home safe, and earlier than if you walked the five miles back. And because you won't be as tired, you'll be glad to have me call around for half an hour in the evening, won't you?"

"Of course I will," I replied.

Resting my elbow on the bag in my lap, I pillowed my chin on my hand and closed my eyes, remembering the warmth of his touch on my fingers, his arm around my shoulders. I smiled to myself, not caring if anyone noticed. I was in love, and Georgie had proposed. It's true, he looked just a bit ridiculous, when he suddenly went to his knees in front of my chair in the front room. Always the opportunist, he seized the first moment we were alone, when Mum had put down her darning and gone to the kitchen to make tea. He'd unfolded the piece of paper he'd pulled out of his pocket and read the limerick to me. He was so nervous he couldn't lift his eyes from the page. Or maybe it wasn't nerves, maybe he thought if he looked at me, he'd start to laugh?

I slipped my hand into my bag, and took out the paper, tied up with a blue ribbon that Eileen had once given me, when we were children, and I still wore my hair down.

I read his poem for the hundredth time. Its literary merit was so dubious, I couldn't resist a chuckle now. But at the time I'd felt exasperated. "Oh, Georgie," I'd said. "For the love of God, ask me properly!"

And then he did. He fixed those cornflowers firmly on me, and, dropping his note to the floor, took my hand in his. Slowly drawing my hand towards him, he laid it on his chest. The manly warmth of him took my breath away, but the earnestness in his eyes brought my focus back to his words.

"Feel this, Kathleen," he said. "This heart of mine only beats for you. It has only beaten for you since the first time I *really* saw you. I love you, Kathleen. Will you trust me enough to marry me?"

His smile was wide as I nodded. "Yes, I will."

He leaned forward to kiss me, but I gently averted my face, not wanting Mum to catch us. I stalled for time, and asked, "And when did you first *really* see me, Georgie O'Grady?"

His eyes softened with reminiscences in the few moments before he replied. "It was soon after Eileen came back to school, after one of her operations. Something had happened, one of the little kids had been playing with a ball, and it bumped into Eileen, and fell at her feet. She stooped to pick it up, and must have pulled something in her back, because she froze, her face turned gray with agony. You were at her side in a flash, and you took her arm and helped her to a seat. Then you wiped the sweat off her brow with the hem of your pinafore. There was such a look of tenderness in your face; I can see it now. In that moment, you stopped being just some kid with pigtails down your back. And I thought, maybe one day, I'd be worthy of you looking at me like that."

Well, how could I push him away then? Our lips met. And that was when Mum came back in with the tea tray.

Later, while I lay in bed, knowing one day I would be sleeping next to Georgie, imagining being in his arms, I had thought of how Eileen had lain in her bed of pain. Had hovered so close to death that she saw Jesus and Mary; and made the choice to come back. Illness and deformity had mapped out the path of Eileen's life, ensuring she would never know love as Georgie and I would. And yet, her love could radiate to the corners of a room, and fill the hearts of all who saw her.

I would tell her about me and George. I knew she would be excited for me, because she always knew I'd never make a nun.

CAITLIN'S HOUSE, ADELAIDE

"It sounds like quite a romance," said Alex, arching his back, stretching till it cracked. "Whatever happened later, we know they loved each other."

"They must have been a really cute couple." Caitlin looked misty-eyed.

"I never knew you were so romantic."

"Neither did I." Caitlin met her cousin's gaze and suddenly they both giggled.

Alex's mood changed again, and his brows knitted together as he stared at her. "What else don't I know about you?"

She closed her eyes for a moment, thinking. Choosing a secret she felt safe to reveal. "I never believed in saints."

"No?"

"Not really. Like, people who do miracles and stuff, Moses parting the Red Sea, that sort of thing."

"Do you think those things are just stories?"

Caitlin paused, forming an argument in her mind. "You know how people watch superhero movies, to make them feel life isn't hopeless, and it's possible to triumph over evil?"

Alex nodded. "Well, what if the stories of saints are an old version of that, designed to remind people God is all powerful and can sometimes act through people and allow them to succeed against impossible odds?"

Thoughtful, he gazed off into the distance. "Like the Church makes up these stories to keep people in awe of God? Or in awe of the Church because the Church is the intermediary between them and God?"

"Maybe." She shook her head. "I don't know. But now I'm wondering, what if the stories aren't made up? What else did saints do?"

Alex laughed. "I can't claim to have any expertise on saints, Cait. Maybe I should have gone to Sunday school when I was a kid. But they didn't all go around parting oceans. I guess they healed people. Or showed special courage beyond what you would normally expect people to do. Hang on." He reached for his phone and typed something, then held it out for Caitlin to read.

"What do saints do? Oh, Alex, that's too funny."

He grinned and pressed the search button. "Most saints live a life devoted to serving God and people in need. Eventually, their good deeds are recognized after their death and the Pope canonizes them." He shook his head. "Doesn't help much, does it? Okay …" He scrolled. "Oh, look, there's a whole process to officially becoming a saint. Being recognized as living a life of holiness, showing heroic virtue, and doing miracles."

"And all this has to be proven?"

"Yes, the Catholic Church holds special investigations, apparently."

"So, someone could be a saint, but not get recognized?"

"I guess."

"But the first step is that people know someone and think, she's a saint. A saintly person?"

Alex rubbed his eyes. "Looks like it. Otherwise, the whole process wouldn't start, would it?"

Caitlin leaned forward in her wheelchair, her voice low and her face filled with awe. "Our great-great-grandmother Kathleen thought she knew a saint. What did she say? What were the words?"

Alex smiled, proud of his acute memory. "It made an impression on me too. She said, 'I knew in my heart, beyond doubt or reason, we had a saint in our midst'." He typed into his phone.

"No! Please don't google Eileen. Not until after we've finished the tapes. Don't spoil the story. And anyway, there's only one Australian saint; Mary MacKillop, so I know Eileen hasn't made it onto the list."

"Okay, let's keep going then. How about you see what's next in the box?"

Caitlin hesitated.

"What's up?"

"We're going to find some sad things in this box, Alex. Whatever happened to Georgie. Eileen being so ill. If she's not been made a saint, maybe she dies before she can live up to her reputation? And who knows what other suffering is hidden in here?"

He nodded gravely. "Who knows what joy is hidden in there, too? A wedding, and a baby to come, at least. Life isn't just about suffering and dying."

"No, that's true."

"Go on, look in the box."

She smiled back at him and took out a small brown paper bag. She peered inside it, then tipped the bag on a slight angle, allowing a single, silk rose to slide into her cupped hand. Faded pink, mottled with brown spots now, but its heart was protected where the fabric was folded in on itself, and the color was still a deep, coral pink there. A testament to brighter days. She turned it over with care and caressed the tiny brass safety pin pushed through the fabric stem behind the flower. "It was pinned to something once."

"A dress?"

"Maybe."

They smiled to each other and said together, "A wedding dress."

COOGEE–1913

I lifted my skirt just a little as I managed the step onto the tram, not wanting to get marks on my new dress. Mum and I had spent all our spare time in the evenings making the outfit from cream muslin. With a high collar and buttoned cuffs, the blouse was nipped in at the waist. The skirt fell to just above the floor, shaped so it was both elegant and economical in its demand for fabric.

I felt like such a lady when Georgie stepped forward and spread his best white handkerchief over the seat before I sat down. The tram conductor stood aside, watching the show with wry amusement before coming down the aisle to sell us tickets.

"Two of us, myself and my wife," Georgie said, glowing pink with pride.

The conductor winked. "Newlywed, are we, sir?"

"Just this morning." Georgie beamed.

"Congratulations, sir. And you look beautiful, missus."

I blushed as other passengers joined in congratulating us. "Where are you off to on your honeymoon?"

"Oh, we can't take a honeymoon just yet. But we're off to see Eileen O'Connor, seeing as she couldn't come to the wedding."

"Saintly Eileen? Give her my best, won't you?" And he grinned a big cheeky grin at Georgie, while giving me an exaggerated wink. "You're a smart young couple if ever I saw one. If I'd only have thought to get my own marriage blessed by a saint, maybe my Gertie wouldn't be such an old tartar."

The tram erupted into laughter as the conductor moved down the aisle checking tickets. Georgie leaned close to my ear. "He's right," he whispered. "You do look beautiful."

I let my arm nuzzle against his as we sat side by side, the tram rocking us, arms rubbing together, both soothed and excited by his presence. My mind began to drift.

Eileen had been confined to bed for two years now, ever since her father died. Paralyzed in both legs and her right arm, and sometimes blind. I'd been with her during many mealtimes, and knew she barely ate enough to keep a sparrow alive. Other times she couldn't keep anything down at all. And sometimes I would visit, only to find her unconscious. Those bouts of unconsciousness could last for days at a stretch. And through it all, Father McGrath visited her every day, to give her Communion; even if she was unconscious and hadn't held anything down, by some divine providence, she could take Communion.

"You know, Georgie," I mused, watching the terrace houses stream past the window, "The neighbors say they can set their clocks by Father McGrath's nine o'clock visit to Eileen."

"He's devoted to her."

"Yes." I nodded. I'd never forgotten his exhausted face after Eileen's move, when she hovered so close to death. "I wonder if the sheer force of his will helped keep her body and soul together when she was so sick?"

"What?"

"It doesn't matter." I shook my head. "There's something in our Eileen that inspires devotion isn't there?"

He looked perplexed, as if he was not sure what I wanted him to say. "You inspire devotion too," he ventured.

His earnest expression seemed irresistibly funny, and I started to laugh. After a moment of surprise, he joined in, then he took my hand in his, and gave it a squeeze. Later, that night, he would tell me he thought perhaps I was laughing because I was nervous about our wedding night. I didn't have the heart to tell him, I wasn't thinking that far ahead. All my thoughts were on Eileen. It was as if, the closer we got to her, the more I could feel her light shining, ready to welcome us. It was always like that, going to see Eileen. And when I couldn't visit her, especially if I was worried or frightened, I only had to think of her, to feel a peaceful warmth in my chest. It still happens now.

Anne O'Connor beamed at me as she let us in. "Mr. and Mrs. O'Grady, come in, come in." She kissed both my cheeks and even pecked George's.

"Here comes the bride," sang Frank as Mary threw open Eileen's door.

Eileen, propped up on pillows, was smiling and joyful. "You look beautiful, Kathleen. I'm glad you could come." She waved me in closer, with her one good limb. "Come and let me see you better. Oh, how lovely, you wore it! I thought it would be just the thing with your dress." She reached out and touched the pink silk rose she had given me to pin on the waistband of my skirt.

"It is perfect," I told her, humbled by her pleasure. "You have an eye for embellishing dresses."

"It's *The Ladies Home Journals* people bring me to read. I like to keep up with fashion." She reached her hand along the coverlet and passed me a small parcel.

"Thank you," I said, taking it from her.

"Sit here and open it," Eileen urged. Her enthusiasm for presents was legendary, both in the giving and the receiving, and her eyes glowed with excitement as I unwrapped it, keeping the brown paper as smooth as possible so it could be reused. I unrolled a small square of linen, embroidered with a bright pink rose.

"It's gorgeous! Oh, George, look."

"I'll make a little frame for it," George promised, "and when we have our own house, we shall put it in pride of place in the front room, where our visitors can admire it."

Eileen laughed, the happy little-girl laugh that she had when I first met her, over a decade before.

"You're a marvel, Eileen," I breathed. "The workmanship! However did you do it?"

"I've been practicing." She smiled conspiratorially. "I didn't want anyone who looks at my work to know I am only using my left hand."

"You've succeeded, then," I said, and I meant it. No one could tell.

Her smile widened. "I'm glad you like it. It'll remind you that you love each other, and you love me, and I love you. And that *They* love us all." Her tone changed and filled with mischief, as she declared, "And now we are having a party; with cake."

It was like having a second family, as Eileen's mother and siblings crowded into her room with us, bringing tea and little cakes Mrs. O'Connor had somehow made the time to bake for us.

I was perfectly happy that afternoon. I think we all were. Though I did feel sad when I saw Eileen taste a piece of cake—one morsel on a teaspoon, then give a subtle shake of her head to indicate she would eat no more.

CAITLIN'S HOUSE, ADELAIDE

Caitlin cradled the silk flower reverentially in her hands. "It *was* from a wedding dress," Alex said, his voice bringing her back into the kitchen.

"Yes. And it was a gift from Eileen. She must have loved roses, if she embroidered a picture of one too, as their wedding gift."

"We should ask Mum if she has seen that embroidered rose."

"Good idea. Wouldn't it be wonderful if she has?"

"It's a long shot, Cait. It might have gotten tatty and been thrown out decades ago."

"Oh no! What if they threw it away when Nan and your mum were packing up the old house?"

"We'll ask." He turned his head towards the rhythmic thumping on the vinyl flooring in the hall. "Can I get you anything, Uncle Tim?"

"You kids still here?" Tim hopped into the kitchen on his crutches and headed to the fridge. "Thought you might have deserted me by now."

"Where'd I go on a Saturday night these days, Dad?" Caitlin asked, her downturned gaze fixed on her leg, in its awkward brace, sticking out in front of her chair.

He sucked beer straight from the can. "We're a right pair, Cait. Not much use to anybody."

Alex jumped at the bitterness in his tone, as much as at the words, but saw his cousin's expression betrayed no hint of hurt or surprise. He held his tongue while his mind clouded with worry.

"It's okay, Dad. It'll get easier for you when I'm back in action."

Tim surveyed the three cans of beer he'd put on the bench, then the open can in his hand, defeated.

"It's alright, Uncle Tim, I can help you carry them," volunteered Alex.

Tim turned bloodshot eyes on his nephew, and nodded, before making his way back to the couch.

Alex picked up the cans and followed him, a dozen thoughts on what he should do colliding in his head. Caitlin's disclosure that her father had been worse since the car accident took precedence, and he sighed a steadying breath, breathing in beer fumes, as he drew a chair opposite the unshaven wreck in front of him. Revulsion was tempered with a pity strong enough to allow his anger to fade away.

"Are you okay, Uncle Tim?"

"How can I be okay?" Something hostile flashed in his eyes and he brandished the stump of his right leg, just protruding below the hem of his khaki shorts. "I haven't been in one piece since Vietnam."

Caught between the urge to bolt from this unpredictable man, whose deformity and harshness had terrified him when he was a little boy, and his desire to do something—anything—that might make life easier for Caitlin, Alex swallowed and stayed in his chair.

He dropped his voice, making it gentle and caring. "Uncle, I think the car accident must have upset you very much."

Tim stiffened and glared at Alex, who steadfastly held his ground.

"I'm sorry, Uncle Tim. I …" He dropped his gaze, embarrassed to find his eyes filling with hot tears, and dashed them away with the back of his hand. "I tried to swerve, but there wasn't enough time. I couldn't stop. There was nothing I could do to save her."

He gasped as Tim's rough hand grasped his.

"One thing I learned in Vietnam, Alex," Tim said, his gruff voice slurred by alcohol, "is you can't dodge a bullet that's got your name on it. I know it wasn't your fault. That bastard ran a red light. You've got nothing to apologize for. You must have slowed enough or swerved enough to save her life. But her getting hurt wasn't your fault."

Tim felt around in his pocket and brought out a handkerchief, that seemed to have tomato sauce stains on it, and handed it to Alex. Alex sniffed hard and began to wave the handkerchief aside, but something stopped him, and he accepted it, stains and all. "Thanks," he said and blew his nose.

Tim's head was nodding, and his eyes focused far away, at

something Alex couldn't see. His wife dying long ago? His mates who didn't come home from the war? Alex didn't know, but he knew Tim was with his memories now, and he had dismissed him. He reached across the impassable distance between them, and laid his hand on his uncle's shoulder, then left the room without looking back.

Caitlin's worried eyes were upon him as soon as he stepped through the doorway. She had never trusted anyone else to manage Tim's moods, not since her mother died. Her heart lurched at the grief in Alex's face, and her hands gripped the arms of her wheelchair as if she were trying to launch herself towards him. Instead, he came to her and, kneeling awkwardly on the floor, careful of her injured leg, he rested his head on her shoulder and began to sob.

She wrapped her arms around him. "It's all right, Alex. It's all right."

"It's not all right, Cait," he murmured, muffled against her shirt.

She patted his back for a minute. "We've been through all this, Alex. The accident, it wasn't your fault. I saw what happened. I think it would have been worse if you hadn't acted so quickly. And you were very brave. In the car. Waiting for them to cut us out. I—I lost it, but you kept talking to me the whole time and held my hand." She cradled his face in her hands and tilted it to make him look at her. "You were a hero."

He shook his head, not believing her.

"My hero," she smiled. "And now I'm starting to learn to walk again, practicing what the physiotherapist's been teaching me, and when I doubt myself and want to throw in the towel, who is right there beside me, egging me on? Who is still making sure I never give up?"

His gaze was steady now, fixed on her face, echoing his vow. "I am."

"And who's going to vet any guys I might think of going out with in future? To make sure you don't ever have to drop everything and race over to rescue me again?"

"Er, me?" There were still details he didn't know about that night. She never did tell him why she called him then. But, sensing her need to feel protected, he silenced the question on his lips.

"Yes, you again. Aren't you?"

"Yes, I am. I promise."

"Good." She smiled now. "It's a full moon. How about you get up and we can get some fresh air. If you get my crutches, I'll get my butt out of this chair and show you how fast I can walk down the hall. We'll still have time to listen to another track before bed."

Grinning, he brandished the crutches. "I'll race you."

Snatching them, she stared him down. "I'm warning you. I'll cheat."

He pulled a hideous face and, shrieking with laughter, she deftly held a crutch in front of him, blocking the doorway.

"Limbo," he yelled, shimmying his trunk backwards, but losing balance and ending up red-faced on the floor.

Outside, the night air chilled their skin, and he sidled closer to her, letting his arm brush against hers as she balanced herself on the crutches, her eyes glittering with reflected moonlight. He watched her for a moment as she studied the moon, feeling the undercurrent of sadness that never used to be there. But the warmth of her arm next to his stirred his courage. He turned his face to the silver disc of the moon and took a deep breath.

Very gently, he spoke. "You never did tell me why you called me to come and get you in the middle of the night, you know."

She stiffened against him, almost pulled away from his touch. Her shudder alarmed him, and he feared he had crossed some unacknowledged boundary. But the shudder passed, and Caitlin's body relaxed again. He felt the subtle pressure as she leaned against him a little more and waited long seconds for her response.

When it came, he had to lean closer to catch her whisper. "Those bruises I got. They weren't all from the accident."

He frowned, searching for the meaning in her words. His eyes widened in horror. "That frigging lowlife hit you?" he spat. "I thought the weasel just dumped you because you were in hospital. I'll kill him."

A soft sigh of relief escaped from her lungs. "Thanks. But he's not worth it." She shifted the crutches awkwardly so she could rest her head against his shoulder, but they both carefully continued to stare at the moon so they could keep their expressions private.

After several minutes, he broke the silence. "Have you talked to anyone about that?"

"No. Not yet."

"But you will, won't you?"

"Mmm."

"Promise me."

"I promise."

He kissed the top of her head. "Ready to go back inside? It's cold out here."

"Sure. I'd still like to listen to another tape before bed."

COOGEE–1913

Eventually, Eileen, surrounded by handwritten notes, propped up on the chaise lounge in the front room at Restwell, announced everything was ready for Foundation Day, the fifteenth of April 1913, when she would move to the new home to greet the girls and they would celebrate the start of their enterprise, with local priests and community members in attendance. I tried to picture the festive atmosphere Eileen was conjuring up for me, but I couldn't. I turned my face away, to hide my bitten lip as I swallowed down my memories of Eileen's last two moves.

As if she could read my mind, she said, "Father McGrath will arrange an ambulance for me again. And a nurse will travel in it with me. And he promised to walk alongside the ambulance and be praying for me the whole time."

I forced a smile, wanting to reassure her, because I knew well enough, there was never any dissuading Eileen, once she had made her mind up to do something. "It's not very far, that should make moving easier." I tried to sound convincing, even though the last move, which almost killed her, had been short too. I didn't mention how steep and sandy the roads were in places. Not easy for a horse and wagon. Not easy walking either, depending on the weather. Not that Eileen had walked in years. I didn't let myself think how fatigued Eileen must be after helping make all the arrangements, or that she was paler recently, and sometimes her lips looked dusky blue when she was tired.

"Father and I have rented it for a month to begin with. But we are hoping we can buy it."

I blinked. How on earth was Eileen going to be able to buy a big house, even out here in Coogee where prices were lower than in the city?

"Don't look worried." Her smile was as serene as ever, reassuring me. "We're doing Our Lady's work. How can we fail? The Lord will provide."

When Foundation Day came around, Father McGrath's solemn vigil beside the ambulance didn't save Eileen. She was barely conscious and writhing in agony by the time they arrived at 35 Dudley Street. She could be carried no further than the enclosed verandah, because Father and her family couldn't bear the feeble moans of pain caused by the smallest movement. In an attempt to keep things on track, the opening ceremony for the home went ahead, attended by the new nursing recruits, Eileen's family and friends, and several priests.

But how awful it was for the young nurses, who had given up their regular lives to come, to have one founder hovering between life and death, and the other worried sick about her. The promises of a fresh start, a happy home together, and the spiritual rewards of setting up a nursing program for the poor and marginalized, were evaporating before their eyes. They stood around, uncertain and afraid, not knowing where to look, then began to melt away. All but one of the nurses left, never to return. The one who stayed, Nurse Rigney, was already in full-time work at St. Vincent's Hospital and, although she never joined the nursing order, she came every day for weeks, to nurse Eileen herself.

Instead of starting her work in a mood of celebration and promise, with a band of dedicated young women around her, Eileen spent her first night at Dudley Street on her stretcher on the verandah, her only companions a parishioner Father McGrath had arranged to be temporary housekeeper, and her daughter. Mrs. Derrick and her daughter, Mary, to their credit, became an integral part of the early days of the Home. Not only did they care for Eileen, but they came to love her, and I suspect there were times, in that difficult starting period, when they used their own meagre savings to keep food in the house. Of course, that was not something they would ever have told me. But I know for a fact, they worked for love, as volunteers, and were never paid.

Slowly, Eileen's condition improved, although her legs and right arm remained paralyzed. The periods of unconsciousness lessened, and she had enough strength to get involved in the comings and goings of the big house in Dudley Street. But I knew her too well not to notice the pain lines etched into her face. The agreement Eileen said she'd made with Our Lady, to suffer for the salvation of souls, came to mind. And, as always, Father McGrath was never far away, fitting in visits whenever he could, and regularly giving Eileen Communion when she was too ill to go to church.

As soon as she was well enough, she joined him in the work of planning, writing letters, designing uniforms, a thousand details. They worked well together, with great respect and mutual understanding, and a genuine, loving friendship which had them always concerned for the other's welfare. Father would still send promising recruits to see Eileen.

That was how I first met Cissie McLaughlin. Cissie would become the first girl to join the nursing order, and later become the Matron. Later again, she would become the congregation's leader and the first Mother Superior. Not that I guessed any of this back in 1914. She was a beautiful girl, and her star-spangled eyes were round as saucers when I met her at the door. "My cousin brought me," she said shyly, indicating the priest at her elbow. "He asked me if I'd like to visit a *real* saint. How could I say no?"

I wanted to laugh, but I nodded instead and made my face friendly to welcome her. "No one can say no to Eileen," I said and couldn't restrain myself any longer. I winked at her.

A few weeks later, I visited again. I was shown into Eileen's bedroom, to find her propped up against her pillows, holding a telephone receiver in her left hand. Her voice was patient and professional.

"Yes, Mrs. Jones. I can have a nurse come and visit your mother tomorrow. Nurse Cissie. Yes, yes." She smiled at me without breaking her concentration. "That's right Mrs. Jones, at no charge at all. Good afternoon."

As she hung up the broom-handle receiver, which looked too heavy for her, I opened my mouth to greet her but paused as she carefully wrote a few details in her notebook. I remembered her pride at embroidering a wedding gift for me with her left hand. She had obviously learned to write left-handed too. At last, she looked up, her eyes tired but triumphant.

"Word is getting around," she beamed. "We have clients in Redfern and Surry Hills now, not just Coogee."

"How do the nurses get there?"

"They walk. But if they have to go a long way, they don't set off on their rounds till the post has come, in case someone has sent us some money they can use for tram fares." Her eyes were twinkling, and I laughed, picturing the nurses with their bags packed, waiting in the hope they wouldn't have to walk five or six miles to see their patient.

"Well, you see, Kathleen, sometimes we have to give God's Bank extra time to come to our aid."

My mood changed to one of seriousness, as a revelation dawned on me. "You're completely happy, aren't you?"

"Oh yes! I'm doing Our Lady's work. I'm finally making a difference in the lives of the poor and the sick. It's wonderful."

"Yes, that is wonderful," I agreed, seeing how lit up her face was.

"It's not the way I imagined it, you see. I always used to feel I would be useless, only able to stay secluded and pray and suffer. Little Eileen the Pest."

I started to protest at the idea of her being a pest, but she stopped me with a glance. "Look at me, Kathleen. We've only got two nurses, and no Matron yet, so here I am doing my part by answering phones and arranging nurse visits." She waved her notebook at me, as if it were a badge of office. "I meet people, I raise funds, I plan how we can manage things. The girls come in and talk over their days with me as soon as they come home. Sometimes I can even advise them on difficult cases."

Her enthusiasm was contagious but pulled at my heartstrings too. "What do you tell them, Eileen?"

"I have lots of experience of being a patient, of course, so I tell them how they might help someone who is suffering or afraid. When a patient is particularly difficult, I remind them to draw on the grace of Jesus and Our Lady, for whom we are doing the work." She lowered her voice, "And sometimes I remind them to be kind, to work for love and in love, without judging. I tell them the cause of a person's poverty is not theirs to question. The fact a person is poor is the reason you help."

To see Eileen radiating the joy of finding a life of meaning and purpose, despite everything, brought the sting of tears to my eyes. "It's wonderful work you are doing," I said.

"Sometimes, I just listen. There's terrible things the girls get called to see, you know," she said, her eyes downcast for a moment. "Burns.

Someone with a cancer like a cauliflower eating away part of his face. Bitter, broken people. But no matter how appalling their circumstances are, the girls go and visit them, and dress their wounds, and apply salves of loving kindness to their hearts. And sometimes, they pray with them, or sit and keep them company, because no one should have to die alone."

"It sounds like hard work."

"Yes, it is. But we are working for souls. There is nothing more important than that."

I nodded my head in helpless agreement. Mrs. Derrick came into the room with a tea tray.

"Oh, lovely, thank you. Tea, Kathleen?"

"Yes, please." I sat in silent friendship, savoring the view of Eileen lifting her own gilt-edged porcelain cup, decorated with light red poppies, to her lips.

The phone rang, and Eileen made an appointment for a visitor, scribbling away in her notebook again. Then she hung up. "I am so excited about the fete. It's going to be such a busy afternoon, with lots of stalls and games for the children." Her eyes shone. "And for the fundraiser in November, a special performance of Dirty Dick. Such a funny play, about a clergyman who bets on a horse to raise funds to repair his church. Then he tries to dope the horse to make sure it wins."

I giggled. "Eileen, you'd never resort to such measures?"

Her laughter rang out like little bells. "I don't need to. Our Lady has sent me the Governor's wife, Lady Strickland, to be patron. And," she paused, creating a thrum of suspense, "the Gells are going to give us the money to buy this house. They'll give Father and I a cheque each, and we shall buy it half each, because we are the cofounders, after all. So, we won't need to find money for the rent anymore. We'll get all the paperwork finished in December."

"You're very busy, Eileen."

She smiled. "Yes. I'm busy and useful. Who could have imagined such things?"

Something in my heart cracked open. "You were right all along. You are doing God's work. How could you fail?"

CAITLIN'S HOUSE, ADELAIDE

"A cancer eating away someone's face!" Caitlin's mouth puckered with a wave of nausea.

"Sounds awful." Alex checked the time on his phone.

"Even burns in those days were horrific, with no skin grafts, antibiotics, or pain relief. I can't bear to think about it."

"Me either. Let's change the subject."

Caitlin yawned. "It takes me a while to get ready for bed these days," she said ruefully. "But maybe we have time to look at one more thing from the box before bed?"

He smiled. "Sure. See what's next."

She unfolded a fragile newspaper clipping. "Someone, Kathleen, I suppose, has written Freeman's Journal twenty-ninth October, 1914, on this."

"That's about the time the war started."

"It sure is."

She scanned the article then read highlights aloud. "A garden fete in aid of Our Lady's Home, Dudley-street Coogee … blah blah … Marquees were erected in the picturesque grounds, which command a beautiful view of the ocean, and stalls were tastefully arranged beneath them … etcetera … the good work set going for nursing the poor and bringing comfort into their homes. He paid a high tribute to the noble life led by little Eileen O'Connor, who, an invalid herself, had devoted her life to relieving the sufferings of the sick and dying. Eileen and her Brown Nurses had already attended over one hundred cases.

"Oh, listen to this quote. 'She thought the age of miracles could not be over, when one considered what had already come of very small beginnings.' The age of miracles, doesn't that sound wonderful?"

"This is a bit over a year after she moved there. October 1914, you said."

"Yes. Hold on—" Caitlin frowned and reread the article. "That's very odd, Alex. It lists people who were there. Eileen's mother Anne O'Connor, the nurses—in their spotless white uniforms, no less—the stallholders. The priest who did the welcome speech, Father Gell. But according to this, Father McGrath wasn't there."

"But they were inseparable. And he helped her establish the Home in the first place."

"Maybe he was away."

"Then why does Eileen get honored in the article, and no one mentions him?"

"I don't know. Another mystery to solve, it seems."

Alex shrugged. "A great-great-grandfather who died in World War I, but isn't listed in the Commonwealth War Graves data base, and a disappearing priest?"

"Well, we don't know he disappeared. It just seems odd he wasn't there."

"Maybe he was posted elsewhere. Priests get moved to different parishes, don't they?"

"Yes, maybe that's all it is." She didn't look convinced, but her tone brightened. "Well, we know Eileen made a success of the Home, at least for eighteen months or so. And people were talking about miracles, in something connected to Eileen."

Alex grinned. "That's another mystery to solve, then. We'll have to write a list. Was Eileen really a saint?"

"That's enough questions for one day. Let's see if we get any answers tomorrow."

They peered into the living room, lit only by the flickering glow of the television, where Tim was still on the couch, scrolling through channels with the remote.

"Good night, Uncle Tim."

Tim turned towards them with an unexpected smile. "You can work here tomorrow, if you like."

Alex struggled to keep the surprise off his face. "Are you sure we're not in the way?"

"You're not in the way. It's kind of nice to have young voices in the house."

"Sure." A little of the tension in his shoulders eased, and he smiled back at his uncle. "Thanks. I'll see you in the morning then."

"Is there anything you need before I go to bed, Dad?" Caitlin asked, propped on her crutches in the doorway.

"Nah. All good." He turned back to the television.

"What was that about?" Alex whispered, following Caitlin into her room at the end of the house.

"I don't know," she said, mulling her thoughts. "Maybe he's missed having company after all?"

"Maybe. What time do you plan on being up?"

"Breakfast around nine?"

"Cool. Good night, Cait." He softly closed her door behind him and entered the room opposite hers. Seeing the untidy pile of sheets and blankets tossed on the dresser, he began to make up the spare bed.

COOGEE, SEPTEMBER 1914

Eileen's eyes twinkled as she waved a hand over the newspaper report of the success of her latest fundraiser.

"George and I really enjoyed the concert," I said, caressing the comforting gold band on my ring finger. It wasn't getting tight yet. Butterflies fluttered in my stomach at the thought of breaking my news to Eileen, but she was so full of things to tell me, that I was happy to wait my turn. "A full house; how pleased you must be. Miss Ella Caspers was wonderful."

"She really has a voice of gold, Kathleen, just like they say in the papers." She looked like a little fairy, dwarfed in her old-fashioned, metal-framed bed with its blue, silk canopy her mother had sewn with tiny, loving stitches. No, not a fairy: an angel. Though the angels in Bible pictures were never so thin.

"Poor girl. Fancy finding out you have just married a bigamist." I shuddered at the thought of the scandal that had erupted around Miss Caspers, causing her retreat home to Australia from a planned European singing tour.

"Don't speak of such things," Eileen said. "But of course, we shall pray that she finds lasting happiness. She was the reason the concert sold out. And to think, if this dreadful war hadn't started, she would have been on a ship back to tour in Europe, and we couldn't have had her at all."

"They say the war will be over by Christmas." My mouth suddenly dry, I asked her about plans for the fete the next month.

"Everything's in hand," she said. "There will be so many stalls. And games for the children, and lemonade, and cakes. Much more than last year: it'll run over four days."

"Four days? That's a lot of work."

"It certainly is, but we have so many helpers now. We're making the fete our major fundraiser every year. And the Premier's wife is going to open it."

The phone rang. Outside, the sun was getting low in the sky. The shadows were lengthening, beckoning me home, but I wanted to draw out my visit, to enjoy seeing Eileen's enthusiasm. To get her blessing.

Before I could summon the courage to tell her my news, the back door was flung open. Cissie and two of the other nurses must have met on the tram. They chatted in the verandah as they took off their brown cloaks—brown chosen to honor St. Joseph—and pill-box hats, and washed their hands and faces, before coming into Eileen's room in their high-necked, white nursing uniforms, in a cloud of cheery bustle that made me melt contentedly into the background. They greeted Eileen with great affection, calling her Little Mother, and kissing her tenderly.

"Hello, children," she beamed. "Tell us all about your day."

Kit McGrath, Father's sister, had joined the foundation a few months before, and emerged from the kitchen, where she was rostered for the week, with a tea tray for her companions, who gratefully accepted their refreshments. Tired as they were, they helped Kit change Eileen's position in the bed, easing the pressure on her bedsores, and took turns relating stories about the patients they had seen, the wounds they had dressed, the shopping and laundry they had attended to, and a hundred other acts of kindness and service they had offered in the name of love to the dirty, sick, and often-unwanted slum-dwellers of Sydney.

Eileen was keenly interested in all their goings-on and gently reinforced the values she and Father McGrath had envisioned to guide the nurses in their vocation. When one of the nurses commented how afraid she had been to call on a new patient, known for his hostile, drunken attitude, Eileen beckoned her closer to the bedside. "You were very brave, Katie, to go in to care for a patient when you felt so frightened. Tell me, did you remember to pray for Our Lady's help before you went in?"

"Yes, Little Mother. I couldn't have summoned the courage otherwise."

"Our Lady will always help you," Eileen said, with the quiet conviction of someone who knew this for certain. "Remember that in some places, Our dear Lady may have no one else to work through, than our poor and worthless selves. Today, you had the honor of being that person in that place."

Katie's earnest young face was infused with light as she bowed her head in thanksgiving.

After everyone had made their reports, all eyes turned to Eileen, whose own eyes were closed briefly as she drew inspiration. The room was in silence, except for the ticking of the clock, as we waited for her address.

"Well done, my dear children," she began, her soft smile a lantern in the twilight-dimmed room. "Today, through the sick poor, you have slaked the thirst of Jesus, as the Samaritan woman did at the well. You have fed Christ as Martha and Mary Magdalene did, when He returned tired and hungry to Bethany. You have consoled and comforted Him, by bending over the sick and dying in their agonies, as the angel consoled Jesus in the Garden. You have clothed Him. You have helped Him to carry His cross. You have tenderly wiped the sweat from the brow of Jesus and Mary's poor, like Veronica wiped away the sweat and blood of Jesus with her veil."

Her eyelids fluttered closed, and we remained silent, slipping from the room so she could rest before supper.

My place was at home, and I bade my farewells, even though I knew I was welcome to stay, to partake of their supper and conversation, the after-supper sing-along accompanied by the piano Mrs. O'Connor had given Eileen, that was kept in her bedroom. Prayers and rosaries, and Eileen's asking if there were any new names for her list of people to pray for in the night, when pain prevented her from sleeping. Despite their protests, Eileen forbade the nurses from getting up to turn her in her bed at night. She knew how hard they worked during the day, and insisted they needed their sleep. She willingly bore the price of pain and pressure sores, in exchange for their rest.

As I rode the tram home, I was grateful for George's insistence I take the pennies for the fare. The image of Eileen surrounded by her white-clad nurses—the number had grown to five by now—played inside my drooping eyelids as the jolting of the horse-drawn tram lulled me into semi-stupor. Images that were in stark contrast to the growing tide of hostile gossip and muttered accusations about Eileen and Father McGrath. I tried not to listen to the nonsense people were saying, but it was impossible to avoid. Because Father McGrath spent so much time with Eileen and carried her paralyzed, little body—the body he himself saw as a sacred vessel containing a saintly soul intricately entwined with Our Savior and the Blessed Virgin—vile tongues made insinuations that theirs was an improper relationship, and some families forbade their daughters from going anywhere near Eileen. It made my blood boil and brought on an attack of the nausea that had been troubling me lately.

I'd heard whispered allegations Eileen had thrown herself into fundraising for the nurses without first obtaining the proper approvals from the archbishop. I knew Father McGrath had discussed their intentions with him long before the work commenced, and he had not stopped them, but somehow it now seemed he had not given his official permission either.

On top of all this there were developments in the Missionaries of the Sacred Heart that should have had nothing to do with Father McGrath. Father Hubert Linckens, the MSC Visitor General, who had been sent by Rome to examine problems in the administration of the Australian Sacred Heart Missionaries, was detained here indefinitely by the war. The Australian provincial leader and his Council were outranked by this patriotic, Dutch-born, German citizen with a reputation for being a stickler for the rules. Australian independence and propensity to respect only authority that was earned, rather than authority based on mindless protocol and tradition, were attitudes neither Father Linckens nor the Rome-based leaders of the MSC were prepared to tolerate.

The generosity of the Gell's meant Father McGrath's name was on the title deeds of the Dudley Street base of Our Lady's Nurses for the Poor, contravening his vow to poverty. Father McGrath was caught in the center of a storm seeking a spirited Australian priest to make an example of.

CAITLIN'S HOUSE, ADELAIDE

Lying on his back, his hands folded behind his head, Alex stared up at the ceiling in the dim light of the streetlamp that penetrated the thin curtains in the spare room. There were plastic crates stacked along the wall and he casually wondered what was in them. The detritus of Tim's life, he suspected. And by default, of Caitlin's.

He heard Tim hopping along the hall into the next room. Creaking floorboards, then silence for a few minutes.

Muffled sobbing came through the thin plasterboard wall. Mortified, feeling like an eavesdropper, he rolled onto his side and covered his exposed ear with his hand, trying to shut out the sound.

Sometime later, he startled awake, woken by a scream. His feet touched the floor almost before he was awake, and he snapped on the light switch, then stood for a moment, trying to work out where the noise came from. Incoherent mumblings and the jarring squeaks of someone thrashing about on cheap mattress springs. Then he understood: Tim was having a nightmare.

Alex sat on the edge of the spare bed, rubbing his face with his hands, wondering what he was supposed to do. Before he could decide, the noises stopped, and the house returned to a brooding, heavy silence.

His eyes settled on one of the stacks of crates, and, feeling a bit like a detective, and a lot like a sneak, he walked over and lifted down the top crate. It was full of winter clothing. Alex put the lid back on and opened the next crate. An old-fashioned pink floral blouse with a big bow at the throat, a blue merino sweater with a few moth holes in it. Underneath that ... Alex's breath caught.

An ivory wedding dress, wrapped in powder blue tissue. It must be Caitlin's mum's. An image of his Aunt Janet laughing, sitting on a picnic blanket handing Caitlin and him plates loaded with potato salad and cold chicken. He couldn't remember what they were laughing about. Aunt Janet always seemed to be laughing. Using laughter to defend against Uncle Tim's dark moods and memories.

But one day the laughter stopped. He shook away the mental image of Aunt Janet as white as the stiff hospital sheet, tubes and drips running into her. Bald. Caitlin sitting pinch-faced on her father's knee as he held her mother's hand, crying, and whispering something into her ear.

Caressing with gentle fingers yet another family heirloom he hadn't dreamed existed, Alex re-wrapped the dress and put the lid back on the box.

Another crate was full of photographs. And the next of a little girl's toys. As he took the lid off the crate at the bottom of the stack, Alex vowed this was the last box he'd open. On the top were a series of envelopes, all addressed to Tim, in different, feminine-looking scripts. Afraid of what he might discover, and almost paralyzed by the sense of betraying his uncle's privacy, Alex reached out and picked up the first envelope. He paused like a thief, then slipped the letter out and unfolded it.

> *Dear Private O'Grady,*
> *Thank you so much for your letter of condolence. It means more than I can say to hear that Michael wasn't alone when he died, and he was amongst friends who tried valiantly to save him.*
> *I am very sorry to hear of your injury. I will pray for you.*
> *Bless you for bringing comfort to a grieving mother's heart.*

Frowning with deep thought, and now even more curious, he returned the letter to the correct envelope, then opened the next one.

> *Dear Tim,*
> *Thank you for writing to tell me what happened to Bert. It is such a comfort to know he didn't suffer.*

I am grateful for the photograph you sent. It is a comfort to see him looking full of life so soon before he was killed. I am sure our boys will treasure the photo, and the kind words you said about their father, when they are big enough to understand. They are only two and four years old now. The oldest one looks a lot like his dad.

Letter after letter. From the wives and parents of soldiers he had served with in Vietnam. All thanking Tim for his letters of condolence, his little acts of kindness. Some of his correspondents wrote to him over many years, updating him on how his dead comrades' children had grown, or pouring out their grief to *someone who can understand*, or *someone who was there with him when he died*.

Who could have guessed Tim had reached out to console so many people? Yawning and overwhelmed, Alex rebuilt the stack, double-checking to make sure the crates were in the correct order. He crept back into bed. The sheets were cold. He shivered and stared at the ceiling. If Tim still had that soft side hidden somewhere, could he find it again?

COOGEE, SEPTEMBER 1914

I met Mrs. O'Connor on Dudley Street as I walked up from the tram stop. "Hello, Kathleen," she smiled. "Good timing; I've put aside a jar of marmalade for George."

"That's kind of you. It's his favorite."

"I know." She grinned. "I'll get it from the kitchen, when I've said hello to Eileen."

Rags, Eileen's beloved border collie dog, bounded to greet us as we entered the enclosed verandah. I stooped to scratch his head, but Annie O'Connor made a beeline to Eileen's bedroom. A heartbeat later, a scream pierced the calm air, and I dropped my bag and ran to the bedroom. I almost crashed into Annie's back, as she was frozen in the doorway, staring. I stared too. Eileen's bed was empty and unmade. Eileen, who had not left her bed since before her father's death in April 1911, was fully dressed, her face a mask of concentration as she gingerly lowered her frail little body into a chair. My jaw hung suspended, like time, as unnoticed seconds ticked by. Then a tumult of sound, as Eileen's nurses came running from the kitchen, terrified some disaster had befallen their adored Little Mother. The spell was broken, and we all crowded around Eileen, who was breathing hard, but beaming with the contentment of a mountaineer who has reached the summit of their mountain.

Nurse Cissie was the first to regain the power of speech. She turned to Annie, as if she owed Eileen's mother an explanation. "When I sponge-bathed Little Mother as usual today, her thin little limbs were as frail as ever," she mused. "But she asked me to lay out a dress and slippers for her. She's never asked for that before, but I did without question what she asked." Her eyes were round, as were the other two nurses'. They had never seen Eileen out of bed before. "She must have got up and dressed herself."

"It's a miracle." Annie's eyes were bright, and she bent to embrace her daughter. "Thanks be to God."

I was afraid for a moment we must look like the stupid grinning monkeys Eileen had stuck into her scrapbooks to make visiting children laugh. Eileen caught my eye, and she must have thought the same thing, because suddenly we were all laughing and crying, helplessly, but filled with joy.

One of the nurses offered to carry Eileen into the dining room, but she shook her head resolutely. "I'll walk," she said.

It hurt to see how carefully she pushed herself out of the chair, holding its arms to keep her balance, standing with her poor, deformed back disguised by the lacy folds of her pastel blue dress. But nothing disguised how small she was—three foot ten—and the nurses, who had only seen her lying down before now, must have felt like giants beside her. But giants only in size. Eileen's presence was big in a way that made height meaningless. And she squeezed our hands, as, with hesitant, painful steps, she led the way to the dining room, the rest of us following her, silent again for a moment as we took in the enormity of what had unfolded in front of us.

Eileen settled herself into the chair at the head of the table. She took a deep breath and turned her twinkling eyes onto each of us in turn. "Anyone feel like having a party?" she asked, her mischievous gaze sweeping around the room.

The dining room filled with laughter and bustle as we produced china cups and pots of tea, plates of biscuits and a sponge cake Mrs. Derrick had made. There was always food at hand, to cater for the steady stream of nurses' relatives, local children, priests, potential nursing recruits and other visitors. We sang hymns and Eileen's favorite contemporary songs. We laughed at jokes and tall tales.

We were making too much noise to hear the front door but were startled into silence by a roar. Eileen's brother Charlie always came in to visit her after work, and today had found her bed empty. Fearing the worst, thinking his sister must have been rushed to hospital, he was outraged the nurses would make such merriment. He burst into the dining room, ready to chastise us all. And stood transfixed as Eileen rose from her chair, smiling, and said, "Here I am." Charlie would talk about the thrill of that moment, a happy look on his face, almost until the day he died, over fifty years later, with Eileen's name on his lips.

But back then, Charlie recovered from the shock, and went to her side, towering over her as he gently caressed her cheek. "Look at you." He beamed. "Three foot ten tall, and every inch a saint."

***

A few days later, I made time to visit again. Maybe I needed to see Eileen walk again, to make sure I hadn't been dreaming.

"Oh, Kathleen, Frank was too funny for words," Eileen said. "He couldn't believe it when we telephoned him at school to tell him I was walking. We had to drive there so he could see me walk for himself."

"You would have created a sensation at school."

"I did." She grinned. "There was a lad there, limping with a damaged leg. I spoke to him to inspire him. His leg will get better too." She sighed in contentment. "And you, Kathleen, how are you?"

"I'll be needing some new knitting patterns," I said, my cheeks burning. "For bootees and a little shawl."

"How lovely," she beamed. "She'll be a bonnie little lass."

After catching up on news of each other's friends and families, Mrs. O'Connor cleared away the tea things.

I studied Eileen's happy face and lowered my voice. "Can I ask you a question?"

"Of course."

"How did it happen? You walking again? You've been bed-bound for years."

"Well, it's a miracle." Eileen's voice was confident, before her brow clouded with concern. "But there's a reason for it. The work I'm doing for Our Lady needs me to be mobile now."

I watched her, waiting for her to elaborate.

She took a few gasping breaths before continuing. "There's opposition to our work, Kathleen, from within the church. They think we have been wrongful. Father McGrath has been ordered to stop being associated with us and Father Linckens is threatening to send him away."

I gasped with horror. "Why would they do such a thing? After all the good your work has achieved."

"They don't seem to be interested in the good we are doing." Eileen shook her head sadly. "Father Linckens is incensed Father's name is on the deed for this house. He has ordered Father to sign his interest in the house over to some of the nurses."

"But how can he do that?" I hesitated, uncertain how to best word what was in my mind.

Eileen took over for me. "How can he do that, when the girls don't all stay? They try the life here and find it's not for them. Or they are called away due to illness in their families. What if a couple of girls took his share, and left, and then needed money themselves? It'd be a disaster."

"What are you going to do?"

"I've told Father he cannot sign. Legally I need to give my permission to any changes, and I won't give it. Hopefully, that will get Father Linckens off his back until we can convince him we aren't doing anything wrong."

"Anybody who meets you can see you're not doing anything wrong. Won't he come and see you for himself?"

"That's the thing. I rang Father Linckens after Father told me what was going on. He won't come to see me. Neither will the provincial leader or his Council." She squared her fragile, narrow shoulders resolutely. "So, I must go and see them."

I wiped my morning's vomit away with a cloth, spilling the bowl out onto the dirt, away from Mum's clothesline which was groaning under the latest load of washing. The walk from the room George and I were renting to Mum's house had turned my stomach. Or maybe it was my emotions.

"You all right, love?" Mum asked, not looking up. She wound the mangle's handle with her right hand, feeding a customer's sheet through it, guiding it with her left hand, watchful she didn't lose concentration and jam her fingers in the heavy wooden rollers.

"They've gone, Mum."

"Who've gone?"

"Eileen and Father McGrath."

The mangle gears stopped turning. "What are you talking about?"

"Father McGrath has been ordered away. To some mining town, back of beyond in Tasmania. He was given a day's notice." I lowered myself to sit on an upturned crate.

Mum stood frozen, gripping the sheet so it didn't dangle to the ground. "It's as bad as all that, is it?"

"Father was asked to relinquish his vows. He wouldn't. He was ordered to have nothing more to do with Eileen and the nurses. He can't do that either. How on earth would Eileen be able to manage Our Lady's Nurses without him?"

Mum's Irish eyes flashed. "They're doing God's work. We've seen the good they're doing with our own eyes. Is Father Linckens himself going to come in their stead and change the soiled sheets of the dying souls around here? Hold their hand? Bring food? Empty bedpans? And all at no charge." She sighed. "What you need is some nice, sweet tea, my girl, and a crust of bread. Go and get them, will you, while I finish this sheet? And then," her tone became solemn, "you'd better tell me where Eileen went."

I nibbled a piece of crust to settle my stomach. "Eileen's gone with him."

Mum's jaw hung slack for a moment. "Eileen's gone with him?" she repeated, her voice shrill with alarm. I nodded.

"Eileen has only been walking for three weeks, and now she's gone, hundreds of miles *by train and boat*, to Tasmania?" She stumbled as if her knees were about to give way. I hurried off the crate and grabbed her elbow, as she sat heavily, like a load of wet bedding.

Her shock was contagious and suddenly the enormity, not of Eileen going to some remote outpost, but of her being able to go anywhere at all, sank in. Mum's shoulders were shaking, and, thinking she was weeping, I patted her back. "This is the same Eileen who, just months ago, nearly died taking an ambulance ride *around the corner*. Jesus, Mary, and Joseph," Mum expostulated, crossing herself, "will wonders never cease?" And she roared with hysterical laughter, till tears rolled down her cheeks. I caught that too, laughing and crying at the wonder of the restoration of Eileen's mobility, and the sheer courage of the woman to undertake a journey that, a month ago, would have been utterly impossible.

We dried our eyes, and Mum fed the next sheet into the mangle. "You'd better tell me why she went, then," she said. "She must have good reasons. And just before the big fundraising fete, too."

"Well, I think she's partly going to keep an eye on Father; he's beside himself, and I think she's afraid he'll give up his vows. She didn't say so, though. She said she's showing solidarity with Father McGrath. The suddenness with which he has been sent away, and the way he's been forbidden to have anything to do with her makes it look like Eileen is the cause of his disgrace. If Eileen just let him go, she thinks it would feed the gossipmongers. By going, she's making it clear they have nothing to hide and have done nothing wrong. And of course she has to take a nurse with her, to look after her, so she's got a chaperone too."

Mum grunted, her focus on the mangle's jaws again. "If I know gossipmongers, there's nothing she can do that won't feed them."

* * *

Eileen had a busy month. In Tasmania, Father McGrath's new immediate superior gave him permission to return to Sydney in order to apply for a few weeks' much-needed holiday. Eileen, Father, and the nurse who travelled with them, returned to Sydney in time for the fundraiser and for Eileen to take an ocean cruise to the South Sea Islands. The cruise was arranged by the family of a sick parishioner of Father Gell, who had been ordered by her doctor to take the cure. Father Gell and his sister Frances were going to accompany the patient and her family, and arranged for Eileen and her nurse to join them. No doubt, they thought the sea air and the respite from the situation with Father Linckens and the Missionaries of the Sacred Heart, would do her good. Though Eileen, as always, thinking of others, was motivated by the opportunity to offer encouragement to a clergyman she knew, who was considering giving up his vows. Father McGrath had also arranged to join the group.

Unfortunately, Mum's prediction came true. Everything Eileen did fed the gossip.

People, including, as it later was revealed, leaders in the church, claimed to be scandalized by Eileen and Father McGrath. Eileen drew public attention by traveling in the newfangled motor cars of Father Gell and others, often in the company of Father McGrath. True, she sometimes took jaunts to picnic in Centennial Park or at the beach, but that was hardly a crime. She also took trips to comfort patients in the Leper Hospital and St. Vincent's Hospital, but the scandal mongers never mentioned that. Instead, they reported Father McGrath and Father Gell had been seen carrying Eileen, as if a priest having the compassion to carry a cripple was immoral. By the time Eileen's boat returned, the furor had spread beyond the Council of the Missionaries of the Sacred Heart, right to the Archbishop of Sydney, whose complaints against Eileen included that he had seen Father Gell give her a bunch of flowers and she did not have an episcopal sanction for the Brown Nurses, so should not have given them a religious name.

* * *

I visited Eileen soon after she had settled back in her home. She was exhausted, but her eyes flashed with indignation. "They have insulted our honor and reputation."

My eyes widened with incomprehension. "The church has insulted your honor?"

"They say Father has caused a public scandal. Feeding the gossip that Father and I have been more than we should have been to each other." She dropped her eyes, and her cheeks flamed.

I looked at her. Three foot ten tall. As weak as a kitten. Until recently, she had three paralyzed limbs. A distorted spine covered in scars; its inflamed vertebrae so prominent under her paper-thin skin that sometimes I feared they'd poke right through it. Her back was so tender, she couldn't be hugged without being caused pain. A contrasting flash of recollection of myself and George in life-giving ecstasy sped my heartbeat. What on earth were the block-headed church leaders thinking? It wasn't physically possible. But that wasn't the point. It wasn't spiritually possible, neither for Eileen, nor Father McGrath. The love they shared was not that kind of love. It was something altogether different. It came directly from heaven, burning into the very depths of their souls.

My mouth attempted sputtering movements, but I was too outraged to speak. I didn't need to. Eileen knew exactly what I was thinking.

"Thank you for believing in me," she said, and for a moment a tear hung from her eyelashes.

"Of course, I believe in you. I've known you half my life. If the people who were saying nasty things about you, only knew you, they'd believe in you too."

"That's why I kept trying to see them. One look at me is all it would take for them to see how ridiculous these allegations are." She shrugged, the movement taking in all the defects of her body. "But they won't see me, and they won't see reason. I can't allow them to damage the reputation of the Work, Kathleen. How can mothers let their daughters come and live in the nurses' home with me, if such things are said? They have libeled me and defamed my character. I will have to sue them. I've had legal advice. My lawyer is sending the Archbishop of Sydney a letter, demanding an apology, and if he won't apologize, we will go to court. The lawyer will threaten them with ten thousand pounds in damages."

At my next visit, Eileen, propped up in bed, her eyes darkly circled, told me, "It's no surprise Archbishop Kelly is refusing to give me an apology. Though I had hoped he would, of course." She sighed. "I see now, all hope on that front is futile. Father McGrath is getting nowhere with Father Linckens, either. No one here is prepared to give us a fair go."

"Are you going to sue for damages? That seems such a big step, I can't imagine it."

She shook her head, crestfallen for a moment before resolution flowed through her tiny body like steel. "No. They have made it impossible for us to rectify the situation here."

"How?"

"Archbishop Kelly has threatened to excommunicate me, and all of my advisors if I take their slander to court."

My heart sank. "Excommunication? Not to be able to go to church or take Communion or seek consolation or confession—no, Eileen! What will you do?"

"We must go to Rome to appeal and clear our names."

I nearly choked. "Rome?"

Caitlin put down her spoon, looking sideways at her cousin, his muesli untouched on the kitchen table. "Alex, what's up?"

"Just didn't sleep well." He didn't meet her gaze.

She sighed. Secrets, they destroy people.

As usual, he changed the subject before she could ask anything else. "And she suddenly could walk after years of being bed-bound?"

Caitlin calculated, "Her father died three and a half years before this. When he died, she got a lot worse, we know that much. She was paralyzed then." She shook her head. "She was ill her whole life, though, it seems to me."

"What could have happened to allow her to start walking like that?"

"Maybe her mother was right, and it was a miracle?"

"Do you believe in miracles?"

A sense of lightness rose in Caitlin's chest. She'd like to be able to believe in miracles. Who wouldn't? "I'm not sure. But if she really was a saint, then if anyone can live miracles, she could."

Alex tapped the table edge. "Well, we know why Father McGrath wasn't at the fete, anyway."

"Do you believe Eileen could have organized the whole house, the nurses, the fundraising, by herself?"

He shook his head. "No. No one could. But if we know Eileen, and I reckon we do a little by now, she had the capacity to inspire tremendous love and loyalty in the people around her. She would have had a trusted band of people who would help her."

"Her family, her nurses, her friends?"

"Yes, and then also the people she helped. Having someone come to your home, when things are dire, and help. Maybe make you better, or maybe help your relative to die in comfort … a hundred cases by the time that article was written. She must have been very well known."

"Even the tram driver called her saintly. And yet people in the church were attacking her reputation and her honor?"

His eyes narrowed. "Powerful institutions don't like little upstarts coming along and changing things."

"Even the Church?"

"Especially the Church. It's always used the moral high horse to put people down." His voice dripped acid, and Caitlin scrutinized him acutely, wondering why he was taking it personally. He retreated under her gaze and changed the subject. "You know what happened to Mary MacKillop, right?"

"No. Wait, you mean there's a bit of history you know more about than me?"

Alex grinned and drew himself straight in his chair, ready to impart his knowledge. "She got excommunicated. Only a few decades before Eileen came along."

"You're kidding."

"No."

"Our hypothesis becomes," Caitlin said, thinking out loud, "that a crippled girl and a young priest came up with a scheme to help the poor in their own homes, for free, but didn't go through all the bureaucratic hoops, and the Church hierarchy took offence."

"Sounds about right to me." Tim had hopped into the kitchen unnoticed and was filling the kettle at the sink. "No, no, don't mind me. Keep going. This is interesting. I'll just listen."

Caitlin stared at her father's back. She hadn't heard him say anything was interesting since before her accident. Maybe this was a good sign?

"Maybe they heard gossip about them. Can't have a Catholic priest spending much time with a *woman!* Anything could happen," Alex said.

Caitlin nearly choked on a mouthful of muesli. "She was three foot ten and paralyzed!"

"Details, details," Alex waved them away with his hand, a cheeky grin on his face.

"What you are saying is," she said, frowning, "that the Church wanted to stop her, and separate her and Father McGrath."

"At any cost," Alex agreed.

"Even though they had done nothing wrong?"

"That's probably why they wouldn't come and meet her, to hear her side of the story."

"But that's awful." Caitlin banged her hand on the table, making their coffee mugs rattle. Her face brightened into a wide smile. "Well, she certainly didn't take it lying down, did she?"

"No, she got up from her bed and walked."

"Right up to the Church authorities' doors, to pound on them, I suspect. The stuffy old priests and bishops probably didn't know what hit them."

Tim was still propped against the sink, waiting for the kettle to boil.

"Would you like me to bring that into you, when it's finished?" Alex felt a rush of sympathy, noting the red rims around his uncle's eyes, and knowing it wasn't just beer that caused them.

"No thanks." Tim hesitated. "If you don't mind, maybe I could stay in here for a while. This is getting me curious now."

Alex smiled shyly. "Sure. We'd like that. This is your family story, too."

"You still reckon my great-grandmother Kathleen recorded the tapes?"

"Yes. Eileen's one of her closest friends."

Tim settled into a chair. His eyes lowered as if he was watching the curl of steam rising from his mug. "Well, let's see if I can still recognize her voice, then."

A sharp kick under my diaphragm woke me, and I changed my position. "You all right, love?" Georgie whispered in the dark.

I reached out to find his hand, but it wasn't there, and my stomach sank as I realized he was lying with his hands folded behind his head, staring up into the night. I tugged at his elbow till he released his arm and laid his hand over our unborn child. "Baby woke me."

For a moment, the warmth of his hand seeped into my skin, before he pulled it away and rolled over. I snuggled my belly into his back and put my arm around him. I didn't know what to say, all I could do was hope that if I waited long enough, he would tell me what was on his mind. And eventually he did. "I'm sorry, love. I don't feel like I've got much choice."

The blood in my veins chilled as my stomach tied into a knot. "Choice about what?" I asked, my mouth so dry it was hard to form the words.

"I need to support you and the baby as best I can."

"You are supporting us!"

"It's not enough, Kathleen. And it's only going to get worse. The office doesn't have as much work for bookkeepers when there's no wheat to export. This drought is making things tougher. They are laying people off already. And it could be me next. I can't be out of work—not with the baby coming."

"Surely, we can find a way. We can move back to Mum's. It'll be easier for me to help her with the washing and ironing then: she's snowed under with work."

"A man supports his family himself. And sometimes a man just has to make a stand."

"What do you mean?" Dread sank deeper into my being. The determination in his voice meant he had made up his mind.

"At first, I thought this war was just politics. I couldn't see how some Archduke being assassinated in some place I'd never heard of in the Balkans could possibly bring England into a war. The Irish blood in me was screaming it was senseless to get involved, and I shouldn't have anything to do with it. But I've been reading the papers, and sometimes, a man just has to stand up for what he believes in."

"Georgie?"

"The Germans are bayonetting women and children—babies even—in Belgium. Slaughtering them and who knows what else! And a man gets to thinking. What if soldiers invaded here and attacked our womenfolk? What if they would do that to you? I'd hope someone would come to help."

I lay in the dark, floundering for the words that might stop him, keep him here, safe with us. But I couldn't think of any. I drew a deep breath. "Can you at least wait until after the baby comes?"

He rolled over, wriggling in the bed which seemed ever-narrower as my belly grew, and faced me. He kissed my forehead. "Yes. I'll wait. They say the war will be over soon, but I have my doubts. I want to see this baby for myself before I go."

Relief washed through me. Maybe when the baby came, he'd decide he couldn't leave us. Or maybe the war would be over by then. I'd bought us some time. I put my arms around his neck and kissed him.

He broke away. "When I go away," he sighed, "if I go, if the war's still on when the baby comes … I'd like you to move back to your Mum's then. I don't want you boarding here, without me. Without anyone to help you. Okay?"

"Yes, Georgie. If you go away, we'll live with Mum."

Evie was born on a still, hot day in February, a red-faced, little scrap of a thing, her head covered with black peach fuzz I never tired of nuzzling against my cheek. We were so engrossed in her, I could almost forget the war and its long, shadowy fingers that were reaching to take George in their clutches. But he was obsessed with the newspapers, clipping out maps of Europe and reports of German atrocities.

George became increasingly withdrawn, barely able to smile at either Evie or I, though he would sometimes hold her in his arms, gazing at her sleeping face, and murmuring to her, words I couldn't hear. Or I'd wake in the middle of the night to find him kneeling at the side of the dresser drawer we had turned into her cradle, because the room we were renting was too small for much furniture. One night, in the middle of March, I slipped out of bed and went to kneel next to him. He folded his arms around me, and I couldn't suppress a shudder, because I knew what he was about to say.

"I have to go. I can't rest until I know I've done the right thing."

"I know, Georgie." My throat squeezed tight against the words, but I managed to say them, to bring him what little comfort I could. "We'll be alright." I pulled him to his feet and helped him back into bed.

In the cold, dark night, we lay, holding hands, and talked—really talked—for the first time in days.

Georgie would be paid the usual private's rate of six shillings per day, of which the Army kept one shilling to pay a sum at the end of a soldier's service. Before he went away, he would arrange for most of his pay to be sent to me: four shillings and sixpence. I worried it meant he wouldn't have enough money for his own expenses, but he'd laughed and said there wouldn't be any department stores where he was going. Then his tone became earnest, and he said he was fighting for me and Evie, and he wanted us to be well looked after while he was gone, and not a burden on my parents.

"And if you have any money left over, save it up, for when I get back. We'll set up the little home together, that we've been dreaming of, and you'll be wanting pretty curtains and frills." That's what he said. I lay there next to him, terrified he wouldn't be coming home. Like children holding nightmares at bay, we clung to each other, painting castles in the sky, imagining what our future home might be. A little place in the country perhaps? Or a nice terrace house of our own, near my family and plenty of offices needing good bookkeepers. There'd be work aplenty, and brothers and sisters for Evie, and maybe a pet kitten. Lace curtains in the front room. And laughter, always laughter, because the world would be safe again, when Georgie came home.

* * *

Pipe dreams. That's all they were, but they were my *bon voyage* gift to my husband. There was nothing else I could give him. Except my resolve that I wouldn't cry when he marched off with his kitbag slung over his shoulder. And that I wouldn't cling to him and beg him to change his mind and stay.

While he was in basic training, in the last week of April, the papers reported our soldiers had been involved in decisive and successful action, landing in places we hadn't heard of before: the Dardanelles and Gallipoli. Right at the beginning, the British government wrote to the Governor General congratulating us on the splendid gallantry and magnificent achievements of our soldiers.

Over the next couple of weeks, the tone of the news reports changed, and it became clear this wasn't a simple, valiant victory. Our boys had been under heavy fire and long casualty lists appeared in the papers. Grieving mothers and widows wore black armbands, animating those lists in a way that terrified me.

Georgie sailed away in June, and filled with dread, I feared I'd never see him again.

* * *

And so it was that I lived back at Mum and Dad's, helping as best I could with the washing Mum took in and the housework.

"Bloody idiot," Tim mumbled. He hadn't moved since the track began.

Alex jerked his head round. "What was that, Uncle Tim?"

"George, falling for all those newspaper headlines. Just remember, you can't trust what the papers say, especially when there's a war on."

"Like all those patriotic posters, Dad? *Free Trip to Europe?*"

"Humph." He changed the subject deftly, his tone becoming almost wistful. "It's definitely Kathleen's voice. She was a grand old girl." The tension in his shoulders and jaw melted away.

Caitlin's heart lurched with unexpected hope. Surely, a change of scenery would do her dad some good. "When I can walk better, Dad, do you think you could take me to her grave. To pay my respects?"

"To Sydney?" He sounded incredulous.

Alex grasped the baton. "What a great idea, Cait! I bet Mum would want to come too."

Under siege, Tim looked from one pink, young face to the other. A corner of his mouth twitched slightly before he could control it.

Caitlin pretended she hadn't seen it and changed the subject before he could get defensive. "When should we tell Auntie Cara what we've found out so far?"

"You know how Cara is," Tim said gruffly, eager to hide the conflicted emotions that rose in his chest at the thought of a family trip.

"How is she?" Alex asked, his chin held in defiance.

Tim softened again and chose his words with care. "So far, all we really know about, is Eileen. And that George is going off to war." His eyes clouded. "We know he died on the Western Front. I think you should find out more about him, before you bring your Mum into it."

"You've got a point," Alex conceded. "There's something odd about George's story."

"What do you mean?"

"I did a quick google. I couldn't find his name on the Commonwealth war graves website."

Tim stared at him. "They list everyone, even when remains can't be found."

"I thought so, Dad." Caitlin noted his grim expression. "What are you thinking?"

"We need to know more. The Australian War Memorial has military records online. You could look there."

"That's breaking the rules, isn't it?" Alex grinned at his cousin, knowing how hard she was working to conceal her excitement that Tim was showing an interest.

"Just a quick look. What should we search, Dad?"

"Honor Rolls," he replied, with a confidence that demonstrated he was no stranger to searching for soldiers' records.

Alex typed on his phone. "Here we go, we can search a person … ah, the honor rolls … George O'Grady …" He frowned into the screen.

"What's up?" Caitlin asked.

"He's not on the honor roll. Aren't all soldiers who get killed listed on honor rolls?"

"Maybe he had a different first name?" Tim suggested.

"I'll search with just his surname." He scrolled. "Frederick George O'Grady … no that's World War II. No, no other O'Gradys with George as a middle name."

"Hmm," said Tim, staring out the kitchen window with unfocused eyes.

An uneasy pressure was building in Caitlin's chest. "Something's not right, is it, Dad? Something's not right about George."

Tim remained silent, lost in thought.

"What do you mean, Cait?" Alex asked.

"What if he didn't die in the war?"

"Then why was everyone told he did?"

She bit her lip. "I don't know. But I think we should find out."

He reached for his phone. "Okay. Listen to more tapes?"

"Something from the box first." She unfolded a letter. "It's on stationary from the SS Mooltan ... that rings a bell. It was used as a troop ship in World War I. It was sunk by a torpedo, I think."

"From George?" asked Tim.

"No. Eileen!"

Tim's chair legs screeched on the Lino as he pushed away from the table. "Let me know when you've sorted out what happened to George," he said. "It's nearly time for the game."

She followed his retreating back, grateful for their minutes of connection. Then she read the letter aloud.

> *Dear Kathleen,*
>
> *Just a quick note as I am feeling tired. You must be tired too, by now, looking after your lovely little baby. I am looking forward to meeting her as soon as I get home.*
>
> *I'm sure it is a girl. Do write and tell me as soon as you can. I will send you my address when I get to Rome.*
> *I love you,*
> *Eileen*

"Eileen really went to Rome." Shock sharpened the edges of Alex's words. "She only just started to walk again."

"There's hope for me yet, then."

"Of course, there is. She went to Rome, and you can learn the tango."

"This is early 1915, the war's already on. Eileen's traveling on a troop ship with who knows how many soldiers, maybe through dangerous waters."

"Well, knowing Eileen, she wasn't going to let a war get in the way of her visit to the pope. Between her and George, the suspense is killing me. I think we'd better listen to the tapes." Alex shut his laptop and turned on the audio on his phone.

Evie was asleep in her cradle, in the shade under Mum's Granny Smith apple tree. My brothers and sisters and I had slept in it before her, and it was a definite improvement on the dresser drawer in our old room at the boarding house. I tugged at a sheet in the washing basket.

"You stop that right now, Kathleen O'Grady," Mum chided, appearing at the doorway, hands on her hips, her sleeves rolled up to free muscular forearms.

"I'm alright, Mum."

"And we're going to make sure you stay that way, young lady. You can hang the small things, and you can bring in the dry washing. What would George say, if he knew I was letting you lift heavy things?"

"Your secret's safe with me. I won't tell him." I winked at her and she laughed.

"Even with you not doing the heavy work, I've got to say it's good having a second pair of hands again."

I ran my fingers over a line of assorted shirts; checking they were dry before I unpegged them, folding them into a basket ready to be ironed. "Have you heard from Eileen lately?"

"No, but Cissie promised she'd call in on her rounds today, and if the nurses have had a letter, she'll bring it with her."

True to her word, Cissie arrived that afternoon, not letting her tiredness stop her from smiling. She asked me how I was, then checked Evie, declaring her to be splendid before taking a letter from her nurses' bag. Her eyebrows drew together, puckering her otherwise smooth forehead. "I wasn't sure whether I should show it to you or not," she said. "But I thought you'd maybe worry more if you don't hear anything. And I knew you'd be asking, and I couldn't fib." She hesitated again before handing it to me. "Now, remember this was all a while ago, it took eight weeks for the letter to get through, and Eileen would have telegraphed if she was in trouble."

Dread filled me as I took the letter from her, and I sat on the old crate to read it. It was mostly in Eileen's spidery hand, but I recognized Father McGrath's writing too, in a note in the margin which read: *Eileen's little back has been giving her a lot of trouble, but she is taking it all heroically.*

Poor Eileen, I couldn't imagine what it must be like to travel halfway around the world, let alone for someone so frail.

> *My dear children,*
> *Saying farewell to Father, so I can travel on ahead and see what I can do, is so hard. Nurse Dot is too sick to accompany me. I feel so alone, even though Thomas Cook's found me Joe the man to act as my tour guide and translator. I am a little tired. There are soldiers and wounded men on all the boats and trains.*
> *This trip feels like my own Stations of the Cross. I am so frightened. Please pray for me. You are all in my prayers. I love you and am forever your loving Little Mother, Eileen*

The thought of Eileen, ill, alone, and frightened in faraway lands would have broken my heart, if it wasn't already broken by Georgie having gone away to war.

Uncertainty strangles you, sometimes, in the dark of night, in the fevered search through lists of casualties in the papers, in wondering if every letter will be the last you receive, or the last you write. I reached out and squeezed Cissie's hand.

"We are all praying very hard," she said, unable to suppress the quivering of her lips.

"There is no end to the praying these days." Bitterness crept into my tone, and I saw the look of dismay it brought to Mum's face, as she took the letter to read for herself.

Letters from Eileen became more regular now she was on dry land and no longer having to wait to get into a port to mail them. But they were often short, Eileen clearly didn't have the energy to write much. The nurses and I shared the letters we got. Frances Gell received letters too, as she was now coordinating the funding of the trip, Father Gell having been ordered not to have any contact with Eileen, so sometimes she had news to pass on. Half a world away from the action, we pieced together the story as best we could. Father McGrath's Superior General refused to see Eileen, and, as there was nothing more she could do and the plan was to not be in the same place as Father to avoid further gossip, she would be leaving Rome. Fortunately, Nurse Dot was with her again, but Dot still wasn't well, and Eileen had had a fall, and it was clear she was exhausted and ill. They went to Venice and then Marseilles, where she was uncomfortably close to the war.

When Father McGrath was granted an audience with his Superior General, he called Eileen back to Rome to work on their defense of the charges he was facing. Father credited Eileen with doing most of the preparation of court documents, and working indefatigably. Eileen was always loyal to the Church, no matter how serious the problems some of its officials created, so she never told me the details of the case brought against Father. I learned many years later that he had been charged with four counts of "flight from a monastery with a woman": the trip to Tasmania, the return to Sydney, the South Sea cruise, and the journey to Rome. In other words, the charges implied Eileen had an illicit relationship with Father and lured him away from his religious vows. These were the highest-ranked charges against him, deemed more important than the charges of disobedience to his superiors. No wonder Eileen was so determined to clear her name: what choice did she have, if she were to be in public life, fundraising and recruiting young women for the Brown Nurses? All we knew then, was she was arguing for Father's readmission into his vocation, and that their names be cleared of allegations of wrongdoing. We waited anxiously to hear the outcome of Father McGrath's appeal.

Halfway around the world, Father and Eileen were waiting anxiously too. Eileen kept busy and succeeded in having an audience with the pope to tell him about the work. Then she filled time by honoring her promise to her mother that she would go to Ireland and visit her remaining relatives.

At last, the news came. We were overjoyed to hear Father was a priest again, and Eileen was looking forward to him being able to give her Communion. The nurses expected Father to return to them ahead of Eileen, who was still in Ireland, and chatted happily about decorating the home with bunting and flowers, and baking cakes and scones to welcome him.

Later, we were crushed to hear he wouldn't be coming home after all. His reinstatement had been made conditional on him not returning to Australia, and having nothing at all to do with Eileen or anyone involved in the work.

Despite the shock, Father remained buoyant with relief at returning to his vocation, and was confident that fortune would smile upon him, and the conditions would be dropped. But they weren't. He was not allowed to return to live in Australia until 1941, when he was given a post in Victoria. He was finally permitted to live in Coogee, in the care of his beloved nurses, in 1969 when he was in his late eighties.

Eileen would have to run Our Lady's Nurses for the Poor single-handedly. But she had to make it back to Australia first, the captain of her ship carefully planning his route to avoid enemy boats.

When Eileen left for her mission to Rome, ten nurses and Matron Duffy had farewelled her. On her return, almost a year later, she found only seven nurses. Three nurses and the matron had left during her absence, often due to the pressure put on them by their families who were worried by gossip. Eileen comforted herself by saying the best nurses had stayed.

CAITLIN'S HOUSE, ADELAIDE

"Time to check the tin," Alex pushed it towards Caitlin, stifling a yawn. Caitlin glanced at him tenderly, flooded with gratitude that he had stayed away from his computer long enough to share this project with her, and reached into the tin. "An envelope, with two photographs in it." She took out the first. "It's Eileen. Goodness, you can see how short she is, compared to the men in the photo with her." She held out the picture for him to inspect.

"They look like they're on the deck of a ship." Alex squinted at the picture from his spot by the kitchen bench. Is that man with her wearing a dog collar?"

"Yes."

"On a ship. Who is it?"

"It must be Father McGrath," they said together.

"Hmm, he's not as handsome as I thought he'd be." Caitlin peered into the photo, searching for any detail.

"Perhaps he was seasick," Alex laughed.

"Perhaps he was broken by what happened to him? Needing to clear his name."

"And by worry about Eileen? Traveling halfway around the world with an invalid must have been stressful."

"Do you think this is while they were on their trip to Rome?"

"So *many* questions." Alex winked. "Maybe you should just read the back of the photo."

"You're a typical computer geek, Alex."

"Typical? Me?" He rolled his eyes in mock horror.

"Trying to find the easiest way to get from point A to point B. Cutting out all the side routes."

"You'd stop complaining if you knew how much slower your computer would be if programmers didn't do just that."

"Yeah, yeah." She laughed.

Alex enjoyed the sound. Thank goodness she hadn't forgotten how to laugh.

"There's nothing on the back of this one," she said, disappointed.

"Next," said Alex, grinning.

Caitlin held the next photograph in the space between them, and they both leaned in to make out the details recorded in sepia. Women in long wrap-around skirts by the water's edge. A thatched hut. Lean cattle. And two white-clad figures, a stark contrast against the encroaching jungle.

"That's a surprise," Caitlin breathed, her eyes wide. "Who's with her?" she peered closer. "It's Father McGrath again. Where could they be? Whatever were they doing in a jungle?" Alex's silence caught Caitlin's attention. The color had drained out of his face. She frowned then swallowed, trying to decide what to say. "Aren't you going to tell me to see if something's written on the back?"

"No." He shook his head. "I've not finished looking at the picture." He studied the photo, looking for a memory he couldn't find.

"Are you okay?"

"Yes … just déjà vu … I'm fine. Why don't you see if something's written on the back?" He grinned sheepishly.

She flipped the photograph over; a few words were scrawled in fading brown ink. *The Party (& Natives washing cattle). Colombo 1915.* "Colombo?"

"It's in Sri Lanka." There was a faint tremor in his voice. "Would have been called Ceylon back then. They must have stopped off there on their way to Europe."

COOGEE-1916

"Come in, Kathleen." Mary O'Connor held the door of the Nurses Home open for me as I carried Evie, fast asleep, in my arms. "The tram cast its sleeping spell again, I see."

I was panting with the exertion of carrying the baby on the hilly walk from the tram stop and Mary kept chatting while I caught my breath. "She's growing like a champion. Come and see Eileen, she's having a good day today." She grinned her relief. Eileen had been unwell lately, with several episodes of unconsciousness that had lasted two or three days at a time. "The Nurses have just got back for the day, so it's a bit lively, but Eileen will want to talk to you after she's heard about their patients."

I took a chair by the wall, out of everyone's way, and drank in the familiar scene of the white-clad nurses bustling around their Little Mother and taking their turns to report, not just on their patients, but on how they reacted to them.

Nurse Nell was wringing her hands, her face downcast. "This gossiping and nastiness is hard to bear," she said. "Passengers pointedly change cars on the tram when we get on now. Two men spat on the ground right in front of Katie and me this morning. It's horrid."

"Yes, it's hard to bear, Nell, I know," Eileen said softly. "But we pray to Our Lady for strength, and we remember the sufferings of dear Jesus, who suffered for us a thousand times more. You are doing Our Lady's work, caring for the sick poor who have no one else to help them. It's good work, Nell, and it will be repaid in heaven."

"I can't understand it," I ventured. "The number of poor people you help, the way your patients praise you. You don't charge them, and you don't get paid because you are called to care for them out of love. I can't understand how people can be so hateful to you."

"It won't always be this way," Eileen said. "We have many friends, and, in time, the others will see us with clearer eyes. We even have an Anglican priest who is kind to us, who refers his parishioners to us when he sees their need. And we have Our Lady's promise that She will always be with us." She patted Nell's arm. "And your patient, Mrs. Murphy. What did you do for her today?"

Nell's expression changed to one of compassionate devotion as she recounted her work with Mrs. Murphy, a forty-year-old woman with advanced breast cancer. Nell had arrived with a basket of groceries, washed the patient and her bedding, dressed her ulcerated tumor, cooked a meal for her and her four children, emptied bedpans, swept floors, and scrubbed the kitchen table. She had sat at Mrs. Murphy's bedside listening to her worries about her husband's drinking, and her loss of faith in God.

"No one is poorer than a person who has lost their faith," Eileen said.

Nell beamed. "That's the thing. At the end of the day, Mrs. Murphy said what a comfort it would be to go back to the church and sent one of her sons to the priest to ask him to bring her the sacraments."

"So, dear child, despite all that happened on your way there today, you were like the angel who, through Mrs. Murphy, watched over Christ as He endured the agonies in the garden, and you were like Martha and Mary Magdalene, feeding Him through her hunger."

Nell bowed her head.

After a moment, Eileen continued. "Was there anything else compassion would have you do to help Mrs. Murphy or her family?"

Nell frowned until an idea sparked in her eyes. "Mrs. Murphy's youngest children are only six and eight years old. They have no toys, no special things of their own. Perhaps I could make them each a little collage with pictures from a magazine, to put by their bed."

"That's a lovely idea. I have a magazine you can use after supper when you girls do your handicrafts."

Each nurse was given Eileen's attention. As well as debriefing them regarding their professional work, Eileen took their spiritual development very seriously. She had taken responsibility for it since they had been deprived of pastoral care by the banning of Father McGrath and the other MSC priests from attending them. As was her custom, she asked what topic the Nurses would like to contemplate for their morning meditation. Pain kept Eileen awake at night, and she used the time not just to pray for the many people who requested her to, but also to write daily meditations for the Nurses.

Duties now completed, the girls drifted off to prepare for supper. Eileen turned her big smile at me, and her face lit up. No one else smiled like she did. I suddenly remembered a conversation I'd had with George about it. My heart lurched as I heard his words, so clearly in my head: *When Eileen smiles at you, you know it's you she's smiling at.*

"You're sad, Kathleen? Come and sit here and tell me all that's troubling you."

I settled into a chair closer to her bed, snuggling Evie against my chest. I couldn't answer. My gaze locked on Eileen's face, and I saw myself mirrored in her. I was hot and sweaty from carrying the baby uphill in the afternoon heat. Eileen's face was sheened with the perspiration of illness, and damp patches of darker blue marked the blue fabric of her dress. I had let my sadness and fear for George show in my eyes. As I studied Eileen's countenance, I saw that despite her smile, her eyes held not just compassion, but sorrow of her own. I reached to take her bony hand in mine, tenderly and carefully, always mindful that once someone had broken a bone in Eileen's hand, just by shaking it too firmly.

"You miss Father McGrath very much," I said.

"Oh, Kathleen, they told me I'll never see him again."

"Who told you that?" She shook her head and tears welled in her eyes. She wasn't going to tell me who, but I knew it must be someone in the church. "I'd hoped this would all blow over, and they'd let Father come back to help you."

"They won't let *anyone* help me. The MSC Fathers and Father Gell are not allowed to contact us. We can't even have a priest here without permission, and permission is rarely given. Even when I am hardly conscious, they don't often come to give me Communion."

Her skin was damp as I stroked her hand very gently. "We are both lonely and worried about someone far away," I said.

"Yes," she sighed. "Tell me what is worrying you about George?"

I battled the feeling of disloyalty to George brought by putting my shadowy fears into words, but Eileen's patient gaze was on me as she waited to help me carry my burden, and I couldn't stay silent any longer. "His letters, Eileen, they frighten me. He never says anything about what's happening where he is. And if he does, he makes light of it. I know he's in France and I read the papers. I know it's awful there. But he never says so. He writes all sorts of dreams about how life will be when he comes home instead."

"Perhaps he's being brave and trying not to worry you."

I shook my head in dismay, unable to stop horrid words spilling out of my mouth. "I don't know this man who writes to me anymore. I don't feel like he's my George. He writes with such good cheer, but it feels forced and dark. As if the army cans good cheer and gives it to the boys with their bully beef. It's been like that since he was trapped in that bombed trench. He joked about being 'dug out of the dugout' in one of his letters. I know he was hoping to be sent home, but his injuries weren't bad enough. He was sent back to the Western Front.

"I think he broke. His letters to me are hollow. Like he's trying too hard to believe a fairy tale, and something is missing. *Georgie* is missing. Part of Georgie's soul was buried in that dugout. I'm frightened we won't be able to find it." I choked back a sob. "I've burned most of his letters. I can't have them in the house."

* * *

The war went from bad to worse. Despair had settled over the home front as news of the interminable casualties from Gallipoli reached Sydney, and all the while, more and more boys changed their regular clothes for khaki and marched out of our streets. When the boys were evacuated from Gallipoli in December 1915, and sent for R and R in Egypt, I had hoped our luck was turning, and Georgie would be sent home, and everything would go back to normal.

More castles in the sky.

George was sent to the Western Front. For over a year, I had pored over casualty lists in the newspapers, praying I wouldn't find anyone we knew. Ever growing numbers of mothers and widows wore black armbands and haunted expressions.

The rest of us anxiously waited for letters, to prove our menfolk were still alive. Dead men don't write letters—

"That was odd. The tape seemed to cut out." Caitlin frowned.

Alex glanced at the phone screen. "Perhaps she got distracted."

"She sounded pretty close-lipped, like she really didn't want to talk about the war."

"Some things are hard to talk about, I guess." Alex's gaze was a challenge that made Caitlin squirm.

"Okay. Point taken. But Kathleen is telling her history. Why would she leave the war out?"

"Why is she telling the story in the first place?"

"What are you getting at, Alex?"

"Well, Nan didn't know about these tapes till Mum found them at the back of a cupboard. Let's assume Kathleen recorded all the tapes in hospital and died there. Then the tapes must have been given to Evie, and Evie was busy organizing her funeral and stuff, and overlooked the tapes. Because if Nan didn't know about them, presumably Evie, Nan's mother, didn't think they were very important. What do you think, Uncle Tim?" Tim, hopping into the kitchen, stopped on his way to the sink.

"Your grandmother never said anything to me about any history tapes and I never saw them when I was growing up." His chuckle was unexpected, belying his bleary, red-rimmed eyes, "Though I can't say I ever saw the back of the cupboard under the stairs either. It was always full to overflowing."

"And your grandmother Evie never said anything about the tapes or George? Not even when you enlisted?"

"No. Never." He poured a spoonful of coffee into his mug, and settled in a chair, half-brooding and half-listening.

"Oh, I see." Caitlin pulled together her hypothesis. "The tapes could have just been in with her clothes and papers and whatever, from the hospital when she died, and her daughter might have just bundled them away, intending to listen later, and never got around to it."

"If your Nan hadn't died listening to them, we might have done the same thing."

Alex nodded slowly. "That's true. And Cait, remember back to the beginning of the tapes. Kathleen was telling the nurse about the history of the hospital. Because the nurse was interested, she got tapes made. What if the tapes were copied for the hospital's archives, and Kathleen was given a copy to keep, but Evie just thought it was a history lesson on medical care in Sydney. That's what I thought, when we listened to the first track. I was wondering what I'd got myself in to."

"But then we realized Kathleen was telling her own story." Caitlin's eyes widened. "Evie wouldn't have known that. And she wouldn't have read the exercise book with the hints that Kathleen had promised Eileen she'd tell her story."

"No, she wouldn't. She would have been grieving and felt it would invade her Mum's privacy to read what looked like a diary entry." Alex hoped no one noticed the warm flush creeping up his neck. "So, she just put the tapes, and an old tin of newspaper clippings and other things Kathleen had kept, into a box in the back of a cupboard."

"To be found nearly fifty years later. Right when we needed a special project."

The cousins shared a poignant smile, and Caitlin tilted her head towards her father, who was still cradling his mug with a blank expression.

"It's like someone's weaving us together, from beyond the grave," Alex murmured as softly as if they had just walked into a church.

"Just a minute. Are you sure that was the end of a tape, Alex? It felt like something had distracted Kathleen."

As silence fell in the kitchen, Alex turned on his phone, listening intently. Something in the low whirring sound of the tape turning caught his attention. He hit rewind then play. "Did we miss something?"

"She's not talking, but the tape was still running."

"Shh!" He turned up the volume.

They strained to hear a new sound. A soft sigh, choked with emotion. A gasp.

"I can hear music. I think someone has the radio on in the background. Maybe that's what distracted Kathleen? Listen." Alex increased the volume again, and the words of the song became audible.

"Hold on, I recognize that song, it's *And the Band Played Waltzing Matilda*," said Cait, a shiver tingling up her spine.

The song continued. A cheering crowd waved soldiers off to Gallipoli. There was a ferocious battle against Johnny Turk, and the burial of the dead. A few times, shuddering sobs obscured some of the words, but they could make out the gist of the song. The soldier woke up in hospital after being hit by a Turkish shell and described his horror at realizing what his injuries were. He had never known there were things worse than dying.

"Oh, Georgie, I never knew that either." Then sobbing, until the click of the tape being turned off.

The air in the kitchen grew heavy with shocked silence. Caitlin buried her head in her hands and Alex rubbed his forehead. "Oh, Alex! The poor old woman was thinking back to the war, and they played this song on the radio." Tears swam in Caitlin's eyes. "No wonder she stopped dictating."

"That song was written during the Vietnam War." Tim grunted and heaved himself out of his chair, took a beer from the fridge and left the room.

Alex turned anxious eyes on Caitlin, who shrugged, uncertain what to do. "I've got it," he said and followed his uncle to the lounge.

He returned after a few minutes, relief obvious on his face. "He's okay. He says he just needs to clear his head. Something about trauma echoing down the generations —"

"He said that?"

Alex nodded. "Trauma echoing. That's what he said. Kind of poetic. And sad."

"Poor Dad."

"Poor all of you. Poor everyone."

"I'm alright."

He nodded. "I know."

Caitlin studied a coffee stain on the scratched tabletop. "Alex, I've got a horrible feeling."

"Me too," he confessed, encouraging her to put her thoughts into words.

"Georgie didn't die in the war, did he? He came back. But he was so damaged, it would have been better if he died. And whatever happened when he was back home, was so awful that Kathleen never spoke about it, never even told their only daughter he had survived the war."

Alex sucked his lips in, dismay etched into the angles of his face. "I dread to think what we are going to find, to be honest." He rubbed his chin again, as if trying to scrub away his despair. "Are you okay to work on this? It's not too upsetting?"

"I can do this," she asserted. "We owe it to him, to find out what happened to him. And we owe it to Kathleen too."

"You're right."

"It's like opening Pandora's box."

"Or her toffee tin." Alex attempted levity.

"I think maybe it's time to break the rule. And look up George again."

"Okay. Well, we know he survived Gallipoli and made it to Egypt."

"Yes, and he was still alive and in France, in 1916."

"The Australian War Memorial site?"

"Start there. Let's see what they have."

Alex typed. "Here's the home page ... okay, I'll hit 'people.' Name: George O'Grady. Got him. First World War Embarkation Rolls. Well, that confirms he embarked in 1915."

"What else is there?" Caitlin leaned into Alex's arm, getting as close to the screen as possible.

"Nominal Roll of Honor ... that lists their service details ... okay. Here he is. George O'Grady ... what does R.T.A. mean?"

She shook her head. "I don't know. What other abbreviations do they give?"

"R.T.A. is the most common on this page ... but they have K.I.A. and D.O.W. next to some of the soldiers."

"K.I.A. is killed in action, and D.O.W. is died of wounds."

Alex was reading. "Here we go. R.T.A. Returned to Australia."

"He came home," Caitlin breathed, closing her eyes. "He came home, and Kathleen learned some things are worse than dying."

"It looks that way. R.T.A. eleventh of August 1917."

Alex carried the coffee mugs to the table. "Is the next thing in there about George?"

"It's a page from a newspaper, 1917." She unfolded the yellowed paper, and laid it flat on the table between them, well away from the cups.

"OFFICIAL CASUALTY LIST: The 295th and 296th lists of casualties sustained by Australian troops abroad was issued on Saturday," she read, then began to skim. "Must have been a pretty intense time on the battle fields. Five Officers and one hundred and fifteen Others killed in action, fifty-two died of wounds, two accidentally killed, poor bastards ... almost eleven hundred wounded. Two hundred and thirty-eight missing, two hundred and fifty sick. A few were taken prisoners of war. Six nurses killed."

"Sounds grim."

"Yes," she muttered but she was not listening; she skimmed the article again. "It's broken down into States now. New South Wales ...

Killed in Action ... Died of Wounds ... Died of Illness ... Wounded ..." She turned away from the paper and reached for Alex's eyes with her gaze. Their eyes locked and he stretched his hand across to take hers, before speaking.

"You've found him."

She nodded, frowning. "Private G. O'GRADY. Redfern (second occasion)."

"That's all it says?"

"Yes. Some of them are listed as 'sev,' short for severely. They don't say that for George."

An image of his uncle played on the screen in Alex's mind; screaming in his nightmare, his stump flailing as he yet again relived that other night, long ago, in the jungle. "That's cold comfort, isn't it? He was injured, but maybe not *severely*, and it was the second time the poor bastard was hit."

"What happened to him from there?"

"I don't know. Let's see if we can find out." She reached for her mug and took a few mouthfuls, then pressed the play button on his phone.

What was I thinking? That I could somehow tell Eileen's story, without telling mine? Or that I could tell my story, without telling Georgie's? When our stories are woven together, into one cloth, one tapestry. Backwards and forwards, throughout time …

I've carried secrets for all these years. And now, just when my story is coming to its end, Eileen sent that song to remind me I must tell the truth. Of course, she did. Because long ago, she made me promise her I would. She said she understood why I kept the secret, while you were little, Evie. She agreed it was best that way. But, you see, she valued love, perhaps more than anything else. One day, late in 1920, I went to visit her, we all did, because we knew she wasn't going to be with us much longer.

I remember what she said to me: "What is love? Love is wonderful, a softness, a kindness sent from God."

I couldn't take my eyes off her, Evie. Pale as lilies at a funeral, she was almost lost in her white, lacy bed. She struggled for every gasp of air but was eager to spend that hard-won breath advising me on what to do for the best.

"Love demands that Evie knows the truth, Kathleen," she told me. "When she's old enough to understand. Promise me you will tell her." She reached out a thin hand, to take mine. "I will pray you find the courage you need, when the time is right."

I'm not sure the time's right, Evie. I'm not sure it ever was. But I do know, time is running out. I have no choice now: I must do as I promised Eileen.

I'm sorry Evie. So sorry. Please forgive me.

CAITLIN'S HOUSE, ADELAIDE

Silence on the recording. Alex reached across and hit the pause button. "This is getting heavy."

"You okay?"

"Yeah. You?"

She sighed, then a slow grin formed. "Do you think chocolate would help?"

His snort of laughter sounded loud in his ears. "Everything goes better with chocolate. Have you got some?"

"I got heaps when I was in hospital. I stashed some for a rainy day. In that cupboard by the sink. Behind the tins of baked beans."

He shifted the tins and pulled out a package. "Ooh, fancy ones." He passed them to her.

Caitlin opened the transparent plastic, pausing to take a delighted breath, savoring the rich aroma. She studied the information pamphlet. "Pick what you want." She passed him the list, but he waved it away.

"I'd rather find out what happens next." He took the nearest chocolate and popped it into his mouth. "More tape, or something from the box?"

Caitlin carefully removed the next item from the tin. Several sheets of note paper were folded together, and tied with a very narrow pink ribbon, faded with time. Once long ago, it was red. She untied the squashed bow and opened the fragile papers. "Letters. They're from George. There are a few of them." She spread them flat on the table, and the two heads bent over them, reading in silence.

August 20th, 1915
Darling Evie,

Daddy hopes you are being a good girl for your mother, having lots of long sleeps and doing special funny, baby things to make her laugh and keep her cheerful even though she is worrying about me and missing me very much.

Tell her I miss you both very much too.

I have a nice view of the sea, but not as nice as Miss O'Connor's view from Coogee, and the accommodation isn't as pleasant here either.

When I come home, the first thing I'll do is have a nice bath and shave, and then I am going to hug you and your Mum so tight, I'll never let you go. Except for when you want me to bounce you on my knee.

Give my love to everyone but keep some special love for you and Mummy.
Your loving Daddy

October ?th 1915
Dear Mum,
I don't know what day it is. They're all the same. Just different colors of hell.

Kiss Evie for me while she is sleeping. Please.

Johnny Turk is picking us off, one by one.

I don't know if any of us will make it out of here alive.
Your son-in-law, George

June 16th, 1916
Dear Mum,
You have done so much for me already, taking Kathleen and Evie back in, and making sure they are managing without me.

I need you to do something else. Can you please pass on a message to Archie Moran's wife for me? You'll know by now he was killed. It was a night of terrible shelling, Mum. I'm still more than half deaf. We made a pact, me and Archie, when we saw how intense the bombardment was, that if anything happened to one of us, the other would get a message back to his wife.

Well, poor Archie bought it, not twenty minutes after we made the pact. We were in the trench together, with a billy on for tea. There was an explosion near us, and I crouched down in the mud just where we were. "Not here!" Archie yelled, and he grabbed my arm and pulled me towards a little dugout and pushed me in. Before he could follow me, another shell came right into the trench and exploded. It blew his head right off, part of it went straight up in the air like a football. Poor Archie's brains splattered out all over my back and I had to scrape handfuls of them off my jacket. I found one of his fingers in the billy.

Tell his wife Effie he was a hero, and he died saving my wretched life. Tell her it was quick. He wouldn't have seen it coming and he wouldn't have felt a thing. He was lucky that way. Tell Effie there never was a braver man, nor a truer one, and I am proud he was my mate. And tell her that he loved her.

The other blokes in the trench weren't lucky. Robbie was just screaming and staring at the place his arm used to be, and Jacko lost half of his face, was blowing big red bubbles from a hole where his mouth and nose used to be, drowning in his own blood.

Every time I close my eyes, I see their faces. And know it should have been me.

Your loving son-in-law, George

The cousins' eyes met over the letter. "That's pretty grim." Alex's voice was hesitant, worried about how Caitlin would be taking this, but she seemed strangely calm. Calmer than he was feeling himself. He took a breath and started talking again, "Why would he write to his mother-in-law about that?"

"His mother isn't on the scene. Maybe she'd died by now?"

Alex brushed her reply aside, shaking his head. "That's not what I meant. Why would he write that sort of stuff to *a woman*? We know

Kathleen's Dad was around. If he couldn't write to his own parents, why wouldn't he have written to his father-in-law instead?"

Caitlin shrugged. "I wondered that too, when I studied World War I history. There's a lot of letters from diggers available online. A lot of them are pretty graphic. And a lot of them are written to mothers."

Alex blinked. "Why?"

"Maybe the boys … they were boys, many of them, younger than you are now, living in a nightmare, maybe they needed their mums?"

Heaviness fell on them like a creeping, tainted fog, sucking the air out of their lungs. "I can't imagine how it would feel to get a letter like that."

"Neither can I."

> *June 17ᵗʰ, 1916*
> *My darling,*
> *It's late here, and all quiet now, and I have a little lamp-light to see by, so this can be story-time.*
>
> *Once upon a time, when the war is over, and I come home, you and I will find a little house of our own. Maybe even in Baptist Street, nice and close to your Mum. After everything she has done for you and Evie, it'd be nice if we always live close, wouldn't it? She'd miss you both nearly as much as I do now, if we moved too far away.*
>
> *We'll put wallpaper in the front room, with a pattern of pink roses, if you like. I miss flowers terribly here. And we'll plant a rose bush to match, right by the front gate, so we always see the blooms when we come in or go out. We'll teach Evie about the prickles, to make sure she doesn't hurt her fingers or catch her little frocks on them.*
>
> *If we have trouble paying the rent, we'll take in a boarder for a while. A nice widow perhaps, who lost her husband in the war and needs a family to live with. But in time, we'll fill the house with children, and she'll find quieter accommodation elsewhere. I'll have been promoted by then and we'll be comfortably off.*
>
> *And once a week, we'll pack the children up and travel to Coogee—by tram, no less!—and visit Eileen.*

We'll take a big basket filled with your home-made apple pie and leftover roast mutton, for them to give to the poor, because we will always have plenty to share. And we will enjoy being with Eileen, and sometimes she will have big parties there, and other times it will be just us and her and the Nurses, and we will play cards or sing just like in the old days.

And sometimes there won't be any spare apple pie to take, because your pies are so delicious, I won't be able to help but eat them all myself. I hope you don't scold me too much when that happens. You won't, will you? Because I will look at you with my big blue eyes and you'll realize you can't tell me off.

And in our little house, we'll never get cross anyway, because we will never forget how truly blessed we are to all be together.
Your loving Georgie

Checking that Alex had finished reading too, Caitlin slowly refolded the page. Was Georgie going mad? How could the same man write two such different letters, a day apart? They moved on to the next letter in the pile.

January 12th, 1917
Dear Evie,
By the time you get this it will be your 2nd birthday! Happy Birthday, precious girl.

Every day I think of how big you must be, the funny things you must do, and wonder what new words you are using. Tell Mummy how much I love the lists of clever things you are doing.

I didn't know I would be away so long and miss so much time with you. You'll be able to read my letters for yourself before long!

It's cold and wet here. Tell Mummy the socks and mittens she knitted for me are lovely and warm and make a big difference. In the night, when no one's looking, I pretend it's not her mittens warming my hand. I pretend that she's taking my rough old working hands in her own warm little hands, to comfort me and send away the nasty chill.

I love you both very much.
Daddy

There is a little girl called Evelyn,
I love her more than anythin'.
And when Jerry plays pranks
With his guns and his tanks,
I listen for her voice above the din.

April 29ᵗʰ, 1917
Dear Mum,
I thought it'd be a relief when the weather warmed up, and we weren't half-frozen, or worse. I was wrong.

The smell, Mum. I'll never get used to the smell of dead men and raw sewage.

My darling Kathleen—
There's a big push on.

I have loved you every minute since I've been away. Loving you and Evie takes me away from this place. Lifts me up above the mundaneness and the mayhem. Saves me from madness.

Loving you is the glue that keeps my sanity together in this infernal place.

I remember what Eileen said: Love survives separation. Love survives death. Maybe that's what love is for?

Kiss Evie for me.

"Shit. I'm glad Uncle Tim's not reading these," Alex muttered under his breath. Caitlin was sitting with her hand pressed to her mouth, her eyes wet. Alex slipped his arm around her shoulders.

"I'm okay," she said, through the pressure closing her throat. "It's almost like being there, isn't it? As if something strange has happened to time ..."

"Maybe Georgie's right; love survives death, and it has been waiting to be discovered again?" He pulled the half-empty tray of chocolates towards them.

She shook her head. "No, I can't eat anything just now."

"Okay. Let's hear what happens next."

REDFERN-MAY 1917

Any time we saw the telegram man walking near Baptist Street, we froze. Pale-faced, we watched him come closer, step by step, praying he wouldn't turn in to knock at our own door.

I had just come back to Mum's house with a basket of groceries. I was turning to shut the front door. I saw him. I saw him recheck the house number on the telegram in his hand. I saw the way his face stiffened, set like a mask, any emotion diligently hidden behind his professional attitude. I saw him pivot on one foot, in slow motion, turning, turning, ninety degrees, until he was facing me, looking through the doorway. Our eyes met for a brief moment as my heart ceased beating. The world stood still as I saw his lips move, their shapes making the words *Mrs. O'Grady*.

Fury exploded in my chest, and I slammed the door, bracing my back against it. Holding the telegram man at bay, he and his loathsome piece of paper, that would change my world forever.

Mum heard the door slamming and ran in from the back yard, where she would have been doing laundry, in time to hear the insistent tapping. Before I could say anything, my knees gave way and I slid down the painted timber, becoming a sobbing heap on the floor.

"Kathleen!"

The tapping continued unrelenting, and Mum, steeled by some force I had never before met in her, looped her arms under my shoulders and heaved me away from the door, then opened it.

"Sorry ma'am." The telegram man's muffled voice came from very far away.

Mum snatched the telegram out of his hand and passed it to me. I shook my head, and she ripped it open, fast, like pulling stuck gauze off a graze. "Injured. Praise the Lord, he's only injured," she said softly.

"Where? How?"

"France. He'll be in hospital somewhere by now, love. They'll be doing their best for him."

Waiting. The waiting time began in earnest. I was desperate for news. Where was George? What kind of injury had he suffered?

I was frantic. Mum and Dad did what they could to keep me calm, and I knew George was in Eileen's prayers, but she was suffering herself, in the grip of another bout of sickness, and I didn't want to add to her burdens. I wrote letters to the Red Cross, asking what had happened to him. Which hospital was he in? Was he getting better? Was he showing signs of infection? I received polite replies. Snippets of information. He'd been gassed, his lungs were damaged, and he had a leg injury which needed surgery, but he didn't need an amputation. When he was well enough, he'd be sent home!

Relief filled me. He was coming home. It was only a matter of time till we'd be a family again. Surely, when we were all together, Georgie would become his old self again.

I kept writing letters. Asking when he'd be home, what ship he'd be on. It was like trying to get blood out of a stone, to find out what was going on.

> *Dear Madam,*
> *In acknowledging receipt of your communication of 17th inst., concerning your husband 3897, Private George O'Grady, 19th Battalion, I have to state, beyond the advice that he is returning to Australia, no further particulars are available.*
> *Yours faithfully,*
> *Major, Officer Base Records*

After months of waiting, I heard he'd be on the Ulysses, and he'd be transferred to the Randwick Military Hospital. So close! A quick trip on the tram, or a forty-five-minute walk. And as soon as he was able, I'd bring him home and Mum and I would look after him, and we'd all be together.

Eileen's eyes were smiling, as I told her the news. She touched my hand; her fingers cold, and as weightless as a butterfly's wings. I searched her face, hoping to see signs her health was improving, but her skin was pale and almost translucent, and her chest barely moved with each breath. Her voice as soft as a whisper, she said, "We shall help you look after him. And when I am better, I will come and visit."

Early on the morning the men returning on the Ulysses were set to disembark, Dad sat at the table in the kitchen, reading the newspaper. "You've got your ticket from the staff officer for invalids, Kathleen? Marked W?"

"Yes, Dad."

"The names of cot cases will be posted in the Anzac buffet as soon as disembarkation begins."

"Yes, Dad."

"Relatives can meet them at the hospital."

"I know."

"You're sure he'll be a cot case?"

"I think so."

He looked at me over the newspaper. "Are you sure you'll be alright on your own, love?"

"Of course I will, Dad." I managed a nervous smile.

"That's my girl," he said, folding the paper, trying to hide the article on the artificial limb factory, and the advertisements for Bonox Body Building Fluid Beef. *Makes the finest beef tea,* and Bonnington's Irish Moss, *Soothes and heals the throat and lungs at once!* It was too late, I'd seen them over his shoulder, but I didn't tell him that. "I'll see you tonight." He kissed the top of my head, then pecked Mum on the cheek. Evie, sitting in her home-made highchair with her spoon in her empty porridge bowl, shrieked with laughter as he blew her a loud raspberry. He used a rag to wipe her face clean then kissed her too.

"You're really sure, love?" Mum asked as soon as he'd closed the door, lifting Evie down. "We could get someone to mind Evie, and I could come with you."

I squared my shoulders. I was the wife of a returned soldier now. I didn't know what condition he'd be in, but I'd seen men with missing limbs, and he had all of his. I'd read a new gas was being used by the Germans. Mustard gas, but I didn't know much about it. My eyes flicked to the bottle of cough medicine ready on the mantlepiece, and I nodded. "I'll be fine, Mum. He'll probably be loaded right onto one of the hospital trams. I don't know if I'll even get to see him before the hospital. We can bring Evie to him when he's settled." Later, when we have an idea of what we are up against.

"Perhaps that's best. He'll be tired after the journey. And they say quiet is good for the returned soldiers. We don't want to overtax his nerves, or have Evie become too boisterous."

I smiled for her benefit, but it was more a grimace; I couldn't reply as my teeth were clenched together, and my mind was willing me to keep standing on knees that trembled under my long, camel-colored skirt.

"We'll get him home as soon as we can, love. We won't leave him in that hospital a minute longer than he needs to be." Her voice was fierce, and I wondered why, because I didn't understand the courage she needed to say it. Not then. I was thinking of the castles in the sky Georgie and I had built before he went away, that he had reminded me of so often in his letters.

You see, Evie, I hadn't seen the letters he had written to Mum, and I was choosing to forget the alarm signals in my own brain, the feeling that part of Georgie wasn't there anymore. Choosing to forget the returned soldiers I'd seen sitting like beggars on street corners, limbs missing or shaking uncontrollably. The whispers that Jack or Bill or Paddy wasn't the same anymore, had come home a changed man. I pushed all that into a dark place in the back of my mind and slammed the lid down hard. And locked it. And threw away the key.

Mum smiled and reached across to squeeze my hand, then wiped Evie's fingers before she could touch my Sunday-best blouse, washed and ironed, hanging ready on the door handle.

"Of course we will, Mum. Eileen says the Brown Nurses will come and tend him for me, change his dressings, and make sure everything's alright. They'll look after him better than a hospital full of nurses. And so will we."

CAITLIN'S HOUSE, ADELAIDE

Caitlin closed the laptop, as if making the screen disappear would shut away the results of their online research, the image of the old woman reflecting on her father's shell shock; the sepia photograph of her as a small girl, settled in his lap. The voice from the YouTube clip echoed in her mind.

"My father never got over the terrible trauma of the war. I always remember the noise in the night, his screaming out, my mother trying to calm him. I didn't know any different. I thought everybody's Daddy did that, screaming and hollering in the night and cowering under the bed."

Alex was watching her, but Caitlin was determined to keep her face averted, tidying the growing stack of papers beside the tin.

"That could have been Evie, growing up with a Daddy who screamed in the night, thinking it was normal." Alex shifted his weight in his seat, trying to relieve his discomfort, but it didn't help.

"And having her photo taken, snuggled on his knee."

"But it wasn't to be, was it?" he rubbed his face again.

"No. And the story of the woman whose husband was shot for cowardice, hiding the letter from the Army that told her what happened down her top, and never telling anyone, until she was dying at the age of ninety-nine. Too embarrassed to tell people. It wasn't only Kathleen who felt like that."

"No, obviously not." Alex fell silent, frown lines furrowing his brow.

"It's awful, isn't it?"

Alex nodded. "Yeah, it is." His eyes flicked towards the kitchen door, the passage to the living room where Uncle Tim might have passed out in front of the television by now.

"His letters make it look like George had shell shock. We'll know for sure when we listen to the next tape, I guess." She fidgeted in her chair, wondering briefly if she could put off the next instalment, but, no, it was better to get it over with. Before her dad came back into the kitchen.

"Maybe he was institutionalized when he got back?" mused Alex. "And Kathleen thought it was better to have Evie forget about him?"

"Or maybe he died of wounds, or of influenza in the 1919 pandemic?" Hope sank in her stomach like a rock. Those options might be easier to swallow than whatever they were about to hear.

REDFERN, DECEMBER 1917

George's lips were compressed into a thin line across his gaunt face as he sat leaning forward, holding himself rigid, gripping the arms of the chair. His dread of the pain of having his wound redressed was battling with his need to force air into his damaged lungs and his mouth gaped open as he took a shuddering, gasping breath.

Nurse Mary looked professional in her crisp white dress and apron, with her sleeves rolled up to keep them clean. The trademark brown pillbox was tied on over her dark bun, its veil brushing her broad shoulders. With feet almost silent, she moved across the wooden floor, the practiced art of one who has learned not to startle patients by means of making any loud noise.

"It's alright, Mr. O'Grady, we won't do this until you're ready," she reassured him with a cheerfulness that I am sure she couldn't have felt. "Perhaps I can change the sheets for you, and save Mrs. O'Grady the job? While you get yourself ready."

"Just do it," George urged her. "Just do it, Nurse."

I paused in the task of stripping the bed, and instead sat on its edge, watching. The enamel basin was already full of hot water, and she turned to her bag to take out some gauze. She seemed to take her time about it, so I glanced at her face. Her lips were moving silently, and I realized she was saying a prayer. I read her lips and joined in the Hail Mary.

She sighed and turned back to George. "Well, now's our chance to see how this poor leg of yours is responding to the treatments."

George summoned all his courage and nodded. Just one short movement. He was ready. Nurse dragged the wooden fruit crate into position and carefully lifted his leg and rested his foot on it. She pulled up the cotton leg of his blue and white striped pajamas, past the bulge on his thigh where the bandages were. I saw the slight pursing of her lips as she checked the amount of staining on the bandage, from the suppurating wound below.

With practiced precision, she unwound the bandages, placing them in a small basin ready to be cleaned and boiled for re-use. As she reached the thick cotton pad, the sickening stench of decay wafted into the room. The open window wasn't enough to disperse it, and I watched poor Georgie's face as it fell.

Nurse peeled the pad off his skin, it's under surface slick and green.

"Well done, George. We'll just clean this leg a bit now, and soak the gauze plug so we can get it out of the wound and see how it's getting on."

I was filled with admiration at her cheerful, professional tone. Nausea was rising rebelliously in my own stomach. Without warning, Nurse swung round, holding an empty basin for George while he vomited. His lips were blue and starved of oxygen when he finished retching. I took the basin and emptied it in the backyard privy, thanking my lucky stars that Mum had taken Evie out for a walk. There are some things a child shouldn't see, even if, being not yet three years old, she is unlikely to remember them later.

I breathed deep in the fresher air of the backyard before a wave of guilt washed over me. Georgie couldn't get even a moment of respite from his suffering, and there I was, standing in the summer sunshine, breathing fresh air into healthy lungs. I shuddered and hastened inside, to see Nurse Mary washing Georgie's face and reassuring him. I put the cleaned basin on the table in case we needed it again, and, standing behind George's chair, rested my hands on his shoulders, making sure their weight wouldn't increase the labor of his breathing. And making a statement. I was there with him. I wasn't going anywhere.

"There now," said Mary. "That's it. The gauze is nice and soaked. Are you ready?"

George nodded, and would have gritted his teeth, except he was panting too hard to close his mouth.

Mary made it look easy as she gripped the wide gauze plug in Georgie's thigh with her metal forceps, and gently yet firmly eased it out. The wound underneath it was gray-green and dead-looking, with just a little fresh blood where the exudate had been ripped away with the dressing.

Georgie lurched forward and clutched the nurse's arm. "You won't let them take my leg, will you?" he hissed. "Not that."

Mary's voice was kind, and she patted his hand in its vice-like grip on her arm. "Now, George, I'm only a nurse. But look, the skin around the wound isn't any redder this week, is it? Even though the wound itself is nasty and stubborn, the infection hasn't spread. See? That's a good sign, George. We can keep going with the dressings."

He meekly let go of her arm and settled a little further back in his chair. Not all the way back; he needed to sit upright to get the air into his lungs.

Nurse Mary changed the sheets while I started the dinner. She chatted to George, not minding he wasn't replying, then sat at the kitchen table with him. "How's your embroidery going, George?"

"I haven't done much, Nurse." He shrugged, helpless, like a schoolboy who has been caught out for not doing his homework.

"Oh, George, you know the doctors say it's important to keep busy. And sewing is such a peaceful activity, I hear they're getting lots of returned men to take it up while they convalesce. The Red Cross is selling pieces, so soldiers can make a little money for their families, before they're ready to work." She went to the drawer where we kept George's embroidery stuff: a little sprig of wattle painstakingly emerging on the cloth. "Here, I'll start you off again."

"Thank you." He watched with meek gratitude as she deftly sewed the gray-green outline of a couple of leaves.

"Now, see if you can have filled those in by the time I see you on Friday."

"I will, Nurse."

"If Eileen's well enough, she wants to come and visit you then."

My heart leaped in my chest as I saw George's eyes become more focused. "That would be lovely, Nurse. It's always been a pleasure to see Eileen."

"Make sure that beautiful daughter of yours is here, if you can, George. I know Eileen is busting to see her."

"Isn't Evie here?" George's eyes were a vacant blue as they scanned the kitchen. My heart dropped again.

"Mum took her for a walk, Georgie. To keep her from getting under Nurse's feet."

"I'm used to having children underfoot. The oldest of eleven, I am." She beamed fondly, then sighed. "Two brothers, Ernest and John are overseas now. We nurses are keeping Eileen busy, lots of our brothers are away at the war. She prays very hard for them, and we haven't lost one yet."

"You're very lucky," I said, though my mouth was dry as dust, my eyes resting on George's shoulders, bent over his needle and thread, obediently filling in the first leaf shape. His needle hesitating, as he considered every stitch before he made it, worrying he would do something wrong.

"Would you like to pray with me, George?" Nurse asked, closing her bag.

I followed her into the street when she left, and we stood in the roadway for a few minutes. "How's his leg, Mary?"

"I'm willing to keep dressing it, as long as the infection doesn't spread, and he doesn't get a fever or any signs of gangrene." She swallowed. "It's not getting any better. God willing, we're not doing the wrong thing by humoring him. It sounds dreadful, but I'm not sure if we're being kind, or just letting it draw out."

I nodded, unable to speak for the lump that was blocking my throat.

"You're doing a good job, Kathleen." Her voice was low and gentle.

I nodded again, holding my tears deep inside me. "And his lungs? Will they ever get any better?" I'd asked the doctor the same thing before George came home from the Military Hospital.

Nurse Mary's lips twisted, and she shook her head. "I don't know, Kathleen. I wish there was something I could tell you."

I took my time closing the door, composing myself before I could face George in the kitchen. "Well, it'll be nice to have Eileen come and visit," I said, with forced brightness, into the empty space that had cocooned George, still sitting with his needle frozen in the air, as if he had forgotten he was meant to sew with it.

When they returned from their outing, Mum passed Evie into my waiting arms. "How's our Evie? How was the park?" I asked.

"Evie's a good girl. The park's good. We fed ducks."

"Sounds like you had a good time then." I set her down on the floor in front of her daddy, who put his sewing on the table, and patted his good leg.

"Come sit on Daddy's lap, darling," I said and picked her up before she could scramble on his bad one.

She looked up into those shadowy eyes of his. "Do you like the park, Daddy?"

"Yes," he said uncertainly, frowning as if he was trying to remember. "I used to like going to Centennial Park very much ..."

"Before Daddy's leg got sore," I said into the silence.

She nodded, her eyes solemn. "Poor leg."

"You've got grass in your hair," I interjected, trying to change the subject to something else. Anything else.

"I rolled." Her eyes were as big as saucers. "I rolled and rolled and rolled."

Mum laughed. "So she did. I'll get the stains out of her pinafore later."

Georgie looked at her curly hair, escaping from short braids that ended just past her shoulders. In slow motion he reached with the trembling fingers of his left hand to pluck out a blade of grass. He crushed it with great attention, then held it in his fingertips and put it to his nose. "I'd forgotten what grass smells like." He inhaled again, and helpless tears started to run down his cheeks. He shook his head, his eyes wide and haunted. "There's not a blade of grass left there, you know. Not one."

For a moment, I was rooted to the spot, frozen. Not knowing what to do or say. Wanting to pull Evie away so she didn't need to see her father cry, wanting to comfort George ... conflicting impulses to help and protect each of them clashed in my head, and I could do nothing.

Then Evie slipped her arms around her Daddy's neck and planted a wet kiss on his cheek. "There, there, Daddy. Even Daddies cry sometimes," she said earnestly. "There's lots of grass in the park, Daddy. I'll bring you home some, every time I go."

Georgie made a gurgling, sobbing, whimpering noise, like an animal I'd never heard before, and buried his face into Evie's neck. I felt the warm weight of Mum's hand on my shoulder, before she slipped into the backyard, to give us some privacy. I hesitated for a few moments, then knelt beside his good leg and put my arms around them both, crying into Evie's back.

When Friday came, I was dabbing Evie's face with a damp cloth with one hand, and smoothing her hair with the other, while scanning the kitchen to make sure everything was in order.

Mum smiled as she made her way through the back door with another load of washing. "Eileen will be expecting a hive of activity, you know. Not an immaculate castle."

"I know, Mum, I just want everything to look nice."

I caught the door as it swung closed behind her, preventing the bang, and the thought of everything looking nice replayed in my mind. *Looking nice*, but not *being nice*. What happened to Georgie in the war, had stopped things from being nice. Maybe forever.

"You alright, love?" he asked from his corner, looking up from his sewing. "I need to finish this leaf for Nurse Mary."

I managed to smile at his poor, broken-man's expression. "I'm alright, Georgie. You do your sewing. Nurse Mary will be asking to see it, I'm sure."

"I'm not finished." A note of panic in his voice now, his head shaking. "How long have I got till she gets here?"

"It's all right, Georgie. They're bringing Eileen, so they'll be here a bit later than usual. You've got some time, yet." I kept my voice calm, soothing, in spite of the sudden hot rush of frustration. There I was, I thought, trying to help Mum with the washing, raise Evie, figure out the bills, and look after this broken-spirited man, his dressings, his medicine, always afraid someone would make a sudden noise that would trigger a reaction in him. Up at night when he yelled, and hollered, and sobbed in his sleep. And now he'd got the shakes over an embroidered leaf on a scrap of cloth.

"If Nurse Mary is worried you haven't made progress on your embroidery, love, I'll tell her that it was you who hemmed the handkerchiefs we are giving Eileen for Christmas."

His expression relaxed, like a reassured child's would. "Thank you, Kathleen." And just like that, he turned back to his needle, and for him, the outside world, with me and Evie in it, seemed to stop existing.

"Come on, Evie," I said, turning to her. "Let's make sure the front room is spick-and-span."

"Spick-and-span. Spick-and-span," she sang, excited at the unusual prospect of going into the best room.

"You can dust the side table," I offered, handing her the cloth.

"Thank you." She swelled with importance.

Soon there was a rap at the door. Eileen's bright smile made time stand still, as she beamed her greeting at me, as Nurse Catherine carried her in, nestled in her arms. I stood aside making room for her to be taken through to the kitchen to see George.

Nurse Mary took off her brown cloak and hung it on a peg in the passageway wall. Today she was carrying both her usual bag, and a small wicker basket. "Cissie has been busy in the kitchen." She pressed two brown-paper-wrapped packages into my hands.

"Thank you. Can I offer you all some tea today? It's a special occasion having Eileen here."

"I'm sorry, it's against the rules. We're not allowed to eat on duty." Her face was kind, and I knew she was right. It was always against the rules. Some houses were too dirty for a nurse to risk drinking tea in, and as they only served the poor, most people couldn't afford to feed the nurses. But they'd try, God love them, if there weren't rules in place, and go without feeding themselves. Disappointment weighed heavily in my chest, regardless, just for a moment.

"My goodness, Evie! How you've grown." Eileen's voice brought me out of my moment of depression, like a thrill of melody. I followed in Mary's wake into the kitchen.

George was smiling with genuine pleasure, even looking at peace. Eileen's magic, it must have been. She could always change the atmosphere of a room, just by going into it. Even when she was too ill to be moved, and confined to bed, walking into her room was like walking into peace. Often her visitors, even schoolchildren from St. Brigid's School who were sent over after Mass, would be overcome by that peacefulness, and sit in awed silence around her, wanting nothing more than to experience it.

Eileen was bending over Evie, kissing her head. It seemed unbelievable that Eileen was not much taller than her. "Nurse Mary has brought one of my scrapbooks for Mummy to show you, while we look at Daddy's leg," she said with a grin. "And ham sandwiches and fruit cake, for after we've gone."

Evie's eyes were wide as she turned to see me lay the packages on the table. Mary handed me the scrapbook.

"How about we look at this in the front room? It's too crowded in the kitchen for all of us," I said.

"It's like Christmas!" Evie breathed, because in those days the front room was always reserved for important visitors, Sundays and holidays. She slipped her hand into mine and followed me from the room.

"It's good to see you, George." Eileen smiled and took her tiny steps to his side. "Nurse Mary tells me your leg is no worse. I've been praying for it ever so much."

I was reluctant to leave the kitchen. I knew George was in good, safe hands. But I was closing the door on the company of three kind women, especially on Eileen. Our friendship had lasted despite many challenges over the years, and now I was endlessly busy at home, and she was occupied running a foundation of nurses, it was rare that we had time to see each other.

I settled into the old settee, with Evie close beside me, and ran my fingers along the well-used spine of the familiar scrapbook. In an instant, I was transported back in time, a girl again, sitting in Eileen's bedroom at Telopea Street, watching her stick in pictures sent home by girls from school. A girl without a care in the world.

"I recognize some of these pictures! When I was young, not quite as young as you, Eileen and I used to work on this scrapbook together. See these little doggies? They're called pugs."

"Why?"

"Why are they called pugs?"

"Yes. Why?"

A girl again for a moment, I giggled. "I have no idea. That's just their name."

Evie shrugged. "I have no idea either."

My heart melted, as if it was trying to fill a bigger space in my chest, and I snuggled her close, smelling the soapy scent of her hair. "Well, we don't know how pugs got their name, but we do know they must be very special, because they have always been Eileen's favorite dog. Except for one."

"What's the other one?"

"Ah, well, he's that rascal you met when we went to visit her."

"Rags?"

"Yes. Rags."

"The one that jumped up on her lap and made muddy paw prints on her dress?"

I nodded. "Yes, that's him."

"Of course, he'd be her favorite."

I tilted my head to one side, curious what she'd say next. "Why?"

"Because Rags is a real doggie. And he loves her. These pugs are pictures. They're not real. They can't love anyone."

I hugged her into my side, thinking she couldn't see the tears pricking in my eyes. But I was wrong; she was quick to prove she was too clever for me.

"It's alright, Mummy. Sometimes mummies cry," she said, patting me.

A gentle tap at the door, and Mum opened it. "Dressing's all done. Can we bring Eileen in?"

I dabbed my eyes with my sleeve. "Of course."

Nurse Catherine was carrying her and settled her down on the settee with me and Evie, and Georgie limped in on his crutch and took a seat in the old, overstuffed armchair to the left of the fireplace. Mum and Nurse Mary carried wooden chairs in from the kitchen, and we all sat down.

"Did you enjoy the pictures in my scrapbook?" Eileen asked Evie, but the child felt overwhelmed at the sight of so many visitors, and just nodded, her eyes serious, as I handed the book over to Catherine before she sat in the remaining armchair. "As it'll soon be Christmas, I've brought you a present."

Evie sat expectantly, nodding but still too shy to speak.

"Do you want to open it?"

More nodding, and when I rubbed Evie's back she managed to say, "Yes, please."

"Now, where did I put it?" Eileen's eyes twinkled as she made a show of patting down her dress, looking for pockets. "Ah, here it is!" She pulled out a tiny, pink-wrapped parcel and handed it to Evie.

Evie's pudgy little fingers pulled at the string bow until it came undone, then tugged at the paper, which opened, and a pink satin ribbon slipped out into Evie's lap.

"Thank you," Evie breathed.

"I thought we could be twins." Eileen was all smiles and flicked her delicate fingers to indicate the pink bow tied in the long brown curls at the side of her head. "Would you like me to tie it for you?"

Nurse Mary was rising out of her chair, eager to take care of the ribbon; worried, no doubt, that Eileen would hurt her poor back stretching over to do it, but I gave Evie a gentle push. "Stand in front of Eileen, so she can make sure the ribbon is straight," I said, as innocently as I could.

Mary, suddenly realizing she had almost intruded in a special moment, winked approval at me, as Eileen slipped the ribbon under the hair at the nape of Evie's neck and tied it in a soft, limp bow at the side of her head.

"Thank you!" Evie cried, happy and comfortable again.

Nurse Catherine took something from her pocket. Holding out a little piece of mirror, she asked, "Would you like to come and see how it looks?"

Evie skipped across the floor and studied her reflection. "Do you like it, Daddy?"

"You look just like a princess, Evie." And Evie twirled around in the center of the room, practicing a regal wave, as we laughed and clapped at her.

"I am going to have a garden party, and I do hope you will all be able to come," Eileen said, as the applause died down. "It will be the last one for a while, as I find I must travel soon."

"We'd love to come. Thank you," I said, before I could wonder how to get George there. I snapped alert. "Where are you going?"

"I have to go to India. On business for the Foundation. I'll be meeting Father McGrath in Bombay."

"Father McGrath?" Georgie asked. "He's a good chap. I haven't heard of him in years. What's he doing in India?"

"He's a military chaplain now. So, the ban on him communicating with me the MSC imposed doesn't bind him at present. He's stationed in Mesopotamia and will be able to arrange leave so I can meet him."

George's eyes narrowed, almost like they did three years ago, when she announced she was going to Rome. "Are you sure this is a good idea, Eileen? You're not so well, we know. It's no easy thing traveling in wartime. And *India!* The climate …"

"I am very crook, George. All the more reason to attend to business while I can. Our Lady will keep me safe," Eileen said with a certain smile, no trace of recrimination in her voice at his challenge to her judgement. "I am doing Her work. Father will not be allowed back into Australia. I fear he is very down. I will travel to the ends of the earth to see him, if necessary." There was determination in her eyes.

"You must miss him very much."

She nodded. "He is my friend," she said simply. "My first friend in this work." She leaned towards me, and whispered, making sure the nurses couldn't hear her, "I don't know how much longer I can go on, Kathleen. I've been so ill. I can't leave Father without saying goodbye."

Tears pricking my eyelids again, I searched her face, but there was no sadness in it, just a gentle, radiant composure. Acceptance? No, something deeper than that, and the hairs stood up on the back of my neck. Eileen was my friend since childhood. My dearest friend. And sometimes those childhood memories meant I almost forgot she was a saint. Looking at her glowing face that day, her head upturned to meet my gaze, I remembered. I seized the idea that she would one day die, soon perhaps, too soon, and forced it into the box with all the other thoughts I couldn't afford to think.

Evie was talking again. Creating a safe focus for my mind. She was bouncing from foot to foot. "It's from all of us. But my Daddy made it. Where did you hide it, Daddy?"

Georgie's eyes flashed with the same blue light that used to be there, long ago. He patted down his pajama shirt as if he'd hidden the parcel there, before half-rising in his seat, gripping the arm of the chair, and pulling a package out of his dressing gown pocket. As he sat back down, he turned to Eileen and said, apologetically, "I wished I could have put on proper clothes for your visit, Eileen, but I couldn't fit my trousers over the bandaging."

"Oh, George! Of all people I'm the last one you should worry about seeing you in your nightclothes. I've spent years receiving visitors in my room." Her soft laugh was like a cool breeze in summer, blowing away his sense of humiliation. "Though I do understand the appeal of wearing nice clothes." She smiled as she smoothed her pale pink silk gown over her knees.

"Well, you're certainly looking prettier than me today."

The room filled with laughter, for the first time in a long while. "Do I look prettier than you too, Daddy?" Evie asked, tossing her hair about so the new ribbon fluttered beside her.

"Of course you do, princess."

"Then give me Eileen's present. She's busting to know what's in it."

Eileen smiled and clapped her hands. "A present? I love presents!"

"I know," Evie said, swelling with importance as she handed her the package.

"Oh, I wonder what it could be?" Eileen prodded it with a dramatic air, then sniffed it. "I don't think it's flowers."

Evie giggled with delight. "No, it's too flat for flowers."

"And it's nice and light … it can't be a book. Hmm, I really can't guess."

"Open it! Open it!"

And Eileen did, finding two white cotton handkerchiefs. "Oh, that's just the thing! I will wave one when I am on the deck of the ship, sailing to India, and everyone will be able to see me." Her eyes grew more serious as she inspected the stitching. "It's very neat work, George. I couldn't have done better myself."

His smile of pride at such a simple compliment nearly broke what was left of my heart.

Nurse Catherine had excused herself and left the room for a moment, returning from the passageway with a small, newspaper-wrapped cylinder in her hand.

"Now do be careful because the paper is damp, and if you unwrap it in here you will make a mess," warned Eileen, her eyes shining.

"What is it?" demanded Evie, peering at the parcel from a safe distance.

"Once upon a time, before you were born," Eileen began softly, "your Daddy used to dream of making a little home for your Mummy and planting a rose bush so she would have lovely flowers."

I studied George's face, still lined with pain and horror, but softened with nostalgia now. He nodded along, remembering. "Your Grandparents are very generous and have made a lovely home for all of you here, haven't they?"

Evie nodded, a funny little frown on her forehead. "I thought the garden here would be a good place for a rose. One of my friends has lots of roses in her garden and I asked her for a cutting, and she has been caring for it and growing it for me for months." She caught my eye, and we shared a smile. "It's as pink as Kathleen's cheeks were, when she was a girl, George, and it's a tea rose, nice and tough and won't need much work."

"Thank you." His eyes were turned down, studying his hands, which I noticed were shaking. Perhaps he was thinking about how there were no flowers in the trenches again?

Eileen's eyes met mine once more. "I like the name too. It's *Souvenir d'un Ami*." I looked at her in blank incomprehension, never having learned any French.

"Remembrance of a Friend," she said softly, her tone even and matter of fact.

The heavy grip of foreshadowed grief threatened to close my throat, and I reached across and cradled her frail, thin hand in mine. I blinked away tears and nodded. "It's a beautiful gift, thank you. We'll treasure it, won't we, George?"

"Yes indeed. Mum, do you think we can put it in the front yard, near the gate. So everyone can see the flowers when they come home?" He was still studying his hands, and his voice had a slight tremor.

"What a wonderful idea," Mum agreed without hesitation. I remembered again how very lucky I was to have Mum and Dad to take us in, and resolved to make it clear to them how much I appreciated them.

Caitlin was speaking almost before Alex hit pause on his phone. "That rose!"

Alex glanced up from checking his notifications. "You're sounding a bit excited."

"Your mum's garden. She's got a rose. It's pink and kind of old-fashioned looking, not like the modern roses you get from the florists."

"So?"

"She calls it Kathleen's rose."

He grunted and resumed scrolling.

"Alex, pay attention. Don't you remember it? It's in your garden, by the back fence." Her voice commanded his attention.

He raised his eyebrows at her and shrugged. "I don't garden, Cait, you know that."

"She once said it grew from a cutting from her grandmother's garden. *Evie's* garden, Alex. What if it's Eileen's rose. What was it called?"

"*Souvenir d'un Ami.* Don't look at me funny; I did French at school."

She snatched his phone out of his hands. "How do you spell that?" She typed it in and saw several images of pink roses. "Oh, Alex! I think it could be."

"That's cool," Alex said without enthusiasm.

"Don't you see?" Her eyes filled with tears. "Georgie loved flowers and wanted a pink rose for Kathleen. Eileen knew that and she knew she was dying, so she got a rose, chosen not just for the color, but also for its name: to remember a friend. And maybe that rose has been kept in our family, for a hundred years, by people taking cuttings from the original bush, as a kind of keepsake."

"Ah." His eyes widened. "When you put it that way, it is kind of special."

"Love survives ... Love survives separation. Love survives death ..."

"That's what Georgie wrote in the letter before he went over the top."

"What if the rose survived separation, and the rose survived the death of everyone – Kathleen and Georgie, Eileen, Evie. But it's still here, in our family, passed down through the generations?" Her breath caught in awe. *"Love survives separation. Love survives death. But you have to have eyes to see it and you have to know where to look."*

Alex nodded sagely. *"Souvenir d'un Ami."* Then his face exploded into laughter. "Cait, this family history stuff is addling your brain. You need food!"

After they had eaten, Alex collected up their lunch plates, with the last smears of hummus and crumbs of pita bread and cheese and stacked them on the side of the sink. He sat next to Caitlin and looked at her with a worried frown. "Are you ready to go on? I think we're going to find out what happens to Georgie soon. Can you take it?"

She glanced towards the passageway.

"I checked. He's asleep in front of the telly. Out like a light."

Meeting his gaze, she nodded. "Best done while Dad's not listening."

He squeezed her hand; before he could let go, she laid her other hand over it. "Thanks."

"What for?"

She shrugged and her smile wobbled. "Being here, I guess."

Seriousness settled into eyes which, not long ago, were more used to teasing, or avoiding eye contact altogether. "Don't thank me, I can't take the credit." She waited to see if he would explain more. "It's odd. We haven't spent this much time together since ..." he grinned, remembering. "Since our family reunion at the campsite in Swan Hill. Do you remember? Right by the River Murray?"

"When Dad decided to teach you how to kayak, but you could only go round in circles?"

"I was eleven years old, go easy on me!"

She nodded. "You were saying something's odd?"

He breathed in sharply, peered off into the distance, then shook his head as if trying to clear it. He couldn't beat around the bush any longer.

"Yes. You know what we were saying before, about how someone is trying to weave us together." He watched her nod again. "Things weren't going very well, were they? Uncle Tim hasn't been coping since our accident. I've been feeling so guilty and awful, I can't describe it. You were stuck here with no one to help you, trying to look after him …"

She stiffened, and he waited for her usual retort that she'd been fine. She knew how to manage her dad. She promised her mother she'd look after him. But she didn't say anything. The words died away on her lips, and her eyes softened. She placed her hand on her cousin's arm, as if willing him to keep talking, to let it out.

"A drunk driver running a red light nearly killed you. Nearly destroyed what is left of your family. We were all falling apart. Not just you and Uncle Tim. Me too. And Mum was exhausted from looking after Nan and felt awful she couldn't be here for you guys." He rested his forehead on his arms, folded on the tabletop, drawing comfort from the warmth of her hand. His voice muffled, he continued, "You're going to think I am crazy."

"No, I'm not."

His shoulders heaved as he sighed. "I think it's true. I think somehow Kathleen and Eileen set this up, the tapes. The clues. To be found right when we needed a project to bring us together, to make us talk about stuff."

"To heal." Her reply was almost too quiet to hear but given without hesitation.

Alex snapped up from the tabletop, his gaze riveted onto her face. Not a trace of teasing there. "You're feeling it too?"

"Something happened to George's mind in the war, that was so terrible Kathleen lied to the family about it. He nearly lost a leg. Something happened to Dad in Vietnam. He lost a leg, and he still wakes up screaming in the night. Then the car crash. I nearly lost a leg, Dad's mind nearly snapped. There's a pattern, Alex. Something we don't understand yet, but it has passed down the family like a curse, for a hundred years."

A soft snort escaped through Alex's nose. "The curse of war?"

"I don't know. But it's time we find out." She reached over and planted a tender kiss on his cheek, soft as a remembered breeze, before pressing the play icon on his phone screen.

My eyelids sprang open. I never seemed to sleep deeply then, always on alert for when George would wake up screaming. He'd make sounds—blood-curdling shrieks and heart-rending moans—but sometimes there were words, incoherent and jumbled, or repeated over and over like bullet rounds from a machine-gun. I pieced the words together, and realized George was reliving the awful, waking nightmare of being entombed in a shelled trench, trapped under earth, sandbags, and the bodies of his mates. I was trapped too, caught between wishing I could help him, and hoping to get him to quiet down before he woke Evie, asleep on the trundle beside us, or my parents in the next room, and embarrassment that my husband would create such a disturbance in my parents' home.

Warm nights were the worst, because the windows were open, and I worried the screaming was heard by the neighbors too. I could never have imagined it would be a relief to have my brothers and sister move away, but it was. There were less people in the house whose interrupted sleep I felt guilty about. Betty was training to be a nurse at the Royal Prince Alfred Hospital, living in the nursing accommodation there, and my brothers were away too. Paddy, too short-sighted for the Army, was teaching in Newcastle, and Jo had joined up the year before. Sometimes I'd catch Mum staring at Georgie, with terror in her eyes. I knew she was wondering what Jo would be like when he came home. If he came home.

One night, in April 1918, something was different. Georgie was drenched in sweat and flailing to sit upright in bed. The iron-framed bed was vibrating with his shaking.

I reached over to turn up the kerosene lamp, hoping the light would get through to him, show him he was home, not in some fox-hole far away.

Seeing him, pale and terrified in the gloom, the familiar nausea rose in my stomach. Deep breath in, and I began the routine. In my most reassuring voice, I said, "You're home, Georgie. They can't hurt you anymore. See, there's the embroidered rose Eileen gave us, hanging on the wall at the foot of the bed so you can look at it. Can you see it? We're in our own little bed in our own little room. And I'm right here next to you." I reached out and touched his arm, wet and shivering under my hand.

He shrugged my hand off and twisted around in bed to face me.

Every nerve in my body was screaming beneath my calm exterior. I didn't know how much longer I could take this. God help me, I didn't know. But in that moment, as I looked at this man, whimpering incomprehensible things in the dark, this man who was so changed from the beautiful boy I married, my blood ran cold. I opened my arms and folded them around him, but he pushed me away. Gently. There was no violence in it. Except for the violence in my head, the violence in knowing I could never reach the place where he was hurting.

He continued to shake. "Did you see?" he asked, stammering.

"See what, Georgie?"

"Eileen." His eyes were wild, desperate.

"No, I didn't see anything, Georgie. We're here, in our room. No one else came in."

His eyes became steel in the glow of the lamp. "I know where we are, Kathleen," he insisted. This was different from the nights when he woke convinced he was buried under his dead mates in a trench that had been shelled … or frozen in no-man's land as machine guns spat bullets around him. His terror was catching now, and my guts spasmed.

I swallowed down the vomit that my stomach was trying to expel. "What is it, Georgie?"

His eyes glinted as lamplight reflected off his tears and he shook his head as if he couldn't bear to say the words. "Eileen. It's Eileen. She's ill."

"I don't understand, Georgie," I stammered. "Eileen must be in Bombay now, with Father McGrath."

"She's ill. I saw her, Kathleen. She was standing here, by the side of the bed. She touched the bandages on my leg. Then she smiled and faded away."

The hairs stood up on the back of my neck. "Maybe she just came to help heal your leg?"

He shook his head. "No, not that. It felt like goodbye, Kathleen. It felt like she was ill enough to be dying."

Now he let me put my arms around him, and for a moment he sobbed against my shoulder. Then the words came that chilled me to the bone. "I know it sounds silly, love, but I can't survive this without Eileen."

"Eileen will be home soon, Georgie. Maybe she'll be able to come and visit again. Or we can go on the tram to Coogee, if you feel well enough."

"What if she doesn't come back? Then what?"

"She'll come back," I said with a vehemence I didn't feel. Doubt was gnawing at me, and dread at losing two people I had loved so much, for so long. "It was just a bad dream, Georgie, wasn't it?" I pleaded. "We'll ask Nurse what news there is of Eileen, when she comes to dress your leg in the morning."

He nodded, like a little boy trying to please me. "Yes, ask in the morning," he said. "I'm sorry, Kathleen. I didn't mean to wake you. Go back to sleep. I'm alright now."

For a moment, I felt the old love flow through me, released from some icy prison in my heart. He kissed my forehead, leaving a smudge of cold sweat there, and reached over me to turn down the lamp. The sickly-sweet scent of fear wafted from the folds of his pajamas as he moved, but I wanted to show him I could respond to this moment of kindness and self-control he was creating. I slipped back under the covers and yawned.

"Good night, my love," he whispered.

"Good night, Georgie," I replied, reaching to hold his hand in the narrow space between us. I kept my body rigid so he couldn't feel me sob.

The next morning, Nurse Nell hung her brown cloak on the peg in the hallway, then followed me into the kitchen. "Good morning,

George." Her voice was cheerful, but her eyes were red-rimmed and tired. "How are you?"

George didn't reply, sitting silent and hunched over at the table.

"George has been fretting about Eileen being away." I knew he needed me to frame the question he could not. "He wanted to ask if you have had any news of her?"

An odd expression crossed Nell's face, draining away her usual professional demeanor. She collapsed into the nearest chair.

"Are you ill, Nell?" I stepped forward, concerned.

She shook her head. "No, no, I'm right as rain," she protested. "Just surprised by the question, that's all. You see, we had a telegram yesterday. Little Mother is very sick, and so far away."

George found his voice. "What's happened to Eileen?"

"Little Mother has had terrible pain in her heel. She had an X-ray, and the doctor said the bone was so infected it couldn't wait till she came home. She had an operation on her foot, in a hotel room in Bombay. It wasn't a success. She's been unconscious ever since. Father sent us the telegram and asked us to pray."

"Is she going to die?" George barked.

Nell flinched and pressed her hands to her mouth, shaking her head.

"She's been ill enough to be unconscious many times before. Even when she was a child, living in the house over the road," I said, trying to calm her. "She's always come good again."

Nell nodded and let her hands fall into her lap. "It's just hard, with her being so far away."

"Of course, it is," I soothed. "How about a nice cup of tea?"

"I can't," Nell said in a tone filled with familiar regret.

"I know. It's against the rules." I grinned at her.

"I'll tell you, when we hear any more news."

"Thank you. We'll be praying for her too."

"Thank you." She smiled bravely and opened her bag.

I poured hot water from the kettle into a basin as she prepared to change George's dressing.

"How did you know something was wrong?" she murmured.

"I saw her last night."

"A dream, he had a bad dream," I said, too quickly.

"It wasn't a dream," George protested, adamant. "It felt real."

Nell's brow knitted. "No, I don't think it was a dream, Georgie. One day, Little Mother said to one of the nurses, she'd had a busy night with her brother who was on the Western Front. Then, later, the nurse got a letter from her brother. He said he had seen her, in the trenches, on a night of terrible shelling."

The hairs stood up on my neck again. "Did she save him?"

"Yes, that's what he said. A few of our brothers say they've seen her on the Western Front."

Despair grew in the pit of my stomach. George had said he couldn't survive without Eileen. What if he was right, and it wasn't a dream? What if Eileen had come to say goodbye? What if George was right, and he wouldn't be able to manage without Eileen's comforting presence? Could things really get any worse?

* * *

Evie nestled into Georgie's lap, resting her curly head against his chest. He sat stiff and rigid, his injured leg stuck out at an angle, away from his body, to protect it from any sudden moves Evie might make. But his face was relaxed, and he smiled as he nuzzled into her brown hair, whispering some story from his own long-forgotten childhood to her.

I turned away from them, to wash the dishes in the ceramic bowl, one at a time, taking every care that I didn't bang any together.

"Tell me again, Daddy," Evie's voice chimed.

"Again?"

"Yes, the part about how the frog turned into a prince."

I checked over my shoulder. George was still smiling. His breathing seemed comfortable, it fluctuated – worse when he was anxious or ill, or if the air was cold or smoky. I sighed and went back to my dishes, enjoying the soft murmur of his voice telling Evie how the kiss of a princess could transform a frog.

"Can it really, Daddy?"

"I don't know, Princess."

"If I kissed a frog, what would happen?"

"You'd get slimy lips. And the frog would squirm and hop away, I reckon."

Her face screwed up in disgust. "Why?"

"Even a princess can't turn a frog into a prince, no matter how hard she tries."

"Why not?"

Curious, I watched his face as he thought up his next answer. His expression softened, then he replied, "Because only saints can do that."

"Do we know any saints?"

"Only one, and she's far away now."

The shadows were darkening under his eyes, so I took a step towards them, drying my hands on the dish towel. "I think Daddy might need a rest now, Evie. He's getting tired." I held out my arms and she slid off his lap obediently.

"She's alright, love." Georgie made a feeble protest. "She's a good kid."

I picked her up and hugged her. "Yes, she is. Do you want to help Granny with the washing? It's nice outside in the yard today."

Evie shook her head. "I'll help you."

I put her down beside me. "Now, be careful then. No banging things."

She stood very still, and I handed her the dish towel and a spoon to dry. Piece by piece, she meticulously dried the cutlery and laid it in the dresser drawer as if she was afraid to break it.

George returned to his silent state, staring off into space in his corner of the room. I wondered where his mind had gone. Perhaps it was better not to know.

Evie put away the last fork. I turned back to the washing up, yawning. I didn't notice her come back to my side until her hand darted up to take a cup. I stiffened, a little involuntary gesture. I never let her dry the china, just to be safe. She recoiled. The cup flew out of Evie's hands, it's blue and white pattern spinning as it revolved through the air in slow motion. Evie's face crumpled in horror, her mouth open in a wail. I leaped to catch the cup, my fingers stretching towards it, but it grazed my fingertips and crashed to the floor, erupting into a thousand splinters like shrapnel that shot around the room.

Evie's whimpering was drowned out by the screeching of chair legs across the floor, then the chair teetered over sideways, it's back passing a fraction of an inch from her skull before it clattered to a stop on the floor beside us. I grasped her to my chest, trying to soothe her, pressing her face against my shoulder to shield her from the terror in her father's eyes, and, worse, the terrifying absence in his gaze, the awful certainty that he was suddenly blind and deaf to us—to anything but the sights and sounds replaying in his own mind.

Mum rushed in from the yard, her apron hanging limp and heavy from water spilled from the wash. Her eyes wide and alert, she surveyed the kitchen then plucked Evie from my arms. "Come outside, there's a good girl. Mummy will want to clean up the floor, so you can't cut your little feet."

Once Evie was safe behind the closed door, I gingerly dropped to my knees amidst the broken porcelain, and peered uncertainly under the table, praying for inspiration on what to do next.

"Georgie?"

No reply; just his harsh, panting breath and the acrid reek of fear. I brushed away some broken china, then crawled in under the table and sat beside him. Fresh red blood was seeping into the blue and white flannel of his pajama leg. He must have dislodged the dressing in his scramble, ripping its stuckness off part of the wound and making it bleed. That's a good thing, I thought. Fresh bleeding is a good sign in a wound.

I wrapped my arms around my knees, and rocked, wondering how I could help.

"It's alright, Georgie. You're home now. See, I'm here with you, we're in the kitchen. Under the table, in the kitchen," I said, keeping my voice patient and quiet. Trying to call him back to the present. To me.

No response.

I waited. Minutes ticked by, yet the only sound was Georgie's breathing, labored as his panic upset the delicate state of his lungs. I tried to calm my respiration, slow my racing heartbeat, hoping somehow that would affect him, help him to calm his own. But it was hard enough to manage my visceral reactions, let alone his. A deep slow breath, and I wondered what Eileen would tell me to do. Taken ill in India and then confined to a hospital in faraway Melbourne for months on her return to Australia, I'd never missed her so much as I did in those long moments. Oh Eileen! Tears of desperation welling in my eyes, I turned inwards, searching for her whispered wisdom.

Give me a heart, able to love as you love. Help me to look after the poor and the sick, in my own home.

"Georgie, what can I do to help?"

Silence.

"Please …" Something in my pleading caused a reaction. A new dimension of horror and revulsion showed in his face as he turned unseeing eyes on me. I reached out a hand to touch his arm, but he recoiled, violently shaking his head.

Watch and pray. Watch with him in his loneliness, in his pain and sadness. Speak to him and comfort him. Watch and pray.

"Georgie, it's me, Kathleen. You're here in the kitchen with me, in Redfern, far away from the war now, Georgie. You're safe."

A clear, warbling voice rode the breeze through the window. "A-tishoo, a-tishoo, we all fall down." Evie had forgotten her shock and was singing in the yard.

For a moment, seeing myself and George huddled under the kitchen table, amidst scattered wreckage, almost made me laugh. But I swallowed that cynical humor back down, into the space where I hid all my other emotions. Evie kept singing, and George seemed to become calmer. After a minute, I slid my arm around his shoulders. He didn't resist.

"We all fall down." His lips moved in time with her refrain.

"Yes, we did," I said softly. "But we can get up again."

He looked at me as if he couldn't quite understand.

"Let's get up, shall we? Out from under the table."

He nodded.

"You wait there just a moment, and I'll straighten things up first."

He nodded again like an obedient child.

I shuffled out and picked up his chair, then took the broom and swept the shards away in case he cut himself. He'd been hurt enough.

"There. All done," I bent to look at his slumped form under the table and stuck my hand out to him. "I'll help you up."

I settled him in his chair and made him a mug of tea. Sitting beside him, I wondered what to say. I tried to hold his hand, but he withdrew it from reach.

"I could have killed her, too," he mumbled.

"Too?"

He shook his head. Thought for a moment, then started again. "The noise. Like a shell."

"That frightened you."

"The noise. You take cover from shells."

I just nodded. How could I even know what to begin to say to him?

"The noise. I thought I was back there again. I ducked for cover."

"Yes. Yes, you did."

He turned his eyes on me, locked me onto his gaze. I read the desperation and horror in them and was filled with dread. "I could have killed her. Evie. The chair. I forgot she was there. I …" Fat tears splashed down onto the table. "I think maybe the chair nearly hit her head."

I couldn't open my mouth to answer him.

"Did it, Kathleen? Did the chair nearly hit Evie's head?" His gaze was relentless, demanding an answer.

I nodded, a tiny nod, almost imperceptible.

He closed his eyes, the tears squeezed out under his lashes. I used to think his eyelashes were gorgeous. "I could have killed Evie. Not on purpose. I don't ever want to hurt any of you. But by accident. Because I can't control …" his shrug encompassed all of him, his body, his behavior, his shattered mind. "I can't control my reactions. And I could have killed her. She's too little. If the chair had hit her head, I could have killed her."

I had thought my heart was already broken, but I was wrong. "Oh Georgie. The chair missed her. You didn't hurt her."

"But I might have." His voice cut across mine, and I gave up. How could I reassure him? I knew he was right.

"Shit!" Alex pushed his phone away. "That's shell shock, right?"
Caitlin nodded.

"How's shell shock different from PTSD?"

"I don't know. Back in World War I, people weren't prepared for the psychological impact of the trauma of war. They thought it was cowardice or insubordination, and some soldiers were shot for cowardice, for refusing to go over the top.

"Shit."

"And then doctors thought an explosion nearby could damage the nervous system, that's why it got the name. But some soldiers got really weird symptoms, and the idea hysteria was involved grew up too."

"What do you mean by really weird?" He was too uncomfortable to sit still; trying to cover it up, he put the kettle on.

"Well, I watched some videos from a mental hospital. Some of their patients couldn't walk properly. Doctors classified the symptoms, gave them bizarre names like hysterical wire spring gait and hysterical dancing gait. They treated people with electric shocks and hypnosis, and they could walk normally again."

"Electric shocks? That sounds a bit barbaric."

Caitlin shrugged. "Hold on, I'll find the videos." She pulled her laptop towards them and turned it on. "Here we are. Look."

Their heads leaned close together as they watched grainy, silent footage of young men struggling to walk. Subtitles described the gait abnormalities and later announced treatment has been completed and the film showed the same young men walking normally. Then another title slide. A man, who was deaf to everything except the word "bombs", sat beside his hospital bed. A doctor was talking to him, but he was blank and unresponsive. Then the doctor said the word "bombs" and the unfortunate man flew out of his chair and cowered under the bed.

They turned away from the screen and looked at each other, stricken.

"I'd forgotten that one. He's just like George." Caitlin dropped her eyes and picked at her fingernails.

"It must be time to see what's next in the tin," Alex suggested, keen for a break from the tapes.

She pulled out a much-folded piece of paper and opened it out into a long strip of foxed beige. "I don't know what this is."

"It's a piece of streamer."

"Streamer?"

"You know, long paper streamers like you throw at parties."

"Oh, yes. Or passengers throw them off boats, to their families on the shore, seeing them off."

Alex fingered the paper as if the memories it held could pass through his skin. "If soldiers were throwing streamers back to shore, as their boat was departing, people would have kept pieces as souvenirs."

"This must be a souvenir of George's embarkation. Kathleen must have kept it. Maybe as a reminder of the bonds that tied them together."

"Maybe George kept one too, for the same reason."

Caitlin sighed and jiggled the string of her teabag. "But all the while they were being ripped apart by things they couldn't control." Alex flinched at the bitterness in her voice, but it was better than tears.

REDFERN — 1918

Evie climbed up from the chair onto the table and stood obediently in the white enamel basin. Georgie leaned forward in his chair and held a scrap of flannel over her eyes as I poured warm water over her head and lathered her hair with soap.

"You don't want soap getting in your eyes, do you?" he asked.

"No, Daddy, it stings." She pressed her lips together while I rinsed the soap from her hair.

"Step out now." Georgie held her little hands as she lifted her leg over the edge of the basin, so she couldn't slip, then wrapped her up in a towel and she giggled as he started drying her off. He patted her unruly hair down on her head and swung her off the table onto his good knee. The exertion made him cough, but she was used to that and waited patiently until he caught his breath again.

"I'm all clean now," she beamed.

"Yes, you are."

"When my hair is dry you can tie my nice ribbon."

"Yes, I can."

"Did you see my sore foot?" She wriggled a plump little foot out from under the folds of the towel and waved it at him. She had scraped a small patch of skin off the day before, running around in the yard.

His face drained of color, and he clutched at his chest. I stood paralyzed on the spot, as he sat in silent horror. Long seconds later, he turned desperate eyes on me and held the child out to me at arms' length.

"Dress it, Kathleen. Quick! Foot wounds can be dreadful."

Evie was frightened now, crying, and I caught her up into a hug. "It's alright, darling. Your foot is fine. It just reminded Daddy of some of the nasty things he's seen." Reggie Saunders down the street was discharged with trench foot, and was still in hospital months later from it, which meant I had some idea of the horrors George would have seen in the trenches. "It's alright, George. I used Lifebuoy Disinfectant soap, that will kill any germs. It's just a little scratch. She'll be fine."

But he wasn't listening. His eyes were blank, and he was chewing at his thumbnail. It was bleeding. Relief flooded me when Mum came in with a basket of laundry. I handed Evie, still sniffling, to her, and put both hands around George's wrist. I pulled his hand away from his mouth, despite his resistance.

"That'll be getting sore, love," I said, cradling his hand against my stomach. "Don't hurt yourself."

"She's so little. So little. So little," he said, over and over. And then he began to cry. I held him against my chest, as he sobbed, and the sobbing led to coughing. Powerless. All I could do was hold him and pray.

Mum dressed Evie and took her out into the yard.

"She's so little. So little. Something could happen to her."

"She's safe, Georgie."

"I could have hurt her."

"You won't hurt her, Georgie."

"With the chair. I could have killed her."

"You didn't hurt her." Fear and frustration meant I had to fight raising my voice, and instead filled it with steely determination. I pulled away from him and bent forward to look into his eyes. "Listen to me, George. *You did not hurt her.*"

"I could have hurt her. Could have hurt her. She's so little."

"George?"

Nothing. No response. His eyes were staring out into space and wherever his mind had gone, I couldn't reach him.

My hands were shaking as I picked up the basin of water and took it into the yard to pour onto Mum's apple tree.

"You alright, love?" she asked, her face worried.

"I don't know what to do, Mum. I can't help him."

Mum dipped a battered tin cup into a bag of wheat under the porch. "Can you feed the chickens for me, Evie?"

Evie took the cup, cradling it in both hands, and trotted towards the four red hens scratching under the tree. "Chookie, chookie, chookie," she called and sprinkled the wheat a few grains at a time to hens who were delighted by the unexpected treat.

Mum hugged me to her for a moment. "You're doing a great job, Kathleen. The best. It's hard. He's got his appointment at the Repatriation Hospital next week. You can talk to the doctor then."

I nodded. "I'll ask again. Maybe he will have something different to suggest now, because Georgie's nerves are getting worse."

"Maybe he could go into hospital for a while? Give you a rest and get some medical attention?"

"Oh Mum, I couldn't send him to hospital again. He gets more depressed there, and he dreads the place. He's paranoid that they'll take his leg off if he goes back into hospital. I can't do it to him."

I could see the unasked question in Mum's eyes.

"No. I can't send him to a lunatic asylum. I can't."

"I know, love. Maybe they can change his nerve medicine, then?"

"Maybe."

"And in the meantime, take a deep breath and put on your bravest smile, love. And go in there and give him a dose of his nerve medicine. That's a good girl."

I sucked my lips in, then maneuvered them into a sort of frozen smile.

"That's my girl." Mum gave me a reassuring pat on the shoulder, which also served as a gentle push in the direction of the kitchen door.

"Here we are, Georgie. It's pill time." I took a glass of water and his tablets to him. His eyes were still vacant, staring into space. "Georgie, love, take your tablets."

He blinked and obediently opened his mouth, and I popped the two little pills onto his tongue. He swallowed them down. "There, that'll help you feel better," I said, in the same tone the Brown Nurses used. "And how about a nice cup of tea?"

I poured hot water from the kettle, left on the wood stove, into the tea pot. Beside the kettle, the lid of a large pot jiggled as bursts of savory chicken-scented steam escaped into the kitchen. The bird had belonged to a neighbor. She kept hens for eggs, and when one succumbed to old age, she brought her to us. She's too tough to be of any use besides making broth, she said, and offered the scrawny, plucked carcass for me to make something nourishing for George. I'd offered to pay her for the bird, of course, but she'd drawn herself up very straight and retorted that it was the least she could do. She knew we'd help her if one of her sons came back injured, she said. And indeed, we would. But in the meantime, I was praying they would come back whole and healthy. Any time I wasn't talking, it seemed there was one long prayer of intercession running through my head, an ever-lengthening list of names of relatives, friends and neighbors who needed protection, healing, solace, or to find eternal peace in their final resting place. Special prayers for Georgie, and Eileen, who was still in Melbourne, not well enough to come home. Pleas for strength and patience and inspiration for me.

I glanced at the faded image of the Virgin Mary hanging on the wall, before pouring two cups of tea, one for me, one for George. I added cold water to his, so he couldn't burn himself if he spilled it, and spread dripping onto a piece of bread.

"Here you are, love. Keep your strength up." That forced cheeriness grated on my ear drums, but Georgie looked up with a forlorn smile.

"You're the one who needs to keep your strength up, my love. I don't want your health to suffer. I see you working day and night, nursing me, and raising Evie, and helping your Mum with her work, and cooking, and who knows what else. It's more than I can bear to watch."

"Oh Georgie!" My heart sank as I watched his face crumpling. "Please don't cry. I don't mind hard work. We're a family, love. We want to stay together."

I yearned to put my arms around him, bring him some comfort if I could. But he folded forwards, his head slumped on his arms, resting on the table. Shutting me out, as his shoulders heaved, and he fought for breath.

I sighed and spread dripping on another half slice of bread. Standing in the doorway, I held it out to Evie. "Here, have a picnic in the garden."

Evie ran up to me and took the bread.

"Mind the chickens don't pinch it," I cautioned her.

She scrambled up onto the woodpile, like a little monkey. "I'm the king of the castle," she declared. "They can't get to me now."

"Good idea." I turned back towards my husband, determined to make this moment normal, a cup of tea shared by a married couple, snatching a moment of peace while our daughter was busy outside. I sat at the table and smoothed my skirt across my knees. "George, I've been thinking." Could that cheery tone suffocate me one day, like a lump of cement slowly drying in my throat?

A tiny shrug of one shoulder was his only response. I ploughed on, regardless, eager to fill the silence in the kitchen with the sound of chatter.

"I thought maybe we could grow a couple of lavender bushes under Eileen's rose. We can get a few slips from Mrs. Chen's garden. She's offered me some before. And it'll look pretty against the pink flowers, when they come."

He shook his head. "One lavender, if you like it. But rosemary, Kathleen. Rosemary's for remembrance."

I swallowed the dryness that threatened to choke me. "Eileen will get better, George."

He coughed as if the lining of his lungs was tearing, then with a sheen of sweat on his forehead, insisted in a voice as weary as a graveyard, "These are times for remembrance, Kathleen. We have so many people to remember."

I thought I understood. "You're right, Georgie. I'll get a piece of that big rosemary bush that grows down the road, you know the one with the pale mauve flowers? It will look pretty with pink roses."

"We'd have to trim it, so it doesn't get too big."

"We can do that." I smiled. The thought even of having George standing on the front doorstep and issuing directions on where to prune it made my heart throb. The monthly visits to the Repatriation doctor were the only time he left the house. "And perhaps you'll feel up to visiting Eileen when she gets back. She might be needing to rest for a bit then, with her poor foot." No response. Deep breath. "Here you are, Georgie, won't you keep me company while I drink my tea?"

He shook himself, like a dog shaking off water, or a man shaking off secret horrors. His hand trembled as he reached for his cup, but I refused to notice it, just as he never seemed to notice I only ever gave him warm tea, never filled to the top of the cup.

He sipped his tea, then rubbed his lips with the back of his hand. "It's good tea," he said, as if searching for conversation.

"It's a new one. It's a blend of Ceylon and Indian and China tea." I kept talking, hoping the sound of my voice would hold his attention in the present, even if I couldn't think of anything interesting to say. "It's flavored with Orange Pekoe. I've never heard of that, have you?"

A gentle smile spread across his face. "Jacko was a grocer. Some nights when we were crouched in the trenches waiting to go over the top, you know nervous-like, or waiting for the Huns to start shelling, he'd talk about tea. He could have talked the hind leg off a donkey. I guess it was a special interest of his. Orange pekoe is a kind of black tea, from India and Ceylon. And it's named for the size of the leaves, not the variety."

I smiled back, enjoying an island of connection between us, in the ocean of distance. "It's not a special orange flavored variety then? I wondered why it doesn't taste citrusy."

"No, teas are graded by leaf size, that's all."

"I never knew that."

"You never needed to. You've only bought tea, not sold it."

For a moment, I thought we might chuckle together, but the levity passed. I tried again. "That's why Jacko knows his tea, then."

Georgie's jaw set and my stomach clenched in on itself, knowing I'd said the wrong thing. Cursing myself. His cup shook violently, spilling tea onto his trembling hands.

"Knew," he murmured, so softly I had to lean closer to hear him. "Knew his tea."

CAITLIN'S HOUSE, ADELAIDE

Alex stopped rubbing his face and took another chocolate. Caitlin removed the next item from the tin. "More letters ... Oh, hold on a minute."

"What is it?" Alex asked, his mouth still full.

"The tea expert. Jacko? Was that his name?"

"Hmm, I think so."

"Wasn't that the guy whose face got blown off?"

"Shit." He swallowed hard, as if he couldn't bear having the sweet in his mouth a moment longer. Turning to letters they had read previously, in their neat stack next to the tin, he rifled through them. "Yeah. Jacko. Poor bastard."

"I'll never feel the same way about a cup of tea again." She sighed, watched him put the letters back in order, then opened out the next few sheets of paper, which had been folded together.

> *My darling Kathleen,*
> *I was going frantic to get word from you. Six weeks with no letters. You have no idea how much it means to a bloke to get letters from home.*
>
> *And then today, they all came at once. Twelve letters from you, and six from your Mum. Three from your Dad, even. I can't decide whether to read them all at once or spread them out and just read one a day in case the mail is held up again.*
>
> *I even had a couple of letters from my Dad. He's trying to make light of it, but he doesn't sound well and his writing's shaky. I know he's really never been the*

*same since Mum died. He's in a sanitorium now, up in
Queensland. I'm very grateful your parents are so kind to
me. Be sure to give them my love.*

*How grown-up Evie must look now, with her hair
long enough for you to braid it. I hope there will be a photograph of her soon.*

*It's horribly muddy here. Lots of rain and starting to
get cold, but I am perfectly healthy, and you don't need to
worry. I wish this war would end tomorrow, so I could
come back home to you.*

Don't ever forget that I love you. Both of you.
Your devoted Georgie

She glanced at Alex, who was taking another chocolate. "He
doesn't sound himself, does he?"

"No. He sounds depressed. Closed off."

"Unreachable. That's how Kathleen described him, wasn't it, that
his mind was in a place she couldn't reach?"

"Maybe it was better that way."

"What do you mean?"

"That war was unbearable. If she knew what he'd been through,
how would it have helped her?"

Creases formed in Caitlin's forehead. "I see what you mean. There
was another letter folded in with this one."

"Okay, let's read it."

Dear Mum,
It's a miracle any of us are still here.

*Fritz is shelling us ferociously. A shell landed right in
our trench and a few of the lads were buried. We all used
our fingernails to dig them out. Two of them died, and
two more off to hospital. And last week there was a flying
duel. There've been a lot lately and our boys are getting
very good. They shot the German plane—must have been
in the petrol tank, because the plane caught fire. The two
Jerries jumped out of the plane to escape the flames.*

We stood, paralyzed, watching them plummet 6,000 feet to the ground. Their bodies were there one moment, and the next there was mincemeat splattering about. I will never forget the awful thud, if I live to be 100. Not that that seems likely at the present.

We had to drag what was left of them into the trench and search them for maps or plans or anything useful. Then we buried them, near our fallen comrades. United in death.

Kiss my girls for me, George

"You've got a point, Alex. Maybe it is better he didn't talk to Kathleen."

"I'm still shocked he's talking to her mother, though. Wouldn't he have wanted to spare her feelings?"

"What happened to his own family? He said his mother died."

"No idea. His dad was sent to a sanitorium. Maybe he had tuberculosis?"

"He had never been the same since his wife died, George said. And his hands were shaking. We know it couldn't have been shell shock, he didn't go to war."

"You're thinking he was an alcoholic?"

"I don't know. But it seems likely to me. Maybe Dad would know."

Tim paused on his way from the lounge to the bathroom. "What might I know?"

"What happened to George's parents?"

"Who?" He blinked, bleary-eyed.

"Kathleen's husband George, who served in World War I. What happened to his parents? He said in a letter that his mother died, and his father was in a sanitorium in Queensland."

"A sanitorium?" Tim laughed cynically. "Destitute asylum more likely."

"You know about him?"

"Not much. I asked Kathleen once, why her husband's folks hadn't stepped in to help her when she was widowed in the war."

"You talked to Kathleen about that?"

"Only a little." He hopped into the kitchen doorway. "I was a teenager at the time. Kathleen had said something about how lucky I was to have a family supporting me. That I should always remember to be grateful for that. I'd had a big row with my dad, you see. He wanted me to go to university. I couldn't see the point, what with the draft and everything. Anyway, I asked Kathleen, hadn't she always had her mum and dad to help her, when Evie was little? She said she had, but not everyone was so fortunate. She wished George had had parents that cared for him. That's all she said, then. But she said something else, a few years later."

The cousins leaned forward in their seats.

"I didn't know I was this interesting." Tim's voice was laced with sarcasm.

Alex pushed the chocolate box towards his shadowy, backlit form. "Have a chocolate, Uncle Tim, in exchange for telling us everything you know about George."

"You're a cheeky sod." His expression still severe, Tim nevertheless made his way to a chair and sat down, then focused on unwrapping a chocolate and put it in his mouth. "Payment in advance, because I don't know very much."

"Deal," said Alex. He winked at Caitlin. "They're Cait's chocolates anyway."

A chuckle emerged from somewhere deep in Tim's chest. "Okay, I knew my great-grandfather George went off to war just after my grandmother, Evie, was born. Kathleen never mentioned him much. But when I was in hospital after …" he waved his hand at his stump. "Well, of course, I lived in Sydney then, so Kathleen came to visit me in the hospital. Poor old girl, it wasn't long before she died. She took it hard. Seemed sort of freaked out. She sat and looked at the place my leg should have been and started to cry." He filled time by taking another chocolate. "I've earned another one?"

"Sure, Dad," Caitlin said breathlessly. "That must have been awful for you, having her cry like that."

"It was." He met her eyes. "She must have been eighty years old. You know, it was odd. She caught a taxi to the hospital. By herself, she didn't let Evie come with her. I always thought that was strange. Evie never let her out of her sight."

The two cousins exchanged a meaningful glance.

"What? What did I miss?"

"Sounds like she was hiding something," Caitlin said.

He snorted. "Do you want to speculate about stuff, or hear the rest of my story?"

Caitlin grinned. "I paid you an extra chocolate remember?"

Tim grinned back. "You know, you're starting to look healthy again. You've almost got some color back in your cheeks."

"This family history project is good for her, Uncle Tim."

Alex jumped with surprise when Tim patted his shoulder. "You two always were as thick as thieves when you were little. You're good company for her."

Feeling awkward, Alex dropped his gaze. "Thanks."

Tim's voice was firm, and a little too loud. "Look at me, boy." He waited till Alex turned towards him again. "I know it was a bloody accident. A drunk driver ran a red light. What happened to her isn't your fault."

Alex nodded once. "If I've learned anything in my life—and that's debatable—it's that guilt and blame only make things worse." Tim's eyes wandered towards the fridge.

"Cup of tea, Dad?" Caitlin suggested before he could make up his mind.

A quick frown, then Tim's face relaxed. "Yes, why not? It'll keep my head clear so I can finish this yarn."

"I'll do it, Cait." Alex was already up and putting three mugs on the bench, before Tim could change his mind. "What kind?"

"Peppermint for me, thanks," said Caitlin.

"Make it two, then. With a bit of cold water."

Tim fiddled with the string of his teabag for a moment before deciding it was still too hot. "Right, back to Kathleen. There she was, sitting beside me, frail as gossamer, as if a puff of wind could blow her over. Tears streaming down her cheeks. She hadn't been well. And she seemed to be living in the past, you know, like maybe she was a bit senile. I don't know how she talked Evie into letting her come and visit me alone. She said my injury reminded her of someone she knew in the war, who also got a leg wound. She told me she knew how hard it was, that things happened in wars that stayed in a man's mind for a long time. That it was natural I'd be having trouble adjusting. And then she changed; she became stern and seemed very strong. Just for a moment, it was as if she had grown bigger. I can still see her now, her brown eyes reflecting the fluorescent lights, her face was like an old-fashioned crab-apple, all wrinkled and flushed pink. She said she had learned something in her life, that made it possible to survive the impossible things that happen. She was going to tell it to me now, because it was important for me to know it."

"What did she say?" breathed Caitlin, her eyes rivetted on her father's unshaven face.

"Find something you believe in, that gives your life purpose, and never forget what it is. To fix that purpose so firmly in my mind, that whatever happened, I wouldn't forget it. Then it would guide my footsteps through darkness."

"Did you do that, Dad?"

Tim's eyes clouded over. "Yes, I did. I believed in your mother."

Her eyes filled with tears. "Oh, Dad."

Tim swallowed. "But we're getting off topic. She gave me something." He paused dramatically and the cousins leaned forward in their seats.

"What?"

"I think this is worth another chocolate."

Alex groaned but his eyes were smiling. He'd do anything he could to keep them connected. He pushed the chocolate tray further towards Tim. "The suspense is killing me."

Tim grinned, enjoying the attention. He took a chocolate but didn't unwrap it. "A photograph. In a frame ... of Evie."

"Evie?"

"As a little girl. Maybe two years old."

"Why?"

"She said she had hoped it would have been enough to get George through the war. And maybe it would help me."

Alex shook his head, confused. "To get George through the war?"

"Something like that. It didn't work."

"But George came home, Uncle Tim."

"No, he was killed. You just haven't found the details online yet."

"No, Dad. Kathleen talks about him on the tapes. He came home.

We knew something was wrong when we couldn't find his grave listed on Commonwealth War Graves. He came back in 1917."

"No kidding?"

Alex fixed his gaze levelly on his uncle. "No kidding."

Tim chewed his lip. "Well, I can see I've been missing a lot. I should stick around for a while. This is getting interesting."

Caitlin's voice was uncertain. "He had shell shock, Dad. And a leg wound. He was terrified he'd lose his leg."

Tim became morose. "I can understand why. Poor devil."

The atmosphere in the room became heavier as Tim sank into his own memories. Alex glanced around for inspiration, ignoring the chocolate box. "Do you happen to still have that photo?" he demanded suddenly.

"As a matter of fact, I do. It's on the tray table in the lounge. When you were talking about the family so much yesterday, I thought you might like to see it, so I hunted for it in the dresser. There's someone else in the photo. A woman, I never did find out who —"

Alex was out of the room before Tim finished speaking and returned with a faded sepia photograph in a simple silver frame. He handed it to Caitlin.

"Evie," she sighed, touching the plump little face with her index finger. "Oh look, she's got little braids. And Alex …" Her eyes were shining.

"It's Eileen," Alex agreed, blinking moisture out of his eyes.

"Is it? Kathleen's friend that you were telling me about?"

"Yes, it's Eileen." A smile lit Alex's face. "Look how tenderly she's put her arm around Evie's shoulders. Uncle Tim, do you mind if we take the photo out of the frame?"

Tim's eyes narrowed. "To see if anything is written on the back."

"Sure, why not?"

Caitlin was surprised to find her fingers trembling as she struggled to turn the tiny catches that held the back of the frame in place. She eased the backing board out of the frame and stared at the back of the photograph for a long moment, before swallowing and handing it to Alex.

Tim's eyes fixed on his nephew, cradling the opened frame in his hand, as if it were a sacred relic, making sure the glass front wasn't dislodged. Alex studied the spidery scrawl crammed onto the back of the photo, taking his time. He passed it to Tim who, despite not understanding the profound effect it was having on the others, despite his hands being large and rough, and his nails unkempt and grimy, held the little frame as if it were an injured baby bird, fragile and crushable.

He read it.

> *Dear Georgie,*
> *See what a lovely big girl you have to come home to!*
> *Here's a photograph of her with her hair in braids so you can see. We are sending you all our love and praying for you to come home to us soon.*

"What am I missing? Was this photo sent to George at the Western Front?"

Alex cleared his throat. "Must have been. We have just read a letter he wrote to Kathleen, saying he'd like a photo now that Evie's hair is long enough to put into braids. This must be the photo she sent him."

"That's some coincidence."

"No, Dad. There are no coincidences, not in this."

"What do you mean?"

"Eileen is in the photo, that's a sign. It can't be more than half an hour since we read the letter Georgie wrote, asking for a photo. And now we're looking at that same photo and discovering you had it here all along, Dad."

Tim looked skeptical. "That's getting weird, I'll grant you." He frowned. "Hold on, this photo was sent to the Western Front, but then it came all the way back to Kathleen?"

"Yes."

"You're sure George really did come home?"

"Yes, Kathleen is talking about it on the tapes now."

"She wasn't just telling a fairy story? Something to make Evie happy?"

"No, Tim. We found a record that confirms he was returned to Australia in 1917. But even if we hadn't, Kathleen made the tapes in 1974. When she was sick and in hospital. Evie was well past fairy stories then."

"1974?"

"Yes, the nurse states the year at the beginning of the first tape."

His voice was distant, thoughtful. "A lifetime ago …"

The cousins exchanged a worried glance.

"Uncle Tim, when did she give you the photo?"

He laughed. A strangled staccato sound. "1973. Not long after I got back from Vietnam."

"She must have got sick very soon after that."

"Bowel cancer. It was inoperable." He released his breath in a soft sighing gush and looked piercingly at Alex. "I always thought the shock of what happened to me was what killed her."

"Oh, Dad! She was over eighty years old. It wasn't you."

"I know that now, I guess." He half-smiled. "I've spent over forty years working out what I should feel guilty for, remember."

"Uncle Tim? Can you just go over what Kathleen said to you when she gave you the photo again? Please?"

Tim stiffened with his first impulse, to shrug off the question. But the earnestness in his nephew's young face, handsome despite its scars, was mirrored in the pale face of his daughter. He sighed as he let his guard down and repeated what he could recall. "She said she'd hoped it would have been enough to get George through the war. And something about maybe it would help me."

"Can you remember why she thought it would help you?"

"A photo of a little girl … maybe she thought that would represent the future? A time when maybe I would have a little girl of my own?" His voice trailed off in wonder and he stared at his daughter. "She couldn't have dreamed you up, could she?"

"I don't know, Dad." Caitlin smiled indulgently. "What else? Did she say anything about Eileen?"

"I don't remember anything about Eileen."

"Please think. Did she say anything about why the photo had someone other than Evie in it?"

"You know this was nearly fifty years ago, right?"

Her eyes were wide with excitement. "I know."

"All right, all right. Give me a moment." He closed his eyes and took a few breaths. "She was a practicing Catholic. She said she'd been praying to a saint for me."

"You're sure? A saint?"

He paused, before saying with growing certainty, "Yes. A saint."

"And Eileen's in the photo! She's the saint Kathleen was praying to for you." Her excitement drew the eyes of the two men, who watched her with slight concern.

"Don't get too excited, love," Tim cautioned.

"Don't you see? It's come full circle. A hundred years ago, Eileen was praying for George. Fifty years ago, Kathleen was praying to Eileen for you. Then she was seeing her in the hospital, when she was old and sick. And now, Eileen's back, in this family."

Alex rubbed his face nervously.

"Are you going to say I sound crazy again?" she demanded.

"No. But I don't know what it means."

"I don't know what it means either. But what if it's not weird? What if it's wonderful?" The light that shone in her eyes warmed Alex's heart and was strong enough to disperse their remaining private doubts.

"I've said it before, this family history thing is good for you," said Tim. "It lights you up."

"Literally," agreed Alex, with a hesitant grin. Returning to solid ground, he turned back to his uncle. "Would you like us to fill you in on George?"

"And his secret return from the war? And why he was removed from the family record? Yes, yes, I would."

"Cait warned you before. It's not a pretty story. Awful shell shock, a nasty physical wound," He turned his eyes on his uncle in mute appeal. "Things are looking grim for him, Uncle Tim. It's … kind of upsetting. And I think we're about to find out what really happened. If you don't want to listen to the tape with us, we can give you the gist after."

Alex saw Tim's initial defensiveness melt away in the face of his own genuine concern. "It's okay, son. I can take it." Tim settled back into his chair as Caitlin pushed across the photograph of George at the pyramids for him to look at while Alex summarized what they had learned thus far.

Unexpected panic dug its fingers into my chest, snatching at my heart. With no time for explanations, I stooped and swung Evie onto my hip. "I want to walk, Mum," she protested.

"Sorry, love," I panted. "We're just going to see how fast we can run home, see?"

My heart was pounding on the inside of my ribs as I flung the front door open and dropped Evie and the wicker basket full of shopping on the floor. In three flying steps I was in the kitchen. Empty. My eyes flickered around the walls, over George's empty chair. The back door was closed. And in the center of it, secured by a nail driven through it, was a piece of paper.

My feet felt like lead as I crossed the room, slowly, slowly, as time froze. I heard Evie shuffling in the hallway, not sure what to do. I heard my pulse crashing in my ears.

I couldn't understand why anyone would have nailed a note to the door. Drowning. Something was sucking me under water. Some demon from the undersea world, pulling me deeper and deeper. Somehow, I read the first words, in bold block letters.

KATHLEEN GET HELP

DO NOT COME INTO THE OUTHOUSE

I didn't stop to read the rest. I didn't stop for anything. I wrenched the door open and, on legs as wobbly as jelly snakes, I flew towards the outhouse, past the washing Mum had hung before doing her rounds to collect more.

The outhouse door was closed, and something was jamming it from inside.

Summoning strength I didn't know I had, I strained my shoulder against the timber, inching it open. The darkness behind the cracked door was too deep after the blazing sun in the yard. I couldn't see. A final grunting heave, and the door opened enough for me to get in. Sunlight followed me, and I saw him.

Like a madwoman, I threw my arms around George's hips, bracing his weight. A part of my mind was grateful that I had closed the kitchen door behind me, and Evie was too short to reach the latch. The sound of screaming filled my ears.

Neighbors, summoned by my noise. Arms around me, pulling me out of that confined, awful space. I resisted, desperate to take the strain off the rope around my husband's neck. He needed air. If we loosened the rope, he'd be able to breathe, wouldn't he? A man's arms, stronger than mine, took George's legs from me. Gentle, kind words, but I couldn't make out what they were. Couldn't ask him to repeat them because something had stopped working in my mind.

Women's arms now, forcibly turning my face away from the scene, drawing me inexorably away from my husband, with his hideous, swollen, purple face. They dragged me towards the house.

Someone was making tea. The smell of warming black leaves curled into my nostrils, and my stomach heaved. I jerked myself free of my friends and folded double, as the acrid taste of vomit filled my mouth, and gushed onto dirt made bare by chickens scratching.

CAITLIN'S HOUSE, ADELAIDE

Caitlin's crutches crashed against the doorframe. Rustling movement. Harsh retching noises. Alex and Tim exchanged a glance, uncertain who was the best person to follow Caitlin to the bathroom. Tim grunted as he heaved himself up from his seat and hurried down the hallway.

Balancing himself against the door frame he surveyed the scene. Caitlin was standing on one leg, clutching the edge of the sink, still retching. Careful not to bump her injured leg, Tim used the towel rail as support, and standing beside her, scooped her hair back with his free hand, just as vomit splattered into the sink.

Still in the kitchen, Alex frowned as he turned his attention to the latest folded letter Caitlin had taken out of the tin. She had untied its thin black ribbon and started to open it out before her precipitous escape. He picked it up, trying to understand. The back of the letter was rough. Torn corners of paper radiated out from a central hole. With one questioning finger he probed it, then turned the paper over and opened it out, holding it flat.

> KATHLEEN, GET HELP. DO NOT COME INTO THE
> OUTHOUSE.
> I can't control myself, Kathleen. I can't hold the pieces
> of my mind together. I'm so sorry.
> I cannot take the chance that I will do something that
> would hurt Evie. And what sort of a father am I? She'll
> be better off without me.
> And so will you. I can't bear to see you, exhausted

and worried every day. The toll this is taking on you is
unbearable.

You deserve much better than this. Than what I can
give you. Please forgive me for everything. I think it's best
that you and Evie forget about me.

I am setting you free. I will always love you.
Always, Georgie.

Alex buried his head on his arms. "This is getting pretty effed up," he mumbled to the tabletop.

In the bathroom, Caitlin wiped her mouth on the facecloth Tim handed her. Water spiraled down the drain, taking her stomach contents with it.

He handed her a cup. "Rinse your mouth, love."

"Thanks, Dad," she said, then gargled and spat.

He settled himself against the shower screen. "Feeling better?"

Nodding, Caitlin ran her free hand through her hair. She was not ready to let her thoughts go back to Kathleen, to Georgie. She started talking, expressing the first competing thought that popped into her head. "You know something, Dad? When girls go out drinking, they always say it's their best friends who hold their hair out of the way when they spew."

He waited, a slight frown creasing his brow. "How did you know to do that?"

A soft snorting outbreath. "Your mother."

"I didn't think she drank!"

He shook his head, a soft light in his eyes. The light that came, sometimes, when he thought of his wife. If he was sober. "She had the most awful morning sickness when she was pregnant with you. We had to take a bucket with us wherever we went, for months. Eventually she got into the habit of keeping her hair in a ponytail all the time. But even then, sometimes the end would get in the way. She had beautiful long hair. Just like yours."

Smiling sadly, she stretched to pat his arm. "Thanks, Dad."

His eyes searched her face. "What happened?"

"The letter. Georgie's suicide note. I think that's the next one from the tin."

"You didn't open it. How did you know?"

"There's a hole in it. Like a nail was hammered through it. I could feel the hole. Then … well, it all became a bit too real."

"I know how that goes." He stared at the frosted glass window.

"Are you okay with this, Dad?"

He rubbed his face then ran his hand through his hair. Just like Alex, Caitlin thought. I wonder why I didn't see that before.

"It's a bit of a shock. I never gave much thought to George. He was just a name I'd heard occasionally when I was a kid. Or maybe I'd think of him on ANZAC Day: another bloke in the family who'd done his bit in a war. And if I thought any more about it, it was what a shame it was he never came home. My grandmother never knew her Dad, that must have been tough."

"It's not fair."

"Nothing is fair when it comes to war." Businesslike now, Tim reached across the bathtub and opened the window, letting fresh air in to disperse the acid stench.

"You guys alright down there?" Alex's voice called their attention back to the kitchen, where the kettle was boiling again, as if steam and hot tea could hold back the events that overwhelmed them.

Caitlin smiled in answer to her father's unasked question then maneuvered into the hall. "Yes, we're fine."

"Good," he gave her a lopsided, uncertain grin. "I've got some peppermint tea on. It's good for the digestion."

"Thanks, cuz!"

"I read the note." He faced away as he poured steaming water onto teabags.

She waited for him to go on.

"I think you guessed what it was?"

"Yeah. Sorry. It was kind of a bit much."

"No need to apologize. It's distressing." He looked at them both, his cousin, her brown hair dampened with cold sweat at the temples. His uncle, silent and brooding, but different somehow. Alex couldn't place it. Until a spontaneous show of affection, and Tim reached out to take his daughter's hand. That's it, he realized. Uncle Tim was more present, accessible somehow. Like when you have been wondering what's in an overgrown garden, hidden behind a tall brick wall, then come across a place where the brickwork has begun to crumble, and you can peer through to the other side. Alex turned back to the mugs of tea, blinking hard, wondering. Maybe Cait was right. Maybe he did share some characteristics with George? He'd never had such a poetic thought before … "Umm, cold water anyone?" he asked, careful not to let his voice betray his emotions.

Feeling safe again, behind peppermint scented steam and a plate of shortbread biscuits, Alex stepped into the lead. He met in turn the two pairs of eyes fixed on him. "Are you both okay with this?"

"I am," Tim asserted, his demeanor calm and confident, then glanced at his daughter.

"Yes. I am too."

"Good. Is there anything you need to say? Or shall I read you George's note?" He rubbed his hand over his face.

Unexpectedly, Caitlin grinned. "You know, you two share that habit? Dad does that too."

"Do I?"

"You just did it in the bathroom."

"Maybe it runs in the family," Tim teased.

Maybe it runs in the family? wondered Alex. Maybe George did it too? He took a deep breath and ordered himself to stop imagining things. "I guess lots of things run in families …"

"Well, secrets and lies seem to run in this one," Tim said, his lips pressed thin. "It's high time we sorted them out."

"Not just secrets and lies, Dad. Don't forget, there's a saint in this story too."

"Humph. She wasn't a relative, was she? Our family has been lied to and keeping secrets for a hundred years. I'd like to get to the bottom of it. Read the note."

After he finished reading to them, Alex looked from one to the other. Both faces were sorrowful. But Alex could see they were alright. Caitlin had already guessed what was in the note, and was looking resigned, and Tim was staying in his seat, not heading for the fridge. He passed the paper to them, and they studied it in silence.

Tim looked deeply moved, his eyes downcast, keeping his reactions private. He shivered and gulped his tea. "Well, that's how the secret started, then. Poor George got PTSD and couldn't cope. Not surprising, in those days. The medics had no clue about it."

"He sounds like he was deeply depressed. He really thought they'd be better off without him …" She jiggled her teabag string. "How awful. Poor George."

"Poor everyone." Alex sighed. "I bet Kathleen had her own PTSD after that."

"I wouldn't be surprised," said Tim, shuddering as the haunted faces of widows of some of his fallen comrades surfaced from his memories. "And then there was Evie. Growing up without her father."

Caitlin nodded. "She was three years old in 1918. She wouldn't remember him much at all. Especially if everyone stopped talking about him, acted like they'd forgotten him, like he wanted them to do." She shuddered.

"It's awful. How Kathleen managed, I can't imagine. If he's not on the honor roll, I'm willing to bet she didn't get a war pension. Not for suicide." Tim sighed.

"That's not fair!" Caitlin articulated each word to emphasize her outrage.

"Fair doesn't come into it."

Caitlin folded the note back into thirds and tied the ribbon around it. Her eyes glazed over, as she became lost in thought for a few moments, then she cleared her throat.

"This story isn't just about secrets and lies, is it?"

Two faces turned to her, surprise flickering across them.

"This is an unconventional love story. On many levels."

Her audience waited, both unsure what to say.

"Eileen, a saint who dedicates her suffering to the service of others. Kathleen, who adores her as one of her oldest friends. George, who believes he might accidentally harm his daughter, and that he's a bad role model, and his family will be better off and safer without him. It's heart-breaking."

She watched the two men whose attention was rivetted on her. Almost grinned when they both rubbed their foreheads as if somehow that would clear their thoughts so they could follow her meaning.

"But it's not just heartbreaking, is it?" Her eyes were bright. "It's all about love. Not the *you'll love this chocolate biscuit* kind of love. Real love. Something from the soul."

I scrubbed my face, determined to remove every trace of vomit, then scrubbed my hands. Throwing off the steadying hands of neighbors, I ran up to my room. Making sure to grasp them with only my fingertips, so I didn't have to hold them in my hands, I pulled all the sheets and blankets off my bed. My marriage-bed. And dumped them on the floor. Tearing off my clothes, adding them to the pile on the bare floorboards. Standing naked, I shivered even though the weather was warm. I took my clean set of underclothes out of a drawer and dressed myself again. Ignored the gentle rapping on the door. The soft call, "Mrs. O'Grady, are you alright, love? Can I come in?" The alarmed sobbing coming from Evie, somewhere downstairs.

Still using my fingertips in a pincer grip, I bundled the clothes with the sheets and blanket, into an impromptu swag, and tied the corners. I picked it up and opened the door.

The neighbors' faces, crammed against the wall of the narrow passageway by the top of the stairs. Pale and anxious. Sympathetic.

"I have to wash all this," I said with quiet conviction, in a small voice that seemed to come from very far away. "I have to wash everything."

Another neighbor blocked the kitchen door. "I'll take those for you, dear," she said, her voice pinched and kind. "Don't go in there. Not just now. Evie's in the front room. She needs her Mum."

"Evie." My voice echoed empty in my ears, and I obediently handed over my bundle, entering the sitting room. Yet another neighbor was in there, sitting in Dad's armchair, cradling Evie on her knee. She rose and passed the child, worn out now with crying, into my arms. I squashed her to me tightly, rocking back and forward, pressing my nose into her hair. Breathing in the soapy, child scent of her. I sat down, still rocking.

In time she fell asleep on my shoulder. I rocked her, under the tired, sympathetic eyes of women I exchanged snatches of conversation with every day, whom I had known since childhood. Women who had seen my birth, my marriage, my motherhood. My widowhood.

Mum stumbled into the room and knelt at my side, folding her arms around me. "Oh, Kathleen!" Waylaid in the street by someone who was brave enough to tell her of the tragedy that had unfolded so suddenly, when we had all gone out and left Georgie alone. He must have had this all planned. How long for?

"Georgie's gone, Mum. Georgie's gone."

* * *

I looked into Eileen's eyes, which reflected the brightness of the sky, as we sat in the gardens at her house in Coogee, overlooking the deep blue sea. A soft breeze stirred the leaves of trees, and birds chattered amongst themselves. With Rags the dog bounding in close pursuit, Evie was crawling across the grass after a beetle. Time slowed down, stood still as the peace that always seemed to emanate from Eileen soothed me, body, mind, and soul. She reached to balance her delicate, pink teacup on the table beside her.

"I am glad you came." She smiled. Always smiled, no matter what.

"I am sad you were so ill when you got to Father McGrath in Bombay. We were all so dreadfully worried about you, needing those operations on your poor foot. How are you?" I only knew about the severe infection in the bones in Eileen's heels at first, but later, more worrying still, Cissie had confided her heart was badly damaged.

"The pain has been terrible." Her breathing betrayed her and revealed the effort it cost her to speak. "I'm putting the Home's affairs in order, Kathleen, because the pain is so bad, I don't think I can live much longer."

I studied her face, which had become more beautiful even as she became frailer, until I couldn't bear to look at her any longer and tore my eyes away.

My voice failed me. I didn't think she could live much longer either, but I couldn't imagine losing her. Her eyes were on me, but I still couldn't meet her gaze. I just nodded, to let her know I understood.

"I am sorry I was laid up in hospital in Melbourne for so long after I got back from India. This has been such an awful time for you. I've prayed very hard for you all, and for Georgie."

"Thank you," I mumbled, then hesitated. Eileen, of course, could read me like a book.

"What is it you want to tell me?"

"He knew you were sick, you know. Before we heard anything. He started having nightmares about you being ill. He was praying for you."

"That was kind of him." She held me in her steady gaze, a sad smile playing around her lips. "We were praying for each other. God always listens, but we cannot control how He answers our prayers."

She reached out her hand to take mine. It was so thin I could count the little bones of her wrist, clearly visible under her translucent skin. But her touch was like a lifeline to a drowning man, pulling me out of dangerous currents. Tears swam in my eyes but didn't spill over.

"Georgie was a good man, Kathleen. He truly loved you and Evie." Her eyes were still fixed on me, coaxing memories out of the recesses of my heart. "What did you love about him the most? Tell me about him."

I recoiled from the question. I didn't want to talk about George, about loving George. I was afraid it would hurt too much. But, as my gaze roamed over Eileen's face, soft with gentle encouragement, and the garden full of patterns of moving, leafy shadows and memories of long afternoons, the chatter in my mind eased. I breathed in air tinged with sunlight and relaxed just a little. How natural it suddenly seemed, to be talking of my lost love. "He was such fun, Eileen, he had such a gentle artistic side. And was willing to put aside his ambitions to make an honest living. The thing I loved most about him? It sounds silly, but that way he had of rubbing his face when he was thinking hard. As if he was clearing cobwebs away." I smiled in spite of myself, seeing his handsome, earnest face in my mind's eye. "Do you remember the time he stopped me from falling into the street and being hit by a car?"

She nodded. "That was before you started courting. He saved you then. And he looked out for you ever since."

Out of nowhere, bitterness erupted in my gorge. I swallowed hard. A voice in my head was screaming, *Well, he's not looking out for me now! He's left me all alone now. Me and Evie.*

"What was frightening him?"

"His nerves were bad, Eileen." I wrung my hands, unsure of how to continue.

"Bad nerves would never have made him leave you and Evie, Kathleen. We both know that." Her voice was soothing and gentle. It was like that old fable about how the wind once wagered he could snatch a cloak off a young man, but the more the wind blew, the harder the man held on to his cloak. The sun ended up winning the bet, because his gentle warmth persuaded the man to take his cloak off. And so it was with Eileen. Her patient kindness shone in her eyes, and I loosened my grip on the defenses I had built up around my heart. "Don't we?" she persevered.

I nodded helplessly. I told her about how he had reacted when Evie dropped the cup in the kitchen. "He never stopped worrying that something would happen, and he would accidentally hurt Evie. He couldn't get the idea out of his mind that the chair could have hit her."

"Poor George." Her voice filled my pause and encouraged me to keep talking.

"He left me a note. He said he couldn't bear the toll his illness was taking on me, how tired I was. And that he couldn't be a good father. And we'd be better off without him."

I studied Eileen's face, watching her eyes—shadowed, deep-set in their sockets—mist with tears, then clear again. "It would be different, wouldn't it, if there had been treatment that could help him get better?"

"There was nothing. The doctors gave him nerve pills, but they didn't help. And what would have happened to him if I'd sent him to a lunatic asylum? Should I have sent him, Eileen?"

Her sympathy hit me with a tangible force, like slapping the cheek of a woman in hysterics. "Of course not. He was a man, Kathleen. Not an animal to be locked up. He would never have been happy in an asylum, away from you."

"But would he have been alive?"

"Perhaps. Perhaps not. Nothing is certain, Kathleen. But it wouldn't have been a life that suited him. You knew it wouldn't. That's why you never sent him."

The knot of guilt in my guts loosened a fraction.

"It would have been different if there was treatment available," she repeated. "But there wasn't, was there?"

I shook my head, as despair threatened to swallow me.

"Well, if you accept there was no treatment available, that nothing could be done to help George get better ... Was there truth in the things that he said in the note?"

My eyes widened, as I allowed myself to feel the horror of George's situation, through his eyes. I nodded almost against my will. "I was exhausted, all the time. He'd wake up screaming several times a night. I'd try to soothe him. He'd hear a noise in the street, and dive under the table. I'd sit under there with him, till he could come out. I was struggling to help Mum with her washing work, because she was taking in more to help support us. And trying to look after Evie."

"And you never once complained, or wished Georgie wasn't there, did you?"

"No. How could I?" My cheeks burned hot. "I know I never wanted him to go, but he went to war because he believed it was the right thing to do. To protect women and children he never even knew. None of us knew what that would mean, or what it would do to him. They said it would be a short war. The men would come home heroes." I paused to check the emotions expressed on her face. She was as calm as ever, waiting for me to finish. I closed my eyes and took a breath as the next round of words came to my tongue. "I married Georgie because I loved him, and I meant my vows. For richer, for poorer. Well, I never expected riches, did I? Not that I ever expected to be living off Mum and Dad. In sickness and in health. I made those vows, but I had no idea what was coming. How could I?"

"You couldn't, none of us did." Her voice was very gentle. "But you made your vows, and you honored them, and you did everything you could for Georgie. We all know you did."

Her words sank into my understanding, like a sugar lump sinking into a bowl of congealed porridge, dissolving and adding its sweetness. "Are you sure?" I asked.

"I'm sure."

My shoulders lifted a little bit, and my back straightened. "I'm sure too." The words were out of my mouth before I could stop them. The initial thrill of surprise faded away as Eileen nodded encouragement. "There was nothing else I could have done."

"And?"

I frowned at the questioning look she gave me, uncertain what she was getting at.

"And was there anything you could have done differently?"

"I couldn't have sent him away to an asylum."

"No, definitely not."

"And even if I hadn't gone shopping while Mum was out, and Dad was at work …" My words were slow, matching my laboring thoughts. "He was waiting for an opportunity, wasn't he? Which means, even if I would have been there that day, he would have found another time. He had decided what he was going to do."

"Yes, I believe he had."

"Poor Georgie."

"Poor you, and Evie. Poor everyone." Eileen turned her head to look out over the distant ocean. "I'd like to pray. Would you like to join me?"

I nodded. What else could keep me going?

CAITLIN'S HOUSE, ADELAIDE

Caitlin wriggled in her chair, as if shifting her weight could ease the pressure in her mind. She glanced sideways at her father, worrying he would have found the tape confronting, searching for a light-hearted distraction. He rubbed his face then ran his fingers through his sparse gray hair. She grinned. "It does run in the family then."

"What does?" Tim's voice was sharp as his gaze snapped onto her, searching for meaning, wondering if she was thinking mental illness ran in the family.

"This." She rubbed her face with her hands and winked. "You and Alex and George."

"And you too, apparently." Alex picked up the mood of playfulness, aware of how protective she had always been of her dad. She frowned at him. "Just now. You did it just now, too."

She shook her head. "No, I was just copying you guys, demonstrating what I was talking about."

"Just copying us, hey, cuz? Well, we will be keeping a close eye on your mannerisms from now on, won't we, Uncle Tim?"

"I guess we will." A slow smile spread across his face and reached his eyes, which then drifted towards the clock. "What are you kids doing for dinner?"

"I've got some mince out to defrost. How about spaghetti?

"Spag bol? Awesome. I know how to make that. I'll play chef." Alex stood up, smiling.

"Thanks, Alex." Caitlin's smile was warm. "I still struggle with the stove."

Alex reached into the pantry and found two onions. He tossed them to his uncle. "Chop these."

Tim moved around the kitchen to get a knife and chopping board. He paused, then headed to the fridge. The cousins watched him. A collective sense of disappointment passed between them, then turned into curiosity as the rustling of plastic bags came from the vegetable crisper. Tim threw a bag of salad greens at Alex.

"I bought those a couple of days ago. I keep thinking we need to make a bit of effort to build Cait up again, with good healthy food. But I don't seem to get around to it." He sighed. "I need to try harder."

"We all do," agreed Alex, his own sense of guilt written on his face.

While frying mince and tomato sauce flavored the air, Caitlin set the table. "I wonder how it felt to pray with Eileen?" Her voice was low, inviting the others to think she was talking to herself, rather than asking for an answer.

"Is that meant to be a rhetorical question?" Alex rummaged in the fridge for salad dressing.

She shook her head. "I've never been religious."

"Me either." He watched her straighten the last place setting, to mathematical precision. Something in the vulnerable angle of her neck, the excess attention she gave to making sure the knife and fork were parallel and set at exact right angles to the table edge pushed him to continue. It was easier to confess while she wasn't looking at him. "I prayed for you, while you were in the ambulance."

Her head snapped round, and she fixed soft wide eyes on his face. "Did you?"

He nodded. "Yes, and when you were in the hospital."

A smile lit her eyes. "Thank you. That's nice."

Tim, hovering in the doorway, laughed mirthlessly. "Saw a lot of that in Nam. Men who never spent a day in church in their life, praying when they were scared or hurt. Like God is just someone you call on when you're in trouble but ignore the rest of the time."

Alex's cheeks flushed pink as he stirred the sauce with unnecessary vigor. He looked up as Caitlin reached across to pat his arm. Her face was full of sympathy, and her eyes showed him she understood through experience how Tim's harsh words made him feel. "I'm glad you care, Alex. About me, I mean." A whisper, hidden from her father by the fridge door.

He grinned at her. "You're my favorite cousin."

"I'm your only cousin," she laughed.

"No slacking off, just because you haven't got any competition. Dinner's ready."

They took their places around the table, helping themselves from the saucepan of spaghetti and the salad bowl. Tim's eyes caressed the food and the cousins, bent over the pasta in their bowls. We're eating a hearty dinner just like a real family, he thought, and for a moment he was too choked up to eat.

A few minutes later, Caitlin leaned across the table towards him, as he was forking spaghetti into his mouth. "What is it that makes people pray when things are tough, even if they don't normally?"

Tim paused, chewing with deliberation, and she relaxed back into her chair, knowing he was going to give her a thoughtful reply. "You know, I used to think a lot about this, once." He wiped the back of his hand across his mouth. "In the middle of the night in the jungle, when I couldn't sleep, and every noise of a bug would set my heart pounding. And I'd hear some of the boys mumbling to themselves, praying under their breath. And sometimes I'd even do it myself." His breath snorted softly through his nose. "And I'd wonder why. And there was no logical explanation that I could ever find. But I decided it was because humans want to pick and choose now. Once upon a time, you'd go to church and a priest would tell you what God was and how you were supposed to act around Him. Then we got a generation where people didn't want to be told what to think. They wanted to be independent and beholden to no one, not priests, not God, no one at all. The first generation where people questioned what God was, or if He was there at all."

Alex rested his chin into his hand, elbow braced on the tabletop.

Tim surveyed them both, and delivered a crooked grin that twisted his mouth, as if behind the humor there was something a little sinister. "You see, once you question whether God exists, it becomes tricky. You're not going to just take anyone's word for it anymore. Do you know what people could do next?"

"No," they answered in chorus.

Tim laughed, a short, cynical noise. "Neither did they. So, they just made up God. A God on their terms. The feminists were sick of a male God and went for the Goddess. And no one wanted a God that allowed bad things to happen, so they went for Love and Light. They forgot to look through the history books, that pretty much prove love and light are rare commodities on this planet." He waited for them to nod. "Now, I ask you, if you wanted to create a God on your own terms, with no reference to what God really is by nature, then would you create a God that helped you out every time you got your sorry self into a fix?"

"Well, yes. I guess I would," Alex ventured.

"And if you were creating a God to suit you, when you were lazing about by the pool, or doing things you knew in your bones were not the right things to do, you'd want God to clear off and leave you in peace, wouldn't you?"

Caitlin watched her father with wide eyes, remembering evenings when he and her mother would have conversations after dinner, when they thought she wasn't listening. "And you think that's what people did?"

Tim laughed again. Mirthless, but not malicious. He looked Caitlin straight in the eye. "Turn on the television or look up the news on the internet. That's all it takes to prove it, I reckon."

Alex twirled spaghetti round his fork. "You've got a point, Uncle Tim."

"In other words, what you're saying, Dad, is we have chosen a God of convenience?"

Tim threw back his head and roared with laughter. "Yes, that's it. The God of fast food from the drive thru. A burger and thick-shake when they're hungry. No substance. And no one *really* wants fries with that, do they, because they don't want to face the heat?"

Alex's fingers combed through his hair. "What's the alternative?"

Tim winked at him. "I've said my piece. You kids can figure it out."

"Do we stick to the food analogy?" Caitlin helped herself to more salad.

"If you want."

"Non-GMO," Alex grinned, indulging himself in the game of words. "No crap, no artificial stuff. No fake flavors. You need to know it's all real."

"Gluten free, fat free, sugar free, you'll love it," quipped Tim.

Giggling, Caitlin tapped her fork on her plate like a gavel. "The judge's verdict is that the world needs to be accountable to an organic

God, who is permanently present, but only takes note of you when you give permission, is very nourishing and comes with the proper nutritional information so everyone knows exactly what they are getting themselves into."

"Thank you, Judge Judy." Alex bowed to her.

Tim pushed aside his plate. "There's a match on the telly. Thanks for making dinner. That was pretty good."

Pleasure painted Alex's face pink right to his hairline. "You're welcome."

"Do you want to see what's next in the box, Dad?"

"Nah. Fill me in at half time." He paused at the fridge for a beer, thought the better of it, then disappeared down the hall.

"That's a different side of your father," Alex observed, his voice low, ensuring Tim couldn't overhear him before he got lost in his sports. "I didn't realize he was so smart and funny."

Caitlin turned shining eyes on him. "He stopped showing it when Mum died. He used to be like that a lot."

"Well, I never knew that. Here, I'll just do the dishes, you can look in the box if you like."

"I'll dry, then we'll look in the box together."

> *April 23, 1919*
> *My dearest Kathleen,*
>
> > *Sorry it's been so long.*
> >
> > *I was awfully proud of my nurses when they all chose to serve the sick poor who had Spanish influenza. We hastened to make caps and gowns and masks, and they worked day and night for two weeks. They saved many lives with their heroic care and sat and comforted the dying. But then five of the nurses fell ill, and we have had to quarantine them. We are looking after them ourselves.*
> >
> > *Poor Matron Hawkshaw died yesterday. We are terribly sad to lose her and so sorry for her family. Did you know that once when I was very ill, she sat up with me and held me in her arms almost the whole night?*
> >
> > *We couldn't even bring in a priest to give her the Last Rites, because of the quarantine.*

I don't know how we can ever replace her. I must
be acting Matron now. I am praying you and Evie are
spared the contagion.
Please pray for us. Eileen

"And after everything else, the Spanish flu." Alex frowned.

"It was horrible. A global pandemic that killed millions of people. It started at the end of the war, and then spread as the troops came home."

"Oh yes. Didn't it kill more people than the war?"

"I don't know how they can be certain of numbers. But yes, I've read that." She nodded in considered agreement.

"And those nurses went into the homes of people who had it, to help them as best they could. Even though there were no antibiotics or anything in those days?" His eyes were full of admiration.

"Funny isn't it, how history overlooks that kind of heroism?"

He shrugged. "I guess it's not as dashing as the hapless diggers going over the top to be mown down by machine guns?"

"It's not just the story people have made up about God that's crazy, is it? It's everything."

"What do you mean?"

"Building a national identity around a terrible defeat at Gallipoli. Ignoring the self-sacrifice and courage of nurses and doctors going out to look after people with contagious diseases. And it wouldn't have just been them. I'm sure family members and neighbors must have risked themselves to help others too."

"Yes, I expect you're right. I suppose, no matter how crazy things get, people are often kind and compassionate to each other aren't they?"

"Hmm. Humans are a very complicated species."

Alex reached for his phone. "Saves us from being boring, I guess. Let's see how much more disaster we can get through before bed."

"It's as if nature had turned her back on us, Kathleen," my neighbor said bitterly, over the fence as I put out Mum's latest load of washing.

I wasn't paying much attention. I just went through the motions in those days, but she was lonely and didn't need any encouragement to keep talking.

"As if it wasn't enough, getting through four years of war. Our men away, and us having to manage everything and try and make ends meet as best we could. Women like you, being mother and father both, to your kids. And then the men coming back injured, or not coming back at all. Bringing back the Spanish flu with them, and now everyone's getting sick. And Enid's Dennis. Did you hear about him?"

I shook my head and mumbled something noncommittal.

"Got through the war unscathed and was waiting to be sent home. Poor Enid, my sister up in Mount Isa, you know, she was that relieved to know the war was over. She couldn't understand how it could be taking so long to get the boys home, but it's a big job for General Monash to organize, getting thousands and thousands of them back home where they belong, isn't it, what with all the shipping shortages? And of course, the injured ones had to come first. She got a telegram last week. Poor Denny died of the influenza; would you believe it? When he should have been on his way home to his mother. He was poorly for two days and then dead the next." A shuddering breath wracked her stooped body, and she wiped the tears from her face.

I sighed, trying to somehow look sympathetic and yet not to listen to her words. Poor Mrs. Caulfield was never quite right after losing her two sons in the war. She'd often just sit on her front verandah, rocking herself, with tears streaming down her leathery cheeks. I felt sorry for her, as much as I could feel sorry for anyone other than myself.

She was talking about "poor George" now, and I began feverishly repeating prayers and stories in my head, anything at all that would help me block out whatever she was saying. After a few minutes' monologue, she raised her voice a notch. "The Brown Nurses, are you listening, dear? The Brown Nurses are out nursing again. Heroes, they are, walking into deadly danger, day and night. They had planned to take more time off, to recover, after the nurses caught the influenza. And poor Matron Hawkshaw died, such a tragic loss. But they couldn't keep saying no to people who were crying out for help, could they?"

"No, they couldn't," I said sincerely. "They never could see a need without trying to help. Would you like to come in for a nice cup of tea when I've finished the washing?"

"Oh no, thank you, dear. Not while there's all these germs about. The government's closed all the schools and churches and theatres, you know. And I'd feel like I was breaking the law, coming round to your house and not wearing my mask like the government says to do in public."

"I'm not the public," I protested with a weak smile.

"True enough." She laughed, a short, jarring guffaw, cut off too soon. "But I can't drink tea through a mask, dear. And just in case, I'd rather not come over, in case I can pass a germ on to Evie."

Hearing her name, Evie, now four, looked up from the little piles of rocks she was building in the dirt.

"She's a bonny little girl, Kathleen. She looks like you, but she's got poor Georgie's eyes, hasn't she? I suppose she's forgotten her Daddy already. Though it's a blessing, maybe, if she has."

Tears I had worked hard to dam up, spilled down my cheeks, and I clutched Evie to my heart.

"Oh, there now, I've gone and put my foot in it, haven't I? And there I was just trying to bring you a bit of comfort. But there's cold comfort for people like us, eh?" She turned away morosely and shuffled to her back door. Her husband was sitting there, on an ancient kitchen chair, an empty pipe in his hand. I watched as his vacant eyes followed his wife's movements. He took a battered tweed cap off his head and waved it at me. Or maybe he was shooing flies away from his face, it was impossible to tell. His lips parted, and he gripped his pipe between his three front teeth, then jammed his cap back on, covering the few stray strands of hair left on his shiny pate.

Broken, I thought. Quite broken. Five years ago, before the war, they were an energetic, hard-working couple, not much past middle age. Two strapping tall sons, they had, working in the local factories. A daughter, Margie, who became a nurse. Looking forward to seeing them getting married and becoming grandparents. The boys never came back, of course, and Margie died of the flu, in the first wave in April 1919. Mr. and Mrs. Caulfield said they had nothing left to live for and looked like they had aged at least twenty years since 1914.

I carried Evie indoors and sat her on my lap. Her warm body snuggled into me, and her curls tickled my nose as I murmured a fairy-tale into her hair.

Mum came in and swung the heavy washing basket onto the table. She reached behind her head and untied her mask. "You alright, love?"

"Yes, Mum."

Her gaze took in my red eyes and slumped shoulders, but she turned on a brave smile, and said, "That's my girl. Let's put on a good show for your dad when he gets home. He's working that hard at the moment, I don't want him worrying about us too."

I nodded.

"Can't risk him getting overstrained and having an accident in the foundry. It's tough enough already, with so many men off sick."

"I know. Don't worry, Mum, I'll hold it together when Dad gets home."

Her eyes were sad as she studied my face.

My cheeks flamed red, and I defended myself from the guilt I felt at showing my weakness. "It was poor Mrs. Caulfield. She was talking over the fence."

Mum's neck stiffened and she was about to speak, perhaps say something about how she wished people would keep their noses out of other people's business, but I continued, cutting her off. "They're not doing very well, Mum. And now her nephew has died overseas, of Spanish flu, waiting to get home."

Mum moaned, a weary, sympathetic sound. "Is there no end to people's suffering?"

The image of Mr. Caulfield's almost toothless mouth gripping the stem of an empty pipe floated in front of my face. "We need to do something to help them."

"It'll take more than us to fix them, lass. But we can take them a pot of stew tonight, and I'll see if she needs any shopping brought in."

"I think they are going senile, Mum. I think I might ask the Nurses to call in on them, after this flu passes."

"That's a good idea. We're already taking in such a lot of washing, maybe we can do some of theirs, the heavy things?"

"She won't take charity, Mum."

"No, she won't, but we can outsmart her." Mum winked at me and for a moment I forgot the hole in my chest where my heart used to be, and smiled at her, like a conspirator.

She dropped the shirts she was separating from the sheets, and I was surprised when she put her arms around me, hugging me, and Evie, who was still on my lap, half asleep. "Oh, Kathleen, love, it does my heart good to see you smile," she murmured in a strangled little voice. Then, she pulled away. "What are we thinking? All this emotion won't get the work done." But her eyes were still warm and smiley as she fixed them on me. A wave of gratitude washed over me, and I kissed Evie's little head.

"Sleepy, darling?"

Her curls bounced as she nodded, and I carried her to the pile of cushions in the corner and stooped to lay her down. "You have a nice little sleep, my darling, while I help your grandma with the washing." I handed her rag doll to her, and she tucked it under her arm, before nestling into the cushions.

"I can't thank you and Dad enough for everything," I said.

Mum looked up, startled, and I kept talking, while I had the courage and self-control. "What you've done for me and Evie. Taking us in. We couldn't have managed without you, Mum. And what you did for George." I let my voice trail away, but I kept my eyes steady and didn't let my lips tremble.

"That's what families are for," she said sternly. "We stick together."

I nodded, and, nervous as a schoolgirl giving an address at assembly, I said, "And we love each other, Mum."

"Of course, we do, my girl. Of course, we do." She kept her eyes on her sorting, but I could tell she was pleased from the soft pink that flushed her cheeks.

CAITLIN'S HOUSE, ADELAIDE

"Soldiers were dying of influenza before they got home from serving overseas?" A look of horror was on Alex's face.

Caitlin nodded, her gray eyes serious.

"Let me get this straight. A family would be here in Australia, would have celebrated the end of the war and thought thank God their son survived, only to have him die of *the flu*?"

"Yes."

"That's bullshit!" He spat the words out.

"Yes, I've read letters from the time, about exactly that. Some soldiers even died on the boats back from Europe. Of influenza, or of wounds."

"And their families were excited they were coming home at last, and then ..."

Caitlin's eyes were sad. "Yes."

"Shit."

"I know." Her voice was low and thoughtful. "Do you know, Alex, when I was studying World War I, it was just horrible. *Free Trip to Europe* posters to get recruits to join up. The trenches, trench foot. The gas. That the gas would blow into villages and kill all the civilians, if the wind changed. The unimaginable scale of suffering. I used to keep thinking *I can't believe this happened.*"

He looked shocked, then amused. "But it did, Cait. It happened."

"I know. I know it happened. I just couldn't believe anyone would allow something so awful to happen. It does my head in."

"Ah, that I can relate to. The sheer scale of misery would do anyone's head in."

She sighed, then grinned. "So, I'm not nuts, then?"

"I didn't say that. You're still nuts. But nice." His eyes met hers, and for a moment they let their gazes lock on their shared smiles.

She gently punched his arm. "Thanks a lot."

His tone was serious again. "Cait?"

"Yes?"

"I agree with Kathleen's mum, you know. Families should stick together. You and me."

Her heart melted. "Aw, you're the best cousin ever."

"I mean it."

"I know. I mean it too." She squeezed his arm. "Thanks."

"Enough mush!" He gently pulled his arm out of her grasp. "What's next in the box?"

"Another photograph." Caitlin laid it on the table between them. An old-fashioned, white-canopied bed dominated a room full of plants and flowers. A diminutive figure with long hair and a big smile was propped up askew on a pile of pillows behind an Overway table covered in books and papers. "Eileen."

"I was wondering how she ever managed to be matron." Alex pored over the sepia image. "Is this how? Propped up in bed with all the paperwork and administrative tasks?"

"She was special, wasn't she?"

"Absolutely. I wonder if she really was a saint?"

Caitlin studied the photograph again. "Well, when I look at her, I get the feeling she might be."

"Why?"

"I can't explain it. Just a feeling."

"Can I google her yet?"

"No. Absolutely not, Alex. That'd be breaking the rules."

"Oh, come on, we said we'd get this done this weekend. It's 9:00 pm and we still have stuff on the tapes to listen to. Can't we take a shortcut?"

"No." Her voice was stern, but her eyes twinkled.

"I won't be able to sleep till I know."

"Excellent! We can stay up late if we have to." She rubbed her hands together. "Let's crack on, then. Have you got uni tomorrow?"

"No ... but I'm supposed to be doing an assignment."

"Yes, family history, right?"

"You're incorrigible."

"That's the nicest thing anyone's ever said to me."

* * *

Tim, who had been to the bathroom during a commercial break, crept to the kitchen doorway to enjoy their banter without intruding. It seemed like a long time since there was laughter in the house, and he suddenly realized he'd been missing it. I must tell Alex I've enjoyed him being here, he thought. He decided against getting another beer from the fridge, telling himself he didn't want to let them know he'd been eavesdropping, but at the back of his mind, he wondered if maybe he'd drunk enough today. And then, even though his game was playing on the television again, and he didn't want a beer, he found himself drawn into the kitchen.

"I thought you could give me a quick update, seeing as I'm backing a losing horse in there," he said, trying to sound nonchalant.

The undisguised pleasure on the young faces turned towards him caught him by surprise. He dropped his gaze, focusing on the chair he pulled towards him to hide the shame that burned in his cheeks. He felt blessed to have the love of his daughter, even though he feared he was unworthy of it. But the respect he saw in Alex's eyes, that was new; Tim wondered what he'd done to earn it.

COOGEE–APRIL 1920

The sunshine was warm and bright, as Mum took Evie's hand. "We'll play for a while, Kathleen, and give you some peace," she said, leading my growing daughter into the dappled shade under the trees behind Eileen's house at Coogee. I paused, watching them as Mum hid her eyes with her hands and started to count, and Evie scurried into the shrubbery to find her favorite hiding place. I smiled; Mum would play along and look everywhere except the spot her five-year-old granddaughter always chose. Rags, turned out of Eileen's sick room, was jumping around in the garden bed, joyous to be part of the game.

My eyes drifted over the view, down the hillside to the rich blue ocean below us. Taking a steadying breath, I rapped softly on the screen door of the verandah, and let myself in. The nurses were all on duty, so the enclosed verandah was empty, and I tiptoed my way towards Eileen's bedroom, in case she was asleep.

Cissie McLaughlin, her beautiful face strained and tired, emerged through a doorway, her arms full of fresh linen. She smiled. "You've come at a good time. Little Mother is awake and about to have some tea. Come on in." She lay the linen on a nearby table and straightened her crisp white apron.

"How is she?" I asked, my voice quiet, my stomach clenching into knots of worry.

The familiar conflicting emotions crossed Cissie's face, professional reticence at sharing a patient's confidential information, trust in knowing that I was one of Eileen's oldest friends and would not divulge anything she said, and the sweeping relief of being able to confide in someone.

Sorrow clouded her eyes as she half-whispered, "Her back is very bad, and the doctor is very worried about her heart. She has fevers and she can hardly manage out of bed now. She suffers dreadfully with the pain."

I squeezed her arm to show my sympathy. "It must be very hard for you to watch."

Cissie summoned a brave smile, even though for a moment, tears shimmered in her eyes. "She has been terribly ill before and recovered. But I don't know how much longer she can go on." She dropped her voice even lower and pressed her mouth close to my ear. "She spends time every day writing instructions and getting her affairs in order. She's asked me to take over running the Foundation for her."

I hugged Cissie quickly, knowing she was too reserved for a long embrace, then nodded. She had prepared me. I was ready to go in.

"How happy I am that you are here." Eileen's smile lit up her face, even though her eyes were shadowed by dark circles. Her voice was gentle and quiet.

"I'm pleased to be here." I couldn't help smiling broadly in return, even though my heart felt leaden, as, in seeing her for myself, I knew that Cissie was right. Eileen's frailness was undeniable; it frightened me now.

Her mind was clear, however, and she demanded, "Where's Evie?"

"She's playing hide and seek with Mum, in the garden."

"I'd like to see her, before you go."

"Of course."

Cissie came back with a well-stocked tray and began to pour tea into pretty china cups. "Will you eat something, Little Mother? I've made some sandwiches and there's a nice Victoria sponge."

Eileen shook her head. Once, she would have laughed off suggestions of eating to lighten the mood when we worried about her lack of appetite. But the inflamed abscess on her spine was too terrible now, the merest movement made the pain unbearable and Eileen, lover of laughter and mischief, could laugh no more. "Just tea, Cissie dear. I'm not hungry. Save the cake for Evie."

Cissie's frown, though she averted her face from both of us as she picked up a cup and saucer, was enough to make it clear Eileen was barely eating now. I took the cup and sipped hot tea, to cover my silence, as I couldn't think of anything to say.

"No long faces." Eileen's scolding was mild. "Do you remember how you used to read to me, when we were children, and I was feeling poorly?"

"Of course, I do." The memory of quiet companionship in the house across the street brought a nostalgic smile to my lips. "They were happy days. Would you like me to read to you now?" I looked around to see if she had a book nearby.

"After tea. But first, tell me your news."

I had learned long ago it was best to have a few stories to hand, when visiting the sick or the bereaved, because sympathy and emotion can make small talk almost impossible. I told her a story about how Evie had built a little house out of rocks and pieces of a wooden crate, and made Dad take her to Centennial Park to catch lizards. Two little skinks were carried home with tender care, in a jam tin lined with grass. How she had lain on the ground watching the lizards settle into their new house and later wept when they escaped. How fortunate it was that Dad was in the yard, chopping firewood for the stove, and could hold the chickens at bay just long enough for the lizards to escape under the fence, preventing Evie's new pets from being eaten alive.

Eileen smiled, but she was looking tired. Cissie put down her tea-cup, and rearranged Eileen's pillows, before leaving the room.

"Did you see my portrait?"

"No. What portrait?"

"I had a painting done and presented it to the nurses. Something to lift their spirits, after I have gone." Her tone was matter of fact. "They will miss me terribly, Kathleen. I must prepare them, as best I can."

Admiration filled me as I gazed into her calm, drawn, little face. "You are very brave."

"Brave? No, not brave. Mother Mary gives me strength. I have tried so very hard to get better, to be able to stay and guide the Work with the poor. But I think, perhaps, the best thing I can do now is make sure I leave instructions on how it is to continue, after I have gone."

"Is there anything I can do to help?"

"Be a friend to the Nurses."

"Always. Anything else?"

"Be reading to me when Cissie comes back in; I don't want her to worry."

I picked up the novel lying beside her bed and held it ready. When Cissie came back in, Eileen turned to her. "Show Kathleen the painting, will you, Cissie dear? I'd like her to see it. And then she will bring Evie in to see me."

"Of course."

"Oh my, it's wonderful," I breathed, staring at the large portrait hanging on the wall in the hallway, where the nurses would pass it many times a day. Serene and beautiful, Eileen was sitting up on a sofa, her calm focus looking straight ahead. Her long hands were held folded in her lap. The folds of a pale-blue, silk and lace skirt hid her fragile, stick-like legs, and her toes were pointed in blue, silk ballet slippers. A vase of pink and white roses in the corner, a few fallen petals speaking the old language of flowers, reminded us life is fleeting.

Cissie was watching me, as if she were waiting for me to say something more. "It's a beautiful gift to you Nurses," I said. "She'll still be watching over you in a hundred years."

Cissie nodded and dropped her gaze. "She's making all the arrangements necessary. Writing and dictating letters for hours, some that we are to post after her death. She's never given up hope that, one day, we will become an order of nuns."

I studied the painting again, my eyes resting on the ring gleaming on the ring finger of Eileen's left hand, the only possible allusion to her aspirations to be a nun. The rest of the picture was deliberately secular, no religious images, no bible, no crosses. How astute she was. I remembered the story about when one of the city's top lawyers came to see her on business, thinking to offer her his professional advice, based on years of experience. When he left, humbled, he admitted Eileen had told him what to do. I smiled again. She might have been too sick to attend much school, too ill to leave her bed for years, and only three feet ten inches tall, but the lawyer wasn't the only man to meet his match in her. "I'm certain it will happen, Cissie. She'll make sure of it."

"And so will I," she said, determined.

"You will make a wonderful Mother General, Cissie. The best."

Cissie smiled bravely. "There's a lot of water to go under the bridge before that happens."

"That's true. You check Eileen's comfortable. I'll just go and get Evie and then we'll leave her to rest."

"Yes, that's best. She tires easily. You'd better bring that dog of hers in with you."

"Do you like him a little better now?"

"He scares the life out of me, jumping up on her all the time. But he never seems to hurt her, I don't know how. The muddy footprints on everything drive me up the wall." She tried to sound harsh, but couldn't pull it off, and the corner of her mouth twitched into an indulgent grin. "He loves her, and she loves him. I found him licking her hand in the middle of the night, when she was in terrible pain, trying to comfort her." She sighed. "I guess I became his latest conquest."

"Dear old Rags," I laughed. "He's won you over at last."

Evie squealed and bounded across the lawn when she saw me, Rags in hot pursuit. "Come on in, Eileen wants to see you." I held the door open for her and the dog, and for Mum, who moved at a more sedate pace, then took Evie's hand.

"I know the way," she protested, pulling at my arm.

"I know you do, sweetheart. But we need to be quiet, remember, in case Eileen's fallen asleep."

The child frowned. "She's not feeling very well, Mummy?"

"No, she's not."

"She'll feel better when she goes to live with God." Her blue eyes—George's eyes—were wide and serious. For a moment, I didn't know what to say.

Mum stepped in, "Yes, indeed she will, Evie. There's no pain in heaven." She exchanged a poignant look with me, and we slipped into Eileen's room, in time to see Rags bound onto the bed, leaving muddy footprints and a few moldering leaves, and start licking her face. His mistress smiled and patted his head.

Cissie looked horrified, then turned to me and we laughed, subdued, but enjoying the spectacle.

Once Rags had lain down at her side, Eileen beckoned to Evie, who, despite the light-hearted scene on the bed, was half-hiding behind my skirt. Eileen's serene demeanor always inspired quiet awe in children. But Evie was comfortable with her and slipped out from behind me to walk to the bed. She was too short to see over the top of the mattress, and Mum picked her up. Eileen patted the bed beside her, and Evie settled there, careful not to bump her. Like a blessing, Eileen laid a thin hand on Evie's head, and like magic, the child sat still for a minute or two, as if mesmerized.

Then she smiled and held her plump little arms out for Mum to lift her down. Mum and I kissed Eileen's cheek in farewell.

That was the last time I spoke with Eileen alone. As her health deteriorated, I visited often, but word of her precarious state spread, and more and more of her friends, patients and admirers queued to visit her. Sometimes, she would be industrious, writing letters and instructions, fiercely determined to do everything humanly possible to pave the way forward for the nurses she knew she would leave behind. Sometimes, she would be resting, too ill to work, almost too ill to know visitors had come. And sometimes, we would be turned away by sorrowing nurses, who could merely shake their heads to let us know, no, not today. Eileen can't see anyone today.

Her room had the profound silence of a cathedral. We would sit or stand, and pray, and watch her labored breathing. Often, she would reach out and touch us. But she was generally unable to speak. Sometimes, she seemed unable to see us, as her affliction blinded her.

COOGEE – OCTOBER 1920

Evie gripped my hand in a tiny vice, feeling nervous in the milling queue of people that stretched across the lawn in front of Eileen's house. The chubby fingers of her other hand clutched a posy of flowers from our garden, a full-blown rose from the bush Eileen had given us a few years before, sprigs of lavender and rosemary, beginning to wilt in the warm sunshine.

Snatches of conversation rippled up and down the line, that I heard without meaning to listen.

"She's quite unconscious."

"At least she's out of pain, then, bless her."

"Doctor Reddall has been this morning. He gave her twenty-four hours."

"Thank goodness I'm here, then! One last chance to see her."

"She's not eaten anything for days. Just ice cubes and a little milky coffee, but she vomits that back up."

"She's blind now, poor love."

"What a shame, that surgery for her bladder stone didn't help her. It was such a big operation, but it just caused extra suffering."

We inched our way closer to the house, and, as we got near, everyone fell silent, and we were all craning our necks to get a glimpse of her through the door of her room. She was propped up on a couch. She couldn't lie in bed any longer, whether through the agonizing pain in her back, or shortness of breath, I didn't know. Her hair was tied back with a neat blue bow, but it was damp with perspiration, her curls hanging heavy and limp. Her face was ashen and impossibly thin, great shadows around her closed eyes. She was in some kind of merciful slumber, beyond the grip of pain, but her stertorous breathing was harrowing to hear. Evie studied the people in front of us, and when our turn came, she bent and kissed Eileen's marble hand, as she had seen other children do, and laid the bunch of flowers on the lace counter-pane over her lap.

I knelt beside the couch and held my oldest friend's hand as if it might crumble into dust. Tears dripped onto her lacy coverings; I couldn't stop them. "Oh, Eily, oh, Eily," I mumbled. A tiny flicker of her index finger, as if she knew it was me. I began to pray, just as I had prayed with her countless times before, for George. But now, her voice was silent, and I was praying for her.

Aware of the press of pilgrims behind me, and the watchful nurses hovering in the room, overseeing everything and ready to jump to any need of their mistress, I rose, stooped to place a light kiss on her brow, squeezed Evie's little hand and walked straight out of the room, without looking back.

CAITLIN'S HOUSE, ADELAIDE

Caitlin had the next items out of the tin almost before Alex turned off the audio track. Yellowed newspaper clippings, their print faded with age, clutched at the cousins' attention as they leaned in toward the obituaries.

"She was twenty-eight when she died," Caitlin shuddered, pushing the smaller article closer to him, and taking up the larger one.

"Lots of people died young then," Alex mused. "Servicemen, army nurses, flu victims … I can't imagine what it was like."

"I don't want to." Her voice was tight and abrupt. "Maybe we're not living in such bad times as everyone says?"

"People have short memories."

"Yeah. I don't get that."

"It plays into the hands of politicians, I guess."

"Humph."

She turned back to the obituary in her hands, and read aloud.

"What strength of will and fervor of faith can accomplish, even when confined in the frailest of bodies, has been well exemplified in the case of the recently deceased foundress of 'Our Lady's Home for the Poor,' Coogee, N.S.W.—Miss Eileen O'Connor …

"Physical disabilities were, in the case of this young Catholic lady, never permitted to be a bar to the carrying out of a project for assisting the sick poor, which has met with unbounded success, and been, through its late organizer and a band of trained and devoted nurses, the means of carrying healing and comfort into many a miserable tenement, where lay, in dire extremity, the very poorest of a city's sick poor.

"Through the terrible weeks when pneumonic influenza raged, the nurses of 'Our Lady's Home,' Coogee, went forth, morn after morn, to their chosen duties, calmly and bravely, and washed and tended all the sufferers their ministrations could reach, the matron herself finally falling a victim to the awful scourge, although the others recovered, almost each one of the band having the epidemic in her turn. The testimony of a Sydney doctor as to these nurses' heroic work during that time of dread is before me as I write. No sight of neglected slum dwellers daunted them. They were always collected, resourceful and self-sacrificing ..."

"Eileen and her nurses were very well thought of at the time of her death, then. Not just by Kathleen." Alex's brow furrowed. "I can't think of anyone nowadays who would have had such a glowing write-up in the papers."

"No, you're right."

"Lady Di?" Tim had been listening in the doorway. "Mother Teresa?"

"Who?" Alex asked.

"Oh, you young people, what do they teach you in school? Lady Di was Prince Charles' ex-wife. She got involved in the campaign to clean up landmines before she was killed. People adored her, called her the Queen of Hearts."

"Oh, yeah, the car crash in Paris. I remember. She should have campaigned about wearing seatbelts and sticking to the speed limit." His joke fell flat, and he continued, "Who was Mother Teresa?"

"A saint in Calcutta who founded hospices for the poor," said Caitlin.

"Oh, interesting. They've got something in common then. How come you know all this stuff?"

"Because my brain isn't full of information on how computers work. So, I can fit in interesting stuff." She pulled a face at him.

"You'll appreciate me next time your computer crashes."

"I appreciate you now." She grinned before becoming serious again. "Well, now we know when Eileen died. January 1921. Nearly one hundred years ago."

"Can I google her yet?"

"No, of course not." She noticed his mock-tortured expression. "After the next bit of the tape. Maybe."

"How much more do you have to listen to?" Tim leaned against the door jamb.

"Not much, Dad, we're getting close to the end."

"So, Kathleen dictated her memoirs, but stopped sometime in the 1920s, you reckon? Fifty years before she died. That's strange, isn't it? Surely there must have been other things that happened in her life after then."

"I don't think she ever meant to tell her own memoir, Dad. I think she wanted to record Eileen's story. Her part of Eileen's story. Right at the beginning of the tape, she was talking about seeing Eileen while she was in hospital. Evie thought she was hallucinating. And then she started out rambling a bit about the history of the hospital she was in, but she went right back to Eileen. And the more I know of the story, the more haunting the words she used become. *I remember the first time I saw her.*" She shivered as goosebumps tingled along her spine.

"Why would she put more emphasis on her friend, than on her own life?" Tim pulled up a chair and sank into it, his interest growing.

"Well, playing devil's advocate," Alex raked his fingers through his hair, "if Eileen really was a saint, it'd be natural to want to reflect about her. Not everyone grows up with a saint, you know."

Tim wriggled his nose, not willing to speak any opinion about saints for now.

"And Kathleen had a pretty tough life. Maybe Eileen wasn't a real saint, she just seemed like one, because she was calm and full of faith while Kathleen was in such difficult circumstances with George?"

"That makes sense," Tim agreed, but he was frowning as if he didn't want that to be the answer.

"Well, I don't like that theory as much, either," Caitlin admitted, returning to the task of folding up the newspaper articles.

"You think Eileen was a real saint?" Tim asked.

Caitlin stared off into the distance and sighed. "Well, it's obvious there was something special about her. Something so special that she was the most important thing on Kathleen's mind when she was dying fifty years later."

"You've changed your tune," Alex said.

"What do you mean?"

"Yesterday you didn't believe in saints." Alex's tone was half amusement and half accusation. "What's changed your mind?"

She shook her head. "I'm not sure."

Tim leaned closer to her, surprising her with his urging, "Come on, Cait. There must be something going on in that brain of yours."

"I guess I've opened my mind to the possibility, that's all. The way Kathleen talks about her, the reverence and adoration, she must have been extraordinarily charismatic. And then the suffering she went through, the disability, but finding the strength to keep going and the desire to serve others rather than give up and feel sorry for herself. It's a remarkable story."

Tim nodded. "What does it take to become an official saint?"

"Heaps of stuff. The Catholic church does an investigation, documents someone's holiness and miracles they have done."

"Has she done any miracles?" Alex's fingers twitched as if he were struggling to restrain himself from searching on his phone.

Tim looked at his daughter, her face alight with interest, and his nephew, sitting together like old friends, working on a common goal. He glanced at his hands, empty of beer cans. The mist in his eyes surprised all of them. "The three of us, sitting here at the table together, two days in a row, having conversations. Even laughing." He cleared his throat. "Maybe she's doing one now?"

Caitlin stretched across the table, and he took her hand for a moment.

"I was thinking I should go back to AA. I haven't been since before your …" his voice trailed away, unable to say the words *car crash.* "There's a meeting on Tuesday."

"Would you like me to drive you?" Alex offered in a heartbeat, before his uncle could change his mind.

"No, thanks. I'll take a cab. You'll have study to catch up on after this weekend, I imagine."

"Yes, that's true." Alex sighed loudly. "But it's not as interesting as this."

"Can I have that in writing, please? That a history project is more interesting than computer geeking?"

Laughter rang around the table, easing the tension caused by alluding to injuries and alcoholism. "Certainly not," protested Alex. "I have my reputation to protect."

Tears mingled with sweat and dripped from my chin as I stood, clinging to the leather handle hanging from the tram's ceiling.

"Take a seat, love," offered the old woman, starting to lift her basket off her plump lap, making ready to vacate her seat for me.

I shook my head, signaling her to stay where she was.

"Are you alright?" she enquired, concern in her eyes.

Embarrassment flared redder on my cheeks than the sweltering heat of the January day. I struggled to control myself. At last, I was able to say, "I'm all right, thank you," without letting a sob escape.

She was still studying my face. I tried to turn away, but that would mean staring at the chests of the gentleman on either side of me, so I had no alternative but looking her in the eye.

Her expression was kind as she offered me a starched white handkerchief. I shook my head again and returned her smile. Careful not to elbow the men beside me, I pulled one from my own pocket and dabbed my face.

"You got far to go?"

"To Coogee."

She ran her eyes over me, my black dress, too thick for the weather, neat black cloche hat, and puffy red face. Understanding dawned in her eyes. "You're going to Eileen's?"

I nodded and averted my gaze as my bottom lip began to tremble.

"Poor love. You're quite overcome with emotion, aren't you? I can't say I blame you. She'll be sorely missed."

I nodded again, incapable of speaking.

Her voice became sharper. "Were you a special friend of hers?"

Her words were like a ray of sunshine, piercing through my heart and warming me from the inside. I looked at her shyly. "Yes, yes I was." A secretive, watery smile dawned across my face, as I felt a subtle strength flow through me, and I repeated the words with more certainty. "I was a special friend of hers. I've known her since she was eleven years old. We lived across the street from each other back then."

"What an honor for you, my dear. To grow up with a saint."

I had never thought of it that way, but the certainty she was right was like a growing power in my chest. "Yes, yes it was."

"Her house was packed this morning. Probably still will be when you get there."

"You've been?"

"Oh, yes, love. Anyone who knew her is desperate to go and see her one last time."

Her words echoed in my suddenly chilled bone marrow. One last time. Oh, Eileen, I don't know if I can do this. "What's she like?" I whispered.

"The little darling is just perfect. Like a doll. At peace at last." She frowned, and I felt uncomfortable as she scrutinized my unguarded expression again. "You'll be fine, lass. You've seen your share of suffering, I reckon. You'll hold yourself together when you get there." And she winked at me, a big, exaggerated gesture like an actress on the stage.

I felt scandalized for a moment, being winked at by a woman I didn't know, in a tram. And then I started to giggle. I couldn't help myself, as laughter turned back into tears, but suddenly I didn't care that I was making a spectacle of myself in the crowded tram.

A few minutes passed in silence. "Come on, love. It's our stop," the woman said and started to move.

Once we were off the tram, she tugged at my sleeve and turned me towards her. "Give me your handkerchief."

Too surprised to do anything but blink, I handed it to her, and she wiped the sheen from my forehead, right there on the side of the street. She folded the handkerchief into neat quarters and gave it back to me, then took out a tiny glass bottle of cologne from a small, black velvet receptacle in her basket. "Dab some of this on, love, and you'll be as fresh as a daisy."

Obediently, I unscrewed the little lid and put the neck of the bottle to my wrist, then rubbed it with the other one. It evaporated quickly, cooling my skin, and the fresh, citrusy scent penetrated the stuffiness in my nose.

"And your throat. That's it. You're as good as new now. Just as a special friend should be." She popped the bottle back in her bag and turned away. I watched her receding down the hill, calling, "Thank you," too late. I never saw her again.

I turned and began to walk up the hill towards Dudley Street. A crowd was milling around by the gate. A throng of people extended from the street into the garden and towards the door of Eileen's house. I wished my hat was more practical and had a bigger brim, but there was nothing I could do about it now. I set my face into a blank expression and gave thanks for the old lady's kindness. My thoughts turned inwards, as I reflected on my *special* friend. Eileen had been an icon, a comfort, a nurse and protector. She had given herself and her time, abundantly and without hesitation, to so many people. That was obvious by the sheer numbers who had gathered here to pay their respects. But I was in a special position: I had grown up with Eileen. I'd known her when she was still a child. I'd played with her, heard her thoughts as she became more and more convinced she was destined to be a servant of Our Lady, and a comfort for the poor. She had family. She had many friends. She had her heroic, devoted band of nurses. They were all special too. I smiled to myself. But she also had me. And I had her in a very safe place in my heart. Just where she belonged.

My breathing deepened as I relaxed, and the internal voice in my head died away, allowing me to listen to snatches of the conversations around me.

"She was brave right up to the end."

"Sent her poor Mother away a few hours before she died, so she wouldn't have to watch her suffer."

"Such a sweltering, hot day it was, too."

"I just had to come today, before they close the coffin in the morning."

"Her last words were to the nurses. 'All is over,' she said. 'I can do no more. I will give you my last blessing and I will always be with you.'"

I blinked against the sting of tears and breathed deeply through the sob in my throat. The beauty of her last words galvanized me somehow because I knew I had her blessing too, and I knew Eileen would always be with me. I rested my hand on my palpitating heart, eyes closed for a moment in the midst of the crowd.

"Poor Father McGrath. I remember how he used to call on her, give her communion years ago. Such a shame he couldn't be here …"

"Shh, Mavis, I don't think you should talk about him here. She never deserved that spiteful gossip, let's not remind anyone about that."

"It's still a shame."

I sighed and looked around the large grounds, the sweeping lawns with views to the ocean, and the scattered shade trees. My mind wandered back to other times, when the garden was filled with happy people. Garden parties for the children of patients from the poorest districts; the children, Evie amongst them, running and playing. White tablecloths, hidden by bone china plates laden with scones and sponge cakes, and jugs of lemonade. Eileen, feeling relatively well, surrounded by her young admirers, showing them pictures in her scrapbooks. Laughing at their jokes. Listening patiently to their childish problems with a sympathetic smile on her serene face. Eileen impulsively inviting struggling people to dinner, entreating the nurses to make sure they ate a large meal. How those girls ever managed to plan meals I had no idea, but there were plenty of hungry stomachs that were filled because of her. And broken, empty hearts too. The weight of loss made my knees buckle, and I turned away from the crowds so no one could see my face.

Out of the corner of my eye a shadow moved under one of the spreading trees. For a moment, I thought I saw Eileen, sitting in her cane wheelchair, the wind dragging its fingers through her flowing curls and fluttering her pale blue ribbons. She was watching us, then, singling me out, raised her hand in greeting. My breath caught in my throat, and I blinked, squeezing my eyelids shut tight. When I opened them, she was gone. I told myself it must have been the wind moving the leaves. But there was no wind that day, the heat was oppressive and the air heavy and still.

Shuffling across the lawn, after an hour I was standing in the shade of the verandah, halting at the threshold. About to walk into Eileen's house. A house full of people, but Eileen wasn't there to smile at us, to hear our problems, to say the hundred little things she'd said over the years to bring us courage and solace. My breath sucked in as I stepped through the doorway. The people around me became silent, their faces stiffening, lips pale and thin as they were shut against emotion. A few sobs, but they didn't disturb the air of a cathedral that had settled in the house. I studied my shoes, a little scuffed now, and the floor, deliberately keeping my eyes off the mourners ahead of me. They deserved their privacy as they said their goodbyes.

Her room was filled with flowers. The white coffin seemed unnaturally big. Far too big for her tiny body. She looked smaller than ever now, resting there as if she were sleeping. Her hair spread over her shoulders like a veil, she was dressed in a powder blue dress and slippers. Serene and peaceful, her frail form no longer needing to struggle for breath or surrender to pain. I closed my eyes and prayed. "Thank you, Eileen. For … for everything," I murmured, before filing out again, into the blinding sunlight in the garden and slinking away, back to the tram stop. And that was the last time I really saw Eileen O'Connor.

* * *

Two days later, I was packed into Our Lady of the Sacred Heart Church in Randwick. The front rows filled with priests in black robes and white surplices. Eileen's Uncle, Father Kilgallin celebrated the Requiem Mass. My lips twitched into a tight smile as I remembered meeting him at lunch at Eileen's a few years before. The two local priests assisted him. Three priests conducting a funeral service! My smile broadened. Good for you Eileen, I applauded her. The Church wanted to sweep you under the carpet seven years ago, when you started your mission to serve the poor. And look at them now. They're all here, except the Archbishop. Who'd have thought it?

My mind wandered during the service. Pondering. Eileen had seemed like a threat to the church, when she was alive, a laywoman, young, charismatic, unpredictable and uncontrollable. She inspired love and trust, and that meant she was able to attract independent funding, without the intervention of the Church. Maybe that was why they had never managed to sweep her under the carpet. That, and her unswerving faith she was doing what the Virgin Mary wanted her to do.

Things had changed for her during the Spanish flu. Even the most hardened authoritarians had to grudgingly admit Eileen and her nurses had been heroic and selfless and saved many lives in those awful months. From there, they softened further, as the nurses lost their matron to the flu, and Eileen stepped into the breach, running the order from her sickbed.

Now, Eileen was dead. It was clear as day, the local people saw her as saintly and special. If I were cynical, I'd say a dead saint is much easier for the Church to manage than a living one. But I didn't say that back then, of course.

After the funeral, Mum slipped her hand through my arm as we turned away from the graveside in Randwick cemetery. "I'd like a nice cup of tea, before we go home."

My brow creased as I fired a questioning glance at her. Mum never wasted money on cups of tea when she was out.

"And a sandwich," she added firmly.

"Are you sure?"

She nodded. "I just need … I just need a little time to collect myself."

"You're alright, aren't you, Mum?"

"Of course, I am, love. Just a little pick me up." She patted my elbow. "My treat."

"Why not? Evie's at school."

"And she's going to a friend's after school. It's all arranged."

I smiled. "Come on then, Mum."

After we finished in the tea shop, we headed to the tram. Walking along the pavement towards us, came the undertaker. His eyes had a faraway look, and he was shaking his head from side to side, as if he couldn't believe something. Our gazes met as he got close enough to pass us, and he stared deeply into my eyes. I was about to bid him good day and wondering if I should ask if he was alright, but he forestalled me.

His voice full of reverence, he half-whispered, "I buried a saint today." His head was still shaking. His eyes searched mine, like a drowning man looking for a lifeline.

I nodded. "I know."

I couldn't tell if he heard me. He tapped the brim of his hat as he walked on, mumbling to himself, "I buried a saint today."

CAITLIN'S HOUSE, ADELAIDE

The audio stopped. The air in the kitchen was cold and heavy. Caitlin shivered and pulled on the jacket draped over the chair beside her. Alex cocked a cheeky eyebrow at her. "You've got goosebumps."

She crossed her arms. "It's cold." He winked. "I've got them too."

After a few moments, Alex wriggled in his seat, shaking off the silence that hung in the room, engulfing them in their own thoughts. "That's the end."

Tim cleared his throat.

"What do you think, Uncle Tim?"

"I think it's time for bed," he said gruffly. He got up and turned the kettle on. "Anyone for a quick cuppa?"

A telegraphed glance between them, they both answered yes, before he could change his mind and head for the fridge. His back to them, Tim chewed his lip and lined three mugs along the bench. "Is there anything left in that tin of yours?"

"Yes." Caitlin drew the tin towards her and lifted out a fragile scrap of blue notepaper. "This is the last thing." She unfolded it. Something fell out onto the table. A small lock of brown hair, tied with a very narrow ribbon, faded to coffee colors now, but showing a blush of pink in the center where the bow was tied.

The spidery hand they recognized as Eileen's, was very unsteady as it scrawled a few words. Caitlin gasped.

What is death? To go, to be with God.

Her hand trembled as she picked up the loop of hair between her thumb and index finger. With awestruck diligence, she inspected it, then held it up for the men to see. "Her hair. It's a lock of Eileen's hair," she breathed, her eyes shining. "I can't believe it."

"Why would Kathleen have had a lock of Eileen's hair?" Tim sounded incredulous as he poured boiling water over teabags.

"People did that, Dad. Kept locks of hair as mementos of someone. In the 1800s, they even made little pictures out of it or put it into lockets they could wear."

"Eww." Alex laughed.

"It started before people had photos, I guess," suggested Tim.

"That's true." Reverently, she held the hair closer to the unshaded light globe hanging from the ceiling. "But, you know, there's something more intimate in having a keepsake that's a part of someone, isn't there? That's got a different energy than just a piece of paper with an image on it, hasn't it?"

"Energy?"

Her shoulders dropped and she shook her head. "I can't explain it, Alex. You see." She passed it towards him. His first impulse was to refuse to take it, but he held out his hand, open and cupped. "What do you think?"

He shrugged. "It's a bit weird ..." He sat up straighter as light infused his features. "You mean I'm holding hair from a saint? Like a ... a relic or something?"

"Yes."

His brow puckered. "No sh— oh gosh, I can't say that when I'm holding a piece of a saint, can I?"

"Nah, probably better not to." A smile flitted across her face before her eyes became serious again, and she pushed the note over for him to read.

"Eileen knows she is dying, scribbles a note to her childhood friend and puts a lock of hair in it?"

"I don't think so." Caitlin was thinking aloud, formulating the idea as she spoke. "I think Kathleen took the hair some time before, maybe even helped her cut it. The note is later, maybe a meditation. Perhaps even written for her in the early days after George died. Look how feeble the writing is, we know Eileen was desperately ill while she was away, when George was falling apart. It could have been written then, couldn't it?"

"I guess so. And then after Eileen died, Kathleen would have decided the two things belonged together, and wrapped Eileen's hair up in the note about going to God."

"That makes sense. That poor woman had had enough death to deal with." Tim braced himself against the kitchen bench and moved the mugs to the table. "Drink up."

"Thanks, Dad."

"What's your plan for the morning? Apart from sleeping in?" Alex asked.

"You can start googling things."

A cheeky grin lit his face as he reached for his phone. "Now?"

She shook her head, teasing. "You never give up, do you? What are you looking up?"

"Eileen O'Connor … singer, lawyer … no, hold on, Eileen O'Connor Saint. Here we go … she's being investigated as a possible saint right now."

"What?" Caitlin stared at him.

"She's been declared a Servant of God, that's some kind of stepping-stone to sainthood."

"Okay."

He frowned and stared at his phone. "Hey, listen to this. Eileen died in 1921. The nurses were determined she should be buried in her home, with her bedroom as a chapel. It took till 1936 for them to get permission, then her coffin was exhumed."

"They dug her up?" Tim peered over the top of his mug.

"Not just that. They opened the coffin."

"What?"

"Yes, the nurses insisted. The undertakers were reluctant."

"I can imagine," Tim grunted.

"Why?" Caitlin leaned in closer, eager to hear what happened next.

"Even fifteen years later, they wanted to see whatever was left of her. Collect relics maybe."

"And what did they find?"

"Guess."

"Fifteen years after being buried?" Caitlin's face screwed up as if she had smelt something horrid. "It must have been pretty gruesome. A few bones, maybe."

Triumph blazed in his eyes. "No. She was incorrupt, apparently."

"Incorrupt?" Tim repeated. "Really?"

"What does that mean?" Caitlin directed the question to her father, remembering he once went to a Catholic school run by nuns.

"Her body was intact, didn't decompose. It's one of the signs of someone being a saint."

"How does that work?"

He shrugged. "No idea."

They turned back to Alex. "She looked like she was peacefully asleep, her face was unblemished, and her hands were neatly folded across her breast with nice fingernails. Her hair was still shiny, but her dress had faded. One of the nurses exclaimed, 'Oh look at the little darling!' An undertaker declared she was perfect."

"The hairs are standing up on the back of my neck." Caitlin shivered.

"Mine too."

"Careful, Alex, or you'll start believing she's a saint too."

He ignored her jesting and returned to his reading. "Shh, this is what one of the undertakers said, twenty-six years later: 'it was a sight I will never forget, and I must admit to being rather scared and shocked.'"

Tim shoved his chair back from the table. "It's past my bedtime. I'm off to bed. It's an intriguing story you've found yourselves in. Sleep well."

"Night, Dad."

"Okay." Alex was still thoughtful. "We know people who knew her thought she was saintly, and her body was incorrupt. What else does it take to prove someone's a saint?"

"They need to have done a miracle, remember?"

"But how do you define a miracle?"

"Me? Or the Church?"

"Either will do. For now."

Fiddling with her empty mug, Caitlin pondered. "Well, usually a miracle is like someone being inexplicably healed or saved from some disaster ..."

"So, something that cannot be explained, and benefits someone in a tangible way."

She screwed up her face. "That sounds terribly dry. A miracle has to be more," she rummaged in her mind to find the right words. "Sacred ... A miracle should be sacred and give you goosebumps."

Alex typed into his phone. *Miracle = [unexplained sacred healing +/- salvation] + goosebumps.* He handed the phone to her, and she laughed. "Trust a geek to come up with an equation like that!"

"Then make it better."

"Speed. Miracles are always fast. But if someone has a splinter through their thumb, a doctor can pull it out quickly and that's not a miracle."

"Of course not. You can explain it."

"True," her face twisted up again. "But it's not just that. The doctor used tools."

"Tools make it easier to explain."

She shook her head. "You're missing my point. For a healing to be a miracle, I don't think you can use tools."

He chewed his lip as his fingers hovered over the keypad. Caitlin watched him type, then took the phone off him again. *Miracle = [fast, unexplained, sacred healing +/- salvation] + goosebumps – tools.*

She passed it back. "Swap the goosebumps. You get them at the end, when you know all the other components of a miracle are in place. And I don't like the fast bit."

"Why not?"

"It's a bit lame."

"Right. How can we word it? How fast is fast, when it comes to miracles?"

She laughed again. "This is getting technical." No response, so she tried again. "Speed of light."

"Of course!" He typed triumphantly. *Miracle = c[unexplained, sacred healing +/- salvation] – tools + goosebumps.*

"You only added one letter."

"c is the speed of light, in physics, as in E=mc^2"

"Oh yeah. I remember."

"Is that the formula for a miracle?"

"Not quite." She took the phone and typed. *Miracle = c[unexplained, Divine healing +/- salvation] – tools + goosebumps.*

"Happy now?"

"For the moment." She yawned and stretched, her mind clouding with sleep.

"Next question: did she do any?"

"Can't it wait till the morning?"

"No, I don't think so. Not if I want to get any sleep tonight."

"And *you* say I'm OCD!" She chuckled, her pleasure in his company and the shared project tempting her to stay up a bit longer.

He beamed. "Just another half hour. If we can't find anything by then, we'll call it a night."

"A morning," she corrected, dragging her laptop towards her. "I suppose we won't find anything by googling 'Eileen O'Connor miracle'. No, just says she'd need two documented miracles. Cures of terminal conditions that are attributed to her and normal science and medicine can't explain."

Their faces glowed blue in the light of their screens. Silence settled over them for several minutes.

"Oh!"

Alex jumped at the sudden exclamation. "What've you got?"

"Someone else has been reminiscing about Eileen. Listen to this: Kathleen Fitzgerald, another Kathleen, isn't that a coincidence?"

"There are no coincidences, Cait."

"Hmmm. Kathleen Fitzgerald was a three-year-old girl with tubercular meningitis."

"That sounds serious."

"Stop interrupting." She grinned at him, then returned to the words on her screen. "Little Kathleen's father was a surfer. The family lived on a property in western New South Wales, but they came to Coogee for a month every summer holidays. In 1914, while they were on holiday, little Kathleen got sick with tuberculosis. The infection affected the lining around her brain. She was desperately ill, unconscious for two weeks and the doctor thought she would die. Her uncle knew Eileen and asked her to pray for her, and in spite of the danger of infection—hmmm, perhaps she didn't know she already had tuberculosis then?—Eileen insisted on being taken to see her. She laid her crucifix on Kathleen's head and prayed. She turned to the distraught parents and told them, *Kathleen won't die, she'll get better.* And the little girl did. Her parents saw her getting stronger in front of their eyes and called the doctor the next morning. The doctor was amazed and said *'It's a higher power than us. I can't explain it.'* The family always believed Eileen healed her, and no one could ever find another explanation."

"Is that a *real* story?"

"Yes. Yes, it is."

"Oh my God," he articulated the words with careful deliberation.

"Exactly," Caitlin teased, as another wave of goosebumps shivered across her skin. "And it's beautiful too, because her family stayed close to the Brown Nurses, even after Eileen died, and Kathleen became a volunteer driver to take the nurses on their visits, when she grew up. Oh, and she was interviewed for this information in 1991, so she lived to be over eighty years old."

"Wow." Alex stared down at his phone, scrolling. "I've found something else. Every January, there's a commemorative service at Eileen's house …"

Caitlin's eyes ignited with a slow-burning excitement. "That's something to think about," she said, then yawned.

"Yes, it is," agreed Alex. "But right now, I'm going to send you to bed. You look done in."

Caitlin took up her crutches and made for the door. She turned back to Alex, frowning. "The tapes just stopped at the end of Eileen's story. What do you think happened to Granny Kathleen? Did she recover? Did she go on to have a happy life, do you think?"

"Well, she lived into her eighties. She had one daughter, but two sons-in-law, that must have been interesting back then. Then she had grandchildren and great-grandchildren."

"One of whom lost his leg and got PTSD in a war."

"Yeah, I know. It's like there are cycles …"

"Hey, Dad?" Caitlin projected her voice through the living room doorway, talking over the newsreader on the twenty-four-hour news channel.

Tim reached for the television remote to lower the sound. "You're up and dressed early."

"I couldn't sleep."

"What's up?"

"Kathleen. I can't get her out of my head, Dad." She flushed as her eyes filled with unwelcome tears. Old mysteries tugged at her heart-strings, reminding her of Alex's comment about cycles. An image of Kathleen dedicating her life to caring for George, then losing him shimmered in her mind, changing form and she saw her own mother, dedicated to caring for Tim, baffled at what to do to help him, watching helpless as he descended into a spiral of withdrawal, depression, and drink, to a place where she couldn't reach him. Though that wasn't quite true, because her father always emerged back out of his darkness, at least while her mother was alive. He had never completely got lost, nor given up. She was swept up in a wave of gratitude for that, and the uncomfortable question of how his life would have been different, if her mother hadn't got breast cancer and died.

Tim clicked off the television, his full attention captured by the emotions swirling across his daughter's pale face. He was afraid of emotion, afraid to ask, because he didn't know how he could handle her reply, but somehow the question came out of his mouth. "What is it, Cait?"

"George, Dad. He was such a nice man, before the war. And he came back so …" She searched for the correct word, "Damaged. She did everything she could to reach him, to help him. But no one knew what to do." Her pause filled with thoughts of her mother, and even herself, images of Tim on bad days, out of control. Tim shuddered, and Caitlin's gut cramped at the feeling he might be reading her thoughts. Her voice shook, "And then she lost him." She couldn't meet his eye.

Tim swallowed down the reflux of defensive words as tension stiffened every muscle. He ripped his eyes away from the down-turned face of his daughter, and they flicked back towards the blackened television screen. There was nothing on it to distract him, and his gaze fell to the bench the television sat on. Onto the photograph, returned to its new home. Preserved by chance, for a hundred years? Or by some unspoken design? His grandmother, Evie, with her hair in tight little braids. A serious little-girl-on-her best-behavior sort of expression on her face as she looked into the camera. And just behind her, Eileen, her long hair billowing around them, dressed in something pale and lacy. Eileen's face, too, was looking straight at the camera. Straight at Tim, and he felt she was seeing him, peering into his soul. Soothing his soul and reminding him he could do better. He shook himself out of his reverie and snatched a sideways glance at Caitlin. She was still studying the ground. His reflections must have taken less time than he thought. As he rubbed his face, the description of his great grandfather doing the same thing echoed through his mind. In this moment, Tim could make up for what George couldn't: he could be present for his own daughter. He would do it for George. And their other ancestors who were counting on him. Evie and Kathleen. For his mother. And for Eileen. He sniffed, then cleared his throat.

"Kathleen was a grand old woman, Cait." His voice was gruff with memories. "Kind, could never do enough for people. Looked after her neighbors when they were sick. My mother adored her, and so did your Mum and I. We all did. She never complained. She never married again, but she didn't need to, to find love, you know. She said there are many kinds of love stories, and hers had become to love her family, and the people around her who were in need." A thoughtful pause lent weight to his words, "I think, you know, if she didn't have Evie, she'd have made a very good nun."

"You're saying she was happy, then?"

"Oh yes." He smiled fondly, his eyes fixed on long-ago images. "I never heard a complaining word from her. She always had a smile and a kind word to share. And quite often a homemade pie or scones too."

Caitlin's breath sighed out as her body relaxed. "I'm glad."

He nodded, holding the silence, then cleared his throat again. "Cait, could you close the door for me? I think it's time I called my counsellor."

Her smile was soft as she met his eyes, but she said nothing. She grasped the door handle and pulled the door shut.

A few minutes later, Alex wandered into the kitchen to find her resting with her head in her hands. "Are you okay?"

The kitchen light reflected in the wetness on her face, but her eyes shone. "Dad's on the phone to his counsellor. And tomorrow he's going back to AA."

Alex put his hands on her shoulders and stooped to kiss the top of her head. "That's good news."

"And Kathleen was a lovely lady, looking after everyone, always smiling. Dad says she would have made a good nun."

Alex laughed. "I never used to think that was a compliment."

"Neither did I. But it is, isn't it?"

"You're sure all this talk of Eileen hasn't addled your brain?"

"No. I'm sure it *has*, but in a good way." Her smile was contagious. "So, what do we do next?"

"We need to find George."

"What?"

"Well, we know he died in Sydney. He must be buried somewhere."

"In the same cemetery as Kathleen, you'd think."

Tim clicked off the television as the cousins appeared in the living room, looking up at them expectantly.

"Dad, where's Kathleen buried?" She noticed a little of the usual tension had left his shoulders. Maybe he didn't need to fight himself so hard now he'd decided to get help?

"She's in Randwick Cemetery. In South Coogee. Why?"

Alex settled on the arm of the sofa, his gaze fixed on his uncle, his tone gentle.

"Is it possible George could be buried there as well?"

"I went to Nan's funeral. That's the only time I was at the Cemetery. I never heard anyone say anything about George being there."

"Would you be able to find her grave?"

He shook his head. "That was forty-five years ago, kids. It'd be in the Catholic section, of course."

"Okay, we'll look online."

Caitlin returned to her laptop. "Nothing much about the cemetery, but there's a phone number to ring if you're trying to locate a relative's grave."

She reached for her mobile phone. Alex watched her dial then switch to speakerphone once the call went through.

"Thank you for taking my call. I'm looking for the graves of two relatives."

"What are their names, please?"

"Kathleen O'Grady. She died in 1974. She'll be in the Catholic section."

"Great. And the next one?"

"Her husband, George O'Grady. He died in 1918. We're not sure if he was even buried there. There's a family mystery."

"We get mysteries to solve, from time to time, in this line of work." The lady on the phone was still professional, but an edge of interest crept into her voice. "Let's start with what you know."

"We were always told he died in the first World War. But we just found out he didn't die overseas, he came home."

"Oh dear." She tutted professional sympathy.

Caitlin's voice thickened with sudden emotion. "We'd really like to know he's at peace."

"I see."

"He came back injured, umm ... damaged from the war."

Silence on the other end of the phone.

"Could someone who committed suicide have been buried in the Catholic section in 1918? Someone who had shell shock? You hear stories about them not being able to be buried on hallowed ground." Caitlin's voice trailed away.

"I've never heard of there being a suicide section here. It would depend on if he had someone who would have bought him a plot?"

"I'm sure his wife would have done that."

"In, when did you say? 1918?"

"Yes."

"Oh, that's a bit harder. We lost some records to storm damage years ago. I can have a look, but I can't promise you anything. Hold the line please."

"Thank you."

After hearing there were no records to solve their mystery, Caitlin pushed away her phone, disappointment heavy on her shoulders.

"Well, we'll just have to go to the cemetery and see whether we can find anything." Alex's chin was set at a determined angle. "We're not giving up now."

Caitlin's face fell further.

"What's up?"

She rotated her laptop so he could see the photo on the screen. "That's Randwick Cemetery."

He frowned, not comprehending, at the rows of close-packed graves marching up a hillside.

"No paths. I can't get around that graveyard with a wheelchair or a walking frame." Her lower lip trembled.

"How about on crutches?" Alex suggested.

"I haven't been practicing enough."

"I know," Tim spoke from his position against the doorframe. "I can help you. You've healed up enough now and you'll be strong enough to manage them, just like the physiotherapist said. It was only the pain from the surgery on your spleen that stopped you before."

Caitlin's face blanched as her father mentioned the ruptured spleen that came close to killing her. It was easier to keep that blotted out of her mind.

Tim misinterpreted her pallor. "That wound has healed up alright, hasn't it? It's not still hurting you?"

"It's fine, Dad. Just pulls sometimes if I move too quickly, that's all."

Reassured, Tim relaxed again. "You're serious? You're going grave-hunting in Sydney?"

"It feels like the right thing to do."

Tim closed his eyes for a moment. "Yes, yes, it does."

Alex turned to face his uncle squarely. "You'll come with us, then?"

Tim's eyes widened with surprise, but when he glanced at his daughter, the naked longing on her face softened him. "Err ... I don't know. If you're sure you want me to come?" The warmth in Caitlin's smile was enough answer. He surrendered. Looking at Alex, he said, "Your mother will want to come too."

Alex shrugged, deliberately nonchalant. "We'll all fit in her car."

"I suppose we will." Tim retreated to the lounge.

Alex stepped closer to his cousin, peering into her face in a way that made her squirm. "What's going on?"

"What do you mean?"

"You looked like you'd seen a ghost just now. What happened when you had that operation on your spleen?"

"Nothing happened then. It was just surgery, you know?"

His eyes held hers like a magnet, and he wouldn't let them go. "There's something you aren't telling me. Something you remembered when Uncle Tim mentioned that operation." He paused and dropped his voice to a tone of gentle sympathy. "Out with it, cuz. What happened?"

"It was in the ambulance. I think." She sounded uncertain, hesitant. "Or maybe in the emergency room? One minute, I was feeling awful, and then there was no pain. I was floating in the air looking down at myself, lying white on the stretcher. There was light all around me. I don't remember very clearly, but it was incredibly peaceful. Mum was there. She said she loved me, but it wasn't my time." Her face was serene, basking in the memory of being in her mother's presence. She shook her head and continued.

"Someone else was near me. She spoke to me; I can't remember the words."

Incredulity clashed with Alex's air of being entranced. He leaned towards her, holding his breath. He moved his lips but couldn't think of the right question to ask.

"What are you looking at me like that for?"

"You had a near death experience."

"Yeah, I guess ..."

"What did she say?"

"I genuinely don't remember most of it. She said I could make a choice. And if I came back, I'd have work to do."

"Ah. So, who was the woman?"

"I don't know. I didn't really see her."

"But?" he pressed.

"She wasn't very tall. And she had beautiful long hair," Caitlin blurted out, finally letting her eyes drop. He wanted to speak, but she stopped him. "Don't say a word. I don't know."

Alex watched her in awe. Had she really seen Eileen? He let her gather her thoughts in silence, but he knew he had a dopey grin etched on his face, and he couldn't make it stop.

"You don't believe in saints," she reminded him, gently.

"I didn't believe in near death experiences, either, until I discovered my cousin had one."

"People have been talking about them for years."

"It's different when you personally know someone who experiences one."

"A saint, or an NDE?"

"Both, I suppose." He relaxed, and his breath flooded out in a soft gush.

"Good morning!" Cara enfolded Caitlin in a huge hug despite her crutches. "How are you?"

"I'm awake," Caitlin yawned. "Six a.m. is not my favorite time of day. How are you, Aunt Cara?"

"I'm a bit excited, to tell you the truth. A nice family excursion. I'm looking forward to hearing these mysterious tapes. We'll have lots to talk about in the car." Her voice changed, became more self-conscious, wary, as Tim limped up the passageway towards the front door. His gait was uneven on the prosthetic leg he seldom wore. "Hello, Tim. Good to see you." She hugged him stiffly.

"Hey, sis."

"I'll take that," Alex gestured at Caitlin's bag near the door. "Do you need to get to anything in these while we're on the road?"

"No." Caitlin shook her head and indicated the small shoulder bag she was wearing. "Anything I'll need is in here."

"Cool." He pushed the wheelchair to the car, folded it, then lifted it into the back of the SUV. He added their bags and balanced Cait's crutches and walking frame on top. "We can open our own clinic with all this stuff. Are you bringing your crutches, too, Uncle Tim?"

"Yeah." Tim retrieved them from behind the door. "I don't know how long I can wear this blasted thing. But it'll be easier in confined spaces."

"Have you got everything, Cait?"

"Yes, Alex. But now you've asked, let's just check my bag one more time."

Alex sighed, "Sorry." He retrieved her bag. "Here, check again."

She felt in the bag. "Notebook. Folder with photocopies of every-thing. Toffee tin." She checked them off one at a time. She grinned sheepishly. "All in the exact same spots they were in last time I checked."

"They can't jump out of the bag all by themselves, you know," he teased.

"I know, I know."

"Are you going to be alright in the back, Cait?" Cara asked, the frown lines between her eyebrows deepening.

"Yes, of course."

"Hop in behind me. I'll take the first shift driving, and you can nap. Then when Alex is driving, you can tell me the story."

Once they were all loaded in the car, Alex pulled something out of the backpack on the floor at his feet. "Look what I've got for the trip."

Caitlin laughed and wrestled the large box of chocolates out of his hands. "I'll take charge of that. You can have one after breakfast." He handed her a cushion. "Thank you." She snuggled into it, holding it in place between her head and the car window.

"Everyone set?" Cara was smiling, ready for an adventure. She sneaked a sideways look at her brother, unbuckling his prosthetic limb and leaning it against the side of the car. "There are water bottles in all your door pockets. Next stop, Tailem Bend. Breakfast, loo break and driver change over."

"We've got it all planned," Alex grinned.

"Did you make a spreadsheet?" Caitlin murmured without open-ing her eyes.

"No comment."

Tim wriggled in his seat, as if he were trying to get comfortable, but Cara, still furtively glancing at him as she pulled into the traffic, decided he was trying to watch his daughter in the rear-view mirror. Caitlin looked comfortable and peaceful, Cara noted with satisfaction, checking her niece herself.

* * *

While they sat in the café at Tailem Bend, Cara put her phone down on the laminated tabletop. "I promised to text Paul from each roadside stop," she explained.

"How is he?" asked Tim, making conversation while he was alone with her, as the cousins were using the restrooms.

"He's fine. I think he's looking forward to retiring, though. He's tired of flying in and out."

"He would be." Tim pushed baked beans around on his plate. "How long till then?"

"Three years, he thinks. Then he can come on crazy road trips with us and help solve family mysteries."

"Why, do we have any more family mysteries?"

"I don't know, Tim. We haven't solved this one yet."

He grinned ruefully. "I think I'm done with mysteries and secrets, after all this." He watched Alex hold the door in the corridor to the restrooms open for Caitlin, who was maneuvering her walker. "I missed some of the story myself." A shadow crossed his face. "I was … wrapped up in my own stuff."

Familiar sympathy stirred in Cara's heart, chasing away her frustration that she never seemed to be able to solve the enigma her brother had become. She smiled nervously, leaning towards him a little. "But you chose to get involved," she said, her voice soft.

He looked up, caught her gaze. "Cait's getting injured hit me hard, Cara, I admit it. I fell off the wagon."

She nodded. She'd feared as much.

He swallowed. "I've gone back to AA."

"Well done, Tim. That was brave."

"I nearly lost her." His voice was strangled, and she was embarrassed to see tears in his eyes. "Everything came crashing back. Her mother …"

Cara laid a tender hand on his arm, but he shook it off. Not aggressively. She knew he never could bear to receive sympathy.

His voice was grim now, determined. "Those kids … they're great kids, sis. Alex brought laughter back into the house this past week. You must be very proud of him." Pride swelled in Cara's breast, but Tim kept talking so she couldn't respond. "And his being there made me realize something. Caitlin needs me. Really needs me. Look at her, she's so pale, learning to walk again. She needs a bit of looking after. And there I was, wallowing. I can't do that to her anymore. So, when they suggested I join them on this crazy journey, I couldn't escape. I said yes."

Hesitant, afraid to overstep the mark and trigger the defensiveness that had so often driven her away, Cara murmured, "If there's anything we can do to help you, let us know, won't you?"

He nodded curtly and brushed his eyes with the back of his hand.

A sudden impulse arose, and Cara extended her little finger, beckoning with it. "Pinky promise?"

He looked startled, before a chuckle rose up from his belly. He gripped her finger with his. "Pinky promise."

The air between them softened as the low-grade tension melted away. Alex and Caitlin, returning from the bathrooms, stood watching them for a moment. "What happened?" Alex murmured.

"Something good." Caitlin led the way back to the table. "Let's go find George," she said brightly.

"We'll play Kathleen's tapes over the car's audio while we drive." Alex paused, feeling protective. "Mum?"

"Yes?"

"There are some very sad bits on the tapes."

"Yes, I guessed that. But it was all a long time ago." She sighed. "Poor Granny Kath. I remember her, you know. Not very well. I was only about eight years old when she died."

Silence filled the car, as everyone retreated into their own thoughts. At last, Cara asked, "Why weren't we told about poor George? How could something like that be kept a secret?"

"It's complicated. Evie was just three at the time, she would have forgotten him. And George had left Kathleen a note saying that she'd be better off not knowing what happened to him. I guess she must have felt she was honoring his wishes, by keeping it secret. And I suppose, the neighbors and everyone else thought it was the best thing to do too."

"You okay, Mum?" Alex squinted into the rear vision mirror.

"Yes, I'm okay. But it's a very sad story."

"Want to hear the tapes now?" Alex reached towards the stereo controls.

Tim closed his eyes, as the voice of his great grandmother took him back to his childhood. Cara, fifteen years younger than her half-brother, didn't recognize her voice, but paid close attention to Kathleen's soft lilt inherited from her Irish-born parents. She watched, unseeing, as monotonous scrub streaked past the windows, her mind filled instead with images conjured from the words on the tapes, and past and present wove into a new tapestry.

After about an hour, Alex paused the recording. "We'll be at Pinnaroo in twenty minutes. I'll get petrol, and we can all have a stretch."

"Great."

"What do you think of Kathleen's friend?" Alex's eyes fixed on his mother in the rear vision mirror. She studied him back, even after he focused again on the road, tracing the scar below his eye. How lucky he was, she thought, with a shudder. It could have been much worse. She clawed her thoughts back to the present, aware the two young people were awaiting her answer with interest.

"Kathleen certainly was very fond of Eileen." She was hesitant, not sure what they wanted her to say. "She sounds very special. What happened to her?"

"Do you know who she is?" Cara shook her head. "Her name was Eileen O'Connor, Mum."

"Eileen O'Connor ... no, it doesn't ring any bells."

"She's being investigated to be Australia's second saint."

"Granny Kath's best friend was a saint?" Cara's surprise made Alex laugh.

"Yes, it looks like it. Eileen was declared a Servant of God last year, and the Catholic Church is looking for evidence to prove she was a saint."

"Goodness me! Do you have any other surprises for me?"

"Apart from the lock of hair from a future saint, that's in Cait's luggage, you mean?"

"You've got a saint's hair in your luggage?" Cara was incredulous.

"Only a little bit."

"Well, that's alright then," Cara said, grinning.

Their laughter woke Tim, but he kept his eyes closed, and smiled to himself, happy to let it wash over him. Somewhere, in the back of his mind, he heard a snatch of a prayer of gratitude, long-forgotten words he last heard when Kathleen murmured at his bedside in his hospital ward. Christ! he thought, I was younger than these two are now. He opened his eyes and screwed himself around in his seat. "Did someone say something about chocolates?"

Caitlin picked up the box and sliced the cellophane with her thumbnail. "Hard-center or soft?"

"Surprise me."

Soon afterwards, fortified by their pitstop with its mugs of tea and coffee, they headed back to the car. Alex paused in the sunshine to take off his jumper. Caitlin stared at the picture on his t-shirt, an elephant walking into the jungle, a small boy at its side. Unchain the elephants, read the caption.

"Nice shirt," she said. "So, you really are into elephants."

"I love them," he replied, then packed her crutches in the back of the car before she could ask him anything else.

"Right, next stop is Ouyen, for a nice lunch at the pub. Then three more hours and we'll be at Hay. And tomorrow, the big smoke: Sydney."

An hour and a half later, Cara pulled over to the side of the road. "Well, will you look at that?"

"What?"

"Over there," she pointed.

To their right, silvery-blue reflections of sunlight sparkled off a large salt lake nestled in front of a low rust-colored sandhill clothed in gray-green scrub. A statue of a man, dressed in white sunhat and shorts, was running in alarm across the water, pursued by two sharks, or at least two shark fins, protruding above the surface's crust of salt.

"Someone's got a sense of humor," said Tim.

Caitlin took her phone out of her bag and snapped some photos. Her forehead creased in thought. "What if it's not just a joke?"

"What?"

"What if there's a message in that sculpture? You know how comedians can make you laugh at something that would otherwise be too shocking to look at?" No one replied, so Caitlin kept talking. "There's a guy, panicking because he's being chased by two sharks, right? But what if he looked under the water and realized, they were only cut-outs of fins, and there weren't any sharks? He's running away from his false perception that two metal triangles are dangerous."

"Have you taken too many pain pills, cuz?"

She sighed. "He's not running away from sharks. He's running away from his own fear."

"You've got a point," Cara said, her eyes flicking over Tim beside her and then to the rear vision mirror so she could cast a sly glance at Alex and Caitlin. An uncomfortable helplessness settled in her stomach: they were all running from fears that she didn't understand and couldn't help them with. She resolved to pray harder. "We're too stupefied with driving to keep up with your agile brain, Cait," she said with forced cheer. "Everybody ready? Not far to lunch now."

Cara pulled out onto the empty highway to drive the last few kilometers into town. "Lunch at the Victoria Hotel. Caitlin will like it." She winked at her in the rear vision mirror.

"Why?"

"Perfect place for a history buff like you."

As Cara turned the corner into Rowe Street, they passed a building advertising a funeral and monument service, then she parked in front of a long two-story hotel. Caitlin surveyed its balcony with its wrought-iron decorations and its imposing high façade. "Wow, this must have been a busy place once. And now it's almost forgotten."

"Almost. Except we're here for lunch." Cara locked the car after them.

Entering the dark hallway, Alex held open the polished, timber and leadlight door to the restaurant. Original glass light fittings hung from decorative ceiling roses, and art deco leadlight graced timber screens, recalling the grandeur of days long past, and contrasting with modern, red carpet and plain, laminated tables.

After lunch they took a short walk up and down the main street, and Caitlin practiced using the crutches.

"You're doing much better," Tim said, clapping her on the shoulder with a look of pride on his face as they returned to the car.

Alex drove, and, munching chocolates, the rest of them relaxed, soothed by the gentle swaying of the car on the highway, and Kathleen's gentle voice on the recording.

A warm breeze blew little puffs of dust up from the baking dirt and scattered it across the single asphalt path that bisected the grave-yard set on a steep hillside. Caitlin was a lonely figure, parked on the path in her wheelchair, watching as the others fanned out to scour three jumbled rows of burial plots up the hill. She let the crutches, propped against her chair, clatter to the ground and slowly wheeled herself along the path, looking up at towering statues on either side; stopping in front of a life-sized Jesus with his sacred heart on show, crowded by hundreds and hundreds of graves. The traffic noise from surrounding streets faded away. Her skin began to crawl, and she checked the sun's position. Still high in the sky, no risk of them being locked in yet, even if the "Gates Locked at Dusk" sign wasn't precise enough for her.

Stone slabs over some of the burials had cracked and slipped, leaving gaping holes under them like tunnels leading into the graves. Vandalized by time or human hands, she wasn't sure which. She shuddered.

"You right there, cuz?"

She jumped and turned the wheelchair to face Alex. "You sneaking up on me?" she asked, only half teasing.

"Sorry, I didn't mean to startle you. I was going to call out to you that we've found her. But it didn't feel right to holler in a place like this."

"No, I can get that," she nodded. "Show me then."

He pushed her chair along companionably, back to where she had started her exploration. "We found something else, too."

"Some*thing*?"

"Someone. Several someones. All together."

"You're not making a lot of sense."

He snapped on her brakes and handed up the crutches. "Can you manage? The ground's pretty uneven, but it's not far." Tim and Cara were standing together, nearby on the slope.

"Of course, I can manage. Can you bring the flowers?"

He took two bunches of flowers out of a plastic bag hanging off one of the handles of her chair. Pink roses and orange carnations. "You'll be glad we brought two bunches."

"Well then, lead on. Show me why." Her smile was resolute as she balanced on her crutches.

He led her along a rough dirt path with graves on either side and stopped in front of several wide plots, with a low brick edging around them, filled with gravel. Tim and Cara were further along the next row, and Caitlin looked at him, confused.

"Read the markers," he urged her.

Polished, black granite slabs ran along the top edges of the graves, inscribed with words.

In Loving Memory of Our Lady's Nurses

She looked at him in wonder. He nodded and she scanned the names. *"Theresa A McLaughlin … First Mother General of Our Lady's Nurses … oh, that's Cissie! And look, Mary Drohan … could that be the Nurse Mary that Kathleen mentioned?"* She picked her way along the row, reading, "Catherine Lynch. Catherine McGrath." She stopped and her breath caught. *"Reverend Father Timothy E. McGrath. Missionary of the Sacred Heart. Founder of Our Lady's Nurses of The Poor.* Oh, Alex, he's here, with the nurses. He came home at last."

She stood in silence, her eyes moist, for a few long moments. "Leave them the carnations, Alex. I can't do it."

He patted her hand and stepped forward. The flowers were bright against the windswept gravel.

"Come on. There's more to see."

"Is George here?"

"I'm not sure, come and see what you think."

They made their way in silence to the others, Caitlin's breath ragged with the heat and the effort of avoiding accidentally placing a crutch on someone's grave. Understanding she required all her concentration to manage, Alex waited until they were standing in front of Kathleen's grave before he spoke.

"Here she is."

Caitlin's eyes flicked across the wide grave, marked by a low, lichen-encrusted, stone edging. The headstone seemed out of place, newer than the edging, and newer than the other tombstones nearby. It was off center, as if it were marking only one half of the plot. She read in silence.

Sacred to the Memory of
Kathleen O'Grady.
Born 1892. Passed from this life 1974 aged eighty-two
years. Loving wife of George (deceased), and mother of
Evelyn.
No longer alone.

A gilded line ran through the marble, and below it the inscription:

And to her beloved husband George,
Who gave his all for his country
In the Great War.

A great, shuddering sob wracked Caitlin's body. "We found him. He's here. He was here all along!" Tears ran down her face.

Alex and Cara automatically moved towards her but froze at the soft sound of Tim clearing his throat. Her father took a few awkward steps on his detested prosthetic leg, reached her, and held out his arms. Alex caught the crutches deftly as she let them go to hug her father. Tucking them under one arm, Alex draped the other, complete with the bunch of roses, around his mother's shoulders. She was teary too, as they turned around, surveying the cemetery as it rolled away down the hill from them, giving Tim and Caitlin some privacy.

"So poor George is resting in peace with Great-granny Kath, after all. Seems to me, you've done something good this week, Alex," she said under her breath.

"I'm not sure I can take the credit, Mum."

"What do you mean?"

He scuffed his toes in the dirt, then froze in horror as he realized he was on someone's unmarked grave. "I don't know, Mum …" He was reluctant to admit his thoughts. "This will sound a bit weird. It's almost like we've been walking in a saint's footsteps this week. Like this whole thing was some kind of divine set up, to get everyone back together."

Cara studied his face, her expression unreadable.

"You think I'm nuts, don't you?"

"No, I can see you're serious. Stranger things have happened."

"Do you believe in saints?"

She laughed. "I'm a lapsed Catholic. As soon as I was old enough to refuse to go to Mass, I did. I've never been back. I used to sit in Church bored out of my brain. Mum was never that religious. She went to Church, but she never talked about it, you know. She just respected my decision it wasn't for me. Let me come to my own conclusions." She gave a short laugh. "Then I never talked to you about it, and suddenly here you are, teaching me about saints."

"Only about one, Mum, and technically she's not recognized as a saint yet."

"Eileen O'Connor. Great-granny Kathleen's best friend." Her eyes were soft, searching. "Do you honestly believe she came back from the grave, to help our family?"

He flushed crimson but nodded his head. "Yes. Yes, I think I do."

Scrunching noises in the dirt behind them warned them the others were joining them now.

"Are you ready to give Kathleen her flowers?" Tim asked, his face somber.

"Sure. Who is doing the honors?"

"You can, sis."

Alex studied the pink roses as he passed them to his mum. "Oh, I didn't ask you, Mum. Did that pink rose in the garden come from a cutting of Kathleen's rosebush?"

Cara smiled at the memory. "Yes, it did. Your father knew how sorry I was to leave Sydney. He wanted to surprise me, so he asked Evie to give him a cutting, and he grew it up for me and hid it in the car when we drove down to Adelaide. It's definitely Kathleen's rose."

"Eileen gave her that rose, originally. Our family's been growing Eileen's rose bush, all these years. Kathleen and George, Evie and Kitty, and now you," Caitlin smiled. *"Souvenir d'un Ami."*

Cara gasped, washed with gratitude that she'd valued the rose enough that her husband had grown a cutting for her. "I'll get Paul to strike a few more cuttings. Then you can have one, too."

"I'd like that."

They accompanied Cara the few steps to Kathleen and George's graveside. She stepped reverently onto the dusty soil, and bowing her head, bent to lay the flowers right in the center of the plot, like a bridge between Kathleen and her long-lost husband.

Settled in the kitchenette of their apartment, Alex fixed his gaze on Caitlin and leaned towards her chair. "Let's not bury any more skeletons," he whispered in her ear.

"What?"

"No more secrets or skeletons in the closet. Promise?"

She pulled away far enough to scrutinize his face. Her lips trembled for a moment, then she smiled a faint, crooked smile. "I promise."

"Whatever will our descendants have to talk about in a hundred years' time?"

Alex picked up the paper containing a lock of Eileen's hair and turned it to catch the light. "Saint's hair isn't a skeleton, is it? Even if you found it in a cupboard. Maybe they can start there."

Cara burst into the room. "Look what I've found," she exclaimed. "I walked past a Catholic church." She waved a book triumphantly.

Caitlin grabbed the book and stared at its cover, at the color image of a young woman with long brown hair, shimmering with dark auburn highlights, staring serenely direct ahead, as if she were looking straight into Caitlin's own eyes, challenging her somehow. Her hair cascaded over a pale blue gown, with lacy edging, and her long, thin hands were folded demurely in her lap. Eventually, she held it up for everyone to see. "It's the portrait, isn't it? That Eileen left for the nurses to remember her by after she died?"

No one replied, and she flicked to the acknowledgements page. "It is. Painting by Norman Carter, 1920." Forgetting her companions, Caitlin turned to the illustrations. Eileen as a serious-looking child, an adult Eileen standing with other adults, removing any doubt that she was less than four feet tall. A lone, forlorn figure with a large, fur muff, surrounded by pigeons in St Mark's Square, Venice, somehow commanding the attention of gawping passers-by. Dressed in white lace, ready for an audience with Pope Benedict XV. Sitting in the garden with her dog, Rags. The tall figure of Father McGrath.

"Dear Eileen," she sighed. "She has so much to teach us."

"Like what?" asked Alex, cupping his chin in his hand and leaning closer.

"How much time have we all wasted, wishing and praying that things would be different? That we'd be healed, we'd feel better, that bad stuff would magically go away. I've wasted so much effort… wasted it on self-pity, or on fighting things I couldn't change."

Cara opened her mouth to speak, to defend her niece against her own self-accusations.

"It's alright, Auntie Cara. Eileen didn't do any of that. She had a life of pain and illness. Dreadful suffering. But instead of praying God would spare her, she just got on with things and spent her life working, and praying, to alleviate the suffering of others." She lowered her gaze for a moment. "She never said, "Oh God, make me well today, so tomorrow I can serve the poor." She started serving the poor and the sick, right then, right there, right where she was. She saw what people needed, and that was more important to her than anything else, than her own circumstances. And she just trusted she could make a difference, through the Grace of God, in spite of everything." Caitlin looked around the room, making shy eye contact with each of them in turn. "I think that's why she could achieve so much, that now she is being investigated for sainthood."

"That makes sense," Alex agreed. "It seems impossible on the face of it, doesn't it? How could someone who was always sick and in pain, often paralyzed, sometimes blind, who only grew to be three foot ten tall, and died at the age of twenty-eight, possibly get into a position where she might be Australia's second saint? You're onto something."

Cara spoke slowly. "These days people are laboring under false expectations. That bad things don't happen to good people. If we are ill or disabled, we can't be expected to be good and productive. I don't know where those crazy ideas came from, superstitions really. Eileen wasn't burdened with those kinds of thoughts. She was from a different age, where people knew bad things happen to everyone, where people did get sick and die young, or have diseases that couldn't be cured."

"And no one went around asking stupid, victim-blaming questions, like they do now?" Alex asked, an edge of bitterness in his voice.

"Like what?" asked Cara.

"Like so and so's got cancer, it must be because they've not been eating a healthy diet."

"Or I wonder why they manifested that in their life? I've heard people who claim to be spiritual ask that about someone who got into a violent relationship," Caitlin's mouth puckered as if she'd bitten a lemon.

Tim knitted his brows together. "I know what you mean. The things I've heard could blow your socks off. But I reckon it's a way they try to protect themselves. Bad things don't happen to good people, so if I am good—eat healthy, make sure I don't 'attract bad energy'—I'll be a good person and I'll be immune from things going wrong."

They lapsed into a contemplative silence for a while.

"I have a question," Cara said eventually, a catch of emotion in her voice. "Mum was listening to the tapes when she died. You don't happen to know which one, do you?"

Alex nodded. "I spoke to the nurse who was looking after her. Nan had asked her to rewind the tape so she could listen to part of it again. I'll play it for you." He reached across the table and took his mother's hand, squeezing it gently as Kathleen's voice filled the room. Cara's eyes slowly filled with tears as the words soaked in.

I'm tired, Little Mother. I don't know if I can go on.

Your face is as serene as ever. Though somehow, it's changed ... Ah, I see what it is now. The little pucker lines between your eyebrows are gone, smoothed away.

You still understand my thoughts, because you answer me, "There's no pain here, Kathleen. You'll have no pain when you get here."

Do my eyes look as round as they feel, Eileen? "No pain?"

"None at all." Your smile is soft as moonlight and, as you nod encouragement, your hair spills over your shoulders like a curly waterfall and brushes against my cheek ...

THAT SAME FRIDAY–IN COOGEE

Sunshine soaked through Tim's denim shirt, warming his skin as he stood at the top of the curving stretch of paving at Coogee Beach, watching Caitlin pick her cautious way down the steps on her crutches. Alex hovered at her side, ready to catch her if she stumbled. At the bottom step, she hesitated, then lowered a crutch experimentally, pushing to see how far it sank into the pale yellow sand, like a ferryman testing the depth of a river. He smiled to himself, wondering what she'd do when she realized it's impossible to walk on soft sand using crutches.

A look of surprise formed on her face, then her mouth opened, and she laughed, hauling her crutch out of the hole and shaking sand off it. Alex took it from her and laid it on the step.

The brisk breeze picked up Alex's words and carried them to Tim's ears. "Last one in is a rotten egg!" Caitlin squealed as he swung her up into his arms, ignoring the clatter of the second crutch as it fell on the steps. He couldn't run on the beach, carrying her, but he struggled manfully as the sand tried to shackle his ankles, and strode into the breaking surf, the bottoms of his jeans darkening in the water.

Caitlin shrieked with laughter and Tim chuckled. Cara wore a worried frown. "What if he gets her leg brace wet? Or full of sand?"

Tim studied her face: the tiny crows' feet around his sister's eyes, and fine vertical lines above her top lip. Gray streaks that he hadn't noticed in her hair before. A shotgun blast hit his stomach, the realization he hadn't really seen his sister for a long time, hadn't paid attention to her. She was getting older, and she'd been through her own stuff. Alex was injured in the car accident too, broken glass almost cost him an eye, and the scars on his face must have confronted his mother every time she looked at him. Where the hell was I, when she needed me? Tim wondered as self-recrimination burst through him like the shockwave from an exploding grenade. Her eyes were still on him, that strange mixture of a little girl's trust in her big brother, and wariness learned by experiencing his distances and unpredictable moods. She was waiting for an answer, he thought, and swallowed, wondering what he could say.

He didn't say anything. He just eased a little closer to her and slid an arm around her shoulders. She took a sharp inbreath at the unexpectedness of it, then tension melted away from her upper back. She didn't say anything either, but Tim could almost hear her smile. They watched as Alex splashed through the water, up past his knees, and Caitlin held her legs out as straight as she could, above the waves.

"Her brace …" Cara protested weakly as a breaker sped towards them.

Tim's smile was crooked. "They've been through worse," he said, and gave her a squeeze.

Alex turned back to shore, then labored across the sand to the steps, where he lowered Caitlin down, making sure she had secure footing. She was laughing, grasping his shoulder for balance as he panted for breath, bent over and bracing his arms against his thighs.

Cara's body stiffened, preparing to pull away from Tim and hasten down the steps to pick up the discarded crutches for her niece, but a passing tourist did it before she could.

"They've got this, Cara," Tim cautioned her. "They're not little kids anymore."

"No, they're not." Her tone was thoughtful. "They always were good for each other."

Alex sat on one of the steps and tugged at his shoelaces, then pulled his canvas sneakers off his feet. He tipped them upside down, one at a time, a one-man comedy act. He peeled his socks off with difficulty and hammed up wringing them out.

"You're an idiot." Caitlin couldn't help laughing, clutching her crutches with the effort of staying upright.

Cara's fingers twitched with a fleeting urge to take a photo of them, then her hand fell back to her side. Some memories are best stored in the heart.

Walking back to the car, Alex's wet jeans flapped heavily against his calves, and his limp sneakers dangled from his hand.

"I'm not sure I should be letting you in the car like that. You'll get it all messed up," Cara teased as the doors clicked unlocked.

"It's alright, Mum, I've got a plastic bag I can put my shoes in. And I can take my jeans off if you like." He started to unbuckle his belt.

Cara's look of horror made him laugh, and when she exclaimed, "Jesus, Mary, and Joseph, will you just get in the car!" the others joined him.

Laughter still echoing in her ears, Cara glanced at the two young faces reflected in the rear vision mirror. Where does the time go? And when will these two partner up? She recalled Adam, the young man Caitlin was dating, who seemed to have dumped her while she was in hospital after the crash. She'd never warmed to him, herself, but that was a low act, even for him. And Alex? She'd wondered once whether he was gay because he never brought any girls home. Later, she worked out he didn't like to be around most people, would only let a few people get close to him, and preferred to figure out virtual problems, rather than physical ones. Thank goodness he got on this well with Caitlin; she'd be able to be there for him, if anything happened to herself and Paul, she thought with a shudder.

* * *

Alex's Adam's apple bobbed up and down as he cleared his throat. "We made a promise, Cait, remember. No more secrets. Don't you think it's time you told me about that bastard ex-boyfriend of yours?"

Caitlin's heart pounded. Her first impulse was to escape, but there was nowhere to run. The two of them were holed up in her bedroom in the apartment, giving Tim and Cara some privacy to talk amongst themselves in the other room. But looking into Alex's tender, blue eyes, she swallowed back a trite denial. Wringing her hands in her lap, she glanced down before she began to speak, her faltering voice so low he had to lean forward to hear her.

"I didn't understand what happened … I thought he cared about me. He said he loved me." Alex nodded sympathetically. "But he was getting weird. Texting me all the time and getting all clingy and if I didn't answer him, he'd get mad. I tried to explain I was busy with assignments and work, but he kept at me. I gave in and went on another date with him, and it didn't go too well. I decided I should get out of there."

Alex's eyes narrowed as he watched her. What she had said that night didn't make sense, but the accident had pushed it out of his mind. "You said he had passed out drunk, and you didn't want to stay."

She nodded, unable to look at him. "I lied."

"Sometimes, it's easier to lie." His tone was gentle, laced with understanding. "What happened?"

She turned to Alex with mute appeal.

Awkwardly, he asked, "You don't have to tell me."

Alarmed, she shook her head. She wanted him here. She was tired of lies and half-truths.

His question came out raw, through gritted teeth. "You said before that not all your bruises were caused by the crash."

She struggled to find the right words, then surrendered, because there were no right words. Gently though, wanting to protect him because he has been hurt enough through caring for her already. She took a deep breath. "I knew, deep down, something was really wrong, but I thought it would work out. He always said the right things. But that night, he lost it. I was terrified."

The yoke of silence had broken in two and, sliding off her shoulders, fell to the floor.

"Why didn't you tell anyone?"

"Everyone always said he was nice. He went to a good school, he was smart. I thought people liked him. At first, I couldn't believe he would treat me that way. I couldn't say the words even to myself."

"And then?"

"I thought no one would believe me. So, I never said anything."

"I believed you."

"Yeah, thanks." She frowned, wondering again how it could have happened, how it could have been so easy to shut everyone else out.

"When we get home, you're going to make an appointment with a counsellor, aren't you?"

"Yes, Alex."

"And I'll drive you."

Sighing, she let her shoulders relax. "Yes, Alex. Thank you."

"Pinky promise?"

Her voice brightened, and she smiled. "You're incorrigible."

"Thank you." He half bowed, as best he could, still sprawled across the bed. He stretched his legs out across the single bed and wriggled his toes, then folded his arms behind his head and rested them on the wall. "You okay?"

Caitlin perched on the bed, her good leg bent and her injured leg straight. She nodded. "Yeah. Thanks. Let's talk about something else now."

He thought for a moment, searching for the right topic. Their Nan popped into his mind, and his face relaxed into a nostalgic smile. "Did you know all that stuff about Nan, that people told us at the funeral?"

She shook her head.

"Me either. She hand-sewed seventy little gowns for stillborn babies and donated them to the hospital to give to parents who had lost babies. What a story!"

Caitlin's gaze was a challenge. "We all have stories no one hears about, don't we?"

"You certainly did." He parried her question.

Something in her steeled, and he sensed the change of mood and became wary. She turned an unwavering gaze onto him. "So, what's your secret, then? You said everyone has one."

"Me? Why would I have any secrets?" He started to wriggle as if he were about to escape, but she blocked him by moving her braced leg across his shins.

"Checkmate."

He froze, afraid to hurt her. "That's a low move," he complained. "And you don't play chess."

"You've been up to something."

"What do you mean?" He looked away, studying the crinkles in the plain, white bed sheet with unnecessary interest.

"Skipping breakfast to be cloistered in your room with your laptop."

"I had an assignment."

"Nah. All those phone notifications this morning. I heard them, even with your door shut. One after the other, like alarms going off." She swung her leg off his shins and focused squarely on his face. "I told you my secret. Now you're going to tell me yours."

He held his hands up, in mock surrender, and grinned. "Okay. Not here. It's still daylight. Let's ask if we can borrow the car."

The snapping of seatbelts, then Caitlin twisted in her seat. "Where are you taking me this time?"

Alex handed her the biography of Eileen before starting the car. "To where one of these photos was taken."

"Ooh, another mystery?" She flicked through the book to the photographs.

"No. I just thought you'd like to see where one of the photos was taken. The one at Coogee Beach."

"We went to Coogee Beach."

"Not the place she went to; look at the photo. There are rocks, no sand."

"Okay?"

"I checked on the internet. I think I found the spot. I thought you might like to see it. It's a bit further up the hill than where we went before."

"And you're taking me there to distract me from asking about your secrets?"

He let out a slow breath, amused. "No, I know I won't manage that. But I thought if you are going to interrogate me, we might as well have nice scenery. And maybe something sweet and chocolatey at a café after."

They were quiet for the short car trip, each lost in their own thoughts. When they reached the beach, Alex took the wheelchair out of the car boot. "Into your chariot, Madam."

"You're sure I can't use crutches?"

"I don't know what the path will be like. And this way you have a nice comfortable seat to take in the view."

She sighed and maneuvered into the chair. "Do you know where we're going?"

"I don't know the exact spot, there are quite a lot of rocks." He handed over her phone with the map open on its screen.

"Oh look! We're right by Wylie's Baths."

"What?"

"Wylie's Baths. A hundred years ago, there were swimming baths built all along the coast here, like big swimming pools in the sea, but walled off so they were safe. Back then, two Australian women trained for the Olympics here, 1912, I think. Mina Wylie, whose family owned the baths, and Fanny Durack. Their club banned them from swimming in front of men, and they had to do their own fundraising to get to Europe. Fanny was the first woman to ever win an Olympic gold medal in swimming, and the first Australian woman to win gold. Mina came second."

"How do you know this stuff?"

"Just interested in history, I guess."

"In 1912, you said?"

"I think that's right."

"Sounds like they were legends too. I wonder if Eileen knew them. Come on, let's find Eileen's rocks." He started wheeling her across a rough lawn, then onto the path that hugged the cliff edge. The salt air filled with the gentle whooshing of waves lapping over the rocks below. A break in the low bushes lining the path opened onto an uneven shelf of rust-colored rock glowing orange in the late afternoon sunlight. He turned her chair to better admire the view of the flame-tinted horizon, which they enjoyed in companionable silence.

After a few minutes, Caitlin tilted her head to study his profile. There was a faraway look in his eyes, as if he were looking far beyond the deep blue ocean, to somewhere else altogether.

"Where are you?" she whispered.

He shook himself, coming back to the present. "Come and stand on the rocks. I'll help you."

Standing with her arm around his waist, she leaned into his shoulder. A light breeze tousled her hair. "You picked the perfect spot for a story."

"It started with a dream. A couple of years ago, I guess …"

"Go on."

"It's kind of odd."

"Dreams usually are. You can tell me."

"I was in a village; I don't know where. Thatched huts clustered together. There weren't any people, and it felt deserted. I didn't know where I was, but somehow, I knew it was exactly the right place to be."

Caitlin shuffled her weight a little on her good leg, and he offered her his free hand as a walking stick. "There was a path through some bushes, at the edge of the clearing around the village, which led into the jungle, and I felt like I had to take that path. I had to push my way through vines, but the path itself was smooth. Something was ahead, but I couldn't see it, so I followed the path. I stepped out into another clearing, small enough that it was still shaded by the trees. I realized I was all alone, but somehow, I was expecting something would happen."

She snuggled against his shoulder, with a soft murmur of encouragement.

"And suddenly there was this thundering noise crashing through the undergrowth, coming straight towards me. My first instinct was to run, but I couldn't move, my feet were stuck to the ground. Bushes in front of me began to ripple, then a huge elephant exploded into the clearing, coming right at me. I just stood there, right in her path."

"What did it do?"

"She. It was a she." His voice was dreamlike, entrancing.

"What did she do?"

"She came right up to me, then stopped. She knelt in front of me and bent her head down. And just by intuition, I knew what she wanted. I rested my forehead against her forehead. We stayed touching heads, for a long time."

"What happened next?"

He grimaced. "Nothing. I woke up."

"You met an elephant, but nothing happened?"

"Well, I guess I just felt," he struggled to find the right words, "at peace. Like that elephant knew me and accepted me and totally, one hundred percent loved me."

"That's so cool. Did the elephant say anything?"

"I don't know."

"What do you think the dream meant?"

"It was a dream, Cait." He wished he could remember. "I don't know if it meant anything."

"But you knew you had to follow that path?"

"Oh yes. I absolutely knew that."

"And following it, led you, eventually, here. With me. To the place where Eileen came to enjoy the seaside."

His face twisted as he tried to work out what she meant. "What are you saying?"

"Eileen went to India, you know."

"Oh yes, so she did." The hair stood up on the back of his neck. He tried to sound nonchalant. "Do you think she met any elephants when she was there?"

"Well, it would be kind of cool if she did, wouldn't it?"

"Is that all you have to say?"

"Yes, it is. Because I have a feeling that's only the beginning of your story."

"Now you're psychic, are you?"

"No. But you brought me here to tell me what you're doing that requires such intense work on your computer. So, I am assuming whatever project you're working on, is connected to that dream somehow."

"Yeah, you're right," he agreed. He paused, looking self-conscious.

"It's okay. Just say it."

"I couldn't get the elephant out of my head. Then it became all elephants. I researched elephants. I tried to figure out whether she was African or Asian; Asian elephants have smaller ears. I decided maybe she was Indian. I guess you could say I became obsessed."

"Okay."

"But now, I'm not sure if it *was* just a dream."

She waited, coaxing him to go on with her eyes.

"Well, when we saw that photograph of Eileen and Father McGrath in the jungle village ... I felt the scene was very familiar, like I'd seen it before."

"You said something about déjà vu. And you did look a bit odd, as I recall."

"Well, you don't expect to see scenes from your dreams in old photographs, do you?"

"Exactly the same?"

"No, the dream village was deserted." His face creased with the effort of remembering. "There definitely weren't any cattle."

"Okay. So, it wasn't the same village, but it was similar."

"Yes. Like I said, I got obsessed with elephants —"

"You fell in love with elephants," she interjected.

"I guess. I wanted to do something to help them. And then I read about an elephant sanctuary. I decided to raise money for them.

But what's a computer geek like me going to do to raise money while they're trying to do their PhD?"

"Something geeky, I suppose."

"Exactly. I made a share-trading bot."

"A what?"

"A computer program to detect stock market movements so I can trade shares and make a profit to donate to the shelter."

"Clever."

Pride painted his cheeks pink. "Thanks. I am already sending them money and thought I'd start saving to go and visit. They have a program where volunteers stay there and work with the elephants. Help feed them, look after them, that sort of thing."

"That sounds awesome." He beamed at her praise, but there was something in his eyes that made Caitlin ask another question. "Where did you say this elephant sanctuary is?"

"I didn't tell you."

"I know." Her eyes were teasing.

His mouth twitched. "Sri Lanka."

"Sri Lanka? That's where the photo was taken, isn't it?"

He nodded sheepishly.

"When are you going?"

"I was thinking maybe I'd go next year. And then I saw the photo, and I'm sure I'll go there, but maybe not so soon."

"Why?"

"Well, I was thinking about what you said about Eileen: how she just saw what needed to be done, and did it, starting right from where she was. So, instead of putting pressure on myself to save the money quickly, I thought maybe I could find something local to support."

"Like what?"

"I'm going to volunteer for a local wildlife rescue group."

She recalled his calm reassurance when they were waiting for the ambulance. "You'd be great at that."

"Thanks."

"Though Sri Lanka does sound awesome." She paused, studying the ocean for a moment. "Do you think I'll be recovered enough to go with you, when you go?"

"Of course, you'll be recovered by then," he retorted. He shuffled a little, a flush creeping up from his collar. "Though someone else is coming along already."

She pushed herself far enough away from him to be able to see his red cheeks. Her voice was loud, excited. "You've met someone?"

"Yes." Making sure her balance was secure, he withdrew a hand to take his phone from his pocket. He called up a photo onto the screen and handed it to her.

A relaxed, olive-skinned face smiled up at her, a pronounced gap between his top front teeth. Dark eyes, and dark brown hair, short and immaculately coiffed.

"He looks lovely, Alex." Her eyes were warm. "How come all the cute guys are gay?"

"They're not. You'll find someone." He felt her body stiffen against his arm. "Not now. When you're ready."

She grunted. A wave of defensiveness built in her, and tears of grief and rage pricked in her eyes.

"You're hurting now, Cait. But you'll heal. And then you'll meet someone. And Damian and I will suss him out for you."

"Promise?"

"I promise."

She dabbed her eyes with the back of her hand. It was too perfect an evening to spoil with tears for the past. Together, they watched the ocean, settling into deeper shades of midnight blue, as the sun set behind them, until she felt calm again. "Do your folks know?"

"I reckon they must. Mum's pretty switched on. But we've never talked about it."

"You're going to, right?"

"Yes. Yes, it's time."

"Are you nervous?"

He looked into her eyes, and then out to sea again. "No. Not now."

She squeezed his waist and followed his gaze over the water.

"You're getting tired?" he asked.

"Just a few more moments," she begged, letting her gaze rove over the rocks, mottled dark browns and charcoals now. She sighed softly, closed her eyes, and called to mind the photograph of Eileen, seated on the rocks at the front of a group of nurses dressed in their white uniforms, her long hair teased by the unseen fingers of a sea breeze. Looking, unblinking, into the camera, at her, urging her … inviting her? To what? The breeze had become cold; she shivered as she opened her eyes. A long-gone presence seemed to coalesce in the shadows playing amongst the rocks. Caitlin nodded acknowledgement to the shadows, then answered her own question: to trust enough to keep going. To live her own life, whatever it may bring. To find her own kind of love story, just as her great-great grandmother Kathleen had done.

Words Eileen said long ago played the chords of her heart as if it were a harp, and the vibrations filled her body and her soul, and brought fresh, cleansing tears to her eyes. *Remember that sometimes and in some places, Our dear Lady may have no worthier, no better person to work through save my poor worthless self. Or through you, my dear children. There is nothing so wonderful, so powerful … as love.*

The sun's last rays slipped behind the horizon.

I will always be with you, I will do more for you from heaven than I could do here.

Caitlin hugged Alex. When she was confident the tremor had faded from her throat, she grinned and said, "Did you say something about chocolate?"

JANUARY 10, 2020, OUR LADY'S HOME – COOGEE

Her sensible shoes made no sound as the white-haired sister walked through the open, glass doors of the function room at Our Lady's Home, to where the overflowing crowd was seated in the shade of the verandah, listening to the annual service commemorating Eileen's life relayed over loudspeakers. She offered communion wafers to them, all the while, her experienced eye roving over them, her flock.

His chair pushed away from his neighbors, his eyes downcast, a defensive slump to his shoulders, Tim stuck out from the rest. He had agreed to come with Alex and Caitlin, out of curiosity and because he wanted a chance to see Eileen's house, but he baulked at the idea of Mass. He had encouraged them to go into the meeting hall, telling them he'd be much more comfortable out the back. Sister Margaret Mary's eyes barely registered surprise, and she continued passing wafers around without any hesitation in her step. He shook his head without looking up as she stood before him, then watched her slowly make her way back indoors.

As soon as the service was over, Sister Margaret Mary made her way through the milling people in the hall, to the verandah. Checking for him. He was still there, looking awkward, as if his mind was filled with thoughts he didn't know what to do with. His crutches discarded on the ground beside his chair, he looked abandoned now everyone else had been lured away by the promise of tea and scones. Her smile was soft and radiant as she approached.

"Do you ever feel you are getting under foot because you can't walk as fast as other people?" she asked confidentially, continuing before he could respond. "Is it alright if I sit here for a moment, out of the way until the crowd thins out?"

His answer was a brief, automatic nod.

She passed a small card with a sepia photograph on it to him, and even though his first impulse was to push it away, he accepted it, and let his eyes rest on the image. A young woman with long flowing hair caught up by a breeze. Sitting in a cane wheelchair, a smile on her face, but her eyes deeply shadowed.

"Eileen was paralyzed for much of her life, and even when she got better, she was never very mobile, and she had terrible pain," Sister said, with reverence in her voice. "And yet she somehow managed to found this place and fill it with love."

He grunted and shuffled his foot, a feeble protest as if maybe he'd get up and leave.

"Her life was her story. A love story."

Tim didn't reply, but his shoulders dropped. Her solidarity was eroding his resistance. Her smile never wavered, and eventually he let his gaze slide across and see it. *You have a beautiful smile,* he thought, but didn't allow himself to speak. After decades of working with the sick and broken, the alcoholic and the destitute, she knew this was the moment.

"You know, I could badly do with a cup of tea. But not out here, it's a bit too busy, don't you think?"

He nodded his surrender.

"It's a bit too busy for you too, perhaps?"

He nodded again, helpless to resist.

"Can I invite you into the office for a cup of tea?" Sister Margaret Mary's smile was gentle as she pressed home her advantage, and he reached down for his crutches before standing beside her.

"We've all got stories," she said. "I was wondering if you'd like to tell me something of yours? And after we've finished our tea, the crowd in the chapel will be thinning out. Perhaps you'd like to come there with me."

* * *

Caitlin stood with her stick in one hand, and her other hand in the crook of Alex's elbow, watching in amazement as the scene unfolded, and her father followed the nun into the office building.

"How did she do that?" asked Alex, in a tone of wonder.

"I have absolutely no idea."

"What do we do now?"

"I'd like to go back to the chapel. Dad will find us when he's done."

Alex took a sausage roll from a platter a passing waitress offered them, and nodded, munching.

Sitting in the back of the chapel, they watched as Sister Margaret Mary showed Tim to a seat in the second row. He didn't see them, and taking his seat in the pew, bowed his head in thought, or, perhaps, prayer.

Sister was still smiling as she advanced down the aisle. She fixed the cousins with her gaze for a moment, inviting them to follow her.

In the enclosed verandah at the back of the chapel, Caitlin whispered, "My dad … How did you do that?"

Sister Margaret Mary's eyes were luminous. "There are many kinds of love story." Her gaze rested on the back of Tim's head for a long moment before she smiled the smile that can change people's lives. It was her smile, but somehow, it was Eileen's smile too, passed on from nurse to nurse and sister to sister, for over a hundred years. "Loving the poor and the broken, that is my love story." She turned back to the chapel; people were still lining up to kneel at the edge of the hole in the floor, where, ninety-nine years after her death, Eileen's coffin was exposed, decorated with blue satin and tulle, and silk flowers. "It was Eileen's love story too."

EPILOGUE

So, what was my love story? My love story was always about my family. Some of them were poor and broken, too. I couldn't save Georgie. But I came back for my grandson Timothy, and for Caitlin, and Alex. My heart swelled to bursting as I watched those wonderful, young people standing together, watching over Tim. They're going to be alright.

A ramrod-straight figure walked confidently on two sound legs down the aisle of the chapel. He paused to lay an unfelt hand on Tim's shoulder. Unfelt, but some slight sensation registered, and Tim rubbed his face thoughtfully.

He stopped for a moment in front of my darling Alex. Those boys really were dead ringers.

Caitlin's skin tingled as he gently walked right through her. Cornflower blue eyes crinkled into a smile.

My throat clamped tight around a ball of long-forgotten joy. "Georgie …"

He linked his strong, young arm through mine. "It's done, Kathleen. Come into the garden. Eileen's waiting."

AUTHOR'S NOTE

I remember the first time I saw Eileen O'Connor. Well, I didn't see her, not really. Not then.

As you might imagine, there's a story behind this story, about how I found myself writing a novel about a saint.

Years ago, I belonged to a meditation group which had a patron saint. The saint was Mary MacKillop, chosen because she established her order here, in Adelaide. So, when I visited Sydney in 2017, it was natural I would visit the chapel which houses Mary MacKillop's tomb, even though I am not a Catholic.

The hushed, reverential atmosphere at Mary's tomb was irresistible, and I visited it every morning and evening while I was in Sydney. On one occasion, as I sat in silent meditation, an image of Mary coalesced in my mind's eye, and she seemed to walk right past me. For a moment, I made sense of what had just happened by reminding myself that long ago, Mary MacKillop did, indeed, walk through this chapel.

But only for a moment, because Mary turned to look at me over her shoulder and said, "Follow me," then walked away, with her nuns trailing after her. I had no idea what that meant and eventually dismissed it from my mind.

On my next visit to Sydney, in 2018, I again made time to visit the chapel at Mary MacKillop Place. I posted a photo of Mary's tomb on my Facebook page, and an acquaintance messaged me to say if I enjoyed Mary's I should go to Eileen's House. That was the first time I heard of Eileen O'Connor. Fortunately, I was able to get an appointment to visit while I was still in Sydney, and, sitting quietly in the chapel in Eileen's former bedroom at Dudley Street, I was sure I was in the presence of a saint.

I visited the museum, which was then set up in the rest of her house, and was generously given reading material to take home. I devoured the books, then put them safely away on my bookshelf.

I attended a writing conference and pitched my first two novels to publishers in 2019. There I learned publishers didn't want the type of novels I had written. Stung by disappointment, I re-evaluated what I write about: unconventional love stories (not romances) with strong spiritual themes. I needed to find a story in my genre that was more "acceptable" to mainstream publishers. The very next day, Eileen popped into my head. I realized writing about a potential saint was the perfect excuse to write a spiritual love story, and I started planning Eileen's novel.

I contacted Our Lady's Nurses for the Poor to tell them I wanted to write a novel about Eileen. They were very generous in providing more books on Eileen and Fr. McGrath. I was put in touch with Sister Greta Gabb, a former Congregational Leader, who entered Our Lady's Nurses for the Poor in 1958. Sister Greta worked alongside four of the foundation nurses and knew Father McGrath. She has championed Eileen's worthiness to be investigated for sainthood for decades and organized Eileen's papers for the archives. Her love for Eileen is palpable.

In our first conversation, Sr. Greta wanted to impress on me that I couldn't write Eileen properly, unless I understood her medical condition. Eileen had suffered from inflammation of the nervous system, transverse myelitis, due to her TB infection, she said, then caught me off guard by firing a question: "Who do you know who has Multiple Sclerosis?" MS is a comparable neurological condition. I was able to reassure her I was a medical practitioner, and also I had personally known people with MS.

I suddenly saw Eileen had called me. Or set me up, perhaps?

Sister Greta kept in touch with me, generously sharing her experience and very useful information.

With what turned out to be very fortunate timing, in January 2020, I returned to Sydney for the service commemorating the ninety-ninth anniversary of Eileen's death. Armed with sheaves of notes, I walked the streets where she had grown up, tracking down her various homes, and the perfect house for the fictional Kathleen to have lived in. Sister Greta arranged for me to have access to the archives as well as the museum. And very best of all, I was invited to spend time with the sisters, including Sister Margaret Mary Birgan. Sitting with them, experiencing the joy with which they lived their calling, and seeing the smiles which can change the world, was life-changing. I believe the joy-filled, compassionate smiles on their faces were a direct legacy of Eileen's smile, so many years before. A living legacy they and their Sisters pass on, a baton of light in the relay race of life that we all run together.

I was privileged to see Eileen's X-rays when I was in the archives. Unbelievable as it seems, I have held copies of the X-rays of a saint in my very-ordinary hands. I was honored to offer the sisters a medical report on Eileen's health, which they found useful.

Sisters Greta and Margaret Mary both read an early version of the manuscript and, I am glad to say, they were very enthusiastic about the story. I sought their insight and feedback, because it is a great responsibility writing about a saint, even if she hasn't been canonized (yet) and I was committed to portraying Eileen and her spirituality as authentically and respectfully as possible. Their prayers supported the writing and the search for publication of Eileen's novel. Sadly, Margaret Mary passed away in November 2023, leaving the world a poorer place. She had no idea she had a cameo in the novel, until she read the manuscript. She was gracious enough to say she liked it.

I have been as true in my portrayal of Eileen as possible, weaving in her own words and the recorded recollections of firsthand witnesses wherever possible. The undertaker, for example, really did say, "I buried a saint today." The young Eileen was close friends with a neighboring family in Redfern. Mr. Rooney often carried her to their home, where a sofa was reserved for her comfort. She enjoyed being read to by the Rooney children, one of whom later helped in the move to Coogee. Eileen reclines on that same sofa, in the portrait she commissioned for her nurses. The sofa itself was later donated to them by the Rooney family.

* * *

Kathleen and George and their descendants are all fictitious, chosen to facilitate Eileen's journey through the novel right into the present, because she belongs here. A comfort and a saintly inspiration for us all.

**

So, did I see Eileen, in the end? Not exactly. But, like all enthusiastic authors, I wondered what the book cover should look like. I imagined Eileen inviting us to step out from the shadows of our worries and tribulations, into an oasis of love and compassion. Something like the vision Caitlin experiences at the end of the book. I couldn't find an artist who could recreate it for me. "Paint it," said the quiet voice in my head. And so it was, with the aid of YouTube tutorials, I painted my first-ever portrait, a portrait of Eileen. A tribute, working through my poor, worthless self. A labor of love.

**

A note on capitalization. I have retained the old-fashioned habit of using capital letters for some religious words, notably the pronouns for Jesus and the Virgin Mary. Eileen routinely capitalized these words in her writing, as a sign of reverence for the sacred. Her reverence is a part of her story and the sentences don't feel authentic to me without capitals.

**

This is Eileen's book, so let's give her the last word:

There is nothing so wonderful, so powerful ... as love.

SOURCES

T.P. Boland, *Eileen O'Connor for the poor and the poor only* (St. Paul's Publications, 1991).

Rob Ditessa, *Eileen O'Connor: A Saintly Inspiration Second Edition* (News Diary, 2019).

Jocelyn Hedley, *And Here Begin the Work of Heaven: The Spirituality of Eileen O'Connor, Co-Founder of Our Lady's Nurses for the Poor* (St. Paul's Publications, 2011).

Jocelyn Hedley, *Hidden in the Shadow of Love: The Story of Mother Theresa McLaughlin and Our Lady's Nurses for the Poor* (St. Paul's Publications, 2019).

John Hosie, *Eileen: The Life of Eileen O'Connor Foundress of Our Lady's Nurses for the Poor* (St. Paul's Publications, 2004).

John Hosie, *A Lonely Road: Fr. Ted McGrath MSC* (ATF Press, 2010).

John F. McMahon, MSC, *Eileen O'Connor and Our Lady's Nurses for the Poor* (Waverley Press, 1996).

Mary O'Connell, *Our Lady of Coogee: Eileen O'Connor and the Founding of Sydney's Brown Nurses* (Crossing Press, 2009).

The newspaper articles read by the cousins are contemporary reports available online by searching Trove. When I first began researching Eileen, there was almost nothing available about her on-line. Happily, that has changed.

Born in England, **Kate Clinch** has lived in Australia since she was six. After a near-death experience, she left her medical practice and began researching and writing about spiritual matters—especially mysticism and miracles. She's co-authored research papers as a doctor, in the 1990s wrote regular columns on garden history for *Australian Doctor* magazine, and in the 2000s on homeschooling for *Education Choices* magazine. Her unpublished first novel was longlisted in Australia for the Richell Prize for Emerging Writers.

In 2020, after meeting Eileen O'Connor's nuns to discuss *Every Inch a Saint*, she wrote them a medical report to support the investigation into her sainthood. She lives in Adelaide.

MONKFISH
BOOK PUBLISHING COMPANY

We are
Monkfish Book Publishing

...an independent press publishing spiritual and literary books from a diverse range of perspectives. Genres include memoirs, wisdom literature, fiction, and scholarly works of thought. Monkfish books appeal to the seasoned or novice seeker as well as to the general public looking for reliable sources on spirituality. The readers we had in mind when we began Monkfish in 2002 were devoted spiritual seekers, the type whose passion for the spiritual quest would lead them to read across a dazzling array of traditions: Buddhist, Hindu, Jewish, Christian, Muslim, Native American and more. It has always been our intent to publish works of spiritual authenticity for the general public as well as the specialist and scholar.

Our books are available from booksellers everywhere.

Use this QR code to see
recently published books:

Use this one to sign-up for
our monthly newsletter:

www.ingramcontent.com/pod-product-compliance
Lightning Source LLC
Jackson TN
JSHW021414110226
97551JS00005B/1